D0821703

ARCADIA

Also by Jim Crace

CONTINENT
THE GIFT OF STONES

ARCADIA

Jim Crace

ATHENEUM · NEW YORK · 1991

MAXWELL MACMILLAN INTERNATIONAL
NEW YORK · OXFORD · SINGAPORE · SYDNEY

Copyright © 1992 by Jim Crace

Atheneum
Macmillan Publishing Company
866 Third Avenue
New York, NY 10022

Macmillan Publishing Company is part of the Maxwell Communication
Group of Companies.

Library of Congress Cataloging-in-Publication Data
Crace, Jim.
    Arcadia / Jim Crace.
        p.   cm.
    ISBN 0-689-12158-X
    I. Title.
PR6053.R228A89   1992
823'.914—dc20   92-7123   CIP

10 9 8 7 6 5 4 3 2 1

Printed in the United States of America

"The tallest buildings throw the longest Shadows
(thus Great Men make their Mark by
blocking out the Sun,
and, seeking Warmth themselves, cast
Cold upon the rest)."

Emile dell'Ova, *Truismes*
Editions Baratin, Paris, 1774

PART ONE

The Soap Market

1

No wonder Victor never fell in love. A childhood like the one he had would make ice cubes of us all. He lived on mother's milk till he was six, and then he thrived on charity and trade.

On the day that he was eighty, Victor dined on fish. He loved fish best. As he had scaled and silvered with old age, so his taste for fish had grown. Ten live perch from his own stock pool arrived that morning at the station and were driven by cab in a plastic travel-tank to his offices. The kitchen staff were used to Victor and his coddled fish. They planned to cook them steeped in apple beer and serve them cold with olives from his farm. There would be champagne too—the boss's own. And fruit, of course. All this for just five birthday guests. Greengrocers every one, spud traders, bean merchants, middlemen in fruit—and each of them, like Victor, old and slow and hard of hearing. There were—at his request—no gifts, no cards, no cake. He would not tax himself—or any of his staff—with speeches. What old men want is peace and informality, and the chance to talk amongst themselves like smutty boys.

He said he wanted a simple country meal. The fiction in his mind was this: that he would sit surrounded by his friends beneath a canvas awning. There'd be white cloths on a shaky trestle. A breeze. The guests would push off their slippers and rub their bare toes in the dust. They'd twist round on their stools and spit olive stones in the air. Some cats and chickens would take care of crumbs and perch skins. With just a little teasing and some cash, the cook's fat son would play plump tunes on his accordion. That was Victor's ideal birthday meal. Simple, cheap, and attainable for country people living earthbound on a farm, say, thirty years ago; but a dream beyond the reach of checks and fax machines for a man whose home is twenty-seven storeys and a hundred meters up, with views all round, through tinted, toughened glass, and tinted, toughened air, of office blocks and penthouses and malls.

Nevertheless, the man we knew as Rook had done his best to cater for old Victor's dreams. White tablecloths were easy to locate. Rook had the cats. The breeze was air-conditioning. The old men could shake their slippers off and rub their toes in carpet wool. They could spit their olive pips at waitresses. Why not?

They'd have to go without the chickens, reasoned Rook. Victor could not have free-range hens clucking amongst his halting guests. He was not Dali, yet. The accordions were booked. The agency had arranged a band of three, two sisters and a friend. Perhaps, thought Rook, he ought to spray the elevator with aerosols of field dung, or play recorded birdsong on the intercom. He'd have the boss in tears. He'd have the boss in tears, in any case. He had resolved to indulge Victor for the day. He planned to dress a birthday chair for him in greenery, just like they used to in the village where Victor was born. Just like the chair in Leyel's *Calendar of Customs*: Plate XVII, a fogged black-and-white photograph of a small boy from the Twenties, beaming, tearful, overdressed in breeches and a waistcoat, amid the birthday foliage of a high-backed seat. Victor could have the same. Office Security and Caretaking would disapprove—but, surely, Rook could decorate a chair without the building grinding to a halt. A little greenery would do no harm.

So that was Rook's day arranged. It made a change from simply standing by as the old man inked his mark on checks and papers or pointed his icy nose at the latest trading journals or—more warmly—at Alkadier's *Illustrated Guide to Green-*

house Coleoptera which was his bed and desk and lavatory companion. Besides, it released Rook onto the streets for a while. His greatest joy, to let his tie hang loose, to dodge and stroll amongst the people of the city. But earning wages all the time, bleeding Victor's purse, bleeding purses everywhere.

There was a city garden, at the heart of the crop market and not far from Victor's, where there were roses, laurels and all sorts of green-gray, stunted shrubs. It used to be the public washing square, and was known still to all the locals as the Soap Garden. With a logic more poetic than functional, the market which engulfed the garden was known, too, as the Soap Market, though soap was not on sale. The bludgeoned medieval scrubbing stones and the gargoyle fountains of the washing square were still there, though protected from the people by a fence. Seats and tables spilled out into the garden from the many adjacent market bars. And there were lawns, a cake-and-coffee stand, and shrubbery that would make a perfect dressing for a birthday chair. "I could send a chauffeur or a clerk, it's true," thought Rook. But on sunny days like this there were girls spread out across the grass—more and prettier than he'd ever meet in country lanes. "Why waste such prospects on a clerk?"

He told Anna, the woman who ran the outer rooms, hired and fired the staff, and controlled the door to Victor's office suite, that there were "arrangements to be made" and that he'd be gone two hours at the most. "Bring back a cake for me," she said. She was no fool. She knew Rook well. She'd known him hurry out before on urgent morning calls, then caught him sitting idly in his room with nothing on his desk but crumbs. He was not the sort to play the grandee if the staff included him in their gossip or their pleasantries. He did not have a reputation there for hard work, or pride. He was Victor's buffer—and his fixer—that was all. Boss said; Rook did. Though what Rook did and fixed was anybody's guess.

Anna liked the teasing mystery of Rook. Her pleasure showed: her voice amused, her face a little flushed and kindled. She wondered if she would dare to share a cake with him, their mouths and tongues contesting every crumb.

They'd been so close to that a thousand times before—his hand upon the waistband of her skirt or pinching at her flesh, his breath upon her neck, as they stood in line at the coffee or the copying machine; her hand, just playfully, on his, when side by side each morning, when hip to haunch at Anna's desk, they checked the agenda of Victor's day. If this was love, then it was wise, not youthful love, not timid love, not blind romance. And if this was simply passion and no more, then it was in good hands, for Rook and Anna were both old—and young—enough to make the most of passion while time was on their side. For Anna there was pouching beneath her chin, some lines and bruising at the eyes, a softness to her stomach and her thighs, some parchmenting of skin along her inner limbs, the loss of buoyancy, and more, to tell her daily, every time she washed or dressed or ran, that she was over forty and that she should dare to change her motto from the *Careful Does It* of her youth to *Yes and Now and Here.*

For Rook the signs of ripening were much the same, plus listless hair that was blanching at the temples and an asthmatic's prowlike chest as evidence that, underneath the lively tie and shirt, his lungs were shallow and distressed. He saw himself as lean and weightless. His mind was lean. The expression on his face was lean. But—naked in the shower or in bed—his leanness was exposed as thinness. But still he was a tempting, enigmatic man, not dry or beaten like the other men she knew. Anna dared to look him in the eye and contemplate the cake—and more—that they could share. "We'll see," she said, not quite aloud, her fingers church-and-steepled at her chins, her spirit moistened by the prospects of the day. Yes, yes. Yes here. Yes now. Rook recognized himself in her. He smiled at Anna and he asked, "Just name your cake. What can I tempt you with today?" She said she wanted a Viennese with fruit and cream. That would go well with the best champagne which she expected the boss to press upon his personal staff so they could toast him at his birthday lunch. Rook promised to fix it. What he'd do was this. He'd see to it that all the people working in the outer rooms got cakes and drink.

They'd join the aged greengrocers in celebrating Victor's eighty years. The staff could eat a cake, he thought, without the building grinding to a halt, though buildings-grinding-to-a-halt appealed to him.

Thus Rook, on that summer Friday in our city, was armed with errands to gather cakes and greenery, as he descended the hundred meters and the twenty-seven floors by Victor's private lift and walked toward the open air through the pampered, plastic foliage of the atriums which flared and billowed from the building like quilted valances of glass. He showed his face and his Staff Pass at the tasselled rope and stepped between the wings of a revolving door. THESE DOORS ARE AUTOMATIC, announced the sign. It was a warning and a boast: These Doors are Greater and More Permanent than You. They simply swept him in a rotating triangle of processed air into the sun and breeze beyond. All security ended there.

You note he did not choose to take a car. There was a man on duty at the doors who would have been glad to summon one, a taxi or a chauffered company Panache. Rook was valued there as much as Victor's perch—if not a little more—and he was not expected to take his chances on the street. But he preferred to walk. And who would know? Five minutes and he would be amongst the crowds, indistinguishable from all those other duplicates in office wear on work-time errands in the city. What could be sweeter than to pass unrecognized amongst familiar strangers, or to proffer half a nod, a shadow smile, to passersby whose faces rang a bell? What democracy!—to dodge and jostle, tadpoles in the stream. But first he had to walk the hot and empty cloisters of the mall where the noise of distant traffic was waylaid by architectural water. It fell and fountained, day and night, with a rhythmic certainty no mountain stream could match. Rook did not pause, despite the heat and solitude, to sit beneath the award-winning lampposts on the mall, or to play elaborate hopscotch on the colored marble flagstones.

He chose a route which freed him from the shadows. He fixed his eye ahead, upon the skyline, where the unaspiring

towers of the ancient town competed for light and oxygen
with the mantis cranes of building sites and the skeletal scaffolding of half-completed office blocks, draped for modesty
in flapping plastic skirts. Rook said he loved to see the cranes
perched overhead. He loved it best, at Summerfest, when all
the cranes were hung with streamers and with lights and there
were fireworks. Then, for once, the streets were duller, darker
than the night sky. He liked his city noisy, teeming, dressed
in black. He saw himself as lean and black, a cliché creature
of the night. Indeed, that's partly why our Rook was known
as Rook: the black clothes that he wore when he was young
and on the streets. The rooklike nasal cawing of his laugh,
too, his love of crowds, his foraging, his criminality. But
more than that: the puff-chested, light-limbed posture of a
bird.

They said he'd made his money out of Victor—that Victor,
childless, heirless, treated Rook like a son and settled money
on him in lieu of love. A check was Victor's version of a kiss.
"Money is the best embrace," he said. But there the gossip
amongst the secretaries and clerks was way off mark. Victor—
for all his years and for all his understanding of the blandish-
ments of money, of how people could be purchased and caressed by cash—paid Rook a salary, no more. And Rook was
wise enough to keep his office fingers clean. He knew how
frayed and slender was the leash which tied him to the old
man's purse, and, indeed, how loosely that leash was now
held, how easily his boss could let the leash go free. For
two men who spent so much time together, they shared few
sentiments or loyalties. Rook's cheerfulness should not be
taken as fondness for his boss or work, but more as his device
for filling in the silences which were the heavy furniture of
their daily intercourse. Victor did not appreciate Rook's spe-
cial knack of levity, his disregard of silence, his subversion of
proprieties, his aggravating idleness. Victor's simple creed was
this: until a man agrees to dedicate himself to work, then he
will not be rich, or valuable, or admirable, or—best of all—
at peace.

Yet Rook was rich, there is no doubt. A poorer man would

not pass up the offer of a limousine. It takes a man who's certain of his wealth to choose to walk when he could ride. It also takes a man who's used to streets, whose heels have eyes, to know when he is being followed and by whom. As those dismissive, automatic doors rotated Rook into the unconditioned air, a fellow, hardly in his twenties, with a cream and crumpled summer suit, detached himself from the hard shadows amongst the quirks of a colonnade and followed him onto the mall, keeping, catlike, to the sunless walls. He sauntered like a truant, faking interest in the fountains, the streetlights, avoiding joins and fissures in the colored marble flagstones. Here is, his manner meant to say, an innocent abroad. It said, instead, here is a ne'er-do-well at large. Stay clear. Watch out. Protect your pockets when you walk.

Rook's ne'er-do-well was fresh in town. His nails were cracked like slate. His hands and neck were scorched. His eyes were streaming from the wind-borne grit and dust which pecked and spiraled at his face. He hadn't learned the city trick of squinting as he walked. He was jubilant at being there and far from home, and lost, and poor, and free. He had in his pocket an old switch-blade that's spring was slow and temperamental. No cash. Sometime, on Victor's birthday, he'd come face-to-face with Rook. Who'd come off worse? He was an optimist, though in the end, of course—unless there was murder on his mind—a boy like him was bound to come off worse. At best, there would be poverty ahead, and drink, and crime, and selling sex and favors in the street. At least while he was young. And then just poverty and drink.

If we were looking for two poles apart to represent good fortune and bad luck we could not better these two men, the fixer and his shadow, as they ducked into the walkers' tunnel and passed below Link Highway Red which separated the old town from the landscaped decks and platforms of the new. It was a tunnel built for beatings or for rape or for the urgent emptying of bladders or as a refuge from the rain and night for people without roofs. Pillars provided dark recesses for loiterers. Its low lighting winked and buzzed, failed at inter-vals or flared like photographic bulbs. The paper litter scooped and fluttered like a pigeon, trapped and fretful. The smell was urine mixed with street.

Rook thought his shadow might close the gap between them underground and there would be a tussle for his wallet, or he'd be cornered for "a loan." He walked a little faster then, and breathlessly. He wrapped his fingers round his keys, so that any punches thrown by him would be hard and heavy. He was glad to see the daylight spilling down the steps at the far end of the tunnel and to hear the pavement clack of women's heels, the vendor bells, the shop-front loudspeaker touting bargains for the town, the doors and horns and brakes of cars.

2

QUITE SOON HE WAS a different Rook, not yet the firebrand that he'd been when young, not quite the wagging spaniel of the office block, but someone more relaxed than both. His pace had slowed. He strolled. His tie was loose. His shoulders dropped. His birdlike chest no longer heaved for air. There was no tension here, in public space, except the amiable and congested tension of the streets which kept the traffic and pedestrians apart, which made atonal harmonies with honking motor horns for brass, and newsstand yodelers as vocalists, and percussion from the beat of leather shoes on stone. Now Rook's main quests upon this street of salons, boutiques, and restaurants, were oddballs, cronies, pretty girls, anyone to stare at, or anything to buy. He was on the lookout, yes, but not for thieves and trouble anymore, not for the fellow in the cream and crumpled suit. Rook no longer gripped his keys. Somewhere between the new town and the old his ne'er-do-well had disappeared, swallowed raw by the pavement multitude.

Untutored in the waltz, the simple quick-quick-slow of passing through a crowd, Rook's country shadow had been blocked by waiting cars and errand bikes, thwarted by citizens on opposing routes, stopped in his path by shopping bags, and kids, and snack-or-bargain carts. He'd been delayed by brochure touts and leafleteers, tackled at the knees and chest by rubbish cans, hydrants, signs, postboxes, newspaper stands. He'd been bumped and buffeted by the selective tidal chaos of the street which unfooted and swept away those newcomers who did not understand its current or its flow. This was a city at full pelt.

As Rook maintained his pace unerringly and blunderless, the young man in his suit—whose name you'll know before the day is out—was left, a stray, unable even to spot his quarry's browsing head amongst the unremitting throng of citizens. He stopped and window-shopped himself, waylaid by sea gull flights of lingerie, by jewels thrown out across a bed of sand as carelessly as stones, by chocolate truffles displayed like jewels on satin trays, by terraces of boots and shoes, by all the sorcery of *Look, Don't touch*. He pressed his back against the window glass expecting eyes to look him up and down, and disapprove. But there were none. The only eyes that stared at him were in the plaster mannequins. They looked out, day and night, as if they dreamed the street, and all the passersby were figments in the glass.

Who can resist the privacy of crowds? A crowd is people, freely voting for themselves. Rook's shadow joined the crowd and went with it along Saints Row, around the Tower Square, and back again, until it beached him amongst the pavement tables of a bar. He sat. He'd sit until a waiter came, and then he'd hurry off again. He was not bored. The street was cabaret, with mime, and all the spoken badinage delivered stagily, in a whisper or a shout. He'd stay there for a while, he thought, and then go back to where he'd spotted Rook, where there were never crowds, in the ill-lit tunnel under Link Highway Red. That was the perfect spot for the ambush that he planned.

Rook, meanwhile, had gone beyond the bustle of the boutique street. He'd skirted round the boundaries of the Mathematical Park where flower beds were cut for every shape—an octagon of primulas, a perfect circle for begonias, roses in triangles and squares—and Pythagorean climbing frames and wooden seats designed impossibly like Möbius strips. Now Rook was walking through the neighborhood where he was born and raised, the Woodgate district of our city.

Where were the wooden gates that gave the place its name,

those medieval, oaken sentries to what had been an ancient town? Burned down, seventy-four years before, when Victor was a child of six. The incendiarists—so it was said—were city councillors who wanted to "better" what had become a low-rent district of beggars, thieves and prostitutes. Their improving additions were terraces of five-storey blocks—one floor retail, one floor wholesale, two floors apartments, attic, cellar, stables, yard, high rent. In their haste, they'd followed, not replaced, the charred and muddled labyrinth of medieval streets. The Woodgate district was then, and still was on Victor's eightieth, best suited to the horse. Those narrow stable yards and cul-de-sacs, those twisting alleyways that locals called The Squints, were scarcely wider than a mare is long. No motor vehicle could turn about inside The Squints. They were too tight and modest for the cussed constipation of the car.

The Woodgate neighborhood had its vehicles of course. A town must breathe, and there were straighter, wider ways which offered access to The Squints and provided Rook a fast, straightforward route to cakes and greenery. Now he was walking down the road, four mares in width, where he was raised. There were parking bays where he'd once played asthmatic ball-and-tag. The building where his parents had leased a flat was let to businesses—a barber on the pavement floor, an accountancy above, and then three floors of warehousing. The room which Rook had shared with a brother for ten years was wall-to-wall with mats and *phaga* rugs, and druggets from Kashmir. An asthmatic's fibrous nightmare.

Neighborhood was not the word. There were no longer neighbors there. At night the barbers and accountants, and the warehousemen, went home by car and bus and train to suburbs out of town. At night The Squints were dark and dead. But still the buildings were the ones Rook had known when he was small. There were no demolitions yet. And still there was a faint smell in the air, beneath the odor of the cars and the scent of secretaries, of ancient fire. And rotting vegetation, too, as if the area had been built against the odds on the sweet and sour of a swamp. For these were the borders

of the Soap Market. The smell, an airborne punch of cabbage
stalks, figs, olives, beet . . . had belched and yawned along
these streets and down these Squints for six hundred years.
The housing bricks and paving stones, they said, could boil
down into soup; the place was steeped in root, and leaf, and
fruit. So, of course, was Rook. Rook soup would taste as
much of fruit as meat. Just like the merchant's monkey in the
song,

> His testicles were mango stones,
> (Quite normal in the Apes);
> His cock was courgette on-the-bone.
> He . . . shat . . . fresh . . . grapes.

For all his coolness and his suits, Rook was a market boy, a
soapie through and through. His mother and his father made
it so. His parents had rented a market stall and too frequent
were the days when they'd encourage Rook to miss out school
and help them stack and sell their wares. He did not know,
perhaps, the shape of continents or algebra when he was ten,
but he could tell—by smell, by patina, by shape (no easy
task)—a Trakana cherry from a Wijnkers, and know, before
he broke the skin, which aubergines were soured, which peas
had grayed inside their pods.

So it was in a sentimental mood that Rook, on Victor's
celebration day, walked the familiar hundred meters between
his old home and the market rim beyond which, as yet, the
colonizing barbers, the accountants, and warehousemen, had
made no mark. The canyoned pattern of the city ended here
in a huge O-shaped, cobbled court, which could not be circled—Rook could guarantee—by a shallow-winded boy on a
bike in less than fifteen minutes. Except for those few low-
rise restaurants and bars in the Soap Garden which formed
the center of the O, all buildings in the court were wood and
canvas market stalls. The place was open to the sky, and could
have been a medieval harvest fair. Except that Big Vic—as
Victor's office block was known—and the other high-rise
monoliths of the new town cut off the market from the sky-

line hills, and fast and heavy traffic on the Link Highways beat drumrolls across the awnings and the roofs.

Inside the oval, there were no parking bays, traffic lights, or ordered flows. The marketeers parked where they chose, or where the Man in Cellophane (who took it madly on himself to block and beckon traffic) directed them. Their trucks and vans choked paths and access streets. Their barrows and their porter sleds were left where they were used. The wooden produce trays, the emptied sacks, the pallets, bins and panniers which had held vegetables and fruit were piled and stacked unevenly, discarded like the crusts and rinds and eggshells of an outdoor meal. It was safe haven for a sprinting criminal pursued by police in cars.

The odors here were less opaque than those which spilled out, wind-borne, into the streets beyond. To walk amongst the stalls, eyes closed, would be to test one's nose for all the subtleties of countryside and food. The practiced nose—like Rook's—could tell when barrows of potatoes were pushed by or where the garlic nests were hung or whether medlar fruit had bletted long enough and now were fit to eat, or when (the softest, then the foulest scents of all) guavas were for sale, or durians. But why would anybody want to close their eyes? No gallery of modern art could match the colors there, the tones, the shapes, the harmonies and conflicts on the stalls.

The yellow stars were babacos; the Turkish turban was a squash; the pile of honeydews were rugby footballs begging for a kick; red currants, clinging fatly to their spindly strigs, burst and bled; zucchini from Sardinia retained their orange, tissue flowers and peeped out of their boxes like madly coiffured snakes. And dead snakes, sometimes, as green and cold as watermelons, could be found coiled thinly round mangoes or cantaloupes. And thrips and ticks and lice and grubs and flies, the living things that make a living out of market fruit and market crowds. The roaches, bugs and weevils that share our meals and beds.

The first traders, on the outskirts of the market, were the bananamen, the specialists in musaceae. They did not wish to penetrate too far into the maelstrom of the stalls. The snags of fruit weighed far too much to move around, ten, twenty overlapping hands perhaps, each with a dozen fingers to the hand, and each fibrous stem damp and heavy from refrigeration on the seas, from journeying, from ripening, from growing sweet. Bananas were mostly sold in bulk from off the back of vans. They sold them by the hand, and not by number or by weight. The bananamen stood by, foulmouthed, lascivious, and raucous with their yellow-penis jokes. Their fleshy plantains were rewarded with the biggest laughs, the deepest blushes. These traders were the butchers of the marketplace. They each were ready with a knife, like senators at Caesar's death, to cut the hand selected by the customer expertly from the stem. Every knife, and every trader's tongue, was as sharp as limes.

Beside them was the jackfruit van—one jackfruit always sliced in half and cubes cut out so that anyone could test the flesh for creaminess and age. And then the melons and the yams, the gourds, the Herculean beets, the pumpkins, the pyramids of cabbages and swedes. Each had its pitch, exactly and invisibly marked out. God help the reckless cabbage that strayed or rolled into the sovereign kingdom of the yam. God help the greengrocer who scrumped his neighbor's space.

So old and honored were the patterns of the trading pitches that Rook, or so he claimed, could have walked as surefooted as a village cat between the produce and the stalls to the Soap Garden at the market's heart without a glance to either side or to his feet. But Rook was not the man to pass unnoticed or unnoticing through such a place. His eyes were Victor's. This was his boss's empire, the place that made him rich. This market was the keystone to the solid arch of Victor's wealth. Wealth can disappear unless it's watched and husbanded. So Rook was more alert than he had been all day. He watched to see which soapies called out his name and waved, which ones had customers and which had none, what new faces were portering or helping out with sales, who scowled, who hid, who turned away as if they'd never seen his face before, who bid him wish the boss a pleasant birthday

lunch, what fruits there were, what vegetables were new, who
had no right to be there and yet was.

At times, Rook simply stood and stared in wonder at the
wit and artistry for sale and on display—the plump, sugges-
tive irony of roots, the painted, powdered vanity of peaches,
the waxen probity of lettuce leaves, the faith implicit in the
youth and readiness of onion sets, the senility of medlars
(eaten only when decayed), the seductive, bitter alchemy of
quinces which young men bought to soften women's hearts.
Who could pass unfeeling through such splendor? Who could
resist an orange from the pile? Not Rook. He pushed up
against the paper trimmings of a stall. Before him were the
peaks of citruses, the best, most flawless fruit built into perfect
ziggurats with prices marked on flags. There were common
blonds and bloods and navels—oranges from twenty nations
of the world; Cuban green griollas, the yellowish valencias
from Spain, the red sanguinas grown on the southern slopes
of Atlas. Not just oranges in peaks, but foothills too of berga-
mots, lemons, limes, kumquats, and the infinite variety of
mandarins. And all this summer landscape edged in boulders
made from grapefruit, shaddocks and half-caste pomelos. The
fruiterer had made a passing masterpiece of oranges. He'd
added, too, a fringe and diadem of lights, the color and the
shape of citruses. No matter how they shone they were
eclipsed. No light was bright enough to glow more cheerfully
than fruit. No packaging could better them or sing their
praises louder than themselves.

Rook made his choice and took an orange from the cheapest
pile. Its peel, it's true, was blemished, dirty almost. There
was a brownish lunar landscape on its outer crust. The price
was low. But for Rook, who knew his oranges, such blemishes were marks of juice and sweetness. An orange so discolored is an orange which has ripened in the heat, in countries
or in seasons where the nights are warm and bruising. An
orange so discolored would have slaked its daytime thirst
upon the perspiration of the moon. Rook held his purchase
up, and searched for a few coins. The fruiterer just clicked

his tongue and shook his head to signify there was no need for Rook to pay, that he should take this orange as a gift.

Rook scalped the orange at its pig with his teeth. He spiraled off the peel and ate, stepping back and stooping to save his shirtfront from the juice. The flesh left fluorescent lacquer on his lips and chin; the pith made anchovies of flannelette beneath his nails. He let the peel fall to the ground as he walked. The detritus of fruit, the husks and pods and skins, the blousy outer leaves of salad, the blown parsley sprigs, were not considered litter there, but God-given carpeting for cobblestones.

Rook loved it all, this market world, this teeming concourse of cobbles. What good, he wondered, would it be to own this land, as Victor did, and yet not have the legs or lungs to browse amongst the smells and tints and sounds? Yet, don't be fooled. Our Rook was not at ease. The market boy was now a predator. What made Victor a millionaire—the rents on market stalls, the "seeds-to-stomach" stranglehold on wholesale and supplies, the canning and bottling plants—had made Rook wealthy, too. His wealth was surreptitious, though. No penthouses for Rook. No limousines. No coddled fish for lunch. No Rolexes or La Martines. His money was the kind you couldn't spend too openly and couldn't bank. It was the kind that came in cash four times a year, slipped to him in a paper bag with a mango or some grapes or handed over at a bar, a cylinder of notes—all used—and held by rubber bands.

Compared to the trading rents which Victor charged, Rook's "service fees" were small, a modest tithe for peace of mind from every market trader there. A guarantee against eviction. A small amount to pay for Victor's ear. "Pitch money," it was called. A sweetener for Rook: vinegar for those who paid. You could see it on the faces of the men who came to Rook just then—his chin still damp with orange juice, his eyes alight, alert—to make their summer payments for their pitches.

One man peeled off his payment like a sinner giving alms. Another passed his ransom concealed inside his palm. A handshake did the trick. A third—the soapie known as Con—shook openly and tauntingly a sealed envelope in Rook's face, with Rook's name written large and red on it for all to see. Others saw the payment as a trade. They paid, then mentioned problems that could be fixed, if only Rook would talk with Victor. The price of olives was too high. The pears were bruised by the new mechanical pickers that Victor used. The contractors who hosed the market down at night were playing games with the water jet and damaging the decoration on the stalls. "Please let old Victor know our troubles. He can't fix what he doesn't know. And—please—wish Victor Happy Birthday from us all." What was unspoken but accompanied all the cash that Rook received was this: Long may you rot in Hell.

What should we make of Rook, then, as he, shamefaced, proprietorial, pushed through the shoppers and the porters in the medieval alleyways of wood and canvas, of trestles, awnings, stalls, and booths, of global colors, smells and tastes, and reached the bars and lawns of the Soap Garden? That he was bad? Or shrewd? Or simply, like the rest of us, a weakling when it comes to cash?

3

WHEN ROOK ARRIVED at the sunlit respite of the Soap Garden, there were no seats. The bars were full. The lawns were packed with porters and with the low-paid women who weighed, wrapped and sold the city's purchases. Their bosses occupied the shaded chairs. Keeping a fruit or vegetable stall is not an unremitting task. There is free time.

At that hour of the morning, the soapies came for coffee-and-a-shot and to fix and chalk their prices for the day. Some turned away or sank into their seats when they saw Rook. Some watched him blankly. One or two—the older, more successful ones, the ones invited to Victor's birthday lunch—stood up and waved at him to indicate that he should join them at their table, that they'd be honored if he'd drink a shot with them. But Rook had Victor's chair to decorate and Anna's cakes to buy. He'd join them later, when his tasks were done. He went first to the cake-and-coffee stand and chose a dozen cakes from their display—four fruit, four cream, four chocolate. Rook leaned against the stand and studied all the salesgirls on the lawns and then the foliage of the garden while his cakes were gift wrapped in a cardboard pyramid and tied with red and silver tape.

Of all the trees and bushes in the garden, the burgher laurels seemed the best for Victor's birthday chair. Their leaves looked supple, shiny, washable. Besides, their branches were within easy reach and, unlike the roses and the snag trees which lined the lawns, they posed no problem for the naked hand. Rook chose a laurel which grew against the railings of the medieval washing place and threw its shadow across the worn stone sinks, the emaciated gargoyles on the fountains, the cluster of grotesques which nuzzled at the basin rim. Rook, made devil-may-care by his passage through the market, was in no mood to be unnerved by rules or inhibitions. He simply grasped a slender laurel branch, and tugged as if he expected it to snap like celery. His hands slipped, ran free, and stripped the leaves, together with the fledgling buds which roosted at each node. What was that smell?

He took more care with the second spray. He bent it downward at its base, and tried to twist and break it off. It snapped but was too green and sinewy to separate cleanly. He tore it free. He held it by its broken stem, satisfied that it would do for Victor's chair. Quite soon he had a thick papoose of laurel sprays resting on his arm.

Rook was bemused, not by the cussedness of laurels, but by the odor of the exposed wood, a cooking, kitchen smell both unnerving and familiar. He smelled his fingers and then put his nose to the fractured branch. "What's that?" he asked himself, and sneezed. He walked across the grass to the group of traders on the patio of a bar. They were all men that he knew by name, and all about Rook's age, not old or rich enough to dine on Victor's fish. They'd all been market boys together, kicking turnip-balls amongst the lettuce leaves, made shrewd and tough beyond their years by laboring for dad. They'd all been comrades in the market strike a dozen years before. The noisy pair were brothers; bananas were their trade. The balding one was Spuds, a shapeless idle man with wife and kids to match. Another was the man called Con whose envelope of hard-earned cash was in Rook's jacket pocket and who now held court with his account of how, at dawn that day, he'd very nearly had his pockets picked. He stopped midsentence when he spotted Rook. He'd already seen the fellow once too often for the day, a thousand times too often for a life. This was the man, this Rook, who'd betrayed the soapies, who'd led the produce strike and then

abandoned it for pay and privilege at Victor's feet, as if fine
sentiments were not as fine as cash. "That man'd barter every
tooth inside his head," he thought, but said, "Watch out.
Here comes the apple grub." Con was not the understanding
sort. He'd gladly throttle Rook. He'd gladly shake out every
golden tooth. He'd pay to have it done.

The others were more forgiving. They might still have been
Rook's intimates if it weren't that they were always in his
debt. "Pitch" payments had cost Rook a thousand friends.
They smiled at his approach, but not with generosity or welcome. It was simply that their childhood friend looked rather
foolish to their male, no-nonsense eyes: one suited arm
weighed down by foliage; the fingers of the other hand entwined in the fussy, dainty packaging of cakes.

Rook leaned against their table and he sneezed again: a
clearance of the nostrils and a shout of matching force and
volume.

"What *is* that smell?" he asked, wiping his eyes with his
sleeve and placing the laurel amongst their cups and glasses.
They passed the broken branch around the table and put their
noses to the wood. They scratched their heads. Their noses
knew that smell so well, but their tongues could not locate
the name.

"Like coconut," said one.

Another thought it smelled like cake. They called their favorite waitress to their aid. She hardly had to smell. "It's
marchpane," she said, using the country word for marzipan.
She handed back the laurel branch to Rook. Once more he
held it to his nose. The girl was right. He smelled the eggs,
the sugar and the almond paste as perfectly as when he was
a child and helping mother mix and shape the birthday treats,
the balls, the stars, the leaves of marzipan.

"That's it! It's marzipan," he said, translating. "I wonder
if it tastes." He put a broken laurel stem into his mouth.

The waitress laughed and said, "That's poison, that is.
Don't you know? You don't suck that." She pointed at the
beads of sap which were swelling like water blisters where
the wood had snapped.

"How should I know? I'm not a countryman," said Rook, and sneezed again. It was his boast that he would wither out of town. He wouldn't last five minutes away from traffic fumes or crowds.

The waitress was the sort to stand and talk, mulishly deaf and blind to summonses from older, less flirtatious men at other tables.

"Those spoonwood leaves," she said, using once again the country term, "are poisonous. You'll run both ends." Encouraged by their laughter, she embarked upon a tale of how the women in her village used once to boil the poison out of laurel leaves. They'd soak the poison into bread, she said, to bait the rats and mice: "A woman my grandma knew made chicken soup with laurel seeds and laurel sap. They'd use it as fox bait. Or for killing crows. She fed it to her bloke by mistake. He had his bum and stomach pointing at the toilet pan for near enough a week, and then he died. The soup had poisoned him. Nice way to go."

"I've eaten soup like that here," said Con, and winked. This time their laughter was prolonged. They knew this waitress had a second job. She was the kitchen girl as well.

"Bang goes your chance of ever breakfasting with me," she said to Con, and then pressed on with what she had to say about the laurel tree: "My aunt, she had a neighbor who wanted to inherit a little apple orchard when his grandma died. Except she wouldn't die. The older she got the fitter she became. So this man and his wife, they asked the granny round for supper. She got the spoonwood soup. She was shaking like a cow with qualsy before she'd eaten half a bowl. But she was tough. Her heart and stomach were made of wood. They had to pinch her nose and force some second helpings down her throat. Then that was that. She'd gone. He got her apple trees."

The waitress paused so that the point of what she said was not missed or weakened by the laughter that she caused or by the noise of Rook's disruptive sneezes. Then she said, "And no one ever knew the cause of death. Though they took the body to a hospital and experts cut the old girl up to see what they could see. The reason is that spoonwood doesn't leave any traces. Except a rash inside the mouth." She turned to Rook. "You'd better watch yourself," she said.

Rook did not hear. He sneezed again. He looked as pale as chalk. It seemed his tongue and mouth were drier, and more blunted, than they ought to be, though whether this was caused by laurel sap or by the juice of orange he could not tell. He helped himself to water from a jug on the traders' table and rinsed his hands. He took the shot they offered him, gargled with the spirit and spat it out into a drain. He rubbed the stinging corners of his lips. He wiped his tongue on the cuff of his jacket. His mouth was now his most self-conscious part. Rook cursed his luck. He knew the signs of asthma on the march. His sense of smell had failed. His nails—dug in his palms—left deep red weals which would not clear. "You'll live," the waitress said. "It takes more than a lick of spoon-wood to harm a man your size."

Rook placed his pyramid of cakes beside him on the ground. This time the sneeze gathered in his upper nose and fizzed but did not detonate. He took deep nostril breaths to try and burst the bubble forming in his head. He started breathing through his mouth. He sucked in air. He beat his chest as if he'd eaten too much cheese and stomach wind was warring with his heart. The more he tried to let the sneeze go free, the more it burrowed into him, and spread. His sputum was like lard. These were the times he missed his parents most. They coped with him when he was small. They'd ignite an asthma firework for him at the table and let him inhale smoke, his head inside the cowling of a blanket or a towel. They'd massage him. They'd soothe his chest with balsam brewed from cloves and juniper and peppermint. They had been dead for fifteen years.

At first, the market men were unconcerned, amused that Rook was making such a fuss. They did not understand what asthma was or how the trigger of the laurel sap and smell had so alarmed Rook's lungs. His breathing now was panicky and spasmed. The tree of passages, the branches, twigs and sprays, which served the air sacs in his lungs, were swollen. They

were almost blocked. He had to cough. His chest had shrunk.
He did not understand what anyone was asking him.

He could have died. The waitress beat him on the back.
She struck him with the rounded heel of her right hand between his shoulder blades. She thought he'd got a scrap of
twig or leaf lodged in his throat and that he should bring it
up or choke. Her blow knocked Rook onto his knees. It
marked his back. He coughed up pinkish phlegm. "That's
right," she said. His lips, his fingernails, his tongue, his feet
were turning violet. His face was mauve. She struck him once
again. He had the sense, and luck, to roll this time onto his
back so that, unless she took it on herself to punch him in
the stomach or the ribs, or kick him on the ground, he was
more safe. In fact, he found it easier to breathe flat out upon
his back beneath the traders' table. The air went in and out
more freely. The tidal ebb and flow increased. He pinkened,
gasped a little less, then sneezed. His mind was clear. He
understood. He'd been exposed. The grass. Some pollen. The
orange juice. The laurel leaves. Some rural irritant had
stressed his city lungs.

He felt his pockets in the hope that he had brought his
nebulizing spray. It was not there. He'd left it in the top
drawer of his desk. He was too careless with himself. He
should have known. The garden was no place for him. He
couldn't wait to reach Big Vic and his nebulizer's balsamed
mist. He would have hailed a taxi for the journey back, but
there were none. No car or taxi, no ambulance, could ever
reach the garden during trading hours. The market was im-
penetrable except by foot or porter's barrow. Rook took a
napkin and wiped the beads of sap from the laurel stems and
then he took the sheet of a discarded newspaper and wrapped
them round the bunch. He held them downward so that he
did not share their oxygen.

"It's greenery for Victor's birthday chair," he said. "To
decorate it."

The traders watched him blankly, without warmth. Rook
looked at the waitress, expecting that she'd understand. She
was a country girl, after all. But no. Her eyes were just as

blank. She'd never heard of dressing birthday chairs. Now Rook's discomfiture, his sense of foolishness, was changing from embarrassment to irritation and regret: irritation that the men were so open in, first, their mirth and then their coolness at his expense, regret that he was not where he belonged, sitting side by side with them, and laughing at the ink-stained stiffness of some other clerk on trifling errands for his boss, made paranoid and breathless by a dab of laurel sap. For what could be more foolish or banal than these tasks of greenery and cakes, which earlier had seemed to Rook to promise so much freedom and amusement? And what could be more demeaning than the panicked, public face of adult asthma?

Rook took his foliage and his cakes through the maze of market stalls. The journey back, out of the innards of the city, seemed less ordained than the route he had followed in, toward the Soap Garden. He wove a clumsy passage through the shopping crowds, hampered and encumbered with his gleanings and his purchases. He felt displeased, and fearful too. Already he was at the market edge. The banana and the jackfruit men were ready with their knives. The Man in Cellophane waved him on impatiently. Beyond, there was the district of his birth. Beyond, there were the boutiques of Saint's Row, Link Highway Red, the ne'er-do-well, Big Vic. Rook walked, half dreaming, from the old town to the new.

4

ROOK'S NE'ER-DO-WELL was called Joseph. His broken nails and weather-beaten neck and hands were all he had to show for three years of work on one of Victor's farms. He'd purchased the cream and crumpled suit from a catalog. Its light, summer style was marketed as *On the Town*. The fashion model in the catalog had been sitting on a barstool with his sunglasses hooked inside the breast pocket of the jacket. One hand—the one with a single, gleaming ring—was resting on his knee, palm up. The other held the barmaid by the wrist. The gold watch on his arm showed the time as five to midnight, or five to midday. There was a bottle of muscatel on the bar and strangely, promisingly, three glasses, as if another woman had just left, or was expected soon. Or, perhaps, the glass was waiting there for Joseph.

When the parcel with the suit arrived, Joseph had cut the picture from the catalog and put it in the breast pocket as if to equip his clothing with a pedigree and, more than that, an aspiration. The model's empty, upturned palm, the drama of the barmaid's wrist caught by the strong hand of the man, exactly matched Joseph's notion of the casual spontaneity of city life where day and night were all the same, where drink and wealth and women were within easy reach. What else was there to fill his mind each day? Trenching orchards, driving tractors, mucking fields, cutting cabbages, boxing plums was not the work to satisfy a youth like Joseph. The muscles that had hardened in the fields had made him vain. And vanity is stifled in the countryside—the rain, the overalls, the solitary work for little pay, make sure of that.

The only chance he had to flex and strut was at the station every cropping day when he went to load the produce onto trains. Mostly they were goods and freight trains, passing slowly through soon after dawn or late at night, and Joseph's vanity hardly noticed in the dark. But once a week, at 7:10 on Thursday evenings, the Salad Bowl Express, as it was called, stopped at the station with passengers weekending in the city, on shopping sprees or love affairs or binges, or just touring the sights. On Thursday evenings rich women and their daughters pressed their foreheads and their noses to the sleeper-carriage glass to watch the men load on the trays of strawberries or cress or endives, fresh for the busy weekends of hotels and restaurants. Some passengers lowered the Pullman windows to buy fruit in cornets of twisted leaves from country girls whose own weekend did not begin until the moon came up on Saturday.

This was the chance for Joseph, obscured and dramatized by the gelid mists of dusk which pirouetted on the platforms with the sweating vapors of the train, to take his work shirt off and parade for them along the station like a boxer, bare and muscular and young. He'd rest the produce boxes on his head and steady them with his arms raised. He felt his body looked its best that way, his muscles stretched, his stomach as flat and hairless as a slate. Besides, in such a pose, his face was hidden by his arms, and Joseph knew his face was not well made. The noses and the foreheads at the glass were powdered, painted, sweet smelling. Their shapes were good, symmetrical, each ear adorned with rings, the hair poised for a weekend in the city. Joseph's nose and forehead were not so ornamental, not ugly but uncouth through work and poverty and innocence. The corners of his mouth were cracked from sun and sweat. His nose was pitted from the scabs he'd picked. One central tooth was gone. One cheek was blemished by a birthmark, cherry colored, cherry shaped. His chin was far too heavy and his face too drawn to benefit from the thin mustache that he was growing. His was a rural face. But his body, give or take a scar or two, was smart enough for town. He dreamed of the day when he would press his own nose to the steamy glass and glide away on the Salad Bowl Express. He worked, saved his wages, sent for his *On the Town* suit, and planned his escapade.

He was not bright. He could not name exactly what it was he sought in town. But it was *privacy*. In town he'd sit inside a bar at noon, three-quarters full of drink, a woman on his arm, his lighter lifted to her cigarette, and no one there would know his name, or where he lived and worked, or who his family were, or how he coped when he was just a meter high at school, or that he had a magpie reputation there for theft. In town he'd flourish in the privacy of crowds, in the monkish cells of tenements, in streets. His neighbors would be strangers. They'd hardly nod. He'd be a mystery to them. They'd only know the things he chose to tell. And—safely, without fear of what the village folk would say—he could choose to tell his city neighbors lies. In any case, the truth of Joseph did not match the suit. He wore it for the first time on the Thursday evening—the day before Victor's birthday lunch—over his khaki working shirt, his black field boots, and helped to load the produce boxes on the Salad Bowl Express. The women pressed their perfect noses to the glass. This time he did not strip to show his working muscles. His suit was on parade. When the Klaxon blew to mark the train's departure, Joseph lifted his final load—a plastic travel-tank marked UR-GENT: LIVE FISH—and stowed it in the corner of the goods car which carried Victor's name. And there Joseph stayed, as quietly as a slug in fruit, until the Salad Bowl Express set off for town. Smudge-suited, ticketless, naive, Rook's ne'er-do-well migrated from the world of plants and seasons to the urban universe of make-and-take-and-sell.

He found a cigarette to smoke, and there was fruit for supper. His *couchette* was four sacks of spinach leaves. He could not shift the sliding door to urinate upon the line. Besides,

he did not want some cousin's tittle-tattle friend to look up
from his hoe or spade to watch the train go by and catch a
sight of Joseph hosing the dusk. He wanted just to disappear
and be forgotten, not be remembered—immortalized—as the
locomotive pisser in a village joke. But men have shallow,
porous bladders which nag and leak. A shaking train is torture
when they want to piss. Why suffer, Joseph thought. It
crossed his mind to urinate onto the apples or the greens. But
he had spent too many years attending to them in the fields
to treat the crops like that. More fun, more logical, to add a
little water to the fish. He unscrewed the cap which sealed
the tank. He knelt, unzipped the trousers of his suit, and put
his mushroom in the hole. The ten perch, used to hand-feed-
ing with protein biscuits in Victor's stock pool, gauped and
butted at his penis end, but when his bladder got to work
they fled into the cooler, blander depths.

Joseph found blander depths as well. He dozed until the
countryside was gone and woke to find the last dregs of the
night made watery by suburban lights. He shivered at the window of the goods car and looked for signs of poverty and
waste, of power and indifference, of wealth and sex and
violent energy, for signs of destiny. His eyes were sharp
for tall and optimistic buildings, and tall and optimistic
girls, for flashing neon lights and fancy cars. The suburbs,
though, were fast asleep and, much like any habitation at
that hour, showed little appetite for day. A few small cars
were on the move, obeying the traffic lights and not the
logic of the almost-empty streets. A cyclist held the center
of a road. Once in a while, in houses and apartments, a
curtain pattern was illumined from within by someone half
asleep, and out of bed, and taking last night's final piss or
their first coffee of the day. The lights in rows of private
shops fell squarely onto pavements; their goods were on
display for cats and bats.

Joseph was struck by all the stillness of the city night. A
country night is just as busy as the day, but here there were
no trees to bend before the wind. The signposts did not move.
The clouds—if they were racing through the sky—were doing

so invisibly, blacked out by streetlamps, put out of sight by electric light. Rain fell like country rain, but underlit, theatrically. It could not soak into the earth. It slid down tiles. It skirted round the angles of each brick. It raced through gutters, dropped down pipes, consigned itself to drains, turned roadside conduits into streams with discarded snack packets as the sails of its racing dhows. It ducked through iron sumps. It undernavigated roads in airless culverts and joined the curling traffic of water below the town, where sewers emptied into sluices and sluices discharged their flood into much slower and more muscular arteries of water. And thence into the mains. And thence into the reservoir, the treatment plant, the aqueduct, the pipe, the tap, the coffeepot, and down the sink as giddy waste.

It took a simple mind like Joseph's to wonder how it was that city rain was so enslaved. He was not bright enough to ask himself, as low-rise housing blocks and sleepy boulevards gave way to warehouses, shunting yards, high-rise offices, and morning's curdy light, how he could hope to soak into the city's ground, how he could stay afloat and unenslaved when so many young men, just like him, had been unfooted, swept away, down gutters, into drains, by the careless rapids and the all-embracing floods of city life. He did not have the time or temperament to care.

His train arrived at dawn. The van doors were thrown back by porters. It was easy for Joseph—much used to being inconspicuous—to merge in with the workers there, three trays of lettuce balanced expertly on his head, and make his entry into town. And then? What then? He put the trays of lettuce with all the other produce in a market van. When it drove away through early breakfast traffic slower than a country cart, slower than a thaw, he followed it, through streets more futile and more aimless than even he had hoped for, to the Soap Market. Of course. Where else would such a hidebound country boy end up?

The time was six-fifteen. The bustle of the market as the traders fixed their pitches for the day was not the world of catalogs. But Joseph's mission was quite clear. City folk were easy pickings. Rich and careless. Weak. Those pampered noses on the carriage glass could sneeze bank notes. Those clerks and secretaries in their cars had gaping wallets, purses, cash to spare. He'd never had the chance to steal off strangers before. It would be easy, he could tell. He'd not be caught. He wouldn't have to turn his village pockets out for every city coin that got lost. He had no face. He had no name. He had no reputation. It was his lucky day.

He'd known such careless crowds at country fêtes and auctions, so all the bump and jostle of the Soap Market was nothing new to him. He was not lost, or overawed. The stalls and market paths had logic. That distant office building on his right gave him his bearings. He knew that empty barrows wheeled by porters led to the outskirt streets where produce vans were parked. The country boy is used to mapping routes, in hop plantations, forests, in the pleats of fields, in mazes made from furrows, fences, dikes. So Joseph stored and sifted signs—the stall that sold shallots, the music of a radio, the trader with the piebald beard, the Man in Cellophane, the diadem of colored lights, the breeze—to keep a tab on where he was, and where he'd need to run, or hide, if he should chance upon some luck.

He was surprised, it's true, by such a city landscape, fashioned out of repetition and conformity, with matching buildings and matching streets and people dressed the same. He was surprised there were no gradients, no sea, no streams, no fertile land. Some fool had built this city on the flat between the pebble and the clod where nothing grew except the appetite. Some fool, in fact, had built this city on the worst of sites. Where was the fish-stocked estuary, the river bridge, the sheltered harbor, the pass between two hills, the natural crossroads in the land where ancient settlements were meant to be? Where was the seam of coal to make the city rich? Where were the hummocks and escarpments to make the city safe? Where was the panoramic view to make the city spiritual, a holy place? What made this thirsty, ill-positioned city—too southerly to benefit from hops, too northerly for grapes—so rich and large? The answer crowded him at every step. It caught his shins. It bustled him from side to side. The marketplace! A city with no natural virtues is reduced to trade. Seas, rivers, hills, coal seams, make fishing, farming, metal bashing, tourist cities. But cities like ours have little choice except to buy and sell and deal, except to do what Joseph planned to do, to make a living out of theft.

If he had been a wiser man, he would have waited for a while before he embarked on his chosen trade. It was too early for the careless shoppers. The only people in the market at that time were marketeers. This was their habitat. This web was theirs. They noted him—not as a thief, but as a scrumper, one of those who came to breakfast gratis on the fruit. He was never unobserved. And so his luck ran out. He'd seen his chance. The soapie Con had moved an envelope with the one red word *Rook* written on it to the back pocket of his trousers so that he could bend and lift more easily. It wagged invitingly as its owner embraced a sack of carrots. Joseph was fast and skilled, but obvious. His fingers wrapped round *Rook*. He got the envelope—but not before three voices had called out a warning, "Look out, Con!" Con's hand shot back and caught Joseph by his trouser leg. He fell. In seconds he was pinioned to the ground. A crowd had formed. His suit was stained by soil and fruit and leaves. He took the first kick of the day.

"You'll pay for this," Con said, already seeing opportunities for cashing in on this young fool's misfortune.

So there was Joseph, a few hours on, paying for his short-lived, bungled life of petty crime by undertaking the "contract robbery" of a man called Rook. Was this the big-time opportunity he'd dreamed about? Was this—so soon—his golden chance? As instructed, he'd first dogged Rook along the mall, to get to know his face. And now he waited for his return in the tunnel under Link Highway Red. He squatted on his haunches, smoking, and studying the picture Con had given him—a snapshot of a market stall. The man amongst the vegetables and fruit was a younger Rook, smiling, scarf unknotted at his throat, his clothes all black. Here was the man to ambush, frighten, rob. Con's promise was, as he dispatched young Joseph to do his business on the mall, that Rook—as he returned from the Soap Market to Big Vic, and not before—would carry money, hidden, maybe, but cash and notes in large sums. There would be an envelope as well, the one he'd failed to steal. Brown, sealed with tape, and marked in red with Rook's name. Con showed the envelope again to Joseph. "Remember it," he said. "The man you're looking for will have this somewhere on him as he heads back to work." All Joseph had to do was wave his knife and take the envelope, unopened, back to Con's market stall. Anything else he found on Rook was his to keep. If he did this task efficiently, there'd be no police involved. The pocket-snatching rashness in the marketplace would be forgotten. Joseph's Identity Card, which Con had confiscated as security, would be returned. Perhaps, there'd be a proper job for him as well. What job? Con wouldn't say, except "a market job, a job where muscles like the ones you've got won't do you any harm."

Joseph, now out of cigarettes and more hungry in the walkers' tunnel than he had been upon the streets, once more fixed Rook's much younger face onto his memory, and then bent more eagerly to study a second picture in the oscillating light—the illustration from the clothing catalog. Now he and the model in their matching suits were cousins, at the very least. The longer Joseph stared at all its appetizing detail—the suit, the upturned hand, the third and unattended glass—the more certain he became that soon he would be drinking at the bar.

Quite soon Joseph was tired of sitting on his haunches in the gloom. He was hungry, damp, and desperate for nicotine. He was embarrassed, too, by the way the elderly woman who had passed him in the tunnel did so with such nervousness and haste that she had missed the pleasant smile he'd given her. He'd never met a woman of that age before who did not know his name and family, who did not stop to swop a word or two. He called after her. At first a cheerful greeting. Then abuse. She did not turn. She did not seem to hear. Perhaps she was the sort that hates the young.

He was impatient now to prove himself a citizen. He walked toward the daylight spilling down the steps from the street in the hope of spotting Rook amongst the faces in the crowd. Much easier to follow Rook and rob him from behind. But as he turned to mount the stairs he saw Rook descending, in his path, three steps above. His victim was not looking well. He held his chest. The pallor on his face suggested fever or anxiety. He was breathless, too, from walking fast and from carrying through crowds what looked like burgher laurel branches and a ribboned box, a pyramid, which, thought Joseph, promised riches of some kind. That was the moment Rook and Joseph met. Rook, recognizing who it was, alarmed and startled, stepped aside to let his ne'er-do-well climb past. But Joseph did not move. He let Rook step a pace or two into the stench and echo of the tunnel, then placed his left arm round Rook's thin throat and held him—plus a bunch of laurel—as tightly as the model held the bargirl's wrist. "I've got a knife," he said. And to prove that he was honest in his way, he held the pocketknife, last used to stop tomatoes at their crowns, in his right hand and sprang it open just a little distance from Rook's nose.

"Drop the box," he said.

Rook let the pastries fall.

"Now empty all your pockets, one by one. The jacket first."

Rook pulled out the envelopes with both hands, the rolls of bank notes, all the pitch money he had received that day. He held the money up and out, at arm's length, as unthreateningly as he could and as distant from the knife as his shoulders would allow.

"It's yours," he said. But Joseph had no hand free to take possession. One arm was pressed against Rook's throat. The other held the knife.

"Just drop that too."

Rook let the money go. The envelopes and bank notes,

more money than Joseph had ever seen before, fell on the
pyramid of cakes. Con's envelope was in the pile.

"The trousers now," he said. Rook emptied both pockets
and turned their innards out like a schoolboy caught with
sweets. "Let's see what's there."

Once more Rook held out his hands at arm's length. He
held a handkerchief, his Staff Pass, his keys and just a little
change.

"Keep that," Joseph said, and liked the sound of it, the
style, the generosity. He released Rook from his grip, and
stepped away. The laurel branches fell amongst the booty at
his feet. "Turn round. Back off."

Rook turned to face the robber and his knife. He moved
two steps away and waited. The "Keep It" spoken by the
youth had told Rook what he had hoped, that the knife was
for display and not for cutting throats or stabbing chests.
The "Keep It" meant "Live On." Rook's fear made way for
irritation and for shame that he had let this ill-dressed, ill-
shaped hick make such a fool of him on this of all days, when
he'd already—unaided, uncoerced—made himself a public
fool. He wrapped his fingers around his keys. He let the bev-
eled end of one long key poke out beyond his knuckles. He
bit his lower lip—not fear, but anger on the boil. He felt a
little sick, a little drunk, a little like a brute. It was not hard
to take one long step forward as Joseph bent to gather up the
envelopes and cakes, to fix his eyes on that birthmark in
cherry red, and strike this young man in the face with knuckles and with keys.

Rook meant to hit him on the nose or chin, but missed.
He struck him on the forehead, just above the left eye's over-
cliff. The key's sharp end went in. It broke the skin and left
a fleshy pit like those left by the beaks of jays in pears. Rook
struck again. This time his fist caught Joseph on the ear.
Again the jay had left its mark, but raggeder this time. A
tear. A bloody one. The third blow came from Rook's right
foot and left an imprint of the street on Joseph's suit and a
crescent-shaped bruise on Joseph's chest. He toppled forward,

winded, shocked. He crushed the cardboard pyramid. His face was pressed against the laurel leaves, though there was no marzipan to scent his fall. The laurel stems, in fact, no longer smelled. There is no permanence in plants. Their sap, their colors and their odors drain, disperse. The only smell was tunnel dirt. The taste was blood, and tears. He'd wake up soon. He'd find the blood came from a forehead wound. The blood was running down his face. The tears were blood. The laughter lines around his eye, his lips, his hairline on one side, the lapel and shoulder of his suit, were marked in red. The picture from the catalog and the photograph of Rook fell from his pocket, faces up.

Rook's final blow was to Joseph's hand. He kicked the knife away. That kick was delivered with a cough. Rook's throat and chest were heaving like a gannet's. Joseph got up and, empty-handed, ran up the flight of stairs, into the light and safety of the street. God bless the street.

Rook gathered up the things that he had dropped: the bank notes, the envelopes, his Staff Pass, the flattened box of flattened cakes. He picked up Joseph's knife as well. He closed its blade and dropped it in his pocket with his keys. The laurel branches were too battered now for Victor's chair. He kicked them against the tunnel walls. He was surprised at how calm he felt, despite his breathlessness. First, the restoration of his nebulizer. Then, champagne.

He felt no anger for the country boy. That scrap with him had been too short and undramatic for lasting animosity. The asthmatic turbulence that Rook had suffered at the table in the Soap Garden had done more damage than the fight. The mockery had hurt him more. If only those old friends of his—the greengrocers with whom he'd grown up—had seen the scuffle in the tunnel and how the street in Rook had put to flight the mugger with the knife. If only they had witnessed what he'd done. Violence is the perfect repartee, he thought. More dignified, more eloquent than words. He felt in touch again, with boyhood, streets, the town, the universe of laboring. He felt excited, eager for the day. He felt as tough and sentimental as a movie star. He couldn't wait to share a cake with Anna. He couldn't wait to use his fists again.

Rook stooped to recover one last dropped bank note from the tunnel floor. It was moist with Joseph's blood. Next to it was the clipping from the catalog, covered by the photograph which Con had given Joseph. Rook looked at Rook, perplexed. He had not seen that photograph for years. How could it have fallen with his money there? Perhaps some trader, who had paid his pitch money that day, had put the photo with the cash. Why? Some arcane rebuke to Rook, no doubt. Some accusation from the past. It was the sort of petty rebuff he'd expect from bitter, unforgiving men like Con. Rook picked the photo up. The suit, the model and the barmaid, which had been hidden underneath, were now on show. He took a closer look. He recognized the bar, perhaps? The model's face? He put both pictures in a pocket with the knife. He knocked the detritus of laurel from his coat and trousers and headed for the steps.

Rook made his way back to Big Vic and, clumsy and encumbered though he was, he could not disguise the hint of hopscotch in his step as he walked across the colored marble flagstones of the windswept, empty mall. Around him, out of sight, the bankers banked, expeditious every instant of the day; dollars became lira became marks; commodities and futures bobbed and ducked in value, unobserved; screens conversed in numbers on fiber-optic cables like gossips at a garden fence. Above, a restless matrix with its lights like traffic headlamps in the rush, sent out its electronic information into town. The stock report. The city news. A flood in Bangladesh. A birthday greeting for the boss. A puff for Fuji Film. Traffic junctions to avoid. Fly Big Apple—Fly Pan Am.

Rook reached security at last. The automatic doors swept him into processed air. He showed his pass. He tightened his tie at his collar, and summoned the old man's private lift. While he waited for it to fall the twenty-seven storeys of Big Vic, he picked himself a fine bouquet of plastic branches from the gleaming, sapless, perfect foliage of the atrium. He did not have to tug or cut. Each leaf, each twig and branch, was fixed by sleeve joints. The real, reconstituted bark was stuck to moulded trunks with velcro pads. The soil was soil with nothing much to do, except to fool the people of the town.

5

ROOK PUT THE FINAL TOUCHES to the room, while the waitresses and kitchen staff prepared the settings and the food for Victor's lunch. His buoyancy had not been punctured by the tightening of his tie, by the dull proprieties of going back to work. He'd dropped the scuffed and battered pyramid of cakes on Anna's desk and simply said, in response to her surprise, "I had to fight for these!"

Anna asked no questions. She simply filled her lungs with air and closed her eyes and said, "Such gallantry!" Her persiflage was sweet. It was a tease. It was the kind of irony that Anna knew would work on men. Men were clockwork toys when it came to love and sex. You wound them up, you faked a phrase or two; they marched, they danced, they beat their drum. It was her plan to fake some satisfaction, if she had the chance, with Rook. Why not? He was not married. She was now divorced. She was only older than him by a year. He was not short of cash and might have fun if he could spend his money and his time with her.

Rook was an oddball, yes. But oddballs had their appeal for Anna. She liked the stimulation and surprise of men who lived beyond the grid. She liked Rook's secrecy. She was not fooled by his sardonic ways. What kind of man, with power such as his, would spend the morning on the streets and come back laden with squashed cakes and a bunch of plastic leaves? A man worth knowing, she was sure. So Rook and Anna left

it brewing in the air that their flirtations would bear fruit, and
soon, before it was too late, before the heightened passion of
the day, its sap, its colors and its scents had drained and dispersed for good. Let Victor have his birthday first. Let champagne loosen tongues and dilate hearts. Then let Rook and
Anna stay on late, to sort out papers, say, to tidy up, to joust
among themselves as the evening and the office blinds came
down. They'd spoken not a word, but they were old and
wise enough to comprehend the promise and the charge of
"Such gallantry!"

Rook took the plastic branches, a roll of cellophane tape,
some string, into the office storeroom and began to fix them
to the backrest of an antique wooden chair. The molded twig
ends protruded through the spindles of the chair and made
the decoration amateurish, and rushed. Rook tried to bite off
lengths of string so that he could tie the twig ends back. But
the string was just as tough and artificial as the greenery. He
searched the shelves for scissors—and then remembered the
knife he'd picked up in the tunnel, the pocketknife that the
clumsy, birthmarked mugger in that too-large suit had
dropped.

The too-large suit! The thought of it, ill fitting, grim, badly
made, was all it took to solve the mystery of the second
picture Rook had found amongst the debris in the pedestrian
underpass. So that was what he'd recognized. Once more
Rook found the piece of catalog and scrutinized the faces and
the bar. No other recognition, now. Except, bizarrely, for
that suit. Rook smiled at *On the Town,* at its frugal price and
style, at the implication that the early photograph of Rook
himself had come not with pitch payments as he'd thought,
but from the pockets of the young man's suit. He'd been no
chance encounter, then, but targeted. This lad had known,
and God knows how, that he would carry cash in quantity
between the old town and the new. But how the aging photograph tied in with that he could not tell. Some opportunist
soapie? Some maverick inside Big Vic? Some oddball with a
pettifogging grudge? Who knows exactly who one's foes
might be?

Rook held the knife out, sprang the blade and set to work on cutting string and strapping back the plastic twigs. It was then he spotted the eleven worn letters scratched inexpertly on the handle, JOSEPH'S NIFE. He felt he'd like the chance to hand the pocketknife back, not to make amends for the kick he'd landed and the cheating fist of keys which had inflicted such a bloody face, but for the chance to find out who'd set this "Joseph" up, and why. But for the moment he was glad to have the knife at hand, to put its blade to proper use for Victor and his chair. The decoration now was neater. Only leaves were on display. It looked as if the stained, antique wood of the chair, long dead, had undergone a resurrection of some kind, had put down roots and put out foliage, like the farmer's magic chair of fairy tales. A little spit and polish was all it took to finish off the job. The spit took off the office dust. The polish—a *Woodland*-scented aerosol—put back the color and the sheen. Rook's handkerchief buffed up the waxen glimmer of the leaves.

He'd promised there'd be cats for Victor's lunch. They were a part of Victor's dream. The boss himself had three, to chase off pigeons from the roof. Rook had arranged that they should be brought down to the office suite. They'd settled in, two on the sofa, one underneath the desk. The tablecloth was white, exactly as required. The air-conditioning provided just sufficient breeze. In the visitor's lobby the three musicians of the Band Accord were practicing the country dances they would play for Victor. The fruit and cheeses were in place. The champagne was on ice. Rook went through to the inner room and Victor's desk. He telephoned the chef. The perch were cooked and already steeped and cooling in the apple beer. The waitresses were standing by. The five old greengrocers were seated, subdued and patient, in the atrium below, waiting for the summons to the lift. Rook carried Victor's birthday chair into the anteroom. He placed it with its back against a wall, so that the tiara of leaves faced into the room, and the disenchanting clutter of plastic, string and cellophane tape could not be seen.

When the call came that lunch was ready to be served and

that his friends—his guests—were already waiting in his suite,
Victor was in his rooftop greenhouse on the twenty-eighth,
examining the yellow aphids which congregated in an orderly
crowd on the underleaves and along the infant stems, a con-
gregation of busy wingless females plus a single ant which
feasted on their honeyed excretions. Victor hesitated with his
spray. He almost cared for insects more than plants—but not
quite. These aphids were too common to be lovable. He
showered them with toxic milk. The ant, he spared. How
high, he wondered, would he have to build to rise beyond
the pigeons and the flies, to reach above the aphids and the
ants? Forty? Fifty storeys? Would there be oxygen enough
up there, for vegetables to thrive, for bees to come and
pollinate his plants? He looked out through the lichened,
mildewed glass, northward, beyond the mall, the highway
and the high-rise stores, toward the old town, and the suburbs, and the hills. Skyscrapers are the skyline optimists. They
have the first light of the dawn, the final warmth of day.
They get the flattened, cartographic view of towns, the neat
geometry of north, south, east and west.

Victor knew his city like a hawk knows fields. The innards
of the city were laid bare from the twenty-eighth floor, from
what was once the Summit Restaurant of Big Vic but now,
because the Summit diners could not stomach the swaying
flexibility of skyscrapers in wind, was private garden. Innards
are chaos and a mystery to any but the practiced eye. In time,
with study, Victor had got to know the spread-out entrails
of the streets. He knew the bones and organs of the town—
the university, the stadium, the graveyards and the parks. He
knew the Bunkers where poor, delinquent townies lived in
blocks as packed as hives. He knew the yellows and the ochers
of the public buildings, the grand works of the eighteenth-
century trading potentates, the bookend buildings of the police headquarters where once the low-rise slums had been.

The routes and patterns were quite clear. No river—but a
line of pylons and the railway halved the town, and link highways made a rhombus as a frame containing both these
halves. The rhombus, in the midday summer heat, dangled

from the city's flight and swoop of motorways like a box
which swings on ribbons. Beyond the box? The ground-
scraper mansions of the wealthy, crouching behind the thick
masonry of security walls. The suburbs and their trees. Out-
of-town commercial centers with fields of tarmac for the cars.
A threatened cul-de-sac of countryside, earmarked as building
land.

Victor liked the gray and green of boulevards the best,
where lines of trees and central lawns plunged living splinters
into the city's skin. He liked the city humming to itself: the
cheerful plumes of smoke which came from rubbish tips and
factories and crematoriums, the distant drone of traffic, the
cadences of wind.

The suburbs of the city from the twenty-eighth through
Victor's less-than-perfect eyes were patterned fabric, not quite
alive, though shimmering like shot silk in greens and grays
and browns. Nearer to the eye, the striped and garish awnings
of the market, dignified only by the gray-green of the Soap
Garden with its few two-storey trees, seemed capricious and
unnatural, set at the center of the old town's patterned stratagems of startled roofs with their exclamatory chimney pots.

Victor did not like the marketplace. He did not like its
awnings and disorder. He did not like its crowds, so dense
that taxis could not pass. He disapproved of truck-back trading, of noise and inefficiency, of waste. He'd not been to the
market now for seven years—too old, too frail, too numbed
by life—but he could see it every day, a garish blockage at
the center of the city which spurned both logic and geometry.
He'd put it right. Why not? What else could old men do?
He'd stood inside his greenhouse now for fifteen minutes at
the very least. Three times enough for him to earn the money
for a month in Nice, a car, a year's supply of clothes. His
farms and markets, his offices and shares, his merchant capital
crusading in a dozen countries, a hundred towns, earned fortunes by the minute. Thirty millions a month. Morocco's
health and education budget in a year. Enough to build a
dream in bricks. Or stone. Or glass.

His accountants and advisers had been working on him for

a year or more. The marketplace, they said, was out of date.
It did not earn enough for such a central site. It was—compared to canneries and bottling plants—a poor outlet for fruit.
There'd been hints from the city government, that if he were
to seek approval for a plan to renovate, or move the market
elsewhere, say . . . then, there would be no fight. No fight,
indeed! Victor was not so foolish as to think there'd be no
fight if he were to tinker with the marketplace. He knew what
soapies were, an awkward bunch, opposed to any change on
principal. Well, that's Rook's job, he thought, to keep the
soapies quiet. Yet Victor would not share his thoughts with
Rook. He did not trust the man to hold his tongue. He did
not trust his judgment or his loyalty. Rook was no businessman. What businessman would be so sociable? What businessman would settle for such a salary as Rook and for so long?
What businessman could see the market operate and not be
shocked at its trading nonchalance? But Rook, he loved the
Soap Market. He loved its crowds. He'd said as much: "It's
paradise for me." And Victor thought, If that is paradise, that
regimented, noxious crush, that milling battlefield of chores
and errands and anonymity, then that's the paradise of
termites.

Old Victor took his stick and walked quite steadily between
the pots of young peppers and tomatoes toward the lift. And
lunch. He paused to rub out with his thumb the greenfly on
the fessandra bushes which grew in sentinel pots at the rooftop door. He wiped the mush of bodies on the lintel,
wheezed, coughed, and spat a practiced splash of phlegm into
the pot compost. It glistened for a moment like the gummy,
silver residue of slugs. "Good luck," said Victor, to himself.
That's what all good farmers said when they spat in the soil.
The luck was for the soil and for the spitter, too. The luck
that Victor wished upon himself was this: that he would live
into his nineties, long enough to make his lasting, monumental mark upon the city. His age was not an enemy. In fact,
the day that he was eighty seemed the perfect moment to
begin the spending of his millions. He had no family to leave
it to. He had no debts. What should he do then? Leave it all

to charities, and tax, and undeserving skimmers-off like Rook? Or play the geriatric fool and plough the crop back in?

Eighty was the age for second childhoods, so they said. He'd never had his first. He'd never been a boy. He'd only been a baby and a man. So let's commence the childhood now, he thought. Let's be an old man full of impulse, prospects, hope. Let's lay the bitterness aside and die at peace. He spat again—more to clear his lungs than to win more luck than he deserved—into the compost of the second pot.

6

VICTOR'S SIMPLE DREAM of celebrating eighty years in country style could not come true. The air inside Big Vic lacked buoyancy. It was heavy and inert. It was soup. Dioxides from the air-conditioning; monoxides from the heating system; ammonia and formaldehydes from cigarettes; ozone from photocopiers; stunning vapors from plastics, solvents and fluorescent lights. What oxygen remained was drenched in dust and particles and microorganisms, mites and fibers from the carpeting, fleece from furniture, airborne amoebae from humidifying reservoirs, cellulose from paper waste, bugs, fungi, lice. The air weighed too much and passed too thickly through the nostrils and the mouths of the guests at Victor's lunch. They coughed and sneezed and grew too hot. Their eyes began to water, their heads to ache, the rheumatism in their knuckles and their knees to grumble. Big Vic was sick. Contagious, too. It shared its sickness speedily with these old traders, these outdoor men, as they waited for their boss. They blamed their wheeziness, their migraines and their lethargy on nerves. They blamed their dry mouths on embarrassment at the prospect of what had been described on their printed invitation cards as "a relaxed birthday lunch for a few close friends." *Relaxed?* Not one of them could be relaxed in Victor's company unless there was a deal to close or market business to be done. *Close friends?* Were they the closest friends that Victor had? It made them smile, the very thought of it.

But then, who else could he have asked if not these five? He had no family, as far as anybody knew. There were no neighbors on the mall. This was not, after all, the countryside, where people lived so close at hand and in such sodality that they were free and glad to sit in overnight to ease the passage of a corpse, to be the wedding guest, to aid with births or weeping, to help an old man puff his eighty candles out.

"We're here," one aging soapie remarked, "because there's no one else."

"We're here," another said, "because, these days, we have to do what Victor wants. We're here because we haven't got the choice."

It was true they'd been more intimate, at one time, when Victor's empire was as small as theirs and his unbroken dryness had been seen as irony, his silences as only childlike, not malign. But now he was the aging emperor and they the courtiers, obsequious, fearful, ill at ease. Indeed, the whole lunch had been arranged as if this old man were a medieval ruler, addicted to the indulgences and flattery of everyone who crossed his path. He'd been met, as he stepped out of the bright lights of his lift into his office suite, by quiet applause. A respectful corridor was formed for him, so that he could make his progress to the table without the hindrance of his old colleagues. Three accordionists accompanied him across the room with the March from "La Regina," the bellows of their instruments white and undulating like the young and toothy smiles of the staff who had gathered at the door.

The snuffling trader guests closed in when Victor passed and formed his retinue. A waiter or a waitress stood at every chair, except for Victor's. Rook stood there, like the Prince-in-Waiting or the Bastard Son in some fairy tale, clapping both the music and the man. Even Victor felt emotions that, though they did not show, were strong enough to make him sway and lean more heavily upon his stick.

They begged, of course, that Victor should sit down, and then they clapped some more. He asked for water, but surely this was the perfect moment for champagne. Trays of it were brought, for Victor and his guests, for all the workers in the outer rooms. Even the accordionists were given glasses of champagne, though hardly had their nostrils fizzed with the first sip than they were called upon to play—and sing—the Birthday Polka. So Victor sat, the Vegetable King, surrounded by employees, waiters, clients, acquaintances and cats, each one of them dragooned to serve him for the afternoon, as two stout ladies and their friend pumped rhapsodies of sound and celebration round the airless room. Those few who knew the words joined in. The others hummed or simply stood and grinned.

There was an instant, when one of the three cats jumped up amongst the cheeses and the fruits on the table and put its nose into the butter dish, when it seemed that the village ways had made the journey into town. But Rook's raised eyebrow and his nod brought that fantasy and the cat's adventure to an end. A waiter, none too practiced in the ways of cats, removed the creature from the butter, lifting it clear by its hind legs as if it were a rabbit destined for the pot.

The music ended. Rook nodded once again, and all the staff, following the details of his memo to them earlier that day, left Victor's room and returned to their screens, their telephones, their desks, their manifests of trade in crops. The Band Accord played—largamente—at the far end of the room. The guests sat down to the silent whiteness of the tablecloth, while the waitresses served the coddled fish. Rook, bidding everybody bon appetite, left Victor to hold court and joined Anna and her staff for flattened cakes—and more champagne—in the outer rooms. Later on, when Victor had been softened by the meal, he'd enter with the birthday chair.

The meal, in fact, was not as perfect as the cook had hoped. The perch, despite their freshness, were just a little high, a touch too bladdery. They had not traveled well. Only one guest, his palate bludgeoned by the pipe he smoked, dispatched his fish with any appetite. The rest concealed their daintiness by making much of savoring the olives and the bread, or filling up on cheese and fruit. They turned the perches' bones and mottled skin to hide the flesh they could not eat.

It was not long, of course, before the meal was finished
and the waitresses had cleared the dishes, leaving the old men,
freed by champagne and liqueurs, to follow the informal
agenda of the birthday lunch and reminisce. There'd be no
gifts or speeches. That was Victor's stated wish. His hearing
was not good enough, despite his humming, temperamental
hearing aid, for gifts and speeches. But stated wishes of that
kind are only code for something else. No one demands the
gift they want. Instead they say, "No need. No fuss. I'm
happy just to see you here." So Victor's friends had done
their best to translate the old man's code. What gift would
please a frail and childless millionaire about to embark upon
his ninth decade? Something you cannot buy, of course.
They'd had grim fun, these five aging traders, identifying all
those things that can't be bought and which were lost as men
got old. Good health. Good looks. Teeth, hair and waists.
The pleasures of the bed. Patience. Energy. A fertile place in
someone's living heart. Control of wind and bladder. All
these were gone and way beyond the sway of credit cards.
What then for Victor's birthday gift? A place in history? Esteem? These must be earned, not bought.

"A statue, then!" The suggestion had been meant in jest.
A statue to the vanity of age. But the idea was better than
the jest, and soon had the old traders nodding at its aptness.
They'd place a statue with a plaque in the Soap Garden.
They'd raise the funds through subscription. All the traders
in the marketplace would want to give. A good idea. A public
gift to the city to mark the old man's birthday. They'd had
some drawings done by the woman who had cast a bronze
statue (for the entrance of the new concert hall) of the city
senators who died on lances in 1323. They liked her work.
These senators were men in pain. Those lances were as
straight and cruel as Death's own finger. The hands which
sought to stem the wounds or pull out the lances by their
shafts were hands like mine or yours, except a little larger and
in bronze. This was no abstract metaphor. She was no artist
of the modern school. She'd talked to them in terms they
understood: payments, contracts, completion dates, the price

of bronze. Despite his spoken wishes, then, there was a short-ish speech, a gift. The five old men presented Victor with the artist's drawings. "They're just ideas," they said. "You choose. We'll see your statue is in place before you're eighty-one." Victor did not make a speech. He nodded, that is all, and put the portfolio of drawings on his desk.

"I'll find some time later for these," he said, and joined them at the table once again to add his monumental awkwardness to theirs.

They tried in vain to open up some windows and let some town air in. But all windows higher than the second floor were double glazed and safety sealed and only activated by a call to the building's brain, the high-tech deck of chips and boards which regulated everything from heating to alarms. They tried to resurrect the country lunches that they had shared when they were younger, middle-aged, and vying for crops and produce at the small-town auctioneers. They tried to sing along with all the sentimental tunes dished up for them by Band Accord. They tried to grow animated rather than just sleepy with the alcohol they'd drunk. But the office suite was deadening. The headaches and the rheumatism which had made such progress, nurtured by the formal tension of the lunch, deepened their discomfort and the furrows on their brows. Their coughs could no longer reach and clear the tickling dryness in their throats. Their eyes were smarting. Their faces were as red and vexed as coxcombs. Conditions there were perfect for a heart attack or stroke.

Victor sat as deadened as his guests, not by the onslaught of the offices—he was used to that—but by the discomfort that he felt in company. He'd never had the conversation or the animated face to make himself or the people round him feel at ease. He had no repartee, no party skills, no social affability. What kind of city man was he that did not relish the light and phatic talk, the spoken oxygen of markets, offices and streets? He did not care. He did not need to care. A boss can speak as little as he wishes, and stay away from markets, offices and streets. Truth to tell, he did not even relish the joshing and the drink-emboldened flattery that his guests—between their coughs and flushes—were exchanging at the table. He mistook their talk for trivia. He took their wheezing and their creaking and the damp heat on their foreheads as the wages of their sinful lives, their drinking, smoking, family lives, their lack of *gravitas*. He looked on them with less kindness, less forgiveness, less respect than he had looked upon the yellow aphids that he'd killed that day.

Victor's own breathing—papery and shallow at the best of times—had become distressed by the cigarettes and the one pipe smoked with the brandy after lunch. His stomach too was just a little restless from the fish.

"Excuse me, gentlemen," he said, and stood, his brandy glass in hand. His guests stood, too, as promptly as they could, expecting toasts.

"Fresh air," said Victor, his sentence shortened by a cough. "Let's go to the roof."

He led them in a halting, single file across the room to where his private lift waited for his summons. The three accordionists, instructed to "accompany" proceedings until instructed otherwise, tagged on, their instruments strapped on their chests like oxygen machines. The waitress with the brandy—dutiful, uncertain—followed on. And last of all, the cats. They crowded in as best they could. The lift was meant for one. It shook a little on its hawsers as the old men and accordions wheezed in unison, and stumbled intimately against each other on the ascent to the twenty-eighth. But when they had emerged beneath the arch of fessandras into the air and foliage of the rooftop garden, the greengrocers breathed deeply, swallowed mouthfuls of the dirty but unfettered air, turned their faces to the sun and wind, and looked out across the city and the suburbs to the blue-green hills, the gray-green woods, beyond.

The Band Accord stood at the door, their mood transformed. The new note that they struck was sweet and sentimental. They played the sort of joyful harvest tunes that make you dance and weep, their grace notes jesting with the melody. The weaving cheerfulness of the accordion could make

a teacup dance and weep. It is the only instrument strapped
to the player's heart. Its pleated bellows stretch and smile.

The guests spread out, at ease, delighted, cured all at once
by the magic of the place, invigorated by the care and passion
bestowed on every plant that grew on that rooftop. The centerpiece, so different from the sculptured water in the mall,
was a pond surrounded by a path of broken stone. There
were no fish, but there were kingcups, hunter lilies, flags,
and—hunched over, like a heron—the shoulders of a dwarf
willow, providing shade for paddling clumps of knotweed
and orange rafts of bog lichen. There were shrubs all around,
some in clay pots, some in amphoras colored thinly with a
wash of yellow plaster, some in raised beds. A wooden per-
gola, heavy with climbing roses, honeysuckle, creepers, led
toward the greenhouse. The traders followed Victor there and
rubbed the leaves of herbs and primped the seedlings like
owners of the land.

The Band Accord was summoned to the greenhouse door.
"Play on, play on." The waitress poured more brandy. The
old men passed the glasses round like schoolboys on an out-
ing, making sure they kept for themselves the fullest glass.
They all found a place to rest or sit. Some upturned pots, a
wooden bench, some low staging for the plants, made perfect
seats. The cats made the most of the dry and practiced hands,
the bony laps, the strokes and preening that were on offer.
The waitress was a little flustered by the flirting helpful hands
which aided her with drinks. The two stout ladies of the band
and their slimmer friend, on the other hand, were serenading
this impromptu greenhouse gathering with the smiles and gestures of the most intimate nightclub. "To Victor!" And someone added, "May you grow new teeth."

Everybody raised a glass and once again the band squeezed
out the Birthday Polka. Everybody sang the words and passed
their glasses for more drink. Victor stood to say eight words,
no more, of thanks. "Just like the village parties, gentlemen,"
he said, promoting the deceit that he had sap for blood, that
he was just a countryman at heart. "Your health." He looked

out for the second time that day toward the garish awnings
of the marketplace. Before he'd had a chance to sit, he added
one more toast, "Our town!" He swept his hand toward the
market, as if to wipe the townscape clean. He would have
said, if he had been a more loquacious man, "Before I die I'd
like to clear all that! To start afresh. A marketplace. A building worthy of our town." Instead, he said (he could not help
himself), "To business, gentlemen." Again they lifted glasses
up, and drank. "I trust your businesses are well. No problems
that you want to talk about?" No one was in the mood to
answer him. They shook their heads and laughed, as if the
very thought of problems was a joke.

"Well, then," said Victor. "That is as it ought to be. Rook's
paid enough by me to solve and settle problems. . . ."

"By us as well . . ." The man who spoke had meant it
as a joke. He'd never stopped to think before whether Rook's
pitch payments were transactions that he shared with Victor.
Too late to wonder now.

"By you as well?"

"It's nothing much. A gratuity for everything he does."

"What does Rook do that is not already funded by his
salary?"

Victor saw discomfort all round. He read it perfectly. No
wonder Rook thought the Soap Market was paradise. The
market termites droned for him. The man was taking bribes.
Victor knew at once what he must do to this extortionist and
how—a timely gift—it served his long-term purpose perfectly. A man like that, a man who served himself before his
boss, a man, moreover, who could not be trusted should a
market renovation plan be contemplated, could not expect to
keep his job. There was no wickedness in that. It was a duty
for a boss to let the shyster go, just as it was the task of
gardeners to rid themselves of bugs.

"How much exactly do you pay?" he asked. Again, there
were no volunteers to speak. They did not wish to seem the
victims of dishonesty, or collaborators in deceit. Victor took
a notebook from his jacket, and a pen. "Jot down the size of
payment that you make to Rook," he said. "I would not wish

my friends to pay more than they ought." Of course, they did as they were told.

Downstairs, one floor below, Rook and Anna judged—as all seemed quiet in Victor's office suite—that the time was right to seat their boss in his birthday chair, amongst the gleaming foliage, and to raise their glasses in a toast. The chair was carried from the anteroom. The drinks were poured. More champagne, naturally. The chair was placed at the center of the lobby outside Victor's suite where they presumed the birthday lunch was—quietly—still in progress. Rook stood behind the chair, a smile composed already on his face. Anna knocked on Victor's door, and entered. The only sound and movement in the room came from the air-conditioning.

"They've gone," she said to Rook. He came and stood beside her at the door and looked where she was pointing, at the table, at the olive pips, the undrained glasses, the stubbed cigar, the detritus of orange peel and fruit skin and undigested fish. Anna laughed, and—doing so—she dropped her head momentarily onto Rook's shoulder.

"They must have doddered to the roof," he said, and put his arm around her waist. He felt elated and uneasy. The empty room, the woman's reassuring waist, the birthday chair, unoccupied and foolish in the middle of the lobby, were not what he had planned.

"Let's drink the champagne anyway." He turned his back on Victor's door and sat himself amongst the plastic foliage of the birthday chair, satirically, defiantly. He lifted up his glass until Anna, standing at his knees, was still and silent and composed. She raised her glass as well. "Ourselves!" she said. "Ourselves . . . ourselves . . . ourselves . . . ourselves . . ."

7

THE MARKET WAS AS GOOD as gone, and so was Rook. Decisions had been made, that day. The skyline of our lives was changed. Five halting traders, a band, a waitress, and the boss took air and brandy on Big Vic's garden roof, while, on the twenty-seventh floor, Rook and Anna grew tipsy and engrossed with lesser things. There'd be a *romance* (How we love that word!), one *death* at least (We're not so keen); there'd be distress and devilment upon the streets, some fortunes made and lost—and all because a dry old millionaire, alive too long, a little drunk, had fallen foul of that ancient sentimental trap, the wish to die yet linger on.

When Victor offered up his glass and said "Our town!" perhaps the toast was not for what there *was* but for what he *saw* in his mind's eye, the prospects and the dreams. His hand swept up across the distant cityscape. He wiped the market off, as if he was simply clearing steam from glass and looking on the hidden clarity beyond, his place in history.

The story, though, that was running through the city by that midnight was not the one that would change lives and landscapes—unless you were a fish. The story that amused the traders and the porters as they gathered in the Soap Garden for their final coffee-and-a-shot, that so obsessed the chatterlings, the social consciences, the bleeding hearts, the evangelists of social change who talked into the night, was the story of Victor's coddled fish. The fish at Victor's party—or so the

midnight edition of the next day's city paper claimed—were
better treated than his guests. Ten fresh and living perch were
taken from the station to his offices "BY CAB!," was the report. Their plastic travel-tank was lifted by porters onto the
cab's rear seat and the driver was instructed to go no faster
than a hearse. Live perch, it seemed, could lose their sweetness
and their bloom if sloshed about like lunchtime bankers in the
backs of cabs. Their flesh would flood and stress and, no
matter what the chef might do, would disappoint at table,
clinging apprehensively to the bone and tasting faintly bitter.

The cabbie—a little stressed himself, and bitter too at what
he took to be a joke at his expense—adjusted his rearview
mirror so that he could drive and watch the yellowed water
in the tank. He was used to spying into women's laps that
way. He'd earned a little cash a week or two before when he
had spied a politician's hand rest briefly in a woman's silken
lap. The woman was an actress, not the politician's wife, and
the cabbie sold both names to me. You will not mind, I
know, if briefly, after introductions, and having kept myself
discrete thus far, I step back into shadow. This story is not
mine, at least not more than it is every citizen's. I am—I
was—a journalist. My byline was The Burgher. I was, at this
time, the mordant, mocking diarist on the city's daily.

On Victor's birthday, the cabbie phoned me once again and
sold the story of the fish tank too. "By God," he said, "I
swear the water smelled of piss." Here was, I felt . . . The
Burgher felt . . . an amusing illustration of the oddity of millionaires, but only worth a quarter of the fee—and half the
column space—that The Burgher's budget could afford for
hands in laps. The paper ran the story in The Burgher column, on the back page, with a cartoon—a cab completely full
of water, bubbles, weed; a snorkeled diver at the wheel; a
periscope; and at the street corner a well-dressed perch, fin
urgently raised, calling, "Victor's please—and hurry, he's expecting me for lunch!"

Nobody would have the nerve to show the piece to Victor.
Such gossip and such jokes would only baffle him. But Rook

was in the mood for gossip and cartoons. As usual, as a Friday treat, he'd bought the midnight paper from the operatic huckster on the street below his apartment. He had taken the paper back to bed with him, with coffee, brioches and cubes of melon, and had shown it to Anna as if the joke on Victor would wear thin, the newsprint fade, unless she woke and read the paper then. She'd left her glasses in her bag, and where her bag was, amongst the urgent chaos of their clothes, their shoes, their coats, they were not sure. So Rook removed his slippers and his gown and rejoined Anna in his bed to read The Burgher's words aloud. Their laughter led to kisses, and their kisses to the passion of the not-so-young in love. A breeze from the open window rustled and disturbed the pages of the paper which had been thrown carelessly and hurriedly upon the floor. Their faces reddened, their bodies swollen with embraces, their mouths limp and tenacious, they ended their working day much as a thousand other couples did beneath the roofs and chimneys of the town, their cries and promises soon lost amid the hubbub of the traffic and the revelers and the calls of traders in the alleys, avenues, boulevards and streets. The wind. The countless noises in the lives of cities. The climax of the night. The recklessness of sleep.

The marketplace was resting, too, though not silently. The stalls and awnings had been packed away—some in padlocked wooden coffins, five meters long; some decked and lashed like rigging on a boat and riding out the stormless doldrums of the night; some wigwamed carelessly and stacked like bonfire wood. It looked as if a squall had struck, reducing all the trading vibrancy of day to sticks and cobblestones. The noise came mostly from the cleansing teams, the men in yellow PVC whose job it was to operate the sweepers brushing up the vegetable waste, the paper bags, the scraps and orts of the Soap Market like prairie harvesters, and then to uncap the hydrants and bruise and purge the cobblestones with sinewed shafts of pressured water. The quieter group—men, women, kids—foraged for their supper and their bedclothes, gleaning mildewed oranges, snapped carrots, the occasional coin, cardboard sheets and squares of polyethylene before the brushes and the jets turned the market's oval benevolence to spotlessness.

Quite soon the cleansing gangs would go. The night folk of the Soap Market would secure their nighttime roosts. Dismantled stalls and awnings—once the water has run off—provide good nesting spots for people without homes. Cellophane Man—his clinging suit refreshed and thickened by the cellophane he found discarded in the marketplace—stood, vacuum-wrapped, to watch and organize the final vehicles of night. The drinkers had their corner. They did not sleep at night, but sat in restless circles, sharing wine or urban rum and fending off the dawn with monologues and spats. The shamefaced women there, fresh out of luck and cash, kept to themselves, and, desperately well-mannered, slept sat up, their arms looped through their bags, their minds elsewhere. Only the young stretched out—the youths who'd come to make their marks away from home and had ended up as city dips, or tarts, or petrol sniffers. Some—like Joseph—had just arrived. The Soap Market was their first bed-sit, and still they hoped that day would bring good luck. Indeed—again— where else would Joseph be but here? Not sitting at a bar for sure. The pockets of his summer suit were empty still. *Emptier,* in fact. He'd lost his clipping from the catalog. He'd dropped his knife. He'd come off worse with Rook. He slept—young, stretched out—with spinach as a pillow and a mattress made of planks.

At least he slept. For all the bad luck of the day he still retained the knack of easing tiredness, relieving disappointment, with a little sleep. At first he was unnerved by lights and noise; the engines and the headlamps of motorbikes ridden by spoiled young men drawn to the dismantled market by the fun that could be had at speed on cobblestones, and with the "trash" who drank and slept there. But soon the town went quiet—no hoots or yelps to puncture night. He'd lain and watched the city darken as the last few lights in homes and offices had been switched off by insomniacs and caretakers and automatic timing switches. The only lights that

did not dim were streetlamps and the silent conifer of silver
bulbs which stood, unswaying, twenty-seven storeys high
above the town. This Tree of Lights was Big Vic at rest. The
block's computer told which bulbs to shine, and when. It was
the perfect fir—except that those who cared to stare might
see at night a firefly at the summit of the tree, as Victor—
without the knack of sleep—wandered through his apartment
and his office suite, marked as he moved from room to room
by lamps and lights outside the fir tree's grid.

It was his birthday night. He'd had too much to drink. One
glass at his age was too much. His stomach growled. The
pissed-on perch was drowning in champagne. Walking
seemed to ease the wind which pressed against his chest. He
belched to let the champagne free. He knew that in his office
desk there were sachets of kaolin to still his gut. He found
them, and he found the portfolio of drawings, too, the artist's
working notes for the sculpture that his contemporaries
seemed keen to force on him. He carried the portfolio to the
water fountain in the lobby outside his office suite. He
tipped the dry and powdered kaolin into his mouth like a
child with sherbet and washed it down with water from the
fountain. The coldness of the water dislodged the pains inside
his chest. He belched again. He felt quite well at last. Not
sick, at least. Not faint.

Victor put down the sheaf of drawings and looked at each.
Romantic, formal pieces sketched in chestnut pastels. A market vendor weighing out his fruit. A girl with grapes and
flowers. A porter with three produce trays on his head. And
then—alarmingly—a drawing of his past: a beggar woman
with a suckling child, her hand outstretched, the gift of apple
balanced on her palm. He sat, he almost fell, into an aged
wooden chair pushed in shadow up against the lobby wall.
He looked and looked at what he took to be a drawing of his
mother and himself . . . what, almost eighty years before?
His head was flooded now, his face was drained. This was
the statue that he'd have. He'd make his mother once again.
He'd put her back. He knew exactly where she should sit and
beg in bronze, between the Soap Market and the garden. At

last, the implications of his sweeping hand that afternoon
upon the roof became more clear. He'd start afresh, just as
his accountants had advised. He'd build a market worthy of
the statue. A market like a cathedral, grand and memorable.
A market worthy of a millionaire. He would outlive himself
in stone. His mother would outlive herself in bronze. It made
good business sense, though no doubt Rook would not ap-
prove. He'd fight for Paradise.

What better time to start than then-and-there? Decide. Remove all obstacles. Proceed. Victor took his memo pad and
wrote a note in pencil on it. For Anna. She could deal with
Rook. A less generous man would call the police, and let
them sort it out. But, no, let Anna do the job. That's what
he paid her for.

Victor was glad—relieved—to have this task with which to
fill his ninth decade and so engrossed by every touch and
mark upon the artist's page, that he neither saw nor felt the
plastic foliage pressing on his back.

PART TWO

Milk and Honey

1

THERE'D BEEN NO OTHER BIRTHDAY chairs in Victor's life, other than the one that Rook had prepared for him when he was old, other than the one he'd sat upon yet failed to see. Victor was a townie almost through and through. He was not as soily or as leafy as he claimed. He'd fled the countryside when he was three weeks old, when this brusque, gymnastic century was also in its infancy. His dad had died. An epidemic of the sweats had seen him off before his son was born. His home village could barely cope with the sudden glut of widows, dotagers and orphans, all shaken from their tree before their time, all seeking charity at once. A widower could work and earn his keep. But who would go without to feed and clothe the harness maker's wife, or her new baby, when it came? Her husband's skills had died with him. He had left no land or crops for her to sell. The workshop cottage and its yard was only theirs by rent. The landlord's agent let her stay until the child was born, and then—what choice had he?—he asked for payment for the weeks she'd missed. The money that she'd made from selling unworked leather, harness tools, her husband's horse, was not enough to clear the months of debt, and live. The mother and her wrinkled kid were as cold and poor as worms.

At least Victor's tiny gut was full. His mother's breasts were independent of all the hardship in their lives. But she was weak from loss of blood and milk and lack of food. The

best she had for meals was half a block of pigeon's cheese and
two jumps at the larder door.

What of the free food of the countryside? The mushrooms
and the nuts? The stubble grain left over by the thresher and
the harvesters? The berries and the birds? The honey and the
fish? Life's not like that, except in children's books. The free
food of the countryside is high and maggoty before it's ripe;
or else it's faster than the human hand and can't be caught.
What's free and good is taken by the bully dogs and birds.
What's left is sustenance for flies and mice.

So Victor's mother had no choice but to pack a canvas
bag—a bag her husband stitched for her before they wed—
and set off with her baby to the town. She had a distant,
younger sister there, a maid to some rich man. Her address
was *poste restante* at the Postal Hall. Victor's mother asked the
landlord's agent to write a note. It said, "Sister, my husband's
dead, and less than twenty-three years old. I have a child. His
name is Victor. So we must come to you as you are all we
have, and will be with you soon for love and help. Today is
Monday and the 26th of June. God keep you well. Signed
lovingly, your only Em." She begged a postage stamp and
left the letter with the village clerk. There was a mail train
every other day. The letter would soon be in the town. Her
sister would prepare to take the widow and the orphan in,
for sure, and find them food and work.

Em made a sling for Victor and strapped him to her chest
with her shawl. She tied the canvas bag across her back. She
threw some grains of maize—for Thanks and Fare-thee-well—
on the doorstep of her house. She lit a candle. She ought to
carry light from their old home into their new, wherever that
might be. Light is luck. You take it with you when you
move. She lifted it and put it down again. Once. Twice. The
flame drew back. It ducked and shrank. The light would have
to stay. She was not fool enough to think she'd keep the flame
alive out in the wind and night.

"We'll leave it here for him," she told her son. "Your father
always loved the mummery of candle flames." But Victor

cried when he lost the sight of that low flame. It was his first and only toy. He wanted it. Em knelt and snubbed it then, with fingers moistened by her tongue. She let him grip the candle end, a nipple and a finger made of wax. It kept him quiet as they set off on their journey to the town, through valleys made patchy blue that time of year by fields of manac beans. The sky and countryside were fabric from one cloth, and that the color of the Caribbean Sea.

The baby Victor was content with little more than suck and blow. He was happy just to hold the candle end, to sleep or feed, made biddable by the rhythm of his mother's steps, kept warm and coddled by the sling and by her breasts. A child of three weeks old is built to bend and bounce and sleep throughout. And just as well, because his mother's hike to town took seven days and passed through storms and woods and fords which would frighten and dismay children of a greater age. Em feared wolves and chills and broken legs, but Victor filled his empty head with heartbeats from his mother's chest. She washed his soiled and heavy swaddle cloths in streams and let the wet clothes dry and stiffen, draped across her back. By the time they reached the outposts of the civic world, the cemeteries, the rubbish dumps, the gypsy camps, the homes of bankers, and abattoirs, the outer boulevards of town, Victor had regained his birth weight. His mother, on the other hand, was paler, thinner, colder than a cavern eel.

They left the fields behind. They reached metaled roads, and rows of houses with lawns and carriage drives. They came through high woods and found a measured townscape spreading out in grays and reds and browns, with a shimmering mirage of smoke which made it seem as if the hills beyond were chimney products of the city mills and that the sky was spread with liquid slate. This was a different city from the one we know. Less egoistic, more malign.

Em carried Victor down the causeway of trees and grass which split the city's outer boulevard in two, and conducted trams and countryside into the town. These were the days when foot and hoof and wheel were battling for the government of towns, and wheels—because the rich had motor cars—were winning every skirmish on the streets. For peace and quiet the walkers shared the causeway with the trams.

She asked an old man for the Postal Hall. "It's far, you'll have to take a tram," he said, pointing to the tallest part of town. He showed her where the tram would stop and waited while she joined the queue. But, once he'd turned away to dodge a path between vans and carriages which thronged the road, she set off once again by foot along the tramway into the city's heart. She feared the other passengers. She feared the clanking trams with their winding, outside stairs, and their windblown upper platforms which shook and muttered like the devil's hay cart. She trembled in the street. Yet surely these were women just like her, beneath their feathers and their ribbons, beneath their hobble skirts. What had she expected? That city people got about on hands and knees, as country wisdom claimed? She looked her urban sisters in the face, but could not find an eye to match her own. They seemed like modest girls—or sinful ones—who could not lift their eyes, who did not have the energy to smile. Em walked and smiled and sought a welcome from everyone she passed. How could she know how strange she seemed, how disconcerting was her upturned face and mouth? She kissed her Victor on the head. She nuzzle-whispered in his ear the chorus of the nursery rhyme: "Townies, frownies, fancy gownies; noses up is; mouthies down is."

The Postal Hall was not what she had thought. In her world halls were empty spaces defended against the weather and the night by bricks and tiles, and only full for meetings and for feasts. She'd thought the Postal Hall would be a covered clearing in the town. Her sister, unchanged from the young girl who'd emigrated there three years before, would be waiting at the door. Or else, Em thought, she'd simply give the number of the *poste restante*. Someone would press a bell or make a call to summon her sister from her work. If it was simple to find folk in country towns, then think how easy it would be in cities such as this where everything was done so quickly and so well. Instead she found a sandstone building with

many flights of steps, and far too many doors. Her access
was blocked by carts and trams. Opposing streams of people
competed for the pavement and the road. Never had she witnessed so much speed, heard such urgency or encountered
such confidence and hesitation all at once. Never had she seen
so many horses: so at ease and so fulfilled, despite the brassy
onslaught of the motor cars.

Em crossed with Victor in the wake of two fat men in
uniforms. She chose the central entrance to the Postal Hall,
and went inside, through giant columns and great bronzed
doors. At once, she took her hat from off her hair and held
it in her hand. She almost crossed herself and fell down on
her knees to pray. Here was a bloated, oblong hall, sepulchral
and forbidding. What light there was came through high windows in a dome and from gas chandeliers which hissed like
nuns, and were reflected in the polished, veiny marbles of the
floor. There were a dozen mahogany counters and a score of
metal grills and at each one a jostling queue. All the men and
women there had forms or money or parcels or letters in
their hands and, even though they whispered as in church, the
hubbub of the place was louder, deader than the street. No
one seemed to see her there. Their arms banged into hers.
She held the paper out with her sister's number, but no one
stopped to help. She called her sister's name. Her raised voice
upset Victor who had mostly slept despite the city. He pushed
his chin against his mother's breasts, vexed by something.
Wind, perhaps, or by the taste of desperation in his mother's
milk. She pushed him to the nipple once again, but he only
bit it with his gums, and cried like old men cry, his face a
contour map of lines, his eyes squeezed tight. Again she called
her sister's name. But no one came except a postal attendant
who pointed to his badge and then the door and said that she
should leave or "cut the noise."

She joined a queue behind a line of people, most of whom
had envelopes or cards. They moved away from her, her
homelessness, her baby's noise, the smell of urine drying on
her clothesline back.

"Is this the place?" she asked, and held her sister's number up. They saw the two words *poste restante* and pointed to an anteroom. Inside were ranks of metal boxes, each with slits and locks, another counter and another queue. When her chance came, Em held her sister's name and number up against the grill. The woman at the counter glanced at it and disappeared into a closed back room without a word of greeting. She returned a moment later with a letter. It was the one which Em had sent—thanks to the borrowed literacy of the landlord's agent—two weeks before. The clerk said, "That's all there is," and "Identification, if you please."

Em was confused. She said, "My sister, is she here?" She gave her sister's name again. She held a conversation that made no sense and made the people in the queue short-tempered and amused. The counter clerk put her sister's letter to one side. "I can't help," she said. Already she was serving someone else.

Outside again, Em could not find a place to rest and contemplate. "So this is my life now," she thought. "I'm all the Bs—bitched, buggered and bewildered—and far from home!" At least young Victor was asleep again. His mother rolled the end of candle in her hand.

Em walked aimlessly while there was light. She hoped to see her sister on the street. On that first night they slept in stables near the railway yard, but in the morning dogs had sniffed them out and frightened Victor with their barks. Again she walked the streets and looked in all the faces passing by. If she saw women of her sister's age who looked like maids, she stopped them, mentioning her sister's name and asking them for help, advice or work.

"You'll not get work with that," one woman said, pointing at the top of Victor's nuzzling head. "What is it? Boy or girl? There's people in this town who'd pay good money for a kid like that. I can find you someone who will give this kid a proper life." She held Em's arm. "Come on," she said. "I'll take you to place where you can eat and sleep." Em had to shout and struggle to get free.

That second night they slept as best they could on sheltered benches at the tramway terminus. The lights were harsh and there was noise from work gangs cleaning trams. The yard-man said she'd have to move, but when he saw the child he let her stay. "For just one night," he warned. "And then you'd better take the baby back to where your people are. A little dot like that won't last five minutes sleeping rough." Em said she had a sister who would help. She told the man her sister's name and what had happened at the Postal Hall. He shook his head. "You've no idea," he said. "Your sister's just one tiny country bean, buried deep down in the sack. You won't find her by sticking in your hand and pulling ten beans out. This city's big. You've seen the crowds. Your sister, she's as good as dead unless you've got the address of a house."

Later, he came back. She woke to find him watching her. He had some cold fish and some bread.

"You're quite a pretty girl," he said, looking more at Victor and Em's breasts than at her face. "You'd better find some man to take you in. You'd better find a proper father for the child."

Em shook her head and said she didn't want the bread or fish. She had no appetite. She feared the yardman wanted something in exchange for food. His eyes were flared and restless like a pig in heat. He looked—to use her mother's phrase—as if his heart had slipped below his belt. She closed her eyes and pulled her shawl across her chest. At last she heard the yardman walk away. He had not left the bread or fish behind.

Now, her third day on the streets, she did her best to keep her problems to herself. She did not try to match the gazes of the men and women in her path. She did not seek—or trust—their kindness any more. She sat with Victor in the sun on the steps of the Postal Hall. She'd tried the clerks in *poste restante*. This time a man behind the grill had asked for proof of who she was before he'd check the number that she gave. He had looked at her and Victor as if they both were pigeons of disease. She could not stop the tears. She could not stop them running down her cheeks onto her shawl even when she'd fled the Postal Hall and rested in the sun. What should she do? Seek out the yardman? Sell Victor for the highest sum? Head out of town and find her husband's village once again, beyond the sea-blue fields? Perhaps she ought to step beneath a tram. Or try her luck beneath the hooves and wheels of some fast cart. She was too tough to take these easy routes. In those days life was hard. All life was hard. They raised you then on work, debt, hunger, cold. Three days and nights without a bed in town was better than the seven they had spent walking through the fields and woods. So things were looking up and would improve each day.

She nursed the dream of meeting with her sister once again, but set her daily target low. The first task was to find a place of safety. Then to find a place where they might sleep without fear of men or thieves. And, then, a little food perhaps. A good crisp apple, sweet with sun, was what she most desired. This was the country treat for little girls with tears or for children who'd been good. "Cheer up, dear Em," her mother used to say. "Go on. Go to the shed and get yourself a nice ripe apple from the tub." Em smiled at this—the memories of her mother and of treats. It must have been the smile and the charm and snugness of Victor at her breast, that caused the two women passing by to pause and match her smile with theirs. They threw a few small coins into Em's spread lap, and smiled again, and walked away. They looked like sisters, plump, modest girls, with shallow caps pinned to their hair and shoes with little heels. The baskets that they carried—the country market kind, woven out of teased bark—were empty. They looked like rich men's maids, like country girls who'd made their lives in town. Em followed them. It seemed the wisest thing to do. They led her through narrowing streets, past mews, and squints and alleyways, beneath the medieval wooden gates, into the merriment of the Soap Market where they—and Em herself—were soon lost in the crowd. If her sister was a maid to some rich man, then surely she would buy her victuals there, thought Em. Besides, she felt at ease and safe amongst the country products and the smells. What could be more innocent than shopping in the marketplace for food? Ten, twenty times, she thought she saw the plump

sisters once again. But all the women looked alike. They
seemed to dress the same, and walk in pairs. These were the
type of women, as Em had discovered, who would give coins
freely for a widow with a child on milk. She knew that this
was where her fortune would be made.

That night she joined the others without homes, scavenging
for fruit and coins amongst the mats and panniers of the market. She sucked the laxative and discarded fangs of rhubarb
stems. She dined on dates and green tomatoes, while Victor
made supper out of milk. She knew what she would have do
do. At dawn she woke, wet with Victor's urine, and disturbed
by cold and the noise of porters, barrows, market girls. She
turned her palm up for sympathy and cash. A market trader,
fond of children, placed a perfect apple in her palm.

So Victor lived beneath a market parasol for eight, nine
months. His mother found it thrown out. Some flower trader,
at a guess, had given up on it and bought another. Its wooden
pole had snapped in two. Its green and yellow canvas canopy
was torn. She made repairs as best she could without materials
or tools. She made the most of nothing. Women had to then.
A bit of canvas and a broken pole were better quarters than
the trenches that their men would occupy when war broke
out. Em set up her umbrella at the center of the marketplace,
between two bars and near the scrubbing stones. There was
the flat, damp trunk of a snag tree for back support. There
was market waste and mulch to soften cobblestones. Her begging pitch was chosen well. The drunks, the mad women,
the wretched ones, the innocents with visions, the dregs and
cynics, assembled at the steps of churches, and begged for
coins, alms, for Holy Charity, from worshipers, and peni-
tents, and wedding guests. The ones with whistles, tricks with
fire or balls, stayed on the busy streets and entertained the
hangers-out, the tramline queues, the café clientele for cash.
Em's kind of beggar, the kind that is the model of what could
happen to us all, must be clean—and in the Soap Garden there
was running water all day long. Crowds of people, too, with
time to spare. The traffic there was mixed: market traders,
bargirls, their customers, the women and their washing, the

men who came to drink and talk. No one came there without
a little cash. The bars, the girls, the market stalls weren't
charities. Gratitude was not the bargain that they sought.

So Victor's mother did more than beg. She traded smiles
and peace of mind. She did it well. She had a baby to support.
The colored, broken umbrella was the perfect touch. It was
what countrywomen used to shield themselves from the rain
and sun when they came in to town to sell their flowers or
their garlic cloves. Passersby would look down to see what
this woman had for sale. Em's face was hidden by the parasol.
Her breasts were on display—with Victor hard at work. The
child in need. One hand—the one with a single wedding
ring—was resting on her knee palm up. The other pressed the
baby to her chest. She marketed herself. She felt no shame.
Shame is a family, village thing. It doesn't count for much
amongst strangers. Her only fear—and hope—was that her
sister would chance by and look beneath the parasol. She did
her best to beg with pride. It was not sin, like drink or bed,
that had brought her there. She pinned a browning photograph of her husband to the canvas of the parasol with a black
silk funeral rosette. It signified, Here is a widow and her child.
Look at their man. His death has made them homeless, poor.

What of Victor at this time? Are kids of less than five weeks
old so self-engrossed and innocent that nothing in the outside
world makes any impact on their lives so long as they are fed
and warm and free from wind? The truth is, yes. The only
bonding that there is takes place between the nipples and the
lips. Victor was the kind of child who bonded to his mother's
breast with the tenacity and deliberation of a limpet on a
stone. If he was sucking, he was well. Detach his gums, prize
him loose with the gentlest finger, and he would imitate a sea
gull bickering for shrimps, his tiny call—not yet a voice—as
querulous and fretful as a dirge.

Em thought this threnody would earn her cash, that Victor
singing thinly for the breast would move the hardest passerby
to find a few spare coins. If her child could cry like that so
readily she only had to pop her nipples free when people
passed and she would earn a fortune in small change. No one

was mean enough, she thought, to close their ears to babies
in distress. But she was wrong. We in this city are the sentimental sort. We don't like tragedy. That's why the drunkard
at the railway station gates, singing bits of opera in fake Italian
and French, and bothering the women with his arias, earned
more from begging than the trolley man who'd lost a wife,
his mind and both his legs in some forgotten war. To toss
some coins in the drunk's old opera hat was to show one's
liberality, one's worldliness, one's sense that all was well. To
give cash to the trolley man—taken without a word or
smile—was to price a life, a leg, a personality. At what? At
less than one could spare. The coins clattered on the trolley
floor. Enough small change to buy a rind of pork, a two-stop
tramway ride, a piece of ribbon for your hair. The coins paid
for guilt-free entry to the forecourt and the trains. Except, of
course, the gateway where the trolley man lay in wait was
the one least used. His naked stumps, his naked hopelessness,
made people change their routes. The operatic drunkard got
the crowd.

So it was with Em. When she took Victor off the breast,
his protests cleared a space around their parasol. The shoppers
did not look to see what was for sale. They knew. They heard
the baby's screams and kept their eyes away from this private
tableau of distress. It would not do to stare. Or smile. Or
break the moment with some coins in Em's palm. Besides,
what could a coin do for one so young? A coin would not
change its life. What should they do then? Search their pockets
for a little solid love? Hold out their hands and offer to this
pair that spare room, rent free? That job? That meal? That
ticket home? No, Victor's tears—and, here, who will not
pause to note the leaden candor of the words?—were of no
worth. But what could be more appealing than a baby on its
mother's nipple, the two most loved of natural shapes, the
infant cheek, the breast? No need to look away from naked-
ness like that. You could study scenes more intimate in
churches or in galleries. Madonna and her Child. The Infancy
of Christ. First Born. Indeed, there was a sculpture reproduced on the lower-value silver coins of that time. A woman,

Concorde, held an infant to her breast, her tunic open to
her waist, her thighs becoming tree trunk, tree bole, the tree
becoming undergrowth, becoming Motherland. Here, then,
was the sentimental counterpart of comic, operatic drunks.
Em and Victor made a wholesome sight when Victor was
asleep and on her breast. Coins dropped into the mother's
palm or on her shawl were tribute tithes for family life. Em
understood. To earn the pity and the cash of citizens she had
to seem respectable and, more than that, serene—a living
sculpture labeled Motherhood.

2

FOR THOSE MEN WHO were not moved by Motherhood, Em acted Eve. She wore a mask of gormless innocence which was as challenging to them as the pouting and the paint upon the faces of the bargirls who sold real sex for cash. The market traders who passed her frequently and saw the way her expression seemed to fluctuate haphazardly between Eve and Motherhood thought—preferred to think, in fact—that Em was none too bright. They said she hadn't got the sense that God gave lettuce. They labeled her "The Radish." That was the nickname that they used for girls red-faced and odorous and from-the-soil like her. These traders had good cause to doubt the sharpness of her intellect, besides the permutations of her face. She muttered to her baby all day long, and in those slow and well-baked country tones which stretched the vowels and squashed the consonants and made the language sound like morse. Yet there was cunning just below the widow's skin. Almsgivers welcome gormless gratitude. They do not give to people who seem wiser than themselves, no matter whether it be Eve or not. No, Victor's mother was no fool, despite appearances. A fool would have an empty palm, but Em's was always slightly curled and buttoned heavily with the copper brown coinage.

Her looks, of course, were helpful there. She was a radish with a round and childish face. Her breasts were high and firm with milk. Her throat and shoulders were vulnerable and

bare. Her knees were spread to make her lap a cradle for the
child. Her feet and lower legs protruded from her apron skirts
with the unself-consciousness of a small girl sitting in shadow
at the harvest edge. Any man who paused to drop some coins
in her palm had paid for time to stare at her—though if he
stepped too close the parasol would block his view. She did
not lift her face to look these men directly in the eye. A look
from her would make them hesitate, or return the coins they
had found for her in the pockets of their coats. For women,
though, the radish turned its chin and caught their eyes and
smiled. Most shopping women are too timid and too sociable
to fail to match a freely given smile. And having smiled themselves at Em, what could they do? What else but mutter
phrases about the weather or the child, and buy escapes from
smiles and platitudes with coins in Em's palm?

Sometimes the crowds which walked between the market
and the garden were too dense for smiles to work. The shoppers simply dropped their eyes and let the beggar woman's
beams slip by. But Em soon learned the trick of targeting her
smiles with words. "God Bless the Cheerful Giver," she
would say. Or "Lady, Lady!" spoken urgently, as if she'd
spotted danger on the street or recognized a family friend. If
Em could only stop the first one in a crowd and embarrass
her to pause and give, then she could count on gifts in
streams. The first fish leads the shoal.

So Victor and his mother lived beneath the parasol by
day, and slept at night wherever they could find a place
amongst the dozing market baskets or at the back of bars.
They were not rich. Of course they were not rich. How
could they be on gleanings? But they survived, sustained
by charity, by the prospect of Em's sister chancing by, by
the certainty that the city would provide abundantly, by the
sense of awe they felt at being at the center of such a bois-
terous web, by the dislocated optimism of those whose lives
are trembling at the gate.

Was Victor happy? So far, yes. He fed contentedly. He
slept. His domain was his mother's lap. Her nipples were his
toys. But then the muscles strengthened in his neck and arms.

He grew bored with suckling. He wanted to lift his head to
look around at all the movement and the colors in the streets.
He fell back startled from the breast when he heard Em calling
out, "Lady, lady," or when the hubbub of the crowd seemed
more eloquent and urgent than the beating of his mother's
heart. He found he liked those moments best when he was
upright on his mother's knee and she was belching him, sepa-
rating the suckling oxygen from the milk that he had swallowed and which was causing jousting mayhem in his gut.
She had one hand flat on his chest, supporting him. The other
tapped and played a gentle bongo on his back between his
fragile shoulder blades. Or else she beat her tune, not with
her fingers on his back, but with the cracked and graying
candle stub which she would only light again when she had
somewhere to call home. Her son's short neck was creased in
tidal ripples of baby fat. His mouth was hanging open, waiting for the upward storm of warm and milky wind. Some
passing men made clicking noises with their tongues for him,
or comic, pouting kisses with their lips. Sometimes a dog ran
by. Or older children. Always the market offered entertainment to the child—a porter with teetering crates of onions on
his wooden cart, an argument, a snatch of song, some shoving
between friends, and, almost constantly by day, the casual,
tangled flow and counterflow of citizens in search of romance,
fortune, pleasure, food. At times the street around the parasol
was quiet and empty, but then Victor found a butterfly to
watch or sharp-edged sunlight winking on a broken neck of
glass or the flexing toes of his own feet, or spilled water—
parting, joining in its halting, bulbous progress through the
cobblestones.

Once he'd belched he would have stayed most happily, his
head laid back upon Em's chest, his hands encased in hers, a
dozing spectator. But there was money to be earned. His
mother's breasts were Victor's lathe, his workbench, the family spinning wheel. Em put her small son to her breasts. She
put his mouth onto her nipple and she held him there, whis-
pering and pigeoning into his ear to make him calm. It was
a hopeless task. A growing child will not stay calm and supine

all day long. A child is put upon this earth to raise its head
and stretch its legs and grab. Em sang him lullabies. She told
him country tales. She reminisced about her husband, Victor's
dad. But Victor did not care. The docile, suckling infant grew
less tractable. His stomach became distended and would not
clear with belches. His testicles and inner thighs became en-
crusted with a bitter rash, its scaling plaques and lesions made
angrier by the baby's water and his stools. He cried when he
was wrapped inside his swaddle clothes. He thrashed his legs
and pushed his fists into himself.

Em knew what should be done. A nappy rash is not the
plague. It only takes a little air, some white of egg, and patience for the rash to clear. She begged an egg and broke it
into the half skin of a discarded orange. She put tiny poultices
of orange pith, glistening with albumen, onto her son's sore
thighs and testicles. She stretched his legs and let him lie,
naked from the waist down, across her lap. The sun and
breeze were free to sink and curl between his legs. Young
Victor—his flaming gonads patched in orange pith—looked as
if the madders and ochers of a peeling fresco had settled in
his lap. So much for Eve and Motherhood. This sculpture
was not good for trade. Em's outstretched hand was hardly
troubled by the weight of coins now. Nobody caught her
eye. The squeamish men no longer paid to stare at Victor on
Em's breast.

The remedy was simpler than eggs. The problem was that
Em was eating too much fruit. Her diet was the oranges, the
grapes, the grapefruit, the tomatoes and the apples that the
more familiar shoppers and traders tossed to her as they
passed by. She dined on that. Then for supper she fed herself
on what she gleaned amongst the cobbles, the fruit discarded,
bruised, mislaid in the Soap Market. She fed herself on citrus,
pectins, fructose. Her waters were as tart and acid as peat
dew. Her milk was too. It passed through Victor acrimoni-
ously. It turned his gut. It chafed and scalded his most tender
skin. Feeding made him restless on his mother's breast. He
tugged her nipples in his gums. He tried to bite. And then
Em had a problem of her own. Her son had made one nipple

sore. The nipple cracked, and was not helped to heal by all the acid in her milk. She would not let her child feed on that side. She only let him suck milk from the right. But he was bigger now and wanted more. One breast was not enough. He'd passed six months. His mouth and stomach were prepared for solid food—some mashed banana mixed with milk, some peas, potatoes, stewed apple, grain. But Em was frightened of the day when Victor would renounce the breast. She liked the way he clung to her to feed. She simply pushed her child onto her one good breast and hoped his rash, her crack, would heal before the cash dried up.

Em's fruity undernourishment and her fatigue at coping with the child alone reduced her flow of milk still more. Again the baby lost all interest in the outside world. He sucked all day, but still he was not satisfied. He was tired and fretful now, at night. He would not sleep for long. He whimpered and he dozed. His mother's breasts were irritants to him. She would not let him suck the one; the other one was nearly dry. Em was in pain. Her cracked nipple had become infected through neglect. She was feverish. A nut-sized abscess had formed amongst the milk ducts of her breast. It blushed and throbbed. The pain was memorable.

"I'm out of oil," she told herself, picking at the peeling fossil slates which were her nails.

Together Em and Victor rocked away the nights and days. Em's careful presentation of her baby and herself was neglected. The radish face turned yellow-white. The good health of the countryside did not survive the hardness of the town. She had no plan to make a fresh escape. She sank into the shade beneath the parasol and called out above the fretful cries of Victor, "Please help. Please help. My baby's dying." She wept. She tried to seize the trouser legs, the skirts of passersby. She mimed an empty stomach. She put her hand onto her heart. She tried abuse. She called out words she had not known before she came to town.

It did not work. The rich were blind to noisy poverty. The people hurried by. The crazy woman with the parasol would win no hearts like that. She had trembled at the gate. Now the gate was closing on them both. The city was about to lock them in a cell of hunger, sickness and despair. And then their fortunes changed. Em's sister, Victor's aunt, was sent by chance to rescue them.

3

SHE WAS NO RICH MAN'S MAID. She was a beggar, just like Em. And worse. The aunt had lost the kitchen job for which she'd come to town three years before. She'd not excelled at the skivvying which—when her widowed father died—the Village Bench had hoped would "quieten" her. High hopes indeed for such a squally girl. Her face, and tongue, had not found favor with her employer's cook who had taken her teenage dreaminess, her wilful tawny hair, her lack of tact, her pockmarked forehead and cheeks, as insolence.

The hope had been that Aunt could—quickly, cheaply—be transformed from hayseed into scullion. But she was not the curtsy-kowtow kind and had no kitchen skills. "She couldn't boil up water for a barber," cook had said. "That girl's as much use in this kitchen as a cat." Instead, she was the sort who saw the city as a place for play not work. Unlike the country working day the city was ruled by clocks. It had its shifts for work and meals and sleep. And there were shifts when Aunt was free to play. What did she care if cook found single, errant, tawny hairs entwined in dough or curling like a filamentary eel in "madam's" soup? Why all the fuss? Nobody had died from swallowing one hair. And what if there were egg bogeys between the tines of breakfast forks? Or if the skillet smelled of pork? So much the better if the skillet smelled of pork! Anyone with sense or appetite would take a fold of bread and "wipe the pig's behind." She and her older, married sister, Em, fought for such a treat when they were young.

Aunt simply could not understand the odd proprieties, the niceties, of bourgeois city life where more was wasted than consumed, where laughter, yawns and stomach wind shared equal status, swallowed, hidden, stifled by a hand. She did not like "indoors." But she adored the bustle and the badinage of streets, the intimacy of crowds, the hats, the clothes, the trams, the liberty. She had it to herself once in a while—when she was sent by cook to purchase extra eggs or vegetables, when every second Saturday she had a half day off, when—once, at night—she climbed the backyard wall and walked till dawn in those parts of the city where lamps—and spirits—were rarely dimmed. On that occasion Aunt was met by her employer's dogs when she returned. They took her for a thief and, though they knew her well enough from all the times she'd favored them with kitchen slops, they were too dumb or mischievous to let her clamber back into the kitchen yard. Their barking called the Master and the police. For cook this was the final straw. She did not find it likely that the girl had just been "walking" as she claimed.

"You country girls are all the same," she said, " 'Bumpkins do not good burghers make.' " She did not say what she had told her employers, that Aunt was mad, "a leaking pot." She paid Aunt off with the exact train fare—one-way—to the village of her birth, only fifteen months after she had fled it for the prospects of the town. Aunt spent the train fare on a hat.

She skipped around the bars and restaurants quite happily. She wore her hat—a high-crowned, deep-brimmed cloche in straw with dog rose sprigs in felt. It was the fashion for that year amongst young women of a cheerful disposition. It masked the pockmarks on her forehead and made her seem more winsome than she was. She doffed her hat at groups of men who sat on the patios of bars or on the terraces of restaurants. They seemed so bored and so keen to be amused. She only had to smile or comic-curtsy or spin her hat around upon her open hand, to earn a little cash. It was so easy to take money or a meal off men and still stay good.

There were a dozen country girls like her who worked the same neighborhood of the city and who shared a two-room attic in a tenement near the Soap Market, in the Woodgate district. The Princesses they were called, sardonically, by the poor families and the laborers who inhabited the lower floors. They'd all lost jobs as maids or kitchen girls and had finished on the streets. Some stole. Some sold themselves to men. Some earned a little from the sale of matches or doing fetch-and-carry for the posh, frail ladies who took strong waters in the smart salons. Aunt stuck to begging. She was good at it. And soon she had enough each day to pay the pittance rent for a small corner in the Princesses' attic rooms. There was no proper light or water there, or any stove for cooking. But there was camaraderie and candles. We know that poverty's not fun, but if you are young and poor in company then shame, and lack of hope, and loneliness do not increase the burdens on your back. Sharing nothing or not much is easier than sharing wealth.

So Aunt was happy with her life. There was no washing up. No slops. No punctilious, grumpy cook. No silver break-fast forks. They shared—like only women will—their daily gains, their city spoils, their swag. The only privacy they had—if, say, they wished to sit unnoticed on the pot—was to hide behind the lines of washing, strung across the rooms, or to wait for darkness. But why hide away to pee, when peeing in full view of all your friends can cause such mirth and rau-cous joviality? "Hats off," they used to say to Aunt, whose cloche would rarely leave her head. "It's impolite to pee like that in the presence of Princesses." They'd wait until they heard the spurt of urine in the bowl and then they'd say, "Hats off. Stand up . . . and take a bow!" Or "Sing, sing! And show your ring." The communal laughter of these Prin-cesses was laughter with no victim and no spite.

Aunt learned the tricks of begging from their attic talk at night, as each described the day they'd had; how men's brains were unfastened with their braces; how careless waiters were with tips; which restaurant chefs would give a back-step meal to any girl who'd volunteer to mop the floor. You'd eat the

meal—then run; what places were the worst and best for
palming cash from strangers. She learned how just a dab of
zinc and vinegar could make a girl look feverish. It didn't
work with men, but women—older ones—would pay to
make you go away. She learned a gallery of beggars' faces,
how to slide her tongue between her teeth and lips to look
the simpleton, how to fake the single floating eye of the insane, how picking noses is just as good as picking pockets for
getting cash if it is done on restaurant terraces and in a childish, not a vulgar way.

So she did well on city streets. She begged and importuned
enough to count herself—by country standards—well set up.
She was much plumper than the girl who'd skivvied in the
kitchen. She had her hat as talisman and her Princesses for
family. She did not think about the coming day—or much
about the day just passed. She liked to place her hat upon her
head and wander streets as if they were country lanes and she
was simply searching for free fruit. She never tired of putting
out her hand or challenging—this was her favorite trick—the
drinking men in bars to toss and land a coin in the canyon
brim of her straw hat.

Despite the drama of the hat, she was an ill-built, scruffy
girl. The pits and craters on her face were blessings in disguise. They kept the men at bay. She did not have her sister's
looks. But what she had was something better, rarer in those
days than mere good looks. She had a sense of unembarrassed
self-esteem. She liked the way she was. So when she heard
her sister calling from beneath her green and yellow parasol,
"Please help. Please help. My baby's dying," Aunt was not
the least put out. She'd heard a hundred stories of the saddest
kind of why and how her Princesses had fallen on hard times.
Tough tales that made her wonder how animals, as frail as
adolescents are, could surface with such buoyancy from
depths so cold and bitter. She guessed that there was death in
Em's own tale or illness or the loss of work. She was not
shockable. It seemed to fit, not flout, the patterns of the world
that Em, like her, should end up in this place. Fate—the fate
of being born a countrywoman in those days—was not Coin-

cidence, nor was it Chance. The poor take trams. They travel on fixed lines. It's only the rich that go at will in carriages.

Aunt stooped below the parasol and matched her sister with the voice she'd heard. They were the same, except that Em was poorer, thinner than a head of corn that had been stripped of ears. Aunt knew—from just one glance—that her sister was forlorn and ill and underfed. She heard the whimpers of the child. Her niece or nephew, she presumed. She felt content to have a sister once again, to be an aunt. She knew that she could help.

So Em became the oldest of the Princesses—and Victor was their little Prince. Most of the girls were glad to have a child at first. They passed him to and fro and petted him as if he were a cat. They teased him with their little fingers in his mouth and marveled at the power of his gums and lips. They loved to belch him on their knees, his fingers wrapped so bonelessly round theirs, or to press their noses to his head and smell the honey-must of cradle cap. They kissed the baby dimples on his arms, his back, his chin, and called him "Little rogue" and sang "Dimple in chin, Devil within." They made noises like you hear in zoos from those determined that the parakeets should talk. But Victor was in no mood for games. You see, already he was malcontent, and not because of his acid rash alone. He wanted food. Warm lips and murmurs do not serve supper. He tried to push his hand between the buttons of their dresses. He wet and creased the fabric of their blouses with his mouth.

"They're all the same," a Princess said. "Men only want one thing."

Aunt found some floorboard for Em and Victor below the sloping attic roof. She scrounged a little matting and some cloth for blankets. Aunt carried Victor to the street, and within twenty minutes had returned with a topless conserve jar containing tepid mashed potato, manac beans and gravy which she had begged at a restaurant's back door.

"This kid's a gold mine." She crushed the beans and made a mixture with the potatoes and gravy. "There's plenty here for all of us," she said, though softly so that "all of us" meant

Victor, Aunt and Em. She made stew balls in her palms, four large ones the size and shape of eggs, and smaller pellets for her nephew, Victor. His first solid meal. He was almost nine months old. His first milk teeth were winking through the gum.

Together they poked the food into his mouth. It was too dry for him. He coughed. And when he closed his mouth the food was squeezed between his lips and fell into his mother's hand. He did not cry, though. This was not distress. He simply did not have the knack of swallowing such lumps. Perseverance won the day. The sisters had a score of fingers to keep the food inside the baby's mouth. Fingertips are like enough to nipples for Victor to be confused and suck. The sucking did the trick. For every scrap that slithered out across his chin a small amount went down his throat. His sucking dragged the gravy from the mixture. He liked the smell and salt. He had his fill. He slept—for once—without his mother's breast.

Em told her story of how she'd come to town, and how the town had almost beaten her. Then Aunt replied with hers, and how the town was better than a friend. It took more care of waifs and strays than any village in the land. "If that weren't so," she said, "the countryside would be the place for girls like us. The trees and fields would overflow with widows and orphans. But look around you, Em. Look on the streets. It's cities take us in." And then she added, "City air makes free."

They talked like artisans at lunch, about the problems of the begging trade. Their jobs were like all jobs. Why should they be abject? They had their colleagues, rivals, clientele. They had their working rituals, too—and the pride and purpose that such employment brings. The problem was that Em's breasts were nearly dry, and still too sore for comfort. Giving solid food to Victor might give them time to heal—but would the child return to the breast when he and Em were begging once again?

"When Victor isn't feeding," Em explained, "I don't make money on the streets."

"If that's the only problem you've got, then you're the lucky one!" said Aunt. She took her sister by the hand. "Just sleep," she said. "I told you, Victor's gold to us. A baby at the breast earns cash. You don't need milk for that. You don't need spit to stick your tongue inside your boyfriend's ear."

At dawn, while Em and Victor were still asleep, Aunt put on her hat and went down to the bars where the traders, warehousemen and porters had coffee-and-a-shot before they started work. She found the comic angle for her hat. She wore her sweetest, daftest smile. She stood against the walls of bars and called for pitch-and-toss. She'd show the men her plump and mottled knees if anyone could throw a coin in her hat. The man who stepped up to her and softly dropped a coin in, imagined he had got the best of Aunt. She showed her knees. He departed poorer than he'd come, but she, quite soon, had earned enough for food. She bought a bruised banana, cheap. A fresh, warm turban of bread. A bottle of rootwater. A twist of honey. Cheese. She was a cheerful sight upon the street. She skipped like someone half her age. She took the stairs two at a time. She found a dancing path between the sleeping Princesses, and spread the breakfast on the boards. She broke the bread and cheese. She snapped the banana into three, and mashed one third with rootwater in a spangled cup until it ran like gruel and was thin enough for Victor to swallow.

She woke up Em and then woke up Victor too. He was not ready for the day. He wailed like a damp yew log in fire. She pinched him on his arm until tears dropped heavily and he was wide awake and mutinous. Em tried to push her sister back, but Aunt was stronger. She lifted Victor by his arms and held him tightly at her side. He beat her with his wrinkled fists. She said, "Now watch!" She undid the loops of her woollen top, and pushed her clothes aside. She put her index finger in the twist of honey and wiped it on her tiny nipple. The honey sagged like candle grease. Aunt pinched Victor one more time. His voice made pigeons fretful on the roof. Aunt put him firmly on her breast. The silence was as sudden and as comic as a burst balloon. He pressed his mouth and

tongue onto her skin. He sucked and made the noises that
children make when drinking juice through straws. "You see?
He doesn't kneed a knife and fork," she said. "Or milk." She
outlined how they would share the child. They'd work the
boy in shifts. "Four tits beat two," she said. "Ask a cow.
And honey's got the edge on milk. Ask bees."

Em watched her baby nuzzling at her sister's breast, as
fickle when it came to food as adults are with love. He threw
his head from side to side and tried to get a proper grip on
this modest nipple, this impermeable and unswollen breast,
this honeycomb. He was engrossed and sweetly satisfied and,
for the moment, wanted nothing else. Em almost wished that
she and Victor were still marooned beneath the parasol.

4

So this was Victor's life. Two lives, in fact. While other children learned to crawl and pick up what they found as if the world was all a toy and theirs, he shared two women's breasts. His gums grew numb on honey. His nose was flattened by their ribs.

Em still preferred to work the marketplace. She knew the faces there and all the odors were the odors of the countryside, congested and compressed. She'd lost the parasol. Its pole had ended up on someone's fire. Its cheerful canopy was ripped and jettisoned. But she sat cross-legged for harvesting ("We're harvesters. We do not beg," her sister had said) in the usual spot, between the garden and the market, her back against the flat trunk of her tree. It was a comfort when she saw crops of the class and quality that her birth village had produced— "yellows" from the potato fields, carrot clumps, onion sets, the stewing roots, sweet dumpling pumpkins, the dusty shingle of the beans—all so familiar from the days when she and all the other village kids had been dragooned to join the harvesters so that the crop could be brought in quickly and at its best.

She'd known, she would know still, all villagers apart from the shape of their arses. A bean field when the beans were splitting was a field of arses facing bluntly upward as villagers played midwife with the soil. A potato field was much the same. The horse plough turned the soil—and then the village

bums were higher than the noses for the day as harvesters
with trowels sought out the timid "yellows" in the crevices
and punctures of the soil. These townies only dined on such
fresh crops because the country folk were not too proud or
idle to stick their arses in the air. Em slowly had convinced
herself—with Aunt's help—that coins given to her now were
payment for the hours that they'd spent as girls, unpaid, with
blackened hands and aching backs amongst the produce of
their fields.

She harvested the marketplace, less passionately, less urgently, than she had done before her sister arrived. She had
a place to sleep, a family, a group of friends, somewhere to
wash and eat, a simple route to and from her work, free time.
She felt no different from the other working women in the
marketplace and garden, the waitresses and salesgirls, the
prostitutes—that is to say, she felt as bored, inured and dutiful as anyone who has to labor for their pay.

While Aunt slept late, Em took the morning and the midday shift because those were the times when people came to
shop for vegetables and fruit, the times when the Soap Market
and the Soap Garden were most profligate and careless with
their cash. She served her time, with Victor at her breast. She
had a little milk and honeyed nipples to keep her outsized
baby still. And if he tried to raise his head? Or twist to see
the world pass by? She only had to wrap his head inside her
shawl for him to quieten or to doze. The darkness was a drug
for him. His pulse was slower underneath the cloth than when
his ears and eyes were naked to the clamor and the city light.
If he cried, Em simply hushed him with a dab of honey on
her breast, and murmured country comforts to him with her
lips pressed to his cheek or ear. "The squeaky door gets all
the oil," she'd say. "The gabby cat gets cream." She found
rhymes and games to put him on the breast. "Ring the bell,"
she said, and tugged the wayward quiff of hair on Victor's
head. Then, "Knock the door." She drummed her fingers on
his forehead. "Lift the latch": she pinched his nose and—that's
the nature of the nose—his jaw dropped down, his mouth

agape. "And walk right in!" She placed her honeyed nipple
on his lower lip.

In the early afternoon Victor's skipping aunt would come
with bread or cheese to share with any fruit or salad that Em
had harvested that morning. There was no food for Victor
then. He only fed at night. "The hungry mongrel does not
bark," Aunt said. She made these nonsense phrases up, to
mock her sister, to mock herself. She liked to play the country
muse for those foolish men in bars who'd pay for hollow
"wisdoms" such as that. She was not right about the hungry
mongrel—but she was wise to caution against feeding Victor
while he worked. A sated child will not take honey. A sated
child cannot be blackmailed by the promise of a meal. It's
hungry circus seals that sit obediently on tubs and balance
beach balls on their snouts. The more they are rewarded with
a fish, the more they flap and slither out of line.

When Aunt and Em had eaten, Victor was passed on. His
face was pressed against the younger breasts, where the honey
was not mixed with the blood-hot residues of milk, but where
the torso flesh was deeper, softer, less discrete, Aunt tied him
to her with a sash which passed around her neck and round
her waist. His body was not long, but long enough by now
to make Em's sister stoop a little from the toppling ballast of
his weight. Em was now free to walk back to their attic
rooms or buy a little food or bring the family washing to the
public washing square at the center of the Soap Garden, or
sleep.

Her sister carried Victor to her usual haunts, the bars, the
restaurants, the tea salons, of the medieval streets to the east
of the station yard. She wore Victor like she wore her hat,
an accessory to her outfit and her act. She'd show her knees—
at least—to anyone who'd pitch-and-toss some silver in her
hat or place a coin "on my baby's cheek." If any man seemed
slow to search for change, she'd wink at all his friends and
ask, with the innocence of a music hall soubrette, "What's
wrong with him? Has he got a snake in his pocket, or what?"
She'd lean over dining tables with Victor gummed to her

breast like a bloated termite at a grape, and invite the diners—
loosened by the wine or beer—"to place a silver coin on my
baby's eyes if you want fortune and good health." It sounded
like an age-old rite. In fact, she'd dreamed it up. If young
Victor raised his head, to bare his honeyed teeth and scare off
custom with his cries, then Aunt would knock his head back
to the breast with the speed and firmness of a factory foreman,
bent on keeping working children's noses to the loom or press
or lathe. She was not hard. She simply liked the way she was,
and wished to keep it so. What sort of kindness would it be—
to whom?—if she behaved toward the boy as if he were a
rich man's son whose duties only stretched from play and
food to sleep? What money would she harvest on the street
with Victor in her care, if Victor were the normal child, allowed to crawl and scream and play with stones exactly as he
wished, if Aunt was just another "mother" in the town?
Where was the sentiment, the plaintiveness in that? Who'd pay
for such mundanity? So trading says, The child must suck the
breast. Six coins out of ten are lost unless the child is on the
breast. So, Child on Breast! That was the requisition of the
working day.

It was not fair that Victor did not seem a willing volunteer
in this. "This kid's a gold mine," Aunt had said. He kept the
sisters fed and clothed. He kept them decent, free from sin.
They did not have to steal or prostitute themselves or find
thin comforts and escape in drink, while Victor was still
small. They did not have to learn the trade of *dipping*—picking
pockets, that's to say—while Victor's tiny grazing head was
eloquent enough to make hard men and stony women pick
their own pockets of small change.

They used the child as bait, it's true. Put crudely and unadorned like that, it makes the sisters less than kind. But *Less
than Kind* is not the same as *Without Love*. He was their "little
blessing"; their meal ticket, too. They loved him for the gift
he gave them: he saved them from the grinding molars of the
city which seized on women very much like Aunt and Em
and made them old and sick and spiteful within days. Imagine
Em and Aunt without a child. No need. Just think of all the

country girls who lived and begged and starved alone in cities such as ours, across the world, in those dead days before the rich bred consciences, before the telephone, the car, the welfare check, the safety net, the thawing of the civic heart. The lucky ones kept jobs. They labored over stoves. They scuffed their knees in cooling clinkers as they raked out grates at dawn. Perhaps they flirted with a stable hand or—more ambitiously—exchanged embraces with madam's chauffeur. Perhaps they fell in love and, if their half days coincided with their sweetheart's—rare chance, indeed—they walked unfettered for an hour, embraced by city crowds and understanding all too well that this was the best that life in towns would offer them, that there was worse awaiting them, if they should lose their looks or tempers or good luck. They could be roofless, empty gutted, and with no embraces to exchange except those given to their own rough knees, at night.

So why should Aunt and Em not count themselves as blessed in having Victor? Why should they not take care to put him to good use, and love him still, and love him all the more? They liked the independence that he gave. They did not know—he did not know—that they had robbed him of his liberty, that their rib cages were for him two sets of prison bars, their arms his warders, their breasts his sedatives.

They went about their business, dawn till dusk, and ploughed a life. Quite soon—within a year and a half, when Victor was three, with teeth—they had harvested enough to move downstairs, below the attic rooms where the changing cast of Princesses had made the sisters ill at ease. They rented one small room in a crowded family apartment. It was their own. There was a tap and a small coal stove that they could use in the raised courtyard at the back. There was a communal but a proper toilet too, in an outhouse. The sisters took their turn in emptying the "honey can" when it was full. Was this the "citizenry" that they sought? There was no time to ask. There was no time to sit like sisters, face-to-face, and knit a conversation from the warming wool of gossip, hope and love. Em had to be at work before the traders took their breakfasts in the bars. Aunt had to be at work until the restau-

rants had closed and all the rich and drunk had gone back
home. So Victor grew weaker, older, a city child whose landscape was all ribs and cloth and honeyed, female flesh. The
stones and mayhem of the street were ever at his back, a
hidden world imagined only from its hums and dins and
choruses.

What does a small boy know, a child that—by this time—
is barely four? A toddler who has yet to crawl? A little smoth-
ered lad? A boy who is trained to do nothing but drape and
nuzzle like a bean-sized joey in its mother's pouch? How
could young Victor tell that this routine of facing flesh all day
was not normality? He was no revolutionary in bud, no mys-
tic with a notion of a patterned world. He was just worm—
a mouth, an arse, a readiness to bend. He sought the softest
earth, the warmest way, the stone that had no jags, the twi-
light safety of the breast. He had no choice. They'd got him
trained, just like a dog. He knew that if his head went up and
turned toward the lights, a hand much stronger than his head
would push him back. He knew that if he spat the nipple
from his mouth and raised his chin to cry he would not get
what he was crying for, unless he wanted pinches on his legs
or Aunt to hold his nose.

He had no general sense of smell. The cloying odors of the
honey and the herby alkalescence of the breast blanked out
the city smells, the horses and the fruit, the men with pipes,
the scent, the woodsmoke, the urine and the puddled rain.
His eyes were clinkered with the grit of too much sleep. The
underlids were sore from lack of air and exercise. They did
not focus well in light—and streamed at night when he was
fed with solids in the oval, orange thrall of candlelight. His
legs and arms had not grown strong. They'd had no chance
to punch and kick the air. His hands were good for nothing
needing pull or grip. He lived for sound alone. His mouth
was sealed—but his ears were free and open to the world. He
knew the market cries, the trundle of a porter's cart, the curses
of the men weighed down by baskets of crops, the whistles
of a happy man. He knew the tucks and folds of Em's sweet
murmurs from the challenge and the bounciness of Aunt's

street voice. He knew them, but could not clothe them with a shape or form. They were just sounds to him. Sound is air made tangible. No one flourishes on air alone.

As he got older, heavier, so Em and Aunt got tired of harvesting the streets. It was less fun, living in their shrunken home, away from all the toughness and the jollity of the Princesses above. The sisters got on well enough because they hardly met, because they hardly talked. And just as well. If they had met and talked more frequently they would have found what many siblings find when they have fled the nest, that sharing parents is no guarantee that temperaments are also shared. The only thing they did as family was sleep together, sharing mats, with Victor in between. Their bodies were the rails of Victor's cot.

Aunt took the boy onto the streets with less enthusiasm as he grew older, as he passed four. He weighed too much. His body was too long; when he was "feeding" his feet found footholds on her knees. It made no sense to carry him, but Aunt was not prepared to sit with Victor on her lap all day, a fixture on some restaurant steps or at the entrance to a bar, waiting for the harvest to make its way to her. She was the sort who liked to move about, to have a stage, to work (she said) "my mouth and not my bum." She tried to keep him entertained, yet keep him also blind and nuzzling at her chest. She had not learned the sentimental skills of entertaining kids. They liked crude noises, little nonsense rhymes, and songs with simple choruses. What kind of child would understand or like Aunt's running commentary on the world, the adult jokes, the cynicism of her words as she earned money on the streets?

"This one's a soft touch," she would say, as she—with Victor held aloft—approached a woman sitting, waiting, at a table in the garden of a tea salon. "Look at that coat! She's good for a fifty at the very least." And then, "A twenty! God, she's tight. Look at her little walk. You'd think her bum was made of tin. Her boyfriend's out of luck tonight for sure. . . ."

Or else, "Hey! This fellow's giving me the eye. Suck, Vic-

tor, suck. It turns 'em on. Hold tight. I'll give my hat a little
twirl. And show my teeth . . . Aha! He's got his rhubarb up.
What did I say? Two fifties and a wink. I bet his wife don't
know he's got "expenses" in the town like me. She'd have a
fit if she could see her little chap's so loose with cash." Or
else, "Oh dearie dear, here's a fellow looks as if he's wee'ed
on nettles and doesn't like the potpourri. His lady's stood him
up, I bet, or else his boss has stood him down. 'Hey mister!
Put some silver on the baby's eye. Whatever's wrong will
turn out right!' Well, well, we're not surprised. He'd rather
that we went away. It would appear he does not wish to give
to charities like us." Or (Aunt's step and manner quickened
as she saw men outside a bar), "Smiles on parade. This lot
are drunk enough to spit cash in my hat!"

The truth is, Victor grew to like his aunt's brash tones,
despite his inability to understand the words. He liked the
way she walked the streets and joined in badinage and arguments and helped herself—and him—to uneaten titbits from
restaurants. He began to lift his head more often now or find
a sideways view onto the world of streets and bars. Aunt did
not care enough to push him back to feed. She'd tired of
having sticky honey on her blouse, of having this stretched
infant invade her clothes. Life was more comic and more
profitable if she just put him down inside a restaurant gate
and let him topple under waiters' feet while she did routines
with her tongue and hat. Here was an education of a kind.
He learned about the legs of chairs, and shoes. And once—
the final straw—he learned that tablecloths could move, if
tugged. He learned, too, what fun it was to have a bowl of
lukewarm noodles smash onto the floor. He'd never had a toy
so wonderful as noodles and the broken bowl. The mistress
of the restaurant, of course, was not charmed by Victor's
play, or by the mess of tablecloth and food. "I do not care
to see you back in here," she told Aunt, as Victor draped the
noodles round his fingers. "Not unless you're eating à la carte.
Get off our premises. Remove yourselves. Go back into the
haystack where you belong. No beggars here. Understand? If
you don't want to eat, stay on the street."

She took Aunt by the arm and pushed her toward the doorway.

"And don't forget the kid," she said. "You shouldn't have a kid. It's not his fault. Look at the state of him! What kind of person lets their little boy crawl on the floor like that? You shouldn't even have a kid if you can't live respectably. . . ."

"All right," said Aunt, to stifled laughter from the clientele, as Victor stretched the noodles in his hands, as Victor squashed the noodles on his legs. "No need to work up blisters on your lips."

"That could have been a bowl of soup," Em said, when Aunt recalled their escapades that night. "You could have scalded him!" The time had come, it seemed to Aunt, when her sister was a hindrance in her life. Victor, too. He had lost her more than she could earn if she were on her own. At four, at almost five, the boy was far too big for comfort. More frequently she failed to turn up at the marketplace to take the child off Em. Or else she said, "Why don't you keep the kid and stay here longer? You'll get more. You're his proper mum, and people aren't fooled by me. Not anymore."

So Victor lost the chance he'd had with Aunt to lift his head more frequently, to glimpse the world with one eye shut, to study feet and floors. He was back, full-time, where he belonged, an outsized infant on his mother's breast. He was confined again.

5

AND WHAT OF EM? How did she feel? How did she fill her time? She thought of nothing else but getting home, though *home* was not the five-by-five she shared with Aunt, but the sagging country cottage with a yard and thatch and pigs where she herself was raised, or the saddle maker's rented workshop where she had snubbed her husband's candle out. Just as Victor came to live on fictions of the countryside, so Em looked back upon the village she had known. She made a tinseled paradise of it. It was the marketplace transformed, the ranks of vegetables, the fruit, strewn loosely in arcadia. It was a world where everything was ripe and colorful and sweet and free. It was a buffed and shiny version of the village she had known before her husband had—both country phrases—*earth as eyelids,* and his *eternal freehold on a narrow strip of land.*

How wonderful the city had once seemed, how promising. But now she felt that she had reached her highest rung and that her city life was in descent. How long would it be before she was as blunted by the foraging for food and cash as those other mothers she had met? The ones who hired their children out. For what? They dared not ask. The ones who used creams and grease and face ointments to make their kids seem daft or ill or menacing. The ones who kept their aging babies on the breast by stunning them with pods of opium or mandrake tea.

A country beggar such as her must have good looks or
youth or, at least, a helpless infant to hook the passersby.
She'd lost her looks. Her hair was now as lifeless as the leaf
tuft on a pulled beetroot. Her clothes sat on her like a saddle
on a goat's back. Em was so thin—said Aunt, who had a
phrase for everything—that her belly button and her backbone
kissed, and squeaked. She'd lost her youth, as well. Five years
and more of city life could take the paint off carriages or stunt
a country oak, make flowers gray, drain country faces of their
rosy brightness and etch in lines as ploughs put furrows in a
field. She'd still got Victor. What use would he be when he
grew? He was only helpless now because she and beggaring
had kept him so. How long before he turned his back on her
and said, "Enough's enough. I've spent too long already in
your lap. I'm going to open my eyes and stretch my legs and
see this city for myself."

Small children ran past Em when she was begging in her
usual spot, children who were younger than Victor but already had loud voices and strong legs and who were never
still. Yet Victor, as he aged, moved with less frequency, not
more. He was inert, as if these years of falsifying on his mother's breast had robbed him of pluck.

Em knew that you could train or trick a chicken to lay
down dead, as motionless as stone. She'd seen it done when
she was young. It was a common village trick. You pushed
the chicken to the ground. You held its wings. You pressed
its beak into the dust, and drew a hard and short and rapid
line in coal, or chalk, or channeled in the soil, out from its
beak end. The hen was hypnotised. It was geometrically
transfixed. It could not lift its beak clear of the line. You had
to rap the chicken's beak to make it stand again and take part
in the world. They said that without this liberating rap upon
its beak the chicken would just fade away, pressed to the dust
by weights that could not be seen or touched. What should
Em do to lift the weights from Victor's head? She feared that
he would fade away as well, made weak and thin by too
much breast and too much mother's lap, his rigid, geometric
life. Her only remedy—given that to stay in town meant beg-

ging could not end—was to retrace the journey out of town. To walk back down the boulevards until the tram tracks reached the turning gear, and metaled roads grew narrower and rutted, and drains were ditches, and gas streetlamps no longer held their sway amongst the stars or repelled the flimsy light of dawn.

"The first thing you'll see beyond the blue of manac beans," she told her son, her palm outstretched, his hands both tucked and curled beneath her shawl, "is how our village seems to have a mind that's all its own. The river there, it doesn't run fast and straight, not like the drains and culverts of the city do. The river takes its time. It's like a snoozer snake. That's the slowest snake there is. It coils between the fields so slowly that you never see it move. Or else it moves, but only when our backs are turned, at night perhaps, on days when it is raining pips and pods and we are kept indoors. Except your father never stayed indoors. He used to love the rain and stand in it. To get the smell of leather out, he said. He'd wash the leather and the tannin out of him with rain, and let it run off down the gutters of the lane into the snoozer snake, then downriver till the smell and dye on him was swept right out to sea. That's what he said, 'Right out to sea,' though we were nowhere near the sea. I loved it when your father spoke like that. It made the sea seem ours. It smelled like the saddles that your father made."

Em told Victor what fun they had—would have—in fields, at harvest time, with all the fattest rabbits, the lizards and the snakes trapped in the last stands of the corn, how captured rabbits could be skinned and salted for the pot, how lizards could be raced or made to shed their tails, how harmless snakes could cause distress when dropped in people's laps or hidden in a grandma's drawer. She told him how the packers used to—for a laugh—put a snoozer in the top of apple barrels and send them both to market. "To this Soap Market here maybe," she said. They'd laugh themselves as wet as cress at what the market men would do when they dipped in their hands to pull out pippins and reinettes and found the fleshy, yellow fruit of snake.

She told Victor, too, some other time when he demanded "Village Talk," how he had come about.

"We thought you up," she said, "one Sunday afternoon."

It was September and the mushrooms on the beech cobs were getting high and tasty. "Your Dad and me went out to fill a basket. And then—we'd only been married for two months—we had, you wouldn't understand, a kiss and cuddle there and then. It had to be that time because I know that when we took the mushrooms back we found a birth-bug in amongst them. That's a sign, for sure, that you'll get fat with child. Your Dad hung a key on a string above my tummy. It swung clockwise, that's how we knew you were a boy. Anticlockwise is for girls. We picked on Victor as your name straight away. You never were an *it* to us; you were always a *he*. You always had a name. Though your grandad on your father's side—he thought he knew a thing or two. He said it had to be a girl, anticlockwise was for boys, we were muddled up. He got a pair of scissors and a knife. He hid them underneath two bits of cloth on two kitchen stools. He put the stools side by side right in the middle of the scullery. He called me in. He said sit down. Your Dad was there. Your aunt was? . . . no, she'd left already for the maiding job in town. Your grandfather said, 'Select a stool, the one that seems the best for you, the one that's calling you by name. Go on, sit down.' I sat down on the scissor stool. 'That settles it,' he said 'The baby's going to be a girl. The knife's a boy. The scissors are for girls.' They neither of them got to see you born. Both dead. His father first, then yours. When you were born I saw the key was wiser than the stool. I dreamt one night your grandad came back from the dead to see the baby girl. He got a shock. He saw your little dinkle there. I said, 'What kind of clockwise girl is that, she's got a knot between her legs?' I gave your thing a little push. 'What's that then, Pa?' 'I wouldn't know,' he said, and then, 'I wouldn't want it on my eyelid as a wart.' "

She told these stories to her son. He took them in, eyes shut, laid out across her lap. He did not understand the half of what she said, a quarter of the words. What could it mean,

the key was wiser than the stool? That knives are boys and
scissors girls? And rain was pips and pods? And sea was saddle? A normal child of four or five would think it all a strange
and—finally—a tiresome game, to bend words in a way that
was confusing and not funny. Kids of that age would know
the shorthand of the street, the beg and tell of play, the arrow
accuracy of simple words. They'd know how smell and shape
and distance made sense of sound, how words were rounded,
focused tools which served the moment, did the job, and left
no waste. But as we know, Victor was no normal child. For
him the words his mother spoke were two-dimensional, a
sheet of sound, a shallow wash of stories from his mother's
village and the past. He had no role to play except to keep
his head and body still, and listen hard.

He did not know—despite his age—the trick of speaking
sentences or how to make his mark with words. He had not
learned to shout, or tease, or burble rhythmic nonsenses like
other children do. On those few times—at night or when his
aunt was minding him—when he was spoken to by strangers
or Princesses or by the family from whom they hired their
room, he could not form replies. He could not speak. He was
in that respect, and others, too, a baby still. He was comforted
by breast. He did not have the skill to feed himself. His bladder and his bowels had open gates. Anything he chanced
upon—an apple core, a pin, a cockroach case—he tested with
his mouth. He was not happy on his feet. He never ran. He
could not dress himself or tie the laces on his shoes. You
would not guess he had a temper, or that he wanted anything
beyond the milk, the honey and the whispers that seemed to
keep him calm.

In one respect, Victor, in those years before our city was
hustled like so many others into war and weaponry, was more
adult than his years. He had, at least, a muscular and exercised
imagination; that is to say the tales his mother told confused
him, yes, but still they entered him and filled his mind as
music enters infants far too young to grasp its geometric principles, its hieroglyphs, its rhythmic cunning. So when Em
retold Victor for the third? the thirteenth? time how he had

come about—"we thought you up amongst the mushrooms"—he formed a picture in his head concocted from the
wooden tubs of mushrooms which he knew in the marketplace and the single mushrooms which dropped and rolled
from time to time within Em's reach at her station on the
approaches to the Soap Garden. He saw himself a pink but
ragged mushroom, odorous, peaty, one day old. The basket
was his crib. It was a frozen fairy tale for him, an illustration
from a children's book. The tighter that he pressed his eyes
together the clearer the image was; the larger and the pinker
the mushroom; the rounder, the smoother, the waxier the
forests and the fields which were the backdrops to his "thinking up." The world of passersby, of market porters, trundling
barrowloads of cauliflowers, fruit, which Victor saw when his
mother did not talk and he was tempted to turn his head and
lift his lids a little, was chaotic and without pattern when
compared to that village world he structured from his mother's words.

The irony was this, the richness of his life was richness
secondhand. His mother's childhood and her adolescence in
the village landscape was made shiny and intense by distance
and by time. It was Victor's milk and honey now. He fed on
it. It kept him quiet and still and satisfied. He was a country
boy. The city was the dream. He opened half an eye to fall
asleep. He woke to find the nightmares crowding in. He
dozed, caressed by Em's refurbished better times, and by
higher skies and fresher winds and more magical conjunctions
than any city could provide. Imagine what an inner world—
bright and sanitized—a boy would make of all this country
talk, curled up as warmly and as darkly as a sparrow in a
wolf's mouth. It would be nowadays, what? a theme park
marketed as Rural Bliss? The film set for a country musical?
The sort of hayseed Kansas encountered on the road to Oz?

How could a child not be charmed by rural nights when
skies were punctured by white stars, and dreams disturbed by
falling fruit in orchards where the plums and pears and oranges grew side by side in such harmony that it would seem
they shared the branches of one tree? How could he resist the

baffling cussedness of grandpa's anticlockwise cottage door?:
Put the key upside down into the backward lock. Turn it the
wrong way. And lift! What boy would not desire a village
party feast, with a table placed outdoors, or set his heart upon
a birthday chair decked and garnished in the finest greenery
to be his country throne?

"I promise you," Em told her son, "that when the warmer
weather comes we'll put our things into a bag and walk back
home." She rolled the candle stub across his cheek. "We'll
put a light to this. We'll lie awake at night and listen to the
apples drop. When you are six you'll have a leafy birthday
chair." She meant it, too—though it was clear that Victor was
not strong enough to walk much further than the market rim.

She could not carry him. He was too big and badly bal-
lasted. But she was clear what they would do. At night the
marketeers left wooden trolleys parked in the cobbled alleyways between the dormant trading mats and baskets. She'd
help herself to one. The market owed her that. She knew
which one to take. A trader who was kind to her and gave
her fruit and greens when they were cheap possessed a painted
cart which was not unlike a child's perambulator. It had solid
rubber tires and, when he pushed it, it seemed quite light and
maneuverable.

"That's your carriage passing by," she'd tell her son. "It's
full of winter melons now—but soon you'll be traveling in it
like a little king." Em smiled as sweetly as she could at her
innocent benefactor and the means of her escape. It was not
theft to take this cart from such a kindly man. She'd cushion
it for Victor with all their clothes and they'd set off at night.
She was not the sentimental sort, nor given to ungrounded
optimism, yet at those moments when her mood was gray or
stormy she could calm herself with just the thought of Victor
in the cart at that point where the trams and city stopped and
turned, and where blue fields began.

6

IT WAS AT DAWN, in fact, in May, when Victor was a month short of his sixth birthday, that Em at last gained freedom from the town. More freedom than she'd bargained for. She was asleep, and warm enough to have pushed her blanket back and stretched her naked arms beyond the pillow and her head. Her forehead was red and wet with perspiration. Her nose was blocked and whistling when she breathed. She had not been well. A cough had kept her sitting up until the early hours. The floorboards. and the blankets puffed stale air and dust. The room was heavy with the smell of damp clothes and candle smoke and sleep. If she awoke she'd find her head was aching, a ring of pain which was most fierce and unforgiving behind her eyes and in the shallow dell between the tendons of her neck.

Victor had slept, of course. Or lain still, at least, throughout the night. But when the morning light started to infiltrate the room's single whitewashed window glass, he sat up and crawled across the floorboards to the pot. He straddled it on hands and knees and spread his legs. He pissed like donkeys piss but with less steam. He had a donkey's aim as well, and wet the floor a little. He watched his urine sink into the wood and make dramatic grains in what had been a gray and lifeless board. He called for Em to wake and see the patterns that he made. When she did not wake he kicked the pot—in irritation—with his heel, so that the triple waters of the night were spilled.

It was in part an accident, but one which suited him. He knelt and rocked upon his hands to watch the family waters as they sought the cracks and contours. The stewed-apple smell of urine. The apple yellow-green of bladder juice. He let the fluid swell and flow and soak. He let it coil and curl round knots of wood. The snoozer snake again. He watched the stream gain power on the floor until it reached the impasse of a raised timber. It formed a pool; it leaned and strained and then set off at a new angle. It had almost reached Aunt's shoulder when Victor pulled her arm to wake her up. He called, "Water down!" His words made Aunt sit up in alarm and look around, expecting ceiling leaks or Judgment Day. Em was too tired to wake for leaks or Judgment Day. The best that Aunt and Victor could do was watch the urine seep away, as Em slept on and coughed.

"We'd better wash it down," Aunt said at last. "Get the water can." She dressed him in a pair of knee-length trousers and a jacket, no underclothes, no shoes, and put on her own coat and hat above her nightcloth.

"We'll see if we can earn ourselves a nice fresh loaf, as well," she said.

Together they went down the stairs, Aunt first, then Victor, bumping on his bottom down each step. They left the water can beside the tap in the yard and went outside. They walked along the central street, nipped narrow by the district's pair of wooden gates, into a squint too rough and angular for carts or crowds. There was a bakery two streets away. The first loaves of the day were cooling in their tins. The men who sold them on the city streets from shallow raffia trays were gathering to load their merchandise and check that all the bread they took was free of pockmarks, burns and splits. The loaves with blemishes would not be sold and so the tray-men made the baker take them back into his shop. There'd be disputes. And sometimes, when a loaf was badly deformed or split enough to earn the name of Devil's Hoof, the baker would toss it to the pigeons or to the early vagrants waiting there. Most mornings all they had to breakfast on was smell, though even the odors of a fresh, warm loaf are more filling than the scents of other streets where there are riches but no food. As luck would have it that day, the ovens had not let the baker down. His yeast had risen evenly. His dough had not bubbled into caves, or cloven like a devil's hoof, or browned in patches. It all looked good and saleable and—with flour priced the way it was—expensive, too.

Aunt would not carry Victor, though he lobbied her for a piggyback. She made him walk, but let him hang onto her arm or hold her hand. He seemed unnerved to be out on the street and not pressed closely to his mother. He was free—if he wanted—to do what any other boy would do, that is to run ahead into the smell of bread which beckoned them. They moved through the almost empty, almost daytime streets, between two smells. The smell of loaves. And, now, behind them, out of sight, the smell of burning wood.

Which Princess knocked the candle over, or struck the careless match, it is hard to say. The girls themselves all blamed it on the one they liked the least, or else said arsonists (in the landlord's pay) or some spurned man or neighbors with a grudge, had set the attic room alight. Who said that candlelight was luck?

Why there should be matches, candles, arsonists in the apex of that building at dawn no one could readily explain. But what was sure was that there was fire and smoke. By the time the first Princess had woken, the flames had found a carriageway of drafts and were unrolling like a lizard's tongue across the room. Less surreptitious, simpler flames climbed walls and snapped their lips at curtains and at paint. The smoke at first was almost white and then, when the fire had reached the Princesses' mattresses and their clothes and had brewed sufficient heat to peel the blackened paint off window ledges, the smoke became heavier and darker. It was laden with the ash and dust which had been buoyed and agitated by the flames. Its color now was blacker than the worst burned loaf. It smelled and tasted like a new-shod horse.

The Princesses, when they woke—or were woken with a

shake—did not stop to check the cause of the fire. Already
they could hardly breathe, and one or two, the screamers
there, had singed their throats. They ran, not for water to put
out the fire, but for fresh air and safety in the street. The
stairs were narrow. There were falls, and breakages. A young
girl broke her begging wrist (and made a fortune out of that
for the nineteen months she kept the bandage and the splint
in place). Another broke her neck, and almost died before she
reached the bottom step. But not one Princess was licked by
too much flame. Nor did any one of them get left behind,
curled up in blankets, to suffocate in the airless caverns hol-
lowed by the heat. They banged on doors as they went down
into the lower levels of the building. They raised their neighbors out of bed, but no one took it on themselves to check
in every room that there was not a pet cat or a sleeping child
that should be saved. They simply passed the message on,
and messages are bound to end when they reach deaf or hidden ears. Once the refugees had reached the street, and looked
around to check the faces there and comfort those who were
blackened or distressed, no one noticed Em was not amongst
the crowd. In fact, some swore they saw her standing there,
with Aunt and Victor, breakfasting on bread.

Em slept. She was so tired, and dreaming too. The noise
and smoke, they said, must have been the scenery of dreams,
so that they did not threaten her or make her wake. The
smoke—they said, they said—would have sunk into her room
from the attic and curled up where she lay and hugged her
tight and dry before the flames came down the stairs. They
said she would have dreamed her death and felt no pain. But
who can tell? Perhaps the truth is this, Em woke. Who would
not wake when there was so much noise and anarchy, when
the timbers cracked and grumbled like Epimenides the Slum-
berer who woke, stiff and dry and fiery, from two hundred
years of sleep? Her eyes were smarting; from dreams, she
thought at first. But then the smell, the boiling vapors of the
house, the smoke, the drumming hubbub of the flames, made
confusions of that kind short-lived. She would have called at
once for Victor, and gone down on her hands and knees to

scrabble for him where she thought he slept. How long was it before she realized that he was safe? Or thought that he was dead? Or took the chance to save herself and all the rest be damned?

The smoke by then was far too thick and acrid for Em to see the window light, suffused by shadow and by whitewash even when there was no fire. She could only guess where the door was. Perhaps she found the wall and felt along it for the architraves. And then, empowered by some ancient sense of flight, found easy passage through her neighbors' rooms into the hotter, fresh-brewed smoke which furnaced from the few remaining timbers in the flaming, disappearing stairwell. Did she die there, gasping, gaping like a fish on land for moist and icy oxygen and finding only pungent, scalding gas? Or did she simply curl up to drown beneath the fervent, swirling blanket of smoke in her own room, her husband's unlit candle melting in her hand, her family's spilled and puddled urine holding back the flames for just a trice, because she did not wish to live without her son? These are the questions everybody asked—and answered—for a day or two. But no one volunteered the truth, or called the owner in for questioning, or wondered why Princesses should play with fire at dawn. And no one asked, of course, how it could be that sixty-seven people slept in this four-storey house that had been built for ten. Or how they lived with just three taps and no gaslight and just two toilets in the yard. Or where the singed and heated dispossessed had found themselves new "homes." Or why it was that no one came to name or claim the single blackened corpse.

Aunt should not take any blame. She and her nephew were moved away by policemen with the others in the crowd. The policemen did not care if those they moved were gaupers from the neighborhood or residents. "Move on, move on," was all they understood, as if the drama of the streets was a private spectacle, cordoned off to everyone except those few who wore the ticket of a uniform. There were no firemen there or fire appliances. In neighborhoods like that all epidemics, rioting and fires were left to run their course. The buildings, bodies, laws were not worth keeping thereabouts, it was thought. In fact, a city councillor had said the week before, that the best prospect for the city was for all the tenements to be consumed by flames, for all the lawless poor to be dispersed by heat like rodents in a forest fire, for the squalid quarters of the city to be fumigated, cauterized. "Let's build again. From scratch," he'd said.

Aunt and Victor were driven back along the street toward the bakery. Victor was crying from the shock and drama of the fire. He wanted Em. He wanted Mother now. He would not walk a pace, so Aunt was forced to lift him on her shoulders until the policemen judged that they had driven back the crowd to a safe and sterile distance. They turned and watched the smoke knit gray scarves above the roofs, with flecks of dying orange made by airborne sparks. Aunt asked those Princesses she recognized if they'd seen Em. They thought they had. They weren't sure. Yes, yes, they'd seen her standing in the street eating bread with Aunt and Victor just a while ago. Or no, they hadn't seen her, not for days. Em who? They didn't know her by a name.

Aunt did not panic. She was sure that Em was safe. She'd heard it said the building had been cleared. In any case, the fire had started in the attic rooms, and all the attic girls seemed well enough if not exactly dressed for shopping or a ball. Em would have had more chance than them to wake, to dress, to come downstairs, to go in search of her sister and her son. What could Aunt do except stay calm? She was the calmest woman on the street. She was just glad that she had remembered to put on her hat, her battered cloche. It's known that flames make snacks of straw.

The crowds were thickening, drawn by the smoke. Some men were trying to breach the line of police. They lived in houses close to the burning building. They knew that fire had legs and wings and that their rooms and homes were next in line. They'd only come onto the street to see what all the fracas was and, when they knew, to find a certain place of safety for their families. They'd found themselves expelled,

pushed back from their front stairs, spectators to the colonizing heat.

"Let's fight the fire," they begged. "At least let us go home
and save a thing or two, before it all goes up in smoke."

"Keep back," the policemen said.

Their commandant did not organize a chain of buckets or
send for nurses from the sanatorium, or for the water pumps.
He sent instead for mounted policemen and another van of
men. This was his district and he knew that trouble on the
streets would be a black mark in his book.

It was not long before the word was out that the city councillor who'd recommended, just a week before, that tenements
like these should be brought down to earth by fire, had got
his way. How was it that the police were there, at dawn and
in such numbers? Why was it that no one was allowed to
investigate or to fight the fire? The police, the politicians, the
nobs and profiteers who wanted all the city to themselves had
come before the sun was up to make a furnace for the poor.
It was not only hotheads in the crowd who now found cobblestones and staves or started pushing against the policemen's
chests. The neighborhood—in both respects—was now in-
flamed. They'd beat themselves like moths against the cordon
of the law to get nearer to the flames.

If there was fighting to be done, then districts such as this
were good for volunteers. Young men with little else to do
got out of bed and ran into the street. Beggars, hawkers,
prostitutes, the unemployed, the young, the criminals, the
men and women with grudges and with principles, in fact the
sort who had scores to settle with the city and the police,
were glad to add their lungs and muscles to the throng. The
crowds were driven from the rear by rumors and by the more
mature of troublemakers who, hanging back, felt safe to
bruise the air with threats and insults. Their curses and their
slogans, lobbed at the riot from the rear, caused punches,
cobbles, bricks to be thrown at the front.

Riots are like fires. They look their best at night. They
smolder and they flare with greater drama when the sky is

dark. They beckon and they mesmerize. This breakfast riot
was short-lived. The city had no need of it. It had its work
to do, its schedules and appointments to address, its daylight
hours to endure. Those men—and the few women—hurrying
down the pavements at that hour on their way to work—had
only time to poke their noses down the narrow lanes where
they could see the police and smoke and hear the curses of
the neighborhood.

If this had been at dusk, not dawn, with all the duties of
the day dispatched, then only the most innocuous, the wari-
est, would pass the mayhem by. That's something every beggar knows—that breakfast times are dead, that crowds
proliferate when work is done and time is no longer money.
At dusk the riot would have spread out of the narrow lanes,
beyond the burning tenements. It would have helped itself to
food and clothes through the broken glass of windows. It
would have picked on men in carriages or cars and taken
wallets, watches, hats, and paid for them with beatings. It
would have toppled tramcars, and started new and spiteful
fires in districts where the residents were rich. But it was
dawn, and spite was still abed. The police soon gained control
with their horses and their truncheons and their farm-dog
expertise in splitting herds and cutting out the single troublemaker from the pack.

Five buildings burned. The Woodgate district lost its
wooden gates. But only Em was killed. The tiles and timbers
of the tenement fell all around her like the trees had fallen
once across her village lane, that other breakfast time when
the winds had stretched the memory and bent the tallest, oldest pines beyond endurance. The sun fell onto the cobbles of
the street for the first time in who-knows-how-many? years.
The fire-shortened tenements had cleared a path for it. It
thinly penetrated smoke and waltzed like light on water as
the wind gathered, turned and spread the ashy air.

The crowd was now subdued. The ones whose homes were
outside the police lines went home. The unlucky ones stayed
put. And waited. They prayed the wind would settle down
and let the fires die. The residents of the five damaged build-

ings would be happy now to see the wind and flames whip up so that their grief could spread itself throughout the town, so everybody would know what it meant to wake at dawn in purgatory, and without blame, and with no hope of heaven as reward. But there is no patterned justice to the wind or rain. And rain there was, quite soon. It made the timbers steam. It dampened spirits. It cleared and cleaned the streets, so that the rivulets of rain which sped along the gutters took off the ash and dust which had so recently settled.

Em had been roasted and then dusted by the ash. The rain was her undertaker. It showered her. It made her cold and shiny almost, as ready as she could ever be for her discovery two hours later by, at first, a pair of dogs and then a sergeant in the police. By noon they'd brought a box for her. It was not easy to lift her body from the rubble. She was too well cooked. Her flesh was falling from the bone. They wrapped her in a blanket then and lifted her. They kept her in the city morgue, in ice, and out of sight. But no one came and so they gave her earthy eyelids in the common grave and put her on the register as "Woman, unidentified."

Aunt still was calm. She knew where she should rendezvous with Em. The marketplace, of course. Em's place of work. Her pitch where she had sat with Victor on her breast, palm out and up and heavy with coins.

"You have to walk yourself," she said to Victor. "I'm not a donkey. Walk!" She made him stand. She held his hand. "Come on. She's waiting for us. Walk a little way, and then I'll let you have a ride."

Victor was shocked. Not by the fire, and not by fears of losing Em. But by the clutter and the hardness of the streets, by the smoke and horses, by the anger and the weeping, by his Aunt's strange mix of harshness and attention, her calmness and her urgency.

When he was eighty and looked back, it seemed to Victor that this was his first unfettered image of the town, that up till then he'd only glimpsed the city streets. At most he'd seen those dislocated country views of fruit in carts, of vegetables displayed on stalls, of shoppers, traders, bar loafers, from the waists down. He did not like what he was seeing now. He clung to Aunt's hand and her skirts. His cheeks were wet. His chest was shaking, partly from the morning cold and partly from the bubble sobs which he could not suppress. He walked—a little gawkily, of course. He was still young. He was not strong—and wished that he could be elsewhere. His head was full of countryside; the snoozer snake, the falling fruit, the little king returning home in a carriage made for melons, the burning, lucky candle on the step, the birthday chair that's legs were saplings, that's back was green and woven like a wreath.

7

WHEN VICTOR WAS AN OLDER, richer man, a twenty-six-year-old with property and prospects and—already—half a grip on all the riches of the Soap Market, he found the time and sentiment to search the city archives for the bound and brittle volumes in which the local newspapers were preserved. He knew the year and month that Em had disappeared. He knew there'd been a fire and still retained the snapshot memory of being lifted to Aunt's back and watching flames and scarves of smoke across her shoulder.

It was a morning's work to find the thumbnail news item, amid reports of city trade and gossip and a world gone mad with war: "Five tenement houses frequented by itinerants, prostitutes and beggars were fired during dawn disturbances yesterday in the city's Woodgate district. Several rioters were detained and charged with assault and theft following attacks on police, fire officers and local trading premises. The disturbances were initially occasioned, it is reported, by rivalry between criminal groups. The body of an unidentified woman was removed from the debris." The single-column headline was BREAKFAST ARSONISTS DETAINED.

But at the time Victor had no apprehension that his mother might be harmed. His aunt had said, "Come on, she's waiting for us." His only fear was that he would be obliged to walk too far, before his aunt rewarded him with the donkey ride she'd promised on her back. He tugged her hand, so that his

123

walking dragged on her. But she was tough and unlike Em. His tugs earned harder tugs from her. Her grip on his small hand was only soft if he matched steps with her. The instant that he slowed or faltered she bunched his finger bones. "Keep up," she said. Or "Quickly now." He had to run to keep in step. Four trots of his to match her single stride. He'd rarely run before, except in play, and then the distance had been little more than wall-to-wall in their small room. He hadn't realized the urgency, the clumsiness of speed, or how painful it could be.

Who knows what ants or termites feel when boys or bounty hunters kill the queen? Their structures fall apart. The soft, iron magnet lets her fleshy filings go, so even those far from the nest who have not witnessed the sacking of the royal chamber or seen the assassin's needle impale the queen, go listless-haywire at the instant of her death. Looking back, it seemed to Victor that the world that day was a pandemonium of ants, and ants without a queen. How else could he make sense of city streets, or cars and trams and carriages, of random, indiscriminating sounds, of pavement antipatterns in which bodies flocked and fled like cream turned in a whisk, of Aunt once madly kind and now so rushed and unforgiving?

Aunt was quite certain, as she dragged her nephew by his finger to the marketplace, of two things—that Em was waiting in her usual place, that Em had perished in the fire. Or else a nightmare mixture of the two—that they'd find Em, her blackened palm outstretched, her thin, charred back propped up against the usual snag tree on the edges of the Soap Garden.

If they'd found Em, alive and well, their future would have been the past. They would have gone back "home," to the countryside in May. At worst the springs and cushions of a swelling hedgerow are better bedding than the embers of a city fire. But his mother was elsewhere, and Aunt was not nostalgic for the pains and pleasures of the earth. She sat cross-legged all day at Em's worn pitch. She'd give her sister till the night to resurrect herself and then she'd set about the task of finding once again a nesting box. Aunt did not try to put her nephew to the breast, or beg from passersby. Victor was left to shuffle in the garden and the marketplace at will. At last. He loved and hated what he saw. He felt like we all feel when we're first left at school—condemned to a freedom that at first seems narrower and more enclosed than the cell that's family and home. The market paid him little heed, except to bruise and buffet him, and startle him with noise and color.

His aunt was not a callous woman. She guessed the worst when Em did not show up. Her eyes were damp despite herself. But nor was she the sort to mope. If Em had disappeared, had died, was lost, had fled without her son, was lying in a pauper's ward scorched and bruised by smoke and truncheons, then still the world went round, and breakfast followed dawn, and shitting followed food, and life went on. She gave her old straw cloche a whirl. She primped its dog-eared dog rose sprigs in felt. She made its deep brim curl and grin and made a face herself to match. She wiped her eyes and, dutifully, checking one last time for Em, she went in search of Victor; and then, her nephew clinging to her back, she headed for the town.

Street luck is what the city excels at. Aunt's hat (a little passé now), her smile, the boyish burden on her back, attracted comment from the livelier of the men she passed. One followed her—a man about her age, but dressed much older and in the barroom style with patent shoes and collar studs, a soft homburg, trousers with a center crease, a jacket of the latest cut with sloping pockets and long revers.

"What's that you've got on your back?" he asked. "The kid must have seen that hat and thought he'd take a donkey ride!" She answered cheek with cheek. She said the kid was paying for his ride. She was a human tram. "Jump up, if you can find the fare," she said, (and winked). "There's room inside for a little one."

"There's more to me than meets the eye," he said, matching winks with Aunt. "Want to see? Hold on a bit . . ."

"What bit exactly should I hold?"

"Your tongue!" he said.

They called him Dip, though he was known by many other
names. His speciality was crowds. He'd dip a hand and make
off with your purse and the most you'd feel would be a sense
of loss and an unaccustomed lightness in the pocket. He could
unclip brooches, take watches out of fobs and replace them
with stones of matching weight, remove a bank note from a
billfold and then put back the fold, swap a necklace for a
length of string, steal (it was said) the glasses off your nose.
Hard luck the lady who took a helping hand off Dip, who
let him take her arm to cross the street or welcomed his assis-
tance with the too-high step to board a tram. One hand at
the elbow left one hand free to browse the handbag or the
purse. Tough luck the well-heeled man who hovered in the
street when Dip walked by. It only took the slightest nudge
from him, a stumble, an apology. The man would never
guess his pockets had been searched and emptied, his tram
fare and silver tie clip stolen, his saint medallion removed.

At first, Dip's interest in Aunt had been professional. A
woman forced to give a piggyback to a tired child might have
an unattended purse or, perhaps, an outer pocket which he
could open up with just one brushing cut from the pivot blade
of his pigsticker. He'd been surprised when she drew close
how young she was. And poor. And to his taste. He liked
these country girls, their jollity, their give-as-good-as-take,
their dueling repartee. This one was plump and scruffy, it
was true. Beneath the disguise of the broad-rimmed cloche,
her forehead and her upper cheeks were dry and pocked like
grapefruit skin. But she had level eyes, a playful face, a comic
angle to her chin, and—Dip, like every other man, had fantasies too strange to name—she satisfied his liking, his desire,
for girls in hats. He'd never met a woman before who wore
her hat with more flirtatiousness than Aunt. One glimpse of
that had put his rhubarb up.

"Please let me help," he said. "I'll carry him. Where to?"

She shrugged: "Who knows?"

"What's your boy's name?" he asked.

"Victor . . . and, anyway, he isn't mine. You go and tend
your own potatoes. It's not your business who he is." That's

what she said, but what she thought was something else: This man is sent to us to take the place of Em. She let Dip take the boy from off her back and lift him in a flying angle onto his shoulders.

"Where to?" he asked again.

She told him all about the fire and Em and what their life had been; and telling it, she buried it, still warm. Life was too blunt and short to waste it on the dead.

Dip was enthralled by how Aunt spun her hat whenever she was lost for words. He held his breath, as if his lungs were as fragile as frost, when she recounted how the men in bars had tossed their coins in her hat brim to win themselves short glimpses of her legs. Here was a woman, he was sure, who was a gift from heaven and from hell. He jangled stolen coins in his pocket and hoped that he would get a chance to toss them too.

His room, he said, was near. So near that he could smell the market fruit from it. He offered her some floor.

"And what about the kid?" she asked.

It's true, he thought. The kid is in the way. But then, he's small and young. He'll sleep. And when he sleeps? Who knows what might occur?

They put "the kid" to sleep, and then they set to work. Aunt did her best to seem experienced though, truth be told, she'd never suffered this intimacy before. She knew about it, naturally, but only in the way of comic patter, the sexual flirting that it took to beg some coins from a man, the flush and stillness that settled on them when her legs were on display and she was trading winks and innuendo.

Some Princesses—the prostitutes, the opportunists—had kept them all amused one night with stories of their clientele. How one old boy had paid good cash to watch a girl spit on his feet. How others wanted armpits licked ("My wife would never kiss me there!") or asked for entry by the tradesman's door, or took their pleasure spiced with oaths the like of which would shock the guardians of hell. How the teenage sons of bourgeoisie were brought by uncles, godfathers, family friends to girls like them to "taste the fruit" but more

often begged for mercy and their innocence; or wept; or failed
to "stiffen the worm"; or changed their minds when they
found out what, how and where, it all involved; or came into
their underclothes before their trouser buttons were undone;
or wet themselves.

Aunt was prepared for oddities. She was prepared, in fact,
to be amused. Hilarity, it seemed from what the Princesses
had said, was the stablemate of making love, and Dip had
shown that he liked fun. But she soon found herself more
startled than amused. Dip's kisses were the colonizing kind.
His hands—those hands so used to slipping gently and unnoticed into pockets, tucks and folds—seemed suddenly to lose
their expertise. His fingers—adept in crowds at unloosening,
unfastening, unbuttoning—were trembling at the strings of
the nightcloth which she still wore beneath her coat. He
seemed uncertain how to deal with the clips on his braces.
He tried to pass his hands through solid cloth. He seemed
unable, or unwilling, to push his trousers down without
Aunt's help. His breathing had become so uneven and so labored that Aunt began to think that they had better stop before the poor man had a fit and her new dream of moving in
with a good and handsome city thief was ended with a death.
His temperature was fluctuating. His face was red. His levity,
his measured confidence—those two characteristics which had
made Dip so attractive to Aunt—had disappeared. Instead here
was a man who did not seem able to form a simple sentence,
but was behaving with the blunt and charmless urgency of a
child denied the breast. Indeed, quite soon his mouth was
partly on her breast, and partly chewing on her cotton un-
dershift. One hand pulled her heavy coat and nightcloth to
her waist; his other hand was pushed too tightly—and was
trapped—beneath his trouser band, beneath his underclothes.

One gentle shove from Aunt would have sent this Dip toppling like a trussed piglet onto the bare floorboards of his
room. But Aunt was in no mood to shove. Despite her baf-
flement, she was at least gratified to be the center of attention,
to be the focus of Dip's ballet bouffe. It kept the grief of
sisterhood at bay. She let him slide onto the mattress, his

sinking head pressed to her chest . . . her abdomen . . . her
stomach . . . her crutch . . . her thighs . . . her knees. She let
him put his tongue between her toes. She laughed and
laughed. No wonder prostitutes were such a jolly breed.

"Undress," he said. "But not the hat."

8

NOW DO YOU SEE the charm of cities? None of this adventure could have happened on the village green where Aunt and Em had first played tip-and-kiss with boys. There were no flirting, pocket-picking strangers to encounter there, in patent shoes and collar studs, with private rooms. The only available men were cousins all. Or neighbors' sons. Or daft. They were as solid and as passionate as trees, as heroic and original as farmyard hens. That is to say they were all dull and without sin; their only privacy was sleep and shit. But city air makes free—and country pullets can become street cockatoos or fighting birds or songsters once they've shaken hayseed from their wings. So, Aunt and Dip, two village souls gone free and wild in city streets, could no more pass each other by than cats can pass a dish of cream.

The dipping and the begging became less urgent. They lived on love and bed. These were sufficient for a while. So when they woke, curve-wrapped on their mattress like two bananas on one bunch, Dip breathing through the filter of Aunt's hair, Aunt folded like an infant in his arms, it was not often long before they found themselves embracing face-to-face or delving in the blankets for a breast, a testicle, a pinch of fat. Sex was breakfast for these two. It fueled them for the day. Sometimes they breakfasted at leisure, no stone un-turned. At other times Aunt merely turned away and let Dip wriggle into her, to puff and quiver, for a minute at the most, at her buttocks and her back. Aunt did not care for breakfast much. Her appetite for love grew with the day. But she was content to let Dip make use of her after dawn, so long as—in the afternoons, at night—he'd do what she desired.

Every day they washed with water from a jug which Aunt had filled from the public fountain the evening before. They dried themselves on air. They dressed in their best, only clothes, and walked out into town not like the cockroches they were, but eagerly and hand in hand. They had to eat. Aunt dealt with that. She knew which market men would happily part with bruised fruit, which bakeries threw out collapsed or wounded loaves, where trays of eggs were stored and could be reached by someone small and agile like herself, where it was easiest to snatch the bread or chops off diners' plates in restaurants.

They needed money, too. Youth and love are spendthrifts both. Here Dip's expertise gave them an undulating income. One day he'd lift a wallet with enough inside to last the week; and then a week would pass and all he'd get would be "blind purses" containing buttons, tokens, keys, eau de cologne, but not one coin. Dip did not choose his victims well. He'd rather pick their pockets comically so that Aunt—his witness from across the street—would be amused. He did not concentrate. He was on show. He took it as a challenge to remove a worthless glass and metal brooch from the lapel of a stern-faced, clucking woman, and lost all taste for lucrative yet humdrum theft. Aunt satisfied the predator in him. The time would come when he'd insist that she stayed in the room when he went out to work. He'd say she soured his good luck. But in those months when they first met he did not care if business was not good. A note or two, some silver change, would be enough to reunite their hands while they, leaving Victor in the room with blankets for his toys, went off to find a bar.

Aunt had a liking for the clear, cheap, country spirit known then as glee water, but now, of course, tamed and bottled by the drink barons and marketed as Boulevard Liqueur. It did not take a lot to make her drunk. One shot, and she would lay her hat and head on Dip's shoulder, her hand upon his knee, her foot on his. Two shots, and she would press her lips against his ear and say what they'd do to pass the time when they got home, if Victor were asleep. She'd be a "Princess" and she'd let him buy her for the afternoon. She'd be as hard as nails for him. Or else they'd make imagination manifest: "Let's sit apart and masturbate." Or else, "Let's buy some honey, Dip. We'll put it on and lick it off. I'll put some on my breasts and you can feed off me. . . ." Or else, "Do you want to do me in my hat? I'll do a show for you. You toss-and-pitch and watch. For every coin that you land inside the brim I'll take something off."

Once, when she had watched Dip lifting purses from the smarter ladies of the town, she asked, "Why don't you try to burgle me?": "Just like we're in a crowd," she said. "You come up and dip your hands inside my clothes and try to find my purse." For Aunt the narrative of sex, the scene, the characters, were seldom twice the same. Her passions were theatrical. She cast herself in parts in which the heroine was more slender and had better skin than her, in which she was in charge, desired, insatiable, amused, in which she could transcend herself, become any one of those grand or glamorous women on the street.

The Princesses were wrong. *Hilarity* was not the word, though laughter was a part of sexual pleasure. *Euphoria* was what she felt. When she and Dip were making, staging love, it seemed the real world could be kept at bay. She could have kept the world at bay all day! What was the hurry? What was the point in hurtling, like men, through such sustainable pleasures to the brief and unreliable moment when the bubble shudders, bursts? She could not understand how Dip, at breakfast time, was so easily, so speedily, so undramatically relieved. That was his word, *Relief*—"Give me relief," he said. For Aunt not-making-love was not the absence of relief, but a muting of that part of her which found its best expression in the gift of love.

They'd put "the kid" to sleep when they'd first met and kissed. Of course, tired and dispirited though he was, he did

not sleep for ever. For Aunt and Dip to live the life they
chose, to play such parts each afternoon, to spend those hours
drinking glee, they needed privacy, the privacy of two, not
three, bananas to the bunch. A child of Victor's age was old
enough to inhibit anything beyond a kiss. Both Aunt and Dip
had understood, the day they met, that if their passion for
each other was to boil and whistle like a kettle and not steam
and simmer like the water in an open pot, they would require
time to themselves.

"We'll put the boy to work," Dip said, when he had suffered inhibitions for long enough. "He's missing his mum
and this'll give him something else to do."

What kind of work? Aunt raised an eyebrow almost to her
cloche's brim.

"The boy can hardly walk," she said. "And I won't have
him begging on his own. Besides, he's just a baby, though
he's big. He's hardly weaned . . . He isn't bright enough. He isn't
tough . . ."

"I'll fix him up," said Dip. "The streets are full of kids like
him, and doing very nicely, too."

"But doing what?"

Dip hadn't thought it out, but now he had to find a scheme
and find it quickly, too, before he lost his patience with the
boy and showed it with his fists. He settled for the first idea
that came. The boy could build a future out of eggs.

"What eggs?" Aunt asked.

"The eggs you steal from out the back of that big
storehouse."

"Then what? You think he'll build a nest and hatch them
out?"

"We'll boil them up, what else?"

"What else? It's juggling that you have in mind, I guess.
Or sulphur bombs."

"We'll boil them up. Get the kid a little bag or tray, some
twists of salt. He'll have a business on his hands! When I was
little, that was lunch at harvest time, or if we had to travel
anywhere outside the village. One boiled egg. The only salt
we had was sweat. My grandma used to tell our fortunes

from the broken shell. The shell could show how long you'd live. Perhaps the kid can trade in fortunes, too."

"He's hardly seven years of age."

"Seven's an old man in this town."

So it was that Victor first became a marketeer, a soapie at the age of seven. Aunt was his wholesaler. She crept into the storehouse from which she'd stolen—but more modestly—a dozen times before. It was late at night, after the fresh eggs had been brought from the railway station, sorted, placed in straw-lined trays. She lined a muslin bag with paper, lifted the one loose wallboard which provided access from the city lane at the rear of the building, and crept into the midnight room.

On that first night she was afraid. She'd stolen eggs before, but only one or two. A watchman, catching her, would not call on the police or his employer for what it took a hen a day to make. He'd settle for the lecture he could give or, at worst, demand some other recompense.

But on that night she wanted fifty eggs at least, more hen's work than could be shrugged off as "breakages." If she was caught and put away then Victor would be orphaned once again. She did not trust her Dip—left as a sentry in the street with Victor sleeping on his shoulder and her hat in hand—to give the boy a home or love. She'd never seen them touch affectionately. Dip was the sort who having never been a cared-for child himself thought touch and tenderness were simply trinkets with which men could flatter, soften, win their women. But Aunt—persuaded now against all reason that Victor would be *happier* left on his own, the boiled-egg salesman of the marketplace—had made herself the promise that he would "always have a beam above his head at night." If she could guarantee that he was safe and warm at night, then she could put him out of mind by day.

She was the cheerful type. What was the point in brewing guilt? Who'd benefit if she and Victor caressed and hugged all day, and let their empty stomachs shrink and pucker in the cold? It seemed to her, as she gained entry to the storeroom, that stealing eggs for Victor was the greatest gift that she could give because these eggs would free Em's son from her, and leave her free of him.

That night the storeroom was not entirely dark. A late winter moon turned the skylight windowpanes a liquid silver and made the room look colder than it was, as if the ceiling had been tiled in translucent squares of ice. What light there was picked out the thousand brittle, bony skulls of eggs. The shells absorbed the light, reflecting none onto their bedding straw, like button mushrooms butting into oxygen from earth.

Aunt walked as gently as fear allows between the egg trays and the light. The odor was strong, and reminiscent too. The chicken dung, the straw, the timber of the room, the salt-and-semen smell of white and yolk, the moonlight dressing, was farmyard simplified, was field. Aunt took just five eggs from each tray and—counting in a whisper as she worked—filled her bag with sixty eggs. They were the size and weight of perfect plums. The only sounds she heard were Dip whistling in the lane outside—his warning that there were passersby—and, far away, the midnight alarums of the drunks and revelers amongst the final trams and scuffles of the night. There were no rats to alarm her. The watchman slept on undisturbed. But still she was afraid. The eggs were ghosts. They looked like souls or sins encased in sculpted skin. To steal these icy eggs at night made Aunt feel like a grave robber. Each one was someone dead and someone loved. Which were her parents? Which were the villagers who'd been alive when Aunt was born? Which one was Em?

She could not move. Dip whistled without cease, suspiciously and tunelessly. Perhaps there were policemen on the street—then whistling would only bring ill luck to Dip. But if he stopped?

Aunt crouched beside her bag of eggs. A moth flew up from God-knows-where. A bat-moth, black, gray and red. It landed on the back of Aunt's right hand. It closed its wings and rested on her warmth. No great weight, no manacle, could have rendered Aunt more still or breathless than that one moth. Then Victor woke. She heard Dip curse, then whistle once again—a slower, sleepy version of the dance he'd been attempting before. But Victor would not settle to this bogus lullaby. His thin crow voice was raised in protest at the pressure of Dip's hold, the darkness of the lane, his orphanage. "Shut up," Dip said. But Victor knew the power of his lungs and screamed. Nothing would make him happy now. He was alone, at midnight, in the city. Tomorrow he would earn his living—a marketeer at last. But for the moment, but for ever, Em was dead, the eggs were stolen, packed, and Aunt was crouching in that brittle-mushroom field, transfixed. She was not certain what had pinned her there—the screaming or the whistling or the moth. She only knew what everybody knew who'd come from village into town, that midnight is a lonely and ungenerous time when streetlamps blanket out the stars.

She held the bat-moth by the wings and put it on the eggs. She had to take the chance of climbing back into the town. Victor's screaming, Dip's slow dance, were loud and strange enough to bring the army out. She lifted the loose wallboard and looked outside. It seemed safe enough. She clambered through the gap and reached back into the storeroom for the bag of eggs, and then replaced the board to disguise her entry. Dip had seen her now, and stopped whistling. Victor screamed. Despite the hour the lane was busy. Men, mostly alone, were making for a brothel-bar where drinks and women could be bought until dawn. They passed between the distraught child and the woman thief without a comment or a glance. Crime and distress were the common starlings of the street. They could not give a damn.

9

A COUNTRY CHILD OF SIX or seven might work all day at harvest time. Hard work, too, helping with the stacks, or pulling roots, or climbing to the furthest branches for the remotest plums. At dawn it very often was the child who was sent out to slop the pigs or strip the maize for chicken feed. The youngest daughter had the milking stool. The smallest son was sent at dusk to gate the herd or flock, and if he came home empty-handed—that's to say, he'd found no firewood, mushrooms, nuts—then very often supper was withheld. "Empty hands, empty stomach," was the village phrase. At lambing or when the fruit was in its fullest blush, some girl or boy would have to keep the foxes or the applejays at bay. All it took would be a fire, a scare-drum or a horn. A single child in every orchard or each field through-out the day or night would do the job at no expense, so long as they were vigilant and did not sleep. Nobody said, That kid's misused. How could you leave a child so young, alone, for such a time, with so much danger all around? Rather, their childhood seemed ennobled by the tasks they had. Work made them independent, healthy, spirited. Why, then, the fuss when city children worked? Compared to country kids the poorest city children—homeless, reckless on the streets—had an easy time of it. At least they pleased themselves. If they were bored with holding carriage horses for small change, or selling matches, papers, sex, then they could take the time to share a cigarette with friends or join the shoal of sprat-sized thieves and beggars in the Soap Garden. They could vie with pigeons for rinds of bread, or glean the market for discarded fruit, or splash around in the motherly and graying laundry water of the public washing fountain.

Philanthropists, of course, would do their best to net the shoal, to place the best and brightest of the girls in houses where they'd be taught to iron and make the beds. They'd do their best to separate the boys from their bad ways, their friends, their cigarettes, their threadbare clothes, by indenturing them to coach builders, factory men, or anybody wanting hard work for no pay. They thought a hostel was a better place for orphans than the street, yet could not answer why it was that once their orphans had a bed, a schedule for their prayers, once they had work and food, a change of clothes, they still broke loose to join the starlings again.

The answer's tough and simple. It is this: that routes to misery and hell are often much more fun, more challenging than routes to virtue and well-being. Why else, how else, would children such as those who thronged the Soap Garden and the Market, then and now, embrace the destitution of the city streets with such audacity and such appetite? We should not grieve too much for little Victor, then. Not yet, at least. The market was a warm and busy place, more cheerful than a four-walled room, more sociable, more nourishing than the four dry, sweet breasts that had sustained him till the fire. He was bereaved, twice over. He was not strong. Or wise. But he was young enough to mistake mischance for the natural order of his life.

He sat, contented, resigned, before his tray of eggs, exactly in the place—where else?—where he had sat and suckled for so long with Em. His back was set against his mother's tree. It was a home of sorts. And though his face was not well known (how could it be, pressed up against his mother's flesh and shrouded, swaddled from the light?), he knew enough about the tricks of trade to turn his thin mouth up and advertise his wares with what appeared as undesigning smiles. Indeed he was amused. What boy, a few weeks short of seven years of age, would not delight in sixty eggs of which he had sole charge?

Aunt and Dip were his first customers, pretending to be casual passersby. They dropped their coins in his hand and made the most of choosing a well-boiled egg. They smelled the shells. They tapped the shells and held the oval echo to their ears. They ate their eggs exactly where they stood, stooping down theatrically to help themselves to salt.

"Sweet God, these eggs are good," they said, to anyone who caught their eye. "Go on. Buy one. This kid has got the cheapest breakfast place in town."

Victor was glad to see the back of them. It left him free to turn their coins in his hand, to wet his finger for a plunge of salt, to stare into the ranks of eggs, to study all the cracks and stains that came from boiling them, to wait in vain for someone else to stoop and buy.

It was not until he left this home-of-sorts to wander on his weakly and untutored legs amongst the café tables and the market panniers that he began to sell. He did not even have to smile. He did not have to cry his wares. "Boiled eggs! Boiled eggs" was a less eloquent sales pitch than the silent, hardened eggs themselves. Besides, this was a marketplace. No need to state your business here. Display was all it took to do the trick. By late lunchtime, on that first trading day, the fifty-eight remaining eggs had been reduced to three. The salt was gone. Victor's pockets hung like udders with the weight of cash. It was not much in value but volume matters more to kids than value. They much prefer the playfulness of coins to any paper note.

Victor ate the last three eggs himself. He was not skilled at taking off the shells, and had to spit the bony flakes onto the cobbles and flagstones of the Soap Market. He turned to make his way back to the garden, to wash his mouth out in the fountain water. But first he was seduced by the clanking, twig-thin man who sold fruit juices out of spouted cans and called out what was seasonal: "Berries, honey gourds, oranges. Fresh juice. Fresh juice." Victor pointed at a spouted can. He could not tell what juice it held. The hawker rinsed a glass with water from a skin. He shook the glass dry and clean. With practiced shrugs he tilted the can and filled the glass with bluish berry juice. He took a coin out of Victor's hand. Victor stood, struck motionless. He was rejoicing in the simple algebra of buy-and-sell which had so quickly and so effortlessly transformed his boiled eggs into juice.

The street kids did their best, with threats and brittle charm, to make Victor one of them. They had their gangs. The Moths. The Dross. The Market Boys. The Fly-by-Nights. If Victor meant to limp with his burden of eggs between the market pitches or sell them to the café customers in the Soap Garden, then he at least should make his peace with those tough boys and girls who were the gangland chieftains or their generals. They seemed so competent at everything from marbles to manslaughter that, surely, they were the natural allies of any child out on the streets alone. But Victor had been buried for too long. He did not understand the courtesies of life amongst the pack. He did not wish to speak with his contemporaries, or take on board relationships which were not trading ones, which were not serious, which did not earn. These were the sort of boys who made their cash like tough old men, and blued it all on sweets, and toys and cigarettes, not eggs. Victor thought these urchins far too trivial.

At first these gangsters—that's the word—just circled him and nudged as if he were a goldfish in a tank of orfe. They helped themselves to eggs and pelted him with what they couldn't eat. They kicked his shins. They found a name for him. They taunted him with "Vic the Prick," or called him Goose because he walked unsteadily, and had a lot of eggs. They said he had to join the gang, or pay, or leave the marketplace, or else. Or else? They pressed their fists into his face. They burned his wrist with Chinese twists. They knocked his tray so that his eggs cracked on the cobblestones. They meant to illustrate what else might happen to a boy, alone, who did not court the approbation of the gang.

Victor did not understand what blows or twisted arms or threats with fists and knives were meant to signify. Their

language was not his. What did their violence mean? He only
understood that there was chaos on the streets more urgent
than the protocol of gangs. Each day had its uncertainties:
that it might rain. That nobody would want to dine on eggs
that day. That there might be some pointless kindness from
a marketeer who'd give away a damaged pear, or pay for
eggs with too much cash and not require the change. That
there'd be holidays when no one came—the market would be
closed, the cafés shuttered, the cobbles and the sky laid close
and listless, like sheet and mattress on an empty bed. He took
it all. His job was selling on the streets. The eggs passed
through his hands like worry beads. No Chinese burn, no
punch, could deflect his armored single-mindedness. He did
not understand the power of cash yet. He was content that
when he went back to Dip's room at night his pockets were
turned out and all the change removed as "payment for tomorrow's eggs." He had to learn a stranger and a tougher
algebra of trade than the one which fed him berry juice—that
is that all his patience and hard work upon the street could
be so quickly and so effortlessly transformed into beer and
other treats for Aunt and Dip. He was the middleman, the
trading lime—and he was being squeezed.

Of course, Aunt no longer crept at night into the storeroom
to steal the eggs for Victor. It had only taken three days
for the packing foreman to observe that random eggs had
disappeared, and that they disappeared at night.

"You think they're hatching into bats?" he asked. "Or are
we being robbed?"

He and the watchman found the loosened board and set a
trap. They sat on stools behind the entry board with sticks
upon their laps. They shared a bottle of aqua vitae, and sup-
pered silently on pork and bread. One dozed while one kept
watch.

At midnight Aunt arrived, a little slowed and fortified by
drink. She had no appetite for foraging amongst the oval
ghosts. But it was easy money, and Dip was far too tall and
dandified to forage for himself. They'd been amazed how
much their little Vic had earned on his first day. He'd made

enough to win himself not-quite-a-hug from Dip. It was not enough to buy good clothes or meals in restaurants. There was enough, though, turned out from his trouser pockets (the country phrase, again) "to oil their throats and grease their bums."

Aunt was too hurried to remove her hat. Her battered cloche, much loved, clove to her head as tightly as an acorn cup. Dip signaled that the lane was clear. Aunt freed the loose board with her foot and pushed her hat and head straight through the gap. The packing foreman, full of self-esteem and pork, woke up in time to see the watchman's stick make contact with the straw. Aunt's hat fell off, but—good friend that it was—it broke the blow. Her head went back into the town. She tore her chin on wood. She stood. She ran. Though she could have just as safely strolled away. The loose board was too narrow. The foreman and the watchman were twice Aunt's size and had to satisfy themselves with that one battered trophy, that old straw cloche, that disembodied gaiety.

What should Dip and Aunt do now? What could they steal? Where were there eggs to boil for the next day's trade? Aunt took the money that Victor had brought home. She did her sums, and showed Dip how it worked with matchsticks spread out on the floor. They'd buy the eggs from a poultry-man like blameless citizens for such-and-such each egg. Cheap eggs perhaps, not fresh exactly, but not green either. They'd boil them up, and dispatch Victor to sell them in the market-place for such-and-such and such-again. Ten matches spent earned fifteen matches back. And fifteen matches made more than twenty-two. It was safe and legal—and lucrative, so long as eggs were à la mode. If only Aunt could recover her old hat or buy another one, the pair of them would be content again.

So it nearly was. At first they provided and prepared the eggs, and Victor sold them on the streets. But soon they were too bored with boiling them, four at a time, in their one pot. They said to Victor, "It's your job." And so he got them from the poultryman himself. He learned to count the money

out and pay. He begged for charcoal or found wood to feed
the stove in Dip's one room. He boiled the eggs himself, and
took more care than Aunt or Dip had ever done to keep the
shells intact and clean. They shared the profits, but he kept
his merchandise well out of sight. They hardly spoke. They
hardly met. When Dip and Aunt came back at night, Victor
was curled up with stomach pain and sleep. The eggs he ate
each day had made him constipated. His guts were pumped
up with wind. They were as hard and bilious as sated snakes.
His farts were countertenor monotones, as noisy and as regu-
lar as chimes. This was the fiercest smell. But there were
others too—the eerie odors that the eggs released when they
were boiled, the badger-pungency of souring, broken eggs,
the mawkishness of shells. The three of them had sulphur
nightmares, sulphur in their clothes, brimstone breath. They
might as well have slept on Etna or inside the crater of some
soufrière, decapitated like a breakfast egg. The smell was
sweet and hot and aggravating. Victor's guts whined like un-
punctured sausages in coals. Aunt did not snore, but puffed
and hummed all night as if she did not dare to taint her lungs
with inward breaths of air.

Dip hardly slept. He stayed out on the streets all night. He
longed to push his hands in strangers' pockets once again. He
had no appetite for sex with Aunt, or drink with Aunt, or
hatless Aunt. One evening he did not return. He'd make his
fortunes in some other part of town. Then Aunt—her judgment blurred by reckless loneliness—found some other man.
Her sister's boy? She left him with her baggage, unattended,
in what had been Dip's room and now was his. These were
the first days of a life alone.

When Victor was eighty he could not recall his mother's
face, or Aunt's, or Dip's. He could recall the parasol, the
broad-brimmed cloche, the patent shoes, the collar studs. He
could recall the painted cart piled high with greens and melons
which Em had promised would one day take him and her out
to the city edges where the trees began. He could recall his
father's graying candle stub.

He did not talk about these things—though the bricks and

cobbles of the town and marketplace stored all his early life
like walls store moss, and the osmotic gossips of the city had
taken in his life and passed it on to anyone with time to spare.
Victor himself, when he grew to be a man of consequence,
had just one public story from those days of poverty and
waifing eggs. It was the story that he told when he could not
escape the duties of the business millionaire and was called
upon to make a speech to the Commerce Club or talk to
someone from the radio or the financial press, or write a
foreword for the little magazine his staff produced.

They knew he started life with eggs. But then? What was
it drove him onward, up and out of eggs, apart from cramp
and flatulence? How was it that a boy so young could have
the vision to diversify from eggs to eggs and fruit and bread
and cheese, to upgrade his tray with decoration, then with
wheels until he traded off a barrow? Where did he find the
energy, the business zeal, to strip his barrow when the trading
day was done and hire out himself and it for bringing produce
cheaply from the station, until he had two barrows, five, and
twenty-five, and ten boys in his pay, and fruit stalls of his
own, and packing firms and farms, and, finally, before his
fortieth year, the Soap Market itself?

Why not stop when he was crowned the Fruit King of the
city? Why battle on to set up Import/Export firms, and truck-
ing companies, and canneries, to build Big Vic, to spread his
fortune round the city and the world so that each lemon
squeezed for tea by anyone in town would have been packeted
as seed, and grown in soil, and harvested in plantations, and
sent in trucks and trains and boats, and invoiced out of offices,
and sold on market stalls that Victor owned?

"You tend your tree. You get good fruit," he used to say.
Or, "I was born a countryman—and country people always
reinvest their seed." These were both phrases he had taken
from his man called Rook. But that single story from his past
was not Rook's work. It was Victor's own: one evening—he
was nine or ten, Em and Dip were gone, and he was still
surviving on boiled eggs—he ended up as usual in the cafés
and the bars of the Soap Garden. Boiled eggs went well with

mugs of beer—but he had learned there was no point in offering boiled eggs to those who drank the favored clay-red wine
or ordered coffee. Malt and eggs do not do battle in the
mouth—but eggs with coffee or with wine destroy the taste
and smell of both.

There was a man who nearly always bought three eggs and
ate them, without pause, whether he was drinking beer or
wine or coffee-and-a-shot. He paid a little extra to have his
eggs unshelled by Victor. He did not take a plunge of salt.
He dipped his eggs instead into the sugar pot. He halved each
egg longways with his teeth and then consumed each half
openmouthed and without much regard for the spectacle and
mess he made. It was not clear what kind of man he was. He
sat alone, though everyone who served or passed by deferred
to him. He was so fat that he walked with a stick, not because
he lacked the strength to bear his weight, but simply as a
means of maintaining lift and balance should he need to sit or
climb a stair, or—rarity indeed—to step aside. His walking
stick was tarbony and topped in silver, not ostentatious but
smart, and as sturdy as a cudgel. The scroll etching in the
silver was made bold in its recesses by city grubbiness and
verdigris and—who could doubt it?—dried blood.

They said he was a landlord of some sort, a pimp, a man
who'd been a consul in the tropics and had made a fortune
out of gold or slaves or running guns, an impresario, a coun-
terfeiter, an operatic star who had not sung since some scandal
or some love affair had silenced him, an undercover cop. He
hardly ever spoke a word. He took his usual seat, at the margins of the nearest café. It was a seat which did not require
him to negotiate the narrow spaces between tables, chairs and
customers. He drank his drinks. He ate his eggs. He read his
paper or his magazine. He made a note, occasionally, inside
a gray-bound book. He held his stick as if he were a shepherd
eager for the chance to drive away a raven or a dog. He staved
off fullness with excess.

"We never knew his name, or what he did," said Victor.
"The only certainty about this man was that he was worthy
of respect."

So Victor was fastidious. He made certain that the eggs he
sold to him were fresh and free of shell, and clean. He placed
the three shelled eggs, as usual, on the metal bill-and-tip
which the waiter had positioned next to—that balmy night—
a glass of beer, and waited for his payment in small change.
There was always a wait. A fat man finds it difficult to fish
his purse or coins from his trousers or his coat. His right hand
was trapped inside his pocket when someone knocked him
from behind. The table shuddered. And the beer? It spilled a
little and would have fallen from the table had not the fat
man, with the speed and delicacy of a lizard's tongue, shot
out his one free hand and steadied it. He turned as best he
could. His body did not turn, just his head and neck. His
chair and back received another blow and this time the beer
and glass were on the ground before his hand could move.
The eggs began to slide and arc across the tabletop, their
passage eased and oiled by beer. They jostled at the table's
edge like nervous bubbles at a drain, fell off, and then were
split and knocked as tasteless as the cobblestones.

The fat man did not feel the third impulse. Two fighting
men, one pushing with stiff fingers and a spittled mouth,
another walking backward and attempting to defend himself
with kicks, sent the table spinning on one leg, then sprawling,
legs aloft, above the eggs and beer. So far as one could tell
from the stream of threats and imprecations they exchanged,
their differences would not be solved without the death of
one.

They were two market traders, partners, neighbors, old-
time friends—and what they'd fallen out about wasn't worth
a bead of phlegm, let alone the lungfuls that the two of them,
now out of fighting range, were looping at each other through
the air.

The younger of the two had wisecracked with the customers of the older man, the one whose fighting fingers were so
certain and so stiff. He'd teased them, half cunningly and half
in jest, that his neighbor's produce was not fresh.

"He's selling fossils and antiques today," he'd said. The
neighbor swore this foolishness, these lies, had cost him trade.

And more. And worse. He knew for sure that, while his back was turned, the younger one pocketed the cash for onion clumps which they had purchased as partners and whose profits they should share. He did not listen to his friend's defense—that "while my back was turned" meant "while I filled myself with drink, while I let the business, onion clumps and all, slide into hell." There were a hundred other microscopic aggravations between the men that, in the sudden heat of anger, seethed and thrived like viruses. "Go dine on shit," one said. The other held his little finger up, a gesture meant to show disdain, and said, with feeble dignity, "I'll never talk to you again."

The fat man filled his lungs and put some pressure on his stick. His knuckles whitened. It looked as if he were about to show how he could slay these two with just one etched and silver blow. But he was only holding tight so that he could stand. Once up—and once the two adversaries had quietened and were watching him—he dipped his hand into the inner pocket of his coat and pulled out a wallet. He took out one bank note. He unfolded it and held it up, theatrically, for all to see. A blue five-thousand note. A two-month wage. Enough to purchase a good horse, enough to buy a thousand eggs. The fat man folded the blue note in two, lengthwise, exactly as he halved his eggs, and tore it carefully along the crease. What was he then? A conjurer? Would he set fire to those two halves, or chew them up, then make them whole again? Was this a good note? Was it counterfeit?

There was no movement in the Soap Garden. Even waiters, trays aloft, were frozen where they stood. Victor was not the only one who'd never seen a note as large as that before. What kind of man would tear such wealth in two?

The fat man flung out and spread his arms, a half note in each hand. His voice was both bourgeois and everyday. It was surprisingly, for one so large, a little reedy too.

"One each," he said. He shook the worthless halves impatiently. "Come on. Step up."

The younger man was the first to step forward. He did not look the fat man in the eye. He concentrated on the half-a-fortune and the walking stick, expecting there to be some finger trick or some low, crippling blow. He need not have feared. The stiff, blue piece of paper transferred to him with just the slightest reticence where the embossed printing snagged on the fat man's dampened skin.

The elder of the two was also reticent. He recognized the fat man's game. He had children of his own and knew how squabbles were resolved by parental trickery. You broke a ginger stick in half and let the children suck away their moods. Yet half a ginger stick had value on its own. It tasted just as good in pieces. But half a note? He could not formulate exactly what the trick might be, yet he was in no doubt, as he took in the fat man and his neighbor holding half a fortune in their hands, that he would be a fool to walk away. He might as well take half a note. To turn away would not look good or wise. Pride would not allow a market man to jeopardize just half a chance of making random, unearned cash.

He did not move. He put his hand out. Palm up. The cussed supplicant. Let mammon come to him. The fat man was not proud. He did not mind that he would have to move a pace or two. He took three steps. He spread his weight across both legs and leaned his stick against a chair. He rolled the half note in a ball, dismissively, with studied irony. He dropped it on the outstretched, flattened palm. And then he took the market trader's hand in both of his and wrapped the fingers round the paper ball.

"Now talk," the fat man said.

Both traders felt more foolish than they'd done since they were adolescents. They did not hang around. They did not walk away, of course, arms linked, their two half lives already interlocked. They disappeared like cats, their heads and shoulders down, their ears alert, their fur on end. They would not talk that night—but who can doubt that they would trade weak grins the following day and then handshakes? They'd see the sense in being partners once again.

The fat man did not watch them go. He waited for a moment, on his stick, while three waiters put the chairs and table back in place, wiped up the beer, removed the mushy eggs. The proprietor himself brought out a replacement beer, the best. "It's on the house," he said, thankful for the damage and the mayhem that the blue note had thwarted and thankful, too, for all the rich absurdities which they had witnessed.

The fat man started on his beer, as unbothered, it would seem, by the spat which he had ended as by the money he had lost. The no-expression on his face said, Five thousand? That's a morsel for a man like me. I'd throw a hundred of them to the wind just so long as I can have my beer and eggs in peace and quiet. He looked up, then. The thought of eggs had made him lift his eyes and run his baby tongue along his lips.

Victor was standing where he always stood. Hypnotized. The fat man held three fingers up. Victor selected three more eggs. He cracked their shells at their thick ends and peeled them white and bare. He brought the sugar from another table. He stood and took the coins from the fat man's hand. He hoped that he would tear a note in half for him as well. He was not old enough to fully understand what he had witnessed: the fickle, slender contrivances, the artifices, the stratagems of wealth, its piety, its fraudulence, its crude finesse. But—given time—he'd understand it all and make a scripture out of it.

"The fat man taught me," Victor explained, to those who wished to hear or read the complex moral of his anecdote, "that money talks." He did not know that such an insight was old hat and crassly simple. Or that his variations of this insight—such as "Money is the peacemaker" and "Money's muscle"—were simple complications of the truth. What the fat man had displayed was cynicism, if cynicism is the trick of seeming to engage with chance and danger but without taking any risks. Money has no moral tact. It's true, the rich have power to intervene, to heal and damage as they wish. Toss money in the ring and see the drama that it makes of other people's lives. But, more, they have the power, if they choose, to stay more silent and discrete than

monks. The rich—and here was Victor's unacknowledged
dream—can simply make a wall, a fortress shield of wealth,
beyond which the dramas of the world can run their courses
unobserved.

Victor so far—he was nine or ten—had led a life not free
of drama of the tragic kind. The misfortune of his father's
death. The journey into town. The nights beneath the parasol. The fire. The days with Aunt and Dip. The liberation
and the tyranny of eggs. His was a moral tale, an exemplar
of how miserably the small fry of the world can fare. Someone could write a book on his first years and make it stand
for all our city's woes. No wonder, then, that Victor now
wished for something more mundane than poverty. He
wished to be a fat man, too, protected from the city by
what his wallet held. In this, he sought what Joseph, de-
cades later, sought. And that was privacy. He saw himself,
an older, wealthy man, alone and dining in a public place.
At times it was a city restaurant, at other times a trestle in
the countryside, with chickens and with trees. There was
no noise, except the sound of cutlery on plates. He was
quite calm and unafraid. No one around was close enough
to disappoint him or betray him. A waiter, paid to do his
job, was all he needed. He did not need or want a family,
or friends. He did not need the warmth of company or
conversation, or the reassurances of praise. No one could
come and give him Chinese burns. No one could let him
down or disappear. There was no comfort which could not
be bought. There was no problem that he could not solve
by tearing notes in half. What is more eloquent and reassuring than a shield of private wealth?

So Victor now—and almost by design—became an undramatic boy. He had his room, his job, his street routines.
He had ambition, too, but nothing to make good grand
opera from. He set his sights painstakingly on targets within
reach—more sales of eggs, a market stall, an orchard and a
field, a motor van, some staff, some ledgers and a desk. . . .
He told himself that when he was more safe and certain, he
would test the magic of the torn bank note. Not five thou-

sand, naturally. He was the timid sort. A hundred note perhaps. But that day never came, despite the money that he made. Because he never felt that he was safe or certain? Because he was mean and unadventurous? That was the judgment of the town. No one expected such a man—and so late in life—to lower his defenses for a while and toss his money in the ring.

PART THREE

Victor's City

1

IT WAS THE MONDAY after Victor—pent up all his life, between the nipple and the purse—had celebrated being old with a birthday lunch of coddled fish, fresh air, accordions. It was the Monday after he became engrossed in his last, his first, his only *civic* fantasy, to publicly display his private wealth at last by building a market worthy of a beggar woman and a millionaire. A damp and windy morning, just short of nine o'clock—and Victor the Insomniac, a boss who normally was at his desk a little after dawn, was nowhere to be seen.

Rook, with Anna at his side, walked the two kilometers of cobble, stone and asphalt between his apartment and the tunnel below Link Highway Red. Her hand was on his arm. They seemed as fearless as lovers half their age, made adolescent by the comfort—unexpected, overdue—of flesh on flesh. No one would think these two—this sparrow-chested, graying man, this woman, warm and pouchy as a pastry bun— were husband and wife. Such wooing, binary displays belong to fledgling romances. Maturer ones are more abashed, less startled and enraptured by the luck of love. These two fledglings on the street were not the married kind. Their circumstance was clear: here was an out-of-season *grande affaire* between two people almost old enough to be too old, too sleepy for such public love. "Sleepy" is the word the growers use to specify a pear, and other soft-fleshed fruits, which have matured but, though they have their color and their shape,

157

will soon begin to brown and rot and lose their flavor and
their bloom. To taste such fruit is to taste the gamy pungency
of middle age.

As they cut diagonally across the town, between the rush-
hour traffic and the crowds, beneath the ocher-colored
eiderdown of clouds, Rook and Anna seemed misplaced,
late Sunday revelers caught by the Monday morning light.
The hastening single people in the street, toothpaste and coffee on their gums, a day of labor summoning, a desk, a loom,
a till, gave way to them, as if a couple so engrossed and casual
had passage rights, like yachts, to an unhindered channel at
the pavement's crown. We all defer to couples, do we not?
A man and woman hand in hand can make the toughest of
us step aside, can stop a tram.

This couple were not rushed. They were not hungry for
their desks or eager for their colleagues and their phones.
They held each other by the hand, the upper arm, the elbow
and the wrist. They held each other's waists. And when they
reached the walkers' tunnel—just at the spot where Rook had
used his keys and fists and where the mugged and flattened
laurel leaves still lifted in the draft—they took advantage of
the solitude and gloom to kiss. Once they reached the windy
mall, however, they separated by a meter, and walked in par-
allel. The weekend spent in Rook's apartment had been refreshment for them both. They'd hardly left Rook's bed by
day, and then at night they'd taken to the streets and bars
to fuel themselves, with the reckless alcohol of crowds, the
aphrodisiacs of drink, for more lovemaking. Yet now they
walked demurely, chastely, along the colored marble flagstones. It was not wise to love too publicly. Who knew who
might be watching from the greenhouse on the twenty-
eighth, or through the tinted windows of his office suite?
Who knew if Victor—that unimpassioned, loveless man who
seemingly had never tried the luxuries of pressing skin to
skin, who could not understand the pleasures of the thigh,
the tongue, the abdomen, the breast—might take against two
lovers in Big Vic.

The mall was cunning preparation for the lobby of the of-

fice block. It cooled and shrank pedestrians. It echoed with
the click of heels, and the heavy doors of taxicabs, and sighing
ventilation ducts. The shiny brick veneers, the mirrored col-
onnades, the fish-trap cloisters leading to the finance palaces
and the trading brokerages which were the tenants there, did
not invite ill discipline or dawdling. The mall's misanthropy
struck Rook and Anna dumb, just as the deep, cool shade of
conifers will silence those who exit from a field. They did not
speak. They even blushed a little, as if they guessed their
weekend intimacy could not be hidden here. Their entry to
Big Vic was self-conscious, too; Anna's face a little too composed and Rook's—unanswered—greetings to the lobby staff,
the uniformed commissionaires, too hearty for the time of
day. They shared—a shade too clumsily—a segment of Big
Vic's rotating doors. They shared the lift for twenty-seven
floors. But once they reached the office lobby they headed for
their desks as if the only love they shared was love of work.

Rook was in the best of moods, and with good cause. He
was relieved to find his desk was, for the moment, clear.
Normally by that time on a Monday, Victor would have sent
his Fix It list—a sheaf of notes, queries and instructions, re-
criminations. Victor himself did not like to deal with people
on the telephone, or even speak to clients face-to-face. What
was to blame for that? His hibernating temperament? His
hearing aid? His shield of wealth? He read reports. He scanned
accounts. He watched the share and stock prices dance banking quicksteps round their decimals on the office VDUs. If
there was anything to be *done,* then Rook could do it. He had
younger legs and ears. But on that Monday, there were no
tasks for him, no estate manager to intimidate by telephone
("We note that field beans are a trifle mean this year. And
late"), no groundless tension to diffuse amongst the market
traders, no thin letter of regret, refusal, to be composed and
sent, no group executive meetings to be called and chaired
while Victor claimed some old man's malady as pretext for
staying in his room or on the roof.

Such liberty! It suited Rook. He had his own plans for the
day and these involved a little horseplay at the office desk.

He was used to having sex with Anna on his bed. A day or two of anything is time enough for it to seem routine. It had been fun—exhilarating fun—but not adventurous. His sexual needs were escalating. Making love to her at work was what engrossed him now. Big Vic's solemnity was more a stimulation than a restraint. The need for stealth and speed and stiflement would blunt the appetite, you think? Think twice. Lovemaking is at its best when it transgresses social ordinances and strays far from the trodden path into the briars of the undergrowth, where risk and lust run neck and neck.

Rook wanted something more subversive than bedsteading. He wanted intercourse with Anna in the place where he had sat for months and contemplated her. He wanted office sex, with all the office work continuing, and all the VDUs alight, and these two colleagues, ankled by their underclothes, and pressed together like a pair of angler's worms. No one would think it odd if, later in the day, he called Anna to his room for consultations. She'd come, an innocent. He wasn't sure that she would share his eagerness—but from the appetite she'd shown for making bed-top love he had an inkling that she might.

He draped his jacket on his chair and then—with nothing else to do so early in the day—he went to Victor's office suite. The birthday throne was still outside, its plastic foliage evergreen and fresh. It seemed so foolish now that he had wasted so much effort on this birthday gift, for a man who had no appetite for sentiment. He pulled the foliage with its cellophane tape free from the wood. He'd get someone to take it to the atrium and reconnect the stems where he had snapped them free. Or else he'd put them in a pot, a comic bouquet for Anna's desk—a teasing prelude for the courtship that he planned for her in his own room, at his own desk. But first—the bouquet in his hand—he knocked on Victor's door. He knocked again. And tried the handle. The door was locked. The old man's growing soft, Rook thought. He's slept through dawn for once. Rook bent to peer through the keyhole in the door. The inner key was in the lock.

"No signs of life!" he called out cheerily—and inanely—to

the company accountant who, carrying a steaming coffee and a bank of ledgers, was passing through the lobby, tiptoeing through, in fact, as if he wished to keep his presence secret.

"Where's Victor, then?" The accountant shook his head and seemed unwilling to meet Rook's eye or match his cheeriness. "Where's Victor, then?" Rook asked again.

"He won't be down today."

"Why not?" Again Rook had to settle for the shaken head. The accountant went into his room, and slammed the door shut with his heel.

Rook took his bouquet to Reception. The women there were busy at their desks.

"Where's Victor's schedule for today?" he asked. Again he had to ask the question twice.

"It's canceled."

"Oh, yes. Why's that?"

No one could say. No one seemed keen to even talk about this rarity of Victor absent from his desk, his schedule "canceled" for the day. It was perplexing that the staff were unforthcoming and morose when here was opportunity for them to waste a little time with talk.

"What's going on?" Reception shrugged and held its tongue.

"Why so grumpy, then?" Rook asked out loud. "The Monday miseries? Too much to drink on Sunday night? Cheer up, cheer up. It's only a job. 'Work not shirk is life's best perk. So join my harem, said the Turk.' "

Their smiles were thin and stretched. Something embarrassed them. He waited, unsure of what the problem was, but certain that these three women, hired for their public charm and cheerfulness, were ill at ease. At last he said, unflippantly. "What's up with you three, then?" Still, there were no volunteers to look him in the eye. At last the eldest of the women said with a voice that quavered in and out of key, "It's not for us to say."

"It's not for us to say." In other words, this was a private thing, too personal and intimate for them to comment on, despite Reception's reputation as the building's bourse for rumor and hearsay. Rook no longer was perplexed. He guessed what caused their awkwardness, their blushing jealousy. Some office spy had spotted him and Anna out on the town on Saturday, perhaps. Or walking hand in hand toward Big Vic. The word had spread. The word *Romance!* For some reason he could hardly understand this out-of-office liaison was not approved. You'd think this was some tutting medieval monastery, Rook thought (seated for the moment at his desk). Was this just jealousy, or sullen irritation that he'd breached an office code that those in charge and close to Victor should be as continent as him? Or was secrecy the culprit? Did Reception and Accountancy and, come to think of it, the uniformed Commissionary at mall level, resent that Rook had kept his tryst with Anna to himself for one weekend?

"Ridiculous!" He spoke the word out loud. It *was* ridiculous. Unlikely, too. The men and women in Big Vic were magnetized and not rebuffed by any hint of scandal or of secrecy. They loved the ribaldries of life. Particularly the trio at Reception. They wore their grandest, most libertine of smiles when there was gossip to be shared and prurience to trade. They would not drop their voices and their eyes, and act like undertakers' clerks. They would have looked Rook in the eye and said, "What's this I hear?" or "You had a nice time Saturday! A little pigeon spotted you and Anna rubbing noses in a bar. . . ."

What then? What could the problem be? He went through Friday in his mind in search of irritants. What had he said, or done, to set this Monday morning frost? He'd seen that everyone had shared the fun with champagne and cakes. He'd been his usual self, the Prince of Irony and Idleness. What had he done to give offense? Something was irking them, no doubt of that. And, truth to tell, something was irking him as well. His conscience was not entirely clear. Again he ran Friday through his mind and recognized exactly what it was that had stained his day. The subway fight with Joseph. The viciousness of fists and keys. The parting kick. The pleasure that he'd taken in such a squalid triumph. Yet these were private acts, less public than the time he'd spent with Anna.

Who could know and disapprove of what had happened out
of sight and underground and to an ill-dressed clod who had
no contact with Big Vic? Why would anybody care?

Again Rook shuffled through the Friday pack. The pretext
that he'd used to get down to the marketplace. The orange
that he'd peeled. The tugging and the ripping of the laurel
stems. The shaming bout of asthma in the presence of those
men. The creaky birthday lunch. The gleeful coda to the day:
Anna laughing on his bed, delighted by his mordancy, his
teasing hands, that clowning routine with his underpants,
"Ourselves, Ourselves, Ourselves." And yes (I raise my head
above the parapet again), the mocking column that I, The
Burgher, wrote about the taxi and the boss's coddled fish.
All the workers in Big Vic would have seen and laughed at
that . . . and thought, perhaps, The Burgher's source was
Rook? For that was just like Rook, to feed the babblers of
the press. So, then—they would not look him in the eyes
because they thought he had betrayed a fishy confidence?
Again, "Ridiculous!"

A firmer possibility occurred to Rook. He need not search
his diary or his conscience anymore. Of course! The staff's
solemnity could have only one cause. By God, the old man's
dead! he thought. "No sign of life" indeed! Rook almost felt
relieved, as all that morning's oddities were now explained.
The missing Fix It list, the closed, locked door, the empty
schedule, those phrases, "It's been canceled. . . . He'll not be
down today." What apart from death, or at least a major
stroke perhaps, would keep Victor from his work? If he had
tumbled, say, and cracked a hip, his memos would be flying
plumply from his bed like pigeons from a loft. While there
was air left in his lungs and sufficient power in his arm to
hold a pen, nothing would stop him orchestrating his affairs.

So that was it. The stick had snapped at last. Victor had
died, and no one on the staff was senior enough to let Rook
know. Or else, perhaps—this was a possibility—they thought
he knew and were embarrassed by his lack of gravity or grief,
his flippancy. "It's not for us to say," the women on Reception had insisted. And they were right. Rook had been the

boss's eyes and ears, his fixer and his messenger. He was as close, as intimate, as anyone could be to such a cube of ice. No wonder nobody could face him with the news. No doubt the Finance Manager or the Group MD would come up from the floor below to inform Rook personally that there had been "a sad event." Or Anna, even. She was senior enough. Rook sat and waited, hoping it was Anna who would come. He closed his eyes and dropped his chin onto his chest. He felt— for the first time since the Friday night—that he would benefit from sleep.

Rook's door was open. There was no need for Anna to knock so formally on the stained veneer. Yet she was wise enough to knock and wait. He woke from his half sleep and waved her in. Already he had prepared an elegiac face; already he was searching in his mind for what the death of Victor meant to him. Advancement? Displacement? Something in the Will? At least it meant that this was no time to close the office door and push his hands beneath the bands of Anna's skirt and blouse.

Anna did not look at Rook. Her expression was the same as those worn by the Reception staff, by the accountant as he hurried to his room, by the commissionaire who had ignored Rook's airy greeting as he had entered Big Vic from the mall. Now he was sure he had identified the truth. She looked so shocked, so drained, so unlike the face upon the pillow. "Come in. What's wrong?"

"Bad news," she said. She looked as if her knees would give. He held her in his arms. It didn't matter what the staff might think. Her tears fell on his jacket and his tie.

"Sit down. Sit down," he said. He wished to cry himself. He felt so nervous and so powerful. He could not focus on the old man's death.

"What's wrong?"

She took deep breaths, and then she looked him in the face at last. "I wish it wasn't me who had to tell you this," she said.

"I know." And then, "No need to tell me, Anna. I can guess."

"Guess what?"

"It's Victor, isn't it? He's ill. He's dead."

She shook her head. She almost laughed. "He isn't dead.
You'll wish he was. It's you . . . It's us!" She wiped her face,
and took deep breaths until she found her usual even voice:
"He says you've got to go. He seems to know that we've
been meeting out of work. How can he know? It's not his
business anyhow. This isn't sane!"

She handed him an office memorandum. Victor had put it
on her desk, unsealed. Some office rubberneck had read it and
spread the news. It only took one prying clerk, one internal
phone call, to circulate bad news throughout Big Vic, from
the atrium to the twenty-seventh floor. Victor had written the
memorandum—in pencil—late on the previous Friday night,
his birthday night. It instructed Anna to tell Rook: "His out-
of-work contacts and activities are not morally compatible
with the trust invested in him. They have no place in an
organization such as mine where relationships between all
members of the office staff, producers, clients, and customers,
should be based on propriety and honesty. He is dismissed.
Please inform him that he has until midday to clear his desk,
and that there can be no further contact between us except
through the mediation of lawyers." There was an envelope
for Rook—a formal note of termination.

"He's mad," she said. She understood the comforts of hy-
perbole. "He's old and mad and wicked! He's shut himself
away up there like a gutless little kid. Does he think he owns
us all? Can't we have 'contacts, out of work' without the nod
from him?"

But Rook was in no doubt what Victor meant by "contacts
and activities." Someone—he hadn't got an inkling who, not
yet—had spilled the beans. Victor knew now all about the
pitch money which the soapies had paid each quarter and
which had made Rook so rich and careless.

"He isn't mad," he said. "And this hasn't got anything to
do with you, or us."

"We'll fight for you! Come on!"

She was prepared to head an office strike, to draft petitions, risk her job, give Victor merry hell. She was prepared to burrow into Rook, and make a warren at his heart. Rook shook his head. Why fight to lose? Who'd be his ally when the word got out about the scheme he'd run, the money that he'd made, the cynicism of his office jocularity. If he made merry hell, then Victor or his lawyers might make hell of some less cheerful kind. They could inform the police and then the charge might be Extortion or Embezzlement. He'd end up in a cell. The old man hiding in his room had struck a distant deal with Rook that robbed him of his work but not his liberty.

"Anna. Please," he said, and shook his head. "No fuss." That's all he had the heart to say. Already he was letting work and Anna go. He only asked for dignified retreat. He almost packed a bag and just walked out. But Anna would not understand. She stood her ground.

"Do something now," she said.

Her pluck—and innocence—put Rook to shame.

"All right. I'll make him talk to me." He thought there might be just a chance of changing Victor's mind. He'd find a way of justifying the unofficial payments he'd received. The payments were in Victor's interest after all. They kept the traders quiet. They guaranteed Rook's role as intermediary between both camps. "I had to take their money," he could say. "They wouldn't trust a man who wasn't in their pay."

He knocked on Victor's office door again. He tried to call him on the apartment's internal phone, but the day-valet merely repeated that his boss could "take no calls until the afternoon." The truth was that Victor was hiding in the greenhouse on the roof, exterminating aphids once again and primping plants and looking out through glass and rain and wind on distant neighborhoods. What was the point in facing Rook himself, when he could deputize dismissals, and Rook could just evaporate before the afternoon and leave no trace?

Well, Rook could not cooperate. He could not disappear, at least while Anna was around. He could not clear his desk and leave no trace. He planned, instead, to sit it out. He'd stay exactly where he was, his feet up on his desk, his door ajar, his room a mess of plastic leaves, until Victor tired of hiding on the roof. Let him descend. Let them discuss it face-to-face. Let's see, he thought, if Victor has the strength to be a tyrant other than by deputation or by memoranda. Might something, then, be salvaged from the wreck?

At midday Rook was still inside his room, alone and looking out across a rain-lashed city. Already cars and buses drove with full headlights, and the neon on the streets was liquid and intense. The colored awnings of the marketplace could not be seen and certainly no hills or woods or parkland greens, no shafts of natural light, lent any gaiety to what he saw. The city was as gray and formal as an office suit. Rook heard, but did not recognize, a man's voice ask for him by name. He heard a secretary whisper something in reply, then footsteps to his room. Two men, in uniform, one from Security, the other a commissionaire, his face familiar from the entrance hall and atrium, stood at the door.

One coughed. "Are you ready, sir?"

"Ready for what?" asked Rook. Was this the summons from his boss?

"It's midday, sir."

"And so?"

"And so we've come to escort you . . . outside."

Outside! The word was a kidney punch; it winded him. Outside. Out in the cold. Out on his arse.

He shook his head: "Not yet."

"It's midday, sir."

"Not yet."

They came into the room. "Come on," they said.

"I haven't done my desk." Rook opened up a drawer to show he was not ready yet, and rescued his nebulizer from amongst the pens and calculators. He sucked on the mouthpiece. He could feel the spongy alveoli tightening in his lungs.

"We've got our orders, sir. It has to be midday."

They offered him some help. Was it his breathlessness, or were they simply being firm? They lifted him by his elbows.

They pulled his chair clear, and shut the desk drawer. They might have been from the Ambulance Brigade, they were so mild, and Rook so pale.

"You'll have to leave your Staff Pass with us." Rook put his hand into his pocket, to do as he was told. He was resigned to going like a lamb. He fumbled for the sharp edges of his laminated pass, and found instead the old pocketknife, the bunch of keys. How long was it since he'd put Joseph on the ground? Here was an opportunity to use his fists again.

He found and gave them his Staff Pass. He would have ripped it into two if laminated plastic had been more biddable and if he could have controlled his shaking hands.

"We'd better go," they said, and led him through the offices to Reception and the lifts. There was no sign of life. Even Anna had disappeared. Someone had had the cruel sense to ask the staff to keep away while Rook was led "outside." He let them take him to the lift. He let them walk him to the tasseled rope and join him—three to one segment—in the automatic door. He let it sweep him into the rain and wind beyond. He wrapped his fingers round his keys, key tips protruding through his knuckles, so that his punches when they came would do the greatest harm. But the moment never came. Such moments never do, except in books and films. His warders were too proper and too big to fight.

"Thank you, sir," the commissionaire said, deferential to the last, as he watched Rook pass from the dry into the wet. No one offered to summon a company Panache, or a taxi. He was expected now to take his chances on the street. He was of less importance than a perch.

He knew, he felt it in his water and his bones, that already Victor was at work, no longer hiding from the world. Security would call and say, "He's gone!" and Victor could count it safe enough to come downstairs and sit behind his desk as if he had no hand in all the harm that had been done, and would be done. Would he miss Rook? What should he miss? His fixer's willingness to serve? His care and knowledge of the marketplace, his intimacy with vegetables and fruit, his office cheeriness, his social skills? No, Victor had the wealth and power to replace these things, to find another yet more honest Rook, who would be glad to be old Victor's aide. He hardly gave the man another thought. He was too old and crammed.

Beyond the tinted, toughened glass of Victor's suite the wind was fast and strong and sharp with rain. Big Vic was swaying slightly at its top, and whistling. Victor's coffee moved inside its cup. His office door fell open, then fell shut. A paperweight shaped out of polished serpentine slid across the old man's desk. And Rook, once more, was out upon the canyon floor, between the gleaming, swaying, whistling cliffs of glass and steel and stone.

2

WHAT WOULD YOU EXPECT of Rook? That he would decompose without the frigorific regime of the working day? Most city people—men at least—are wedded to their jobs, and when you take those jobs away they soon become as empty and as brittle as blown eggs. Work is for the idle. It gives a chaptered, tramline narrative to life; it empties suburbs and estates and provides the displaced, liberated residents with dramas structured by the clock. It then provides the wages note, the check, the cash, the banking draft which, more than where you're born or live, is what it takes to be a citizen. A salary can make an interloper feel at home; "An empty purse," or so the saying goes, "makes strangers of us all." But no, Rook, weak and self-indulgent though he seemed, was not the sort to crumble like dry pastry. He was—like everybody else with any sense—too selfish and too vain to sacrifice himself. He spent three days indoors, bereaved. He would not answer Anna's calls from work, or let her in when she came round to the apartment in the evenings, or respond when she delivered a snapshot of her—younger—self, inscribed "Let's meet and talk." What was the point? He did not even read the baffled notes which she left in his letterbox to reassure him that "whatever Victor does can make no difference to us." Rook knew better. She would not seek him out once she had learned exactly what his "contacts and activities" had been. Why nourish love when it was bound to fail? He dared not think of her or quantify his loss. He needed first to concentrate on how he could excrete, transmit, the anger that he felt. He was consumed by malice, but none of it was turned upon himself. What had he done, except to be a cheerful pragmatist who'd seen a chance and taken it? He blamed the cheerless millionaire. He blamed the hidebound traders in the Soap Market. He blamed the coward who had gone behind his back to blab. Who blabbed? Rook did not find it very hard to know who told and when. It must have been one of Victor's cronies, one of the five arthritic soapies who had shared the birthday lunch. Which one? He could not tell—so, for the moment, he would blame them all.

He'd once seen a film—*One Deadly Kiss*—in which an English lord had hunted down, one by one, the five male passengers on a country post chaise bound for London. His motive? One of the men—and only one—had "kissed and robbed" his wife as she slept in the cushions of the coach. "Better that all five die than that one blackguard lives to taint again the honor of a lady," the Englishman had said, in those vaulting, vowelly tones that English gentry, and English actors, used to have. He bribed the coachman, richly, to reveal the passenger list, and set off across the country in wild and righteous pursuit. He did not know, as he dispatched another with a pistol or a knife, that all five men were guilty of some other, capital offense—arson, murder, treachery—and so "deserved" to die. He did not know—how simple these films are!—that none of the five had touched his wife. The rapist was the bribed and silent coachman, free, as credits roll, to kiss and rob some more!

The English love these ironies, and Rook took pleasure in them, too. Rook dreamed the film, but in his dream the passengers were greengrocers, the coach was Victor's birthday lunch. Rook became a younger man, the firebrand dressed in black. He hunted down and polished off the five. They fell amongst their fruit. They died on beds of spinach. Who was the coachman, free to sin again? Rook's dream was crowded out by deeper sleep before the credits rolled.

By day, Rook fantasized; and in these angered fantasies he

would avenge the noon indignity of being thrown out, a vagrant, from Big Vic. He would be the English lord, though
more heroic and less mannered. His weapon would be Joseph's knife. He practiced with the blade, and mimed the
damage he might do. He punched the bathroom door. He bit
off the nails on both his hands. He masturbated, but could
not hold the image of a woman in his head. He lay in bed too
long. He stayed up late, and drank too much of the Boulevard
Liqueur he had bought for Anna during the weekend. His
breathing became labored, first with nerves, and then his
asthma took hold in his right-side chest, brought on, intensi-
fied, by his loss of work and income and the anger that he
felt. He nebulized more often than he should. He grew
lightheaded and unsteady from the alcohol and medicine and
from the cheap narcosis of his dream.

At last—for wrath's a sprinter and soon tires—he became
more calm, less frantic. Bruised, he was, discolored by the
blows that he'd endured. But it slowly dawned on Rook, the
self-approving optimist, that he was not weakened as a man,
but made more potent. He was persuaded now that Victor
had freed him from a curse. The job that Rook had lost was
no great loss. Good riddance to it. He'd paid for it a dozen
years before, with . . . what word is there to use but *soul?*
The moment that young Black Rook had taken Victor and
his check by the hand he'd dropped the sanction of the street,
he'd lost the casual chatter of the marketplace. The city sparrow had spread its wings to rise on cushioned thermals beyond the pavement commonwealth and join the austere
governance of hawks. Now he was back on earth again.

He felt too sick to eat, too shaky in the hand to lift a fork
or pour a cup of coffee, but now at least he looked ahead as
much as he looked back. What could he do with this new
potency, this rediscovered soul? He was too old to start a
fresh career. But, surely, he was rich enough to set up a
modest business of his own. He checked the balance of his
savings. He counted all the currency notes which he'd
amassed. He had no debts, no obligations, no family to maintain. His situation could be worse. To be a rich man without

work was not the meanest fate of all. There was no rush. He'd
take a month or two of rest, and keep his eyes peeled for . . .
for what? A bar, perhaps? A shop? He was alarmed by the
dullness in prospect. Could he afford six months of rest? Or
nine? He deserved a little breathing space to plan his future
years. At least the spare time on his hands could be good fun.
He'd please himself and no one else. His tie could hang loose
all the time. He need not wear a tie. He need not wear a suit.
That was the uniform of servitude. He need not hasten
through the city streets, his coffee hardly drunk, to be at work
on time.

Now he was ready to go out. He searched his wardrobe
and he found the black leather jacket he'd once worn. The
skin was scuffed and graying and the cuffs had split, but still
it fitted, and the zip was good. The leather smelled a little of
the marketplace, and the lining was stained beneath the arms
and in the middle of the back from working sweat. He did
not have the working trousers or the shirt to match—but he
had dark and casual office clothes, and these he wore. He felt
transformed. The jacket set him free. He had resurrected the
man he'd been a dozen years before. He transferred his keys
and wallet, his nebulizer, the Joseph "nife" from his suit into
the zipped pockets of the leather jacket. He tidied the apartment, read the notes that Anna had left, put her snapshot on
the mantelshelf, and went into the town.

It was just a week since Victor's birthday lunch, a week in
which he'd rediscovered love, and lost his job, and soared and
plummeted, one hundred meters, twenty-seven floors, onto
the street. All in all he felt winded and invigorated, like some
shaken boy who's just stepped safely from a switchback ride.
He set off for the Soap Market. The sooner he was seen
amongst the stalls and soapies the better for his shaken self-
esteem.

He walked between the banks of vegetables and fruit without a greeting or a glance. He was not snubbed. He was not
recognized, at first. His leather coat was a disguise. It made
his walk more bearlike, from the shoulders, hands in jacket
pockets, collar up. The suited Rook had seemed a little taller,

more loose-limbed, and walking from the hip. But once he sat amongst the traders at a bar in the Soap Garden, his face was known. He heard the whispers, and caught the glances and the nods. The waiter was his usual pleasant self, but waiters do not count. The market workers—the porters and the salesgirls—did not speak to him, but then they never had. He'd been too grand. He'd been the old man's nuncio, his Representative on Earth.

Rook did his best to seem relaxed. But he was not relaxed enough to hold his cup steady with one hand. He shook so badly that the sugar for his coffee trembled in the spoon. He wished he had a newspaper with which to shield himself. He wished that he could hide behind a cigarette, without the smoke occasioning a fireball in his chest. Part of him feared that he would see one of the birthday guests, some arthritic merchant on a stick, and feel obliged, compelled, to make a scene. But mostly he feared what the market men might do to him now that he was stripped of office. He feared their jeers, their ironies, the jabs and punches they might give to him, and with good cause. Those modest tithes, those sweeteners, which Rook had levied every quarter and for which he'd guaranteed clean access to the boss's ear, were now revealed as money down the pan. Rook was further now from Victor's ear than any soapie in the market. He was the only one whose contact with the boss was limited to "the mediation of lawyers."

Mid-morning, though, is not the time for arguments or scenes. The market was too busy and the traders too immersed in chalking prices for the day to spend much time on Rook. It was no secret, naturally, that he had lost his job— but no one there was certain why. The five old men were keeping quiet. Old men have enemies enough, and take more pleasure out of secrecy—their greenhouse secret with the boss—than spreading tales amongst the market hoi polloi. So Rook was noted, but not judged. The men who never cared for Rook, did not abhor him more or less because—or so the rumor was—he'd lost his job. Why would they like him any less because he was dismissed? The traders did not know the

social protocol. His misfortune was, perhaps, good news for
them. It might save them money. Who could tell? But then,
there'd be new Rooks, and tougher ones whose pitch fees
were less modest. They'd rather stick with their asthmatic.
He was not loved but he was witty in his way and had the
common touch. He had, at least, sprung from the marketplace. He'd robbed them, true, but done no lasting harm.
Such is the vagrant logic of the street that Rook was almost
popular with his old foes, just as a bully's popular when he
releases captives from his grip.

Those who'd been on good terms with Rook and considered the pitch payments to be bribes initiated by themselves
felt just as proprietorial now about their "man at Victor's
ear," despite the fact that their man had been sacked. Indeed,
they even felt a little guilty that their market cunning might
have been the cause of Rook's dismissal. They felt a little
fearful, too. What might the old man do? They judged it best
to wait and see. But there were one or two—the younger
ones, the ones who'd had less coffee and more shot—who
went across to Rook. They shook his trembling hand. "A
bad business," they said, inviting Rook to reveal exactly what
had occurred with Victor. And then to end the silence, "Let
us know if you need any help." Or they put a shot down on
the table and invited Rook to stun his bad luck with a little
drink.

So Rook still had a welcome in the marketplace, somewhere
to pass his time while he decided how to spend his life. He
came each morning, exchanged a repertoire of gestures with
Cellophane Man who stood as usual at the market edge direct-
ing people, trollies, vans, and sat amongst his allies there. If
they enquired, "Come on, what did you do to get the push?"
he told no lies. But neither did he tell the truth. He was good
at keeping quiet and hinting with his mouth and eyes that he
was innocent of blame. Within a few days the market men
behaved as if he'd never been their go-between, or in their
pay, or they in his, and just enjoyed his dry sarcasm and his
cawing, nasal laugh when he told stories of the boss amongst
his cats and insects on the twenty-eighth. Market memories

are short so long as debts are settled fast. A lasting grudge is one that's waiting to be cashed.

Rook wandered through the alleys and the lanes of vegetables and fruit with fresh eyes now. He need not be as watchful as before, noting prices, faces, infringements of the market code. He need not be prepared to take pitch payments, surreptitiously, or listen to complaints about the price and quality of olives or pears. If he pushed through the crowds to the peaks and canyons of a citrus stall, no fruiterer would simply click his tongue and shake his head to signify "No need to pay!" He was the public now and he was ruled, like anybody else, by the market creeds which one trader—tired of scrumpers or being asked for credit—had chalked up on his stall: "No Loot, No Fruit," and "We take IOUs, but only in cash!"

Rook was content to be a simple shopper, thumbing, like all the other shoppers there, but with more blatant expertise, the skins of fruit to check their readiness. Or plucking one leaf from pineapple tufts and judging by its reticence the softness of the core. Or testing whether pod beans would snap or bend between his fingers. Or lifting melons to his nose and knowing, from the smell, the rancid from the ripe. Or scratching new potatoes with his nails to see how well the blistered skins would lift. He knew the trick of listening to cabbages: the hearty ones were silent in the ear. He understood the colors of the carrot, and how the reddest roots were soapiest and only good for stews. You could not confuse him with a waxy pear, or with mushrooms "dirtied" with a spray. A butcher might make a fool of Rook with some false cut, some trick with bone or fat, but no one in the Soap Market had greater, wider skill with fruits and roots and leaves.

Why waste such expertise? Why couldn't he return from whence he'd come—the smart son of a marketeer—and become a marketeer himself, a soapie for the second time? Because of Victor? Because he was a snob, who having labored at a desk was not prepared to rise at five to bend and lift and sell? Because he was too old to mend his ways? He was not rejuvenated by the thought of merchant Rook, his thin and graying head peering from behind a gleaming splash of fruit, his fortune measured out in paper bags. But neither was he much seduced by the alternative—a Rook with nothing much to do except to sit and age and spend. If only he could find the heart—and shamelessness—to lift a pen, a telephone, and answer Anna's calls to him, then, maybe, having nothing much to do but spend would seem less mournful.

Rook hoped to meet her on the street, by chance. He was alert for her, for any word of her. Anna's was the only face, he thought, from which he could get pleasure. For sure, he did not hope to see his mugger once again. The boy—whose "nife" he still possessed—had no importance in his life. Yet, on the morning of Rook's tenth visit to the market bar, he encountered Joseph for the second time. The youth was barrowing red sacks of onions, three at a time, from an open truck which was parked amongst the vans and cars at the market edge. Rook was not pleased to see these two adversaries of his in such a partnership, with Joseph working for the man who'd always treated Rook with cold disdain. He was perplexed at first. He could not think what chance, what scheme, what machination, had brought these two together. But his confusion could not last because the moment that he focused on the strangeness of it all, he realized the truth. Rook did not need to draw himself a map. The mugging and the sacking of two weeks before now made full sense. Details that had escaped him returned in trusses and in clusters. Rook remembered now how Con had shaken the sealed envelope of pitch money so tauntingly in his face, a challenge on his lips. Then, within two hours at the most, Joseph—armed with a photograph, a knife—had tried . . . tried what? Tried at Con's behest to resecure the envelope. And having failed to resecure it with a knife, what had Con done? He'd made a call, or sent an unsigned note, that afternoon to Victor. And here was Joseph, still in Con's employ. And here was Rook, disinherited, without a job to do. Those five, blameless party guests! Those harmless, dry old men! Rook found it grimly comic that he'd dreamed of tracking down and wiping out such innocents. So now he knew who'd caused this chaos in his life. If he had half a chance he'd see to it that Con was sent the bill.

But, for the moment, it was Joseph on his mind, not Con. He'd beaten Joseph once before; he'd beat him yet again. So when a few days later Rook spotted him in the Soap Market, he determined they should speak. It was quite late and dark. It was that summer's warmest night and the city had its sleeves rolled up and could not sleep. For once, Rook had outstayed the waiter's welcome at the market bar. The Soap Garden was becoming his backyard. He and three other men had played domino dice until all the other empty chairs and tables had been stacked and the bar staff had changed into their clothes.

The barman closed the shutters and rinsed the final glasses and left the four men in the midnight July gloom to finish off their game. Rook was the last to leave. He was not skilled at dice and he had chanced his stake on one hot throw. He'd won, against three lukewarm throws from his companions. They'd settled up in thousand notes, and Rook had ten of them, folded in the pocket of his leather coat, as he set off for home.

The sweepers and the men with hoses had been at work and what had been a dusty, waste-strewn space, cluttered with dismantled stalls and flattened produce boxes, was now as gleaming and as scrubbed as a spray-washed shingle beach— except that nighttime beaches reflect the white lights of the sky, and smell of medicine, and perform a nocturn, made from water, wind and stone. This washed place smelled more of soup. It honked the jazz of traffic horns and voices in the summer night. It was lit by the yellow, oblong constellations of distant windows in offices and rooms where no one had the energy, in such a heat as this, to pull the blinds or go to bed.

In the summer there was hardly space for all the dispossessed and homeless who came to roost in the dripping troughs and crevices of the Soap Market. Why sleep indoors, in derelicts or hostels or up against the bricks and tiles of bridges, subways, underpasses? Why squat in dark, abandoned flats—your only privacy an unused mattress up against the window or the door—when it's July and there's no rain and the sun has been so fierce by day that all the midnight, city air is swollen with the heat?

There was no need to light a fire from packing debris but there were fires because the poor are always cold in spirit and need the optimistic mesmerism of the flames to take them through the night, to help them kindle just a little desperate joy amongst such misery. Some of the fires would not last long. Their purpose was to shed a canopy like bulbs shed light, making rounded rooms with walls of melting night for children who could not sleep without the fantasy of "home." Some fires would burn till dawn, topped up by sleepless residents whose thirst for alcohol could not be blunted by their desperation or fatigue. One fire gave light for noisy games of cards. Another was the fire where spuds and sweet corn, gleaned from the market floor, were ember-baked on skewers made from cycle spokes. Another warmed the singers' throats—the singing broken up by coughs, those two most humble sounds of human life becoming tangled in the mouth. In this, their simple warmth and light and sound, the nightime soapies were the closest citizens in town to the earth's enduring elements. They understood what every moth must understand, that flame is enemy and friend. Some found in it good cause to smile, but others were expressionless or else astonished beyond words by the scalding visions that the flames revealed. But mostly people sat or slept alone, disgruntled, shamed, made volatile and distant by a life which cast them as the rootless, parasitic clinker weeds amongst the steady stems of native bedding plants. Some slept on cobbles, statuesque, their heads upon their knees, their arms looped round their legs. Some curled on cardboard mattresses with pillowsacks, or nested in the timber and the canvas of the market stalls. Women—rarer, older than the men—looped their arms through plastic bags of clothes and dozed, or pretended to. To seem asleep was their frontier against the raids and sorties of the town. It gave them some respite from their pain—

their swollen feet, necrotic toes, their boils, and coughs, their migraines and their chills. Men talked in voices that were stripped to wire, or muttered madly to their chests, or carried their misfortune squarely, cleanly, without shame. Until they slept, that is. Who could tell the shameless from the lost, when all of them seemed just as thin and innocent and urinous beneath the duvet of the night?

Rook walked as quickly as he could between the starvelings and the vagabonds, the gangrels and the drunks. He was an easy target for their wit or for the begging hands which waved at him or tugged his trouser cuffs, or for their savage mutterings. He did not like the market when the awnings and the stalls were felled, and when the ripe and appetizing day-time colors of the crops were replaced by the moistened grays of night. He did not look when he heard oaths or offers. It was not wise to be waylaid by their ill luck. If he gave cash or time to one, then all of them would rush to him like mallards in the park, pecking for a crust.

Ahead he spotted three young men, as awkward on their legs as day-old foals. They called him to them, but he did not go. He could not quite unscramble what they said. But he was certain he knew what they held inside their paper cups, their shallow plastic trays, their makeshift dishes. These were what people nicknamed the Taxi Cabs, clumsy, noisy, slow and fueled by petrol. They sniffed whatever petrol they could steal. They did not care that nowadays the petrol contained an Anti-Sniff. "Danger" warned the stickers on the petrol caps. "Ethyl Mercaptan." It smelled of skunk. So what? The boys smelled just like skunks themselves. It did not dull their appetite for fuel, not even if the Anti-Sniff made them nauseous, hyperactive, violent. It blocked their tongues, and caused them to tremble like crones and graybeards made helpless by a stair or curb.

Rook did not lift his head to face the Taxi Cabs; or even to trade signals with Cellophane who was still on his feet and summoning Rook, "This way. This way. Then right. And straight ahead," as if Rook were a van that's passage blocked the marketplace. He chose a route which took him to the

market's edge, near the house where he had lived when
young. He liked to walk those streets and look up at the
cluttered windows of the carpet salesmen. Was that cracked
glass the same that he'd pressed his face against, what? thirty
years ago and more? for private, hawkeye glimpses of the
local girls? His mind was already set on women. The July
heat, the weeks since he'd last slept with Anna, made him
wonder what he'd do if some young woman bedded down
on polyethylene amongst the cobblestones asked for money
in return for sex. He did not trust himself. He was afraid.

He walked a little quicker now, the touch of panic and
arousal at his heels. He almost stumbled over Joseph, sleeping
at the market edge amongst the padlocked carts and barrows.
The mugger's face was busy with its dreams. It was not proud
or shy in sleep, but blinked and gaped and made no secret of
its missing tooth, the cherry birthmark on its cheek, the pitted
craters on its nostrils and its chin, the meager, ill-advised mustache, the crusty scar above the eye where he'd been wounded
by a key. The skin was just as cracked but not as bronzed as
it had been when he'd fled the countryside by Salad Bowl
Express. The city life had whitened him. He looked as harmless and as dull as bread.

What made Rook feel again as tough and sentimental as a
movie star? Was it the triumph of his fists, that time so long
ago? Was it the residue of how he felt about old Victor, Anna,
Con? Or just his dreadful appetite for girls transformed to
violence when he saw the sleeping boy?

He thought he'd wake him with a kick. But what if Joseph
yelled? The mob would come. He'd have a tottering circle
made from drunks and Taxi Cabs. Rook was tempted to drop
a coin in the open mouth and creep off to watch the boy
awake, or choke. Instead, he searched his pockets for the
knife. He sprung the blade and squatted at Joseph's side. Just
like a father with an oversleeping child, he squeezed Joseph's
earlobe, a parent's trick to open up the eyes. He waved the
knife across his face, and said, "It's Joseph's 'Nife'—without
the K. Is this your property?" He laid the flat blade on the
young man's nose.

"Don't move," he said. "We owe each other favors, don't we? Don't shake your head. Don't move. I gave you that." Rook pointed at the scar. "And you've scarred me. I ought to hand you over to the police. At least you'd have a decent place to sleep. . . ."

Joseph sat up. He recognized Rook's face at last, despite the lack of tie and suit. He was not frightened by the knife or anything this thin-faced man might do. His own face was wide enough to take more scars. He did not care. He'd snap this man in half for waking him. He'd punish him for being rich when he was poor. Rook stood and backed away, the knife less certain in his hand.

"Have you got money?" Joseph asked.

"What's that to you?"

"Or cigarettes?"

Rook shook his head. Joseph put his hand out, palm up-turned. "You woke me. You'd better watch it, mister. I know you now. You'll pay for what you've done. . . . Come on, give me some money for some food."

"Go to hell."

"Piss off yourself!"

Rook was nervous of the threat that Joseph posed. He knew how strong the young man was. He'd seen him tossing onion sacks as if an onion grew fat and ripe on helium. He should have turned and walked away. Or run. But Joseph's words, "You'd better watch it, mister. You'll pay for what you've done!" convinced him that the two of them should now negotiate for peace.

"All right," he said. "I only meant to give you back the knife." He pressed the blade into the handle and gave it to Joseph. "Hold on!" He found a crumpled nest of notes inside his jacket pocket. He pulled them out one by one, looking for a fifty. But the first ten were thousands, his winnings from the dice. He smoothed them out and held them in his left hand. He found the fifty, let it loop and float onto the cobblestones at Joseph's feet, and then spread out the ten one-thousand notes. He'd put them to good use.

"How'd you like to earn a wad like this?"

"For doing what?" Joseph was certain now that Rook was looking for a man to share his bed. He'd been approached before, but not for so much cash. For money of that kind he'd take a chance. To make a living he would do "bad things"—his simple phrase for kicking down a door or kicking in a rib or letting some dull man pay for his touch. Whatever Rook was offering, there was bound to be a way of cheating on the deal. Ten thousand? What might that buy? What might a man like Rook expect for such a fee?

Rook himself had not yet formulated what he wanted Joseph for. But he was marketwise. He knew that Joseph could be bought, by Victor, Con, by anyone. Rook knew he had to purchase this *On the Town* before he went elsewhere. Here was a bargain too tough and useful to be missed. Buy in haste, use at leisure. He'd take his time dreaming up some useful task for this hireling to *commit,* something to damage Victor, Con, or anyone.

"I'll speak to you again, be sure of that," he said. "Do what I ask and this little bunch of notes is yours."

Joseph was not pleased. " 'If and when' don't butter bread," he said, but for an instant he saw himself as the well-dressed model in the catalog, his pockets stuffed with one-thousand notes. He would—with Rook's fat fee—sit at the bar and hold the barmaid by the wrist. He would drink muscatel from midnight till midday. He held his hand out for the notes.

"Just wait!"

"I'm sick of waiting. Give me something now!"

Rook arranged the ten one-thousand notes so that they made a perfect sheaf. He folded them in half.

"Give me the knife," he said.

The knife had danced between the pair of them so often now that one more time was neither here nor there. Joseph returned the knife. The blade was sprung. Rook slipped the knife inside the notes and cut along the fold.

"Money is the peacemaker!" He mimicked Victor perfectly. "One-half for you. One-half for me." He put one set of severed half-notes in his pocket, and gave the matching set to

Joseph, wrapped round his knife. "So now you know I'm
serious."

"I can't spend this."

"Nor can I!"

"So what's the point?"

"The point, dear Joseph, is that we will have to talk again.
As friends. I've got a job for you. Don't ask me what. But
when that job is done, I'll add my half to yours."

3

VICTOR WAS FLATTERED by the courting of the architects, their optimism. He liked the language that they used; the ease with which they sang of pits and peaks and galleries and foliage travertines and moduled trading canyons, as if the market buildings which they had conceived were ancient caves, or forests, mountains, landscape parks, as if they were importing countryside to colonize the city's heart.

In November—five months after Rook's dismissal—building plans which were jostling for the privilege of standing at the ancient market site were presented to Victor in his offices by men who looked like poets or composers dressed as restaurateurs. Expensive suntans, casual suits, the glistening, barracuda eyes of those who live by their imaginations and their wits. Not one contested that the existing market was diseased. Their diagnoses matched. They were agreed on its ill health, its pathology, what treatment it should get, what surgery. The old Soap Market was a tumor at the city's heart and had to be removed. They prescribed the chemotherapy of the bulldozer, the radiation of the great iron ball. "Reduce the little that is there to rubble. And rebuild."

These architects were far too grand for schools and houses. They boasted of the museums, marinas, hotels and concert auditoria, the bank HQs, the city halls, the celebrated malls, that they had built elsewhere in the city and elsewhere in the world. In Tokyo. And Amsterdam. And Barcelona. And

Zagreb. In tedious, smaller towns which they had placed upon
the map by squeezing in a white-walled university where once
there'd only been some fields, some woods, a run-down
neighborhood.

Great swathes of greased paper with lightly penciled plans
and elevations spread across Victor's desk, and draped his
chairs. Scale models, computergrams and video enhancements
presented new Soap Markets all of which the architects es-
poused like stage evangelists. Axonometrics in 3-D lifted up
the draftsmen's lines and made them real.

Victor had no eye for shape or form. He assessed the buildings by the words that were used for their promotion. He'd
heard it said—and liked the phrase, despite its false extrava-
gance—that architecture was frozen, geometric music. He
judged the tone and rhythm of the plans by how the architects
could sing their wares, what bafflegab they used. Once he'd
made his mind up, then he would allow the managers, the
financial planners, the development engineers, the accountants
in his pay to take command.

Anna made arrangements for the eleven men and one
woman to visit Victor in his office suite. She met each of
them at the entrance from the mall and during the journey
through the twenty-seven floors she gave them strict instructions that they should stay no longer than forty minutes and that they should not be "overtechnical."

"Victor is eighty," she explained. "He's not patient. His
hearing isn't good."

One architect—the first to audition—said his building had
the swagger which was fitting for a marketplace. A forum for
the sale of food, after all, deserved a confident demeanor. No
need to skulk like banks or barracks do. No need for bashful-
ness. A market "hall" could be ambitious, energetic, optimistic, noisy, rash, high-tech. And here his presentation sketch
showed all the anorexic shamelessness of modernism on a
spree, the veins, the innards and the entrails, the ducts and
pipes, clinging thinly to the building's black glass skin.

"Too varicose," was Victor's judgment, though he, or
more exactly Anna, expressed this view more blandly in a

letter of regret which was delivered to the architect that same afternoon.

Others presented plans in the postmodern cocktail style so favored by hoteliers and out-of-city shopping magnates; a dash of Empire grandeur, two shots of common sense, a slug of metal rhetoric, all sweetened and made palatable by twists of pastel ornament.

The woman architect—from the practice which designed the Wall Memorial in Berlin—was a no-nonsense pragmatist. She had no time for curves. Her inspirations were tombstones, bookends, freight containers, washing powder packets, the square black holy Kaaba at the heart of Mecca, the Pentagon, matchstick boxes, wooden packing cases, dice. She most admired the tall, straight democratic canyons of Manhattan. She wished to put up on the market site "a bold and simple slab, free of ornamental flippancy, in which the dogma and perfection of the rectilinear design confronts and challenges the inevitable disorder of the marketplace—and, incidentally, doesn't jeopardize your profit margins."

"Let's not disguise, but celebrate, the probity of rectangles and cubes," she said.

One handsome local architect, a young man much adored by social columnists for his daring disregard of public taste and of the women in his life, called for buildings which were visual metaphors, the city's aspirations made tangible in bloated glass and stone. The metaphor which he'd prepared for the Soap Market was most visible to God. Viewed from above—from a helicopter at a pinch, or even the rooftop garden on Big Vic—its shape was cruciform, a square-winged bird in flight. Its split swallowtail was, for the people on the ground, two tapering wedges which welcomed and embraced its clientele. It guarded them from wind and sun, and led them to the market doors at the swallow's rump.

"This building holds a dialogue with the people passing through," the architect proclaimed. "Its language is the language of the street." Victor was deaf to what it had to say. If he had wanted metaphors for God he would have built a church.

He was more taken and more patient with the Esperanto

architects whose Shanghai–Aztec market halls were decorated
with facades which owed their haywire debts to Marrakesh
and to Mondrian, or to pyramids and pagodas, or to the
paint-by-numbers graveyard classicism of Rome and Greece
and Père Lachaise, or to the Hanging Gardens of Babylon and
the IBM Garden Plaza on New York's Fifty-sixth and Madi-
son, or to spas and fairs and paddleboats. It was amusing to
be guided through these global "theme" environments, to
hear of screens in bamboo and in steel, and roofs in metal-
thatch, and market "trading modules" whose veneered marble
counters were friezed and plinthed like tombs.

But there was never any doubt who'd win the contract once
Signor Claudio Busi arrived and told the old man that his
creed was this: "My allegiance is to what you want. Great
buildings such as this must glorify the vision of the man who
pays. I quote dell'Ova and I say, 'The tallest buildings throw
the longest shadows. Thus great men make their mark.' "

He'd done his homework, God knows how, for Victor's
passions and aversions were not documented, and Anna, in
the ascending lift, was tempting but not helpful. Or perhaps
this Busi simply had the gift of insinuating images into an
empty head with flattery. But, by luck or cunning, everything
he had to say was pleasing and on target.

Claudio Busi was a stringy man of sixty-nine, the eldest
partner in a practice celebrated for its taste and pragmatism.
It was Busi who designed The Riggings, the waterfront development at Port St. Phillips which had been laid flat by Hurri-
cane Eduardo two years before and had not been rebuilt. The
wrought-iron Exhibition Hall in Amsterdam was his work,
too. And so was the Curtains Project in Milan which won
the UN Prize: "A stunning engineering adventure." And the
Centenary Center on the lake in Michigan. His book, *The
World Beneath a Single Roof,* had started a short-lived vogue
for "space as playground, building as event," and had established Busi as a charming, architectural pundit at colloquiums
and on television shows. A lady's man, they said. He had the
kind of peachy voice that could soften stone.

His younger partners had to treat him with respect—but

they had largely forced him from the drawing board. He had become too careless, too passé. He did not understand the functional obsessions of the modern clients who wanted "splendor out and squalor in," that is to say, huge entrances, but offices as cramped and mean as prison cells. He traveled in his olive suits between their studios in New York, Paris and Milan much like a bishop travels his diocese, with great pomp but little power or control. He was a figurehead—and just the man, his partners judged, to win for them the Soap Market contract. A man of eighty could both patronize and trust a man of sixty-nine. So Busi was dispatched from Milan, to be their mouthpiece—and to give them all a break from his phrasemaking and his charm.

Signor Busi would have preferred to be the spokesman for his own designs—but he had convinced himself that this task was his because he was considered by his colleagues and his rivals "a philosopher amongst journeymen." (A journalist had once described him thus, though with the nuance that, perhaps, Signor Busi talked more convincingly than he performed, with buildings and with women, too.)

He took a room at the Excelsior and spent a day looking at the Soap Market and its garden. The team of three from the Busi Partnership who had spent two months on site earlier that year had warned the Signor in their briefing papers that the market was "cheap, inefficient and artificial." Busi thought so too. "Squalid" was the word he muttered to himself. His taxi had abandoned him to walk—all very well in precincts and pedestrianized streets, but here was chaos, a nightmare for pedestrians. To cross the market by foot was to volunteer for service in the bruising labyrinths of an ants' nest. It was—for sure—neither beautiful, nor functional; neither playground nor event. It failed the Busi litmus test. It turned the simple task of buying fruit into an expedition. He marveled at the depth and animation of the crowd and at the patience of the traders obliged each day to erect their stalls, barrow in their produce over cobbles, and then to box and barrow out each night the unsold residue, to end their day dismantling the stalls again. Inane. Insane.

Signor Busi ended up exhausted by the place, his suit disheveled, his shoes discolored. He rested in the Soap Garden but was not happy with the coffee and the pastry that he bought, or with the waiter who was too hurried and lacking in finesse. He tried but could not find his way back to a traffic street. The market was not logical. It had no signs, no thoroughfares. A man in cellophane had sent him deeper in. He had to pay a boy to guide him to a taxi rank. He was elated that the Busi Partnership of New York, Paris and Milan might be the ones to introduce some Order and some Uniformity. A modern, regulated city should be governed not by the impulses of crowds but by the dictates of its tramlines, pavements, traffic lights, timetables, laws. A modern, regulated city would not allow such squalid topsy-turvydom.

When at last they met, Signor Busi complimented Victor on Big Vic and on the mall which was its artery.

"It is gracious and it is legible," he said. "I applaud you that you wish to extend such geometric harmony into the ancient center of the town where, evidently, legibility and graciousness are out of fashion." He waited for an instant to allow Victor an opportunity to respond to these pleasantries. But he saw at once that Victor was no conversationalist and would be silent but attentive, too. He unzipped the black portfolios of draft proposals which he had brought from Milan, shook his body in his suit, and fixed his merchant client with his finest, thinnest smile.

"We have nostalgia and we have experiments," he said. "But you are not the man to like such things. You are a man of *now*. So let's not waste our time with these survivals from the past." His hand dismissed his rivals' plans. He lifted the corners of a design by the Ultra Studios and raised his eyebrows: "And let's not bother either with science fiction. It is dated just as soon as it is built. You see my Ultra colleague—should I talk behind his back?—has designed another Centre Lyons-Symphonique for us, all pipes and tubes and vents, but this one is for cabbages and not for culture. He thinks it's witty to put a building's guts on show, to put the inside on the outside. But this is what I have to say to you: you are a

man of eighty, this I know. Witty is not what you want.
You want a little dignity. You want a marketplace which
comprehends and celebrates your business intellect and not
the artful vision of an architect. I'm right, I think. So, we
dispense with inside on the outside. For you, for this great
marketplace, we put the outside on the inside, we bring the
outdoors indoors."

He spread the drawings over Victor's desk. His partners
had had the sense to keep them small and simple, at one-five-
hundredth scale, so that the spirit of the group's proposals
was more evident than their complexity. For Signor Busi, the
outdoors which they planned to bring indoors was more than
just a scheme to shield the market stalls from wind and rain
and temperature. The "outside" meant the countryside as
well, the world beyond the margins of the town.

"What is a market anyway, but country brought to town?"
he asked. "Let's give the people a country walk right at the
city's heart."

He pointed to the "conceptualizations" which had been
sketched in ink and artist's wash.

"Please, pick them up and take a look," he said. "What do
these elevations recall for you?" He smiled, but furtively,
while Victor shook his head. The design was called the Melting Glass Meringues by colleagues in Milan. Four spectacular
glass ovals which seemed both like cakes and the domes of
viscous mosques filled the Soap Market. Nine tapering barrel-
vaulted aisles—spaceframed in wood and steel, spaceglazed—
radiated from the center without geometric logic but in the
pleasing, balanced way that surface roots spread out from
trees.

"Here is a landscape at the city center," Busi said. "There
are no straight lines in our design, no matching planes or
pitches. Instead we have the horizontal disunities of the natural landscape. We give you hills and plains and ridges made
from curving sheets of glass. We look for coherence. We look
for harmony. We let the natural city light, which is absorbed
by brick and stone, pass through our glass and flood the building in the way that light can flood and warm and make fertile

a country greenhouse. The inner walls are mirrored, and all
the framing is constructed out of reflecting steel or polished
wood, so that the journey of the natural light is not truncated.
We have a greenhouse, then. We have the temperature and
air control to maintain the perfect environment for plants and
shrubs and trees. The walls are breathing walls. Outside, the
city; countryside within. We have glass-bottomed elevators
rising on a scenic ride through the foliage. We have nine trading corridors in human scale. And then the scale is more di-
vine—four domes, the largest fifty meters high and visible from
far away. It is a sculpture made from glass and greenery. It
is a living carapace frozen in metal. It is . . ." (and with a
flourish Signor Busi revealed the project's title) ". . . Arcadia.
But modernized. Climate-controlled. Efficient. Accessible.
Contemporary. Defended."

With this last word, Signor Busi spread his hands, the saddened pragmatist: "Arcadia must be defended. Of course! We
must admit the truth. If it is your wish to lure into Arcadia
those better citizens who have good taste and incomes to dis-
pose, then we must promise them security from . . ." Again
he spread his saddened hands. ". . . from the city itself. You
see we have provided surveillance cameras, antitheft shutters,
suicide netting, commissionaires. The building is a fortress.
A hand grenade would only shake its glass. It can survive the
full impact of an intercontinental airliner. But this is not
enough. We owe it to your customers to keep out drunks and
tramps and demonstrators and people who do not come to
spend, but simply wish to shelter from the rain, or sleep, or
cause unpleasantness. Arcadia—as you will see—is far too
good for them."

He took Victor on a tour, beginning with the two-storey
basement, cushioned in poured concrete and served by a deliv-
ery ramp concealed by lines of trees. He showed where refrig-
erated storage pods kept produce fresh, where ripening units
brought on bananas, apples, mangoes, to the colors judged
best and most tempting for shoppers. Here were the offices,
the basement studios, the service workshops, the market
courtyards, recapturing—intensifying—a medieval market at-

mosphere, with colored awnings, painted signs, terrazzo flooring, augmented natural light. And beds of shrubs, and greenhouse trees, and displays of bedding plants, with ivy, vines and bamboo stands.

The four meringues were joined inside Arcadia by a central hub much as the four seed-carpels of nasturtiums cling fatly to their stems. The hub supported terraces and balconies, with views through foliage of the heads and hats of shoppers, and the "authentic" colored awnings on the fixed-site stalls. On the lower terraces there were bars, a restaurant, an open con-cert arena. The upper balconies were almost out of sight. Below them stretched netting. It hung across the higher chambers of the domes like the billows of a Tuareg tent. Above and beyond the white and green patterns of the net-ting, there would be the largest aviary yet built in which the Busi Partnership envisaged cockatoos and cockatiels and myna birds, who finally, would learn to call like traders. "All fresh today. All fresh today. No loot, No fruit."

"The centerpiece!" Signor Busi produced a final sketch. "You see, we are not charlatans. We have respect for history. We have not torn the medieval washplace down. We have given it new life." The sketches showed what careful restora-tion could achieve, how medieval gargoyles could be rescued by the heroic dentistry of modern masons, how old and pitted stones could have the plaque removed, the cavities disguised, the broken tops replaced. There'd be new fountains, water-falls, where previously the flow had been fitful and controlled by taps.

Signor Busi showed photographs of the bludgeoned wash-ing basins where soap and stone and cloth had for so long made slapping music with the water. Then his new designs: the renewed basins were transformed by lights and plants. They were kept full and busy with piped, pumped, filtered and circulating water, which tumbled from hidden faucets into sculpted pools and then ran into channels to troughs of plants. At night, the air-conditioning, the concourse lights, the water would be turned off and floodlights would shine onto the four meringues. They'd make the innards of Arcadia warm and fathomless with the haywire shadows of pot-bound trees.

"I am a Milanese," said Signor Busi, "but even so I must admit that here we have a building which will be as beautiful and functional, more functional perhaps, than the Galerie Victor Emmanuel II in Milan. You share a name. You are Victor III, perhaps. You share a place in history as well, if you allow the Busi Partnership to make these drawings come alive."

Signor Busi spread his arms and laughed. "No more to say." He left the plans and drawings where they were and put out both hands to Victor. "I am at your disposal until Sunday, naturally. *Tante grazie, Signor Victor.*"

Victor summoned Anna. She took Signor Busi to the boss's private lift and traveled with him to the atrium and to the exit on the mall. He was ebullient and playful like an actor who has triumphed on the stage. He liked the woman at his side. Her perfume and her plumpness and the crowded intimacy of Victor's lift loosened him. His wife was far away. He laid two fingers on her wrist. He said, "I think that your employer will give to me the contract for the Soap Market. Perhaps I ought to celebrate tonight, and you should be my guest at my hotel."

Anna shook her head. "It's very kind," she said, "but far too early for a celebration yet, don't you think? Victor has another three to see."

"My dear," said Signor Busi, letting go her arm, "I feel it in my blood that we shall win. Our plans will be preferred."

"Perhaps Victor will decide to preserve the market as it is."

Busi laughed. "There's nothing to preserve. There's nothing there. There is nothing to demolish. Of course there are the cobblestones to lift and lay again more cunningly. And there are those unkempt small bars and restaurants which cluster round the Soap Garden. Those we have to level off. And then we start from scratch! So we will speak again, I think. And many times."

His car drew up and Signor Busi left Big Vic a happy man. Above him, on the twenty-seventh floor, his plans were strewn across the desk and carpet. Victor stood amongst them, a reference dictionary in his hand. *Arcadia*—a rustic paradise, he read. *Arcadian*—of pastoral simplicity. *Arcade*—a covered row of shops.

Signor Busi waited at the Excelsior for three more days, and on the fourth he received a call. Anna spoke for Victor. She was pleased, she said, to let him know that the Busi Partnership had secured the Soap Market contract. A formal letter would be sent, and Victor would be grateful if Signor Busi would extend his stay for three more days so that a press conference could be arranged and the time scale for construction plotted. He would, too, be sending Signor Busi sketches of a small statue which was a birthday gift to Victor from—how appropriate!—the leading market traders. It was a mother and a child and should be incorporated into Arcadia.

"A small statue? This we will give pride of place!" Busi told Anna. And then, "So, please let me give you pride of place at my table at the Excelsior tonight. Now I think it is not too soon to celebrate."

4

ANNA ATE VEGETABLES like anybody else, but she was not an habitué of the Soap Market. She lived a little way from town—ten minutes on the bus, a forty-minute walk. She did not count herself so poor or so energetic that she need queue at market stalls and then transport her purchases by bag and bus. Within a hundred meters of her home there was a delicatessen with a fresh-products counter and an unhurried clientele, and this she used. Of course there were those times when she preferred to shop in city streets for clothes or shoes or presents for her nieces. Once in a while, after work, she set off down the mall toward the boutiques and the studios, determined to spend money on herself.

On the evening that Signor Busi first met Victor and then ventured to hold Anna by the wrist, she had felt so glad to be herself, so glad to be admired and flirted with (if only by a creaky clotheshorse from Milan) that she went looking for a treat in town. She'd seen a brooch that she wanted, handmade, a galaxy of silver stars, a single moon of pearl. She'd need a darker jacket, too, to suit the brooch. Some Belgian chocolates, perhaps, could keep her company that night. She'd take a taxi home.

The jeweler had her workshop-studio beneath the timber galleries in Saints Row. Anna walked there by the quickest route. She was a little anxious that the galleries might close before the larger stores. But there the owner was, at work on

199

a bracelet, a flight of copper geese. Anna could not see the brooch she wanted on display. She went inside. She asked. The jeweler did not lift her head, or take the magnifier from her eye. She said, "I sold it. Weeks ago."

"Do you have something similar? Another galaxy?"

"I don't do stars and moons, not anymore. What I do now is birds and butterflies." Anna waited for some helpful word, for some expression of regret, for some polite farewell. Instead the jeweler, clearly not prepared to talk, instructed, "You could try elsewhere."

Anna was too vexed to look elsewhere. What kind of businesswoman had such contempt for customers that she could not be bothered to raise her head or lift her eyes. Anna regretted that she had not gone home by bus as soon as work was done. She did not need a darker jacket now. She would not treat herself—and just as well, perhaps—to Belgian chocolates. Or take the taxi home. Instead she'd catch the bus back to her sewing and her television set, and spend the night, as many single women do, as silent and as self-possessed as quails. But first, she thought, she'd take a look at the Soap Market. It was so near, and on the way to her bus stop. Her contacts with the architects and with their plans had made her curious to see exactly what Signor Busi had meant that afternoon: "There's nothing worth preserving there." She'd buy some salad for her sinless evening meal.

Anna had, a month before, turned her back on pasta, bread and rice, and hoped to make her peace with lettuce and with beans. Her only lapse was chocolates. Those times that Rook had pinched her at her waist, the hoop of flesh too loose between his fingers and his thumb, had made Anna discontented with herself. She used to push his hands away. He called it teasing. He thought it was a pleasing intimacy to draw attention to her loss of shape. She counted pinches of that kind as bullying. Men, it seemed, were never satisfied for long with the details of the women that they loved. And that was heartless, was it not?

When Rook was sacked and had ignored her visits to his apartment and the notes she'd left, Anna had found cause to blame herself. She'd frightened Rook with too much passion. She'd slept with him too readily. She'd been the secret cause of his dismissal from Big Vic. Her "details" were not right for him. If only she was slim and thirty-five, then Rook would leave his door ajar for her. Yet he was just as middle-aged and lined as her. At least she was not dry like him. She was not graying, yet. She could breathe without her chest trembling—though it was true that her chest would pout a little less if she shed three kilos, say. She'd learned to blame her weight, and not herself, for losing Rook. She never thought to blame and hate the man himself.

Quite speedily, she'd lost some weight and, if not trim, she was more statuesque and confident. She bought new clothes that fitted her. She had her hair shortened and razored at the neck. She exercised each evening on her *phaga* rug. Now that she was just a trifle lighter and more disguised by what she wore, she felt unburdened. But nothing that she did or ate could take away the pouching underneath her chin, or recompense her for the sudden, hurtful loss of Rook. What use were mottoes such as *Yes-and-Now-and-Here* if *Now-and-Here* were desk and home and bed without her Rook?

She was surprised, however, on that broochless night, how cheerful she was feeling amongst the shopping crowds and how seductive were the market stalls. One soapie dealt only in roots, the gormless starches of the fields. His carrots ranged in color from the red of mutton steaks to the pink of carp; he had carrots as round and bright as fairy lights; he had them straight and long like waxen stalactites; he had them double-limbed. He had potatoes, too—all shades, all shapes, and kept apart in separate buckets. He had whites, yellows, reds, pinks, scrapers, bakers, boilers, friers, cocktail spuds, Idahos, Egyptian, Old Andean, starchy, seedy, sweet. He had potatoes which were grown organically and were presented with the soil intact (to mask the blemishes). He had potatoes slightly greened by light. These were good in salads, raw and shredded with some mayonnaise.

Anna burrowed deep into the Soap Market. She passed the ranks of oranges, the monsoon fruit, the chicory, the sea kale,

the Valentino pears, the commonwealth of apples, and came
into the cooler kingdom of the leaf. She wanted just one lettuce, but she was teased by choice and color. She rummaged
at a stall for a garden lettuce with a tight rosette. She'd never
noticed how they smelled before. The salads at the produce
counter of her local delicatessen were odorless. But here,
banked up in such profusion, the leaves were acrid almost,
funereal. Their odor was precisely that of damp clay newly
turned to take a coffin. The lettuce that she chose was tight
and heavy—an early Wintervale. Its leaf stems were white.
The leaves themselves were strongly ribbed and shaped like
scallop shells. These were the lettuce leaves that the Spirits of
the Field would use as plates at midnight feasts when they
were standing guard against the pinching frost. The soapie
dropped the lettuce in a bag and took Anna's payment as if
the Spirits of the Field had yet to visit him.

Why did she not go now to catch her bus? Because she was
seduced by all the multiformity of food? Because she was
confused by color, noise and crowds? Because Cellophane directed her on some detour? Or because a woman who had
just detected death in lettuce leaves could have no difficulty
picking up the smell of Rook as he sat with his coffee in the
Soap Garden?

Rook spotted her as she negotiated chairs and customers.
At first he watched her idly, thinking simply that she was a
woman to his taste, a trader's stylish wife, perhaps, or the
elegant and tempting boss of some boutique. Then he recognized her, just in time, as she saw him. His chest grew tight.
His trousers, too. The lovers had not spoken for five months.
Or touched. So Rook felt doubly cornered, both by the brutal
carelessness with which he'd treated her and by the meanness
of his sudden concupiscence. He wished to be a thousand
miles away; he wished to be ten meters closer, so close and
wrapped that he digested her, took from her mouth the salty
sauce and fillet of her tongue.

"You've changed," he said. "You've cut your hair." She
seemed embarrassed. She reddened when he complimented

her on how she looked. Was that the red of anger or delight? She did not speak, but put her lettuce on the table, and sat down facing Rook. Let him speak first.

"Am I to take it that there is another man?"

"Why should there be?"

"The way you look, of course."

"Like what?"

"You've blossomed since I last saw you. Is there a man?"

"Of course there is," she said, quite truthfully.

"And who is he?" Rook looked as if his face had lost its bones.

"An architect," she said. "He's asked me back to the Excelsior, no less. To celebrate."

"And what is there to celebrate?"

"The end of all this!" Anna spread her arms and flapped her hands, as if she were an illusionist who could make the real world disappear.

To some extent she was exactly that. Most women are. They are illusionists, at least when they are young. They have the trick of making clocks stand still for men, of making clocks run fast, of lowering the temperature a trace, of raising it, of being so desirable that all the world beyond the bubble of themselves is distanced and diluted. Their narrow heads, their scent, the scissored hairline at their neck, the leafy rustling of their skirts, become bewitchments. So Rook was netted and engulfed, and Anna glorified that she was not too old or large to hold this man in thrall. She laid her hands upon his table. He had the courage and the shame to hold her by the wrist.

"Just like my architect," she said, and then her story tumbled out, how secretive the boss had been, how plans had been passed off as something else, how nine architects—so far—had been escorted up to Victor's suite like prisoners in custody and not allowed to share a lift or chatter with the staff. She told how Victor was obsessed by plans, and how his books on greenhouse pests had been pushed aside by models, elevations and projections for the Soap Market. She told how

Signor Busi had—that afternoon—seduced the boss with sculpted words and how she was convinced—like him—that Busi would be the man to "start from scratch."

"I could have stopped him. I *would* have stopped him," Rook said, more energized and focused than he had been for a dozen years. "But now I've gone, who is there to give him good advice?"

"So, that's why you got the sack? He didn't want you in the way . . . ?"

"What does Victor say?"

"What does Victor ever say? He hasn't said a word. When does he ever say a word? You know what he's like, out of sight, out of mind . . ."

She put her one free hand on top of his so that the three arms on the table made a bas-relief of flesh and fingers. Rook felt reprieved. Anna had not learned about his market fraud from Victor. The ice cube had not revealed the truth. Nor would he. Rook raised his head. He squared his shoulders. He was a cockatoo, all squawk and feathers now, all strut and peck and preen.

"Come home with me," he said. "Let's celebrate."

"I've called round at your home a dozen times," she said. "I've written and I've called. Not one reply."

"So come home now. We'll put it right."

"We'll see," she said. "You're not as fancy as my architect."

"Ah, the Italian, yes." Rook took his fingers out of hers. He held the edges of her coat. "If he wins, I'd like to see his plan."

"He'll win. I'd bet on it." Anna's voice had lost its resolution. She held her breath. She watched his fingertips.

"When will you know?"

"Next week, officially. There'll be a press conference and a presentation of the scheme when the contract is awarded."

"And where?"

"Big Vic."

"I'd like to see the plans before next week, before the press. Can you do that?"

"Do what."

"Give me a preview of the scheme that wins."

"Why should I take that chance?"

"Because I want you to," he said. And (he thought) because the old man plans to put an end to all of this. Because there's no one in Big Vic to stand up for the soapies and the marketplace.

Rook spread his arms and flapped his hands in mockery of her. But there was no illusion at his fingertips—no desire to see the real world disappear, no wish to interfere in the bustling kinship of the citizens who went about their business in the Soap Market with the fitful, browsing innocence of weevils in a cake.

"What can I do?" Anna said. "Victor keeps his room locked. And anyway, those plans aren't small. They're tablecloths."

"And what about your fancy architect?" Rook let her repossess his hand.

"Who? Busi?"

"Yes. He must have duplicates."

Anna nodded, shrugged, as if to indicate she had no access to this man.

"I think," said Rook, his hand pushed through the buttoned vents of Anna's coat, his palm upon her slimmer waist, a finger tucked beneath her belt, "that it might be a good idea to let the signor take you out to dinner. At the Excelsior, no less."

5

ROOK WAS A JUGGLER. He held and tossed five lives. He had to spin and mix them in the air. He had to pitch them so that they arched and fell into his hands with just the angle and the impact he required. Rook had to space the five lives in his grasp, ensure they did not meet or touch, for he was keen to settle scores—deftly, speedily, undetected. He was ready and impatient now to pay off debts and make amends, with Busi, Joseph, Anna, Con, but, most of all, with Victor. Quite what he ought to juggle up, Rook was not sure, though at their simplest and their meanest his intentions were to punish Con and Victor for the job, the private income from pitch payments, the self-respect they'd robbed from him.

The uniformed expulsion from Big Vic tormented him. He had to torment in return. This was unadorned revenge, and revenge is next to lust in its single-mindedness, its self-regard. So Rook did not care that Busi, Anna, Joseph and yes, Con and Victor, too, were mostly innocent of blame for the malfunctions in his life. He'd still be on the twenty-seventh floor and welcome in the Soap Market, sweet with Victor, Anna, Con, if he'd resisted those envelopes of cash, that money in the palm, those bribes. This is something that country people understand more readily than townies. If you sow thorns, then you get thorns. They don't need watering. They flourish and they snag.

Rook would not admit his pettiness, that what he wanted

most was some wounding, simple recompense. He fooled himself that there were nobler motives driving him. The fiction that he made was this: that his months of leisure, free from Victor and Big Vic, had resurrected an old self that had ideals and principles worth fighting for. How could he forget the man he'd been a dozen years before when the produce boycott had been organized? They'd listened to him in the market then. They'd cheered. He'd stood on a platform made from crop boxes, dressed in clichéd black, and made that speech that all the papers had reproduced in full.

"This Soap Market," he had said, "is here to make good salads and fruit pies. To put some muscle into stews, some zest in cake, to keep the city fed. It is not here to make men millionaires. So we traders should let the market die before we let the prices outstrip the common people." They'd flocked to that—and they'd held out on strike for seven weeks. A stirring time. The world turned upside down, with market customers bringing cake and cheese and bread to feed the soapies, and every stall and awning dismantled, and not a scrap of lettuce to be seen.

The striking soapies had given Rook the mandate to negotiate. They'd trusted him. But Victor knew the trick of tearing notes in half. "Why let the market die?" he'd asked, made locquacious by the seven weeks of damage to his wealth. "You only harm yourselves." His agents and his managers had offered Rook a compromise. You lift the boycott, and trade according to the prices we have set, they counseled. And in return we freeze the market rents for two years, maybe three. You traders save a little cash for . . . okay, you win, let it be frozen rents for the full *three years*. You save the marketplace for good.

Rook had said he was only a mouthpiece, that was all, but that he doubted his colleagues would betray their principles. Victor had spoken again. "How much are principles?" he asked himself, but he said out loud, "It would be democratic, don't you think, if my, our, colleagues in the market had some constant spokesman at my side to represent their principles." He had not looked at Rook, but had written a sum in

pencil on a memorandum pad and slid it across his desk so
Rook could see. "That is the kind of yearly sum that we
would pay for such a diplomat." Rook had shaken Victor by
the hand and had taken the stipend of the diplomat.

So now Rook felt he had the chance to make amends, to
piece together once again the man that had been raised within
the odor of the marketplace, that had been schooled in rad-
ishes and rambutans, that thrived in clamor and crowds. He'd
save the Soap Market. He'd be the champion of marketeers.
He'd climb up on the platform once again and "represent their
principles, their fears." But then, once he had sobered from
the fever of the phrases in his head, he thought again, more
clearly. Platforms were for innocents. Speeches only waylaid
passion with fine words. The player with the strongest hand,
the running flush, was not required to show his cards. So it
was in politics—for, yes, Rook was now so inflated with the
altruism of his mission that he'd cast himself as a man in
service to the citizens. In politics you did not need to spout
or strut or speechify if you could quietly slip behind the scenes
to sabotage, to juggle, and to complicate. He had a plan,
unformed but irresistible, which would deliver Anna to his
bed, and damage Con, and punish Victor, and introduce that
muscly Joseph to the truth that brains and money are more
powerful than youth. He'd cause a little mayhem, too, for
Signor Busi of Milan—and leave himself the hero of the
marketplace.

So, four days after Rook and Anna reconnected in the Soap
Garden bar and on the day that Signor Busi won the contract
for Arcadia and once again invited Anna to his table, they
walked to the Excelsior. They'd been together every night
and had slept so deeply, back-to-back, that the dreams and
snores which celebrated their resurrected passion did not wake
them. They were refreshed by the affection that they gave
and got, and Anna took the change in Rook, his liveliness,
his youth, to be a sign that he returned her love. Why else
would she, a careful woman wedded to her work, agree to
dine with Busi and to chance his busy hand so that she could,
for Rook, become a common thief?

Rook had been careless. He should have let Anna walk the final meters to the Excelsior on her own. But she was nervous—as she had a right to be. Dining with a stranger in a hotel such as this would make the toughest of us tremble. Rook had let her hold his arm until they reached the polished marble steps of the Excelsior.

"Aha, my dear. You've brought a companion?"

Signor Busi was standing at the carpet edge, spying on the women in the street. Anna let go of Rook and, at once, wondered why. She held his arm again.

"He's a friend," she said, but had the sense to give no name.

Rook was disadvantaged by Busi's height, his clothes, his age.

"I was just passing by," he said. "Have a pleasant evening." He walked away, but slowly enough to note how Signor Busi had a voice that was as carpeted and marble as the hotel steps.

Rook would never know what happened between Anna and Busi that night, and she would never learn how Rook had passed his time. Though they, of course, would tease each other with alternatives.

It was quite clear to Rook and Anna that they were tethered to the ardor of the night. As they parted, both were charged with the sexual static implicit in the triangle that they formed—the aging, elegant seducer; the apprehensive woman in her finery (bathed, perfumed, bangled, silk-dressed in gold and black); the thin-faced breathless lover transformed to thin-faced, breathless pimp as he dispatched his paramour on her—on his—assignment; the dining table set and waiting with its single rose, its silver tub of ice, its candlelight and its connivance in the creed that all is fair in love and trade; the hotel bedroom with the balcony and matching lampshades, curtains, bedspread; the salacity of wintertime.

Rook had said to Anna, "Do what you can to get a copy of those plans. Do anything. It's up to you." He had not said she ought to sleep with Signor Busi but, then, he had not asked her not to. He was excited, that's for sure, by the power that he seemed to have. He liked to enmesh her in his in-

trigues and to allow the notion, if not the fact, that she would
sleep with Busi if instructed so. How sensual it was, how
riggish, how sportingly loyal, how grandly stimulating that
she might do this thing for him. What would she not do,
now, with Rook in his own bed, on his own floor, if she
could be so dutiful as to serve him with another man?

Anna, for herself, had not contemplated for too long what
Rook had meant by "Do anything. It's up to you." She took
his meaning, but she took it as a joke. She did not want to
think that Rook, despite his recent protestations of affection,
would use her as a bribe, a trinket. She had no wish to be
his representative in Signor Busi's arms. But Rook had spoken
with such passion and such verve about his mission to save
the Soap Market that she had redefined herself as a woman
who, by surrendering and making servile her love for Rook,
could consolidate his love for her.

Of course, she would not, when it came to it, allow the
architect to touch a centimeter more of her than the pale,
unsensual flesh around her wrist. But she had fooled herself
into believing there was no insult in Rook's evident indifference. She did not say, "If that old smoothie has the nerve to
try it on with me he'll get my dinner in his lap," or "If you're
so keen to get a copy of these plans why don't you go and
sleep with Busi yourself. He doesn't seem the choosy sort.
And nor do you." She did not say, "I'm not a prostitute."
She simply let the atmosphere between them stay a little
warmed and moist with the license he had imposed on her to
"Do what you can to get a copy of those plans."

So she had bathed and dressed for the Excelsior in clothes
which she had brought from her own home to Rook's apartment. As she dressed before the mirror, arranging belts and
tights and underclothes, and testing scents and bracelets on
her arm, Rook sat and watched. His breath was shallow, his
tongue was dry, his heart beat fast. Not asthma—but an ail-
ment which nearly every man is martyr to, the subjugation
of all sentiments and resolutions to the tyranny of sex. He
smelled of badger. He felt his penis lengthening inside his
trouser leg. He had to shift his leg and readjust his clothes.

He was not slow to help her with her zip or take the landlord opportunity to wet her neck with a kiss and press himself into her back.

"Not now," she said, and rubbed his trousers with her hand, proprietorially. He was transfixed, entranced, by the prospect of the night. But he had lost the chance of giving full expression and relief to the promptings and the tensions that he felt. He'd happily see the market torn down, and Victor trimphant and untouched, and Signor Busi left to dine alone, if only Anna would agree to turn around and put her face to his. He'd happily—but for how long?—relinquish mission and revenge for five demented, silken, musky minutes in her arms.

She was putting on her shoes, and smoothing down her dress, and searching for her toothbrush in her bag. And they were descending to the street. And they were walking arm in arm like married couples do, respectably. And Rook was looking up at Signor Busi on the hotel steps and saying, "A pleasant evening to you both."

Rook walked down to the Soap Garden and found an isolated chair where he could sit in privacy and think. And drink. What were the diners doing now? Had they reached dessert? Anna liked sweet things and Signor Busi would insist she had exactly what she wanted. No doubt she bubbled; it did not take much drink to make her gamy. No doubt the old Italian was urbane and courteous, and lightly anecdotal in the way that men who are not young must be if they want to charm their juniors. Rook pictured Busi as he lightly put his hand upon his guest's bare arm and called the waiter to the table so that his intimacy could pass as etiquette. Perhaps he asked if she required a *digestif*. A Boulevard Liqueur? Did she stay still? Did she encourage him to leave his hand in place? To stroke her arm perhaps? To take her hand in his?

Rook shook his head, and rearranged the dinner table once again. This time the architect was silent and Anna was urbane and cunning. She kept the conversation light and tempting. She flattered him, his suit, his taste in wine. He boasted of his fame as an architect, the work he'd done to shape the new

Arcadia. She said, I'd love to see those plans myself. He said, They're in my room. She said, Why don't you order some nightcaps and we can take them up.

Again Rook cleared his head. He'd conjured up a harpy, out of character. Anna was not a predator. She'd have to be cajoled upstairs, unwillingly, but with her task in mind, to borrow, steal, a second set of plans. Perhaps she'd asked to see the plans. Busi said, You'll have to come upstairs. He let her know that dinner was not cheap and that Victor would not wish his architect to go without affection in his town. Rook could almost see the plans upon Signor Busi's bed. He saw the look on Anna's face as Busi hung his trousers, creases straight, across a chair, and turned to watch the black and gold on Anna loosen, crumple, drop. Rook saw her, Busi watched her, hold her stomach in as she pushed down her tights and underclothes and stood, in nothing but her slip. Signor Busi cleared the plans and elevations from the bed-spread and then pulled Anna to him by her wrists. "My name is Claudio," he said.

Now Rook, if he had been a younger, fitter, more dramatic man, would have run between the Soap Garden and the Excelsior. Not out of anger, nor jealousy. He was not fool enough to be jealous of these chimeras. But out of lust. He wanted sex; he wanted intercourse. He wanted to express himself before he burst from lack of it. He could not hold his coffee cup. He could not halt himself. He walked unsteadily, a little drunk on his imaginings.

He found a girl—not more than seventeen. A country girl who'd never kissed a man she loved. She took him to a third-floor room two streets behind the house where he was born. She pulled her blouse apart. She pulled her denim skirt up to her waist. She wore no underclothes. She was as thin and unprepared for city life as Anna was mature. Rook said to her, "My name is Claudio." There were two gray patches on the mattress of the bed, where ten thousand knees had been before. Rook put the money on the chair, and did as he was told.

"Undress," she said. Then "Wash."

The water on his penis sobered him, but he was drunk again when she came to him with a sheath and rolled it on. She lay down on the bed. She removed her watch and chewing gum and, pressing the gum onto the watch face, dropped them to the floor.

"Okay," she said. "It's up to you."

She might have been a country girl, but she was as nonchalant and passive in her work as any city laborer or clerk or factory hand. It paid the bills. She held a steady course between professional cupidity and personal disdain. She was wise enough to forge a little interest in the man who paid. The bread won't rise without the yeast. She shook her head or nodded as required. She matched a dozen groans of his with one of hers.

They always looked the same, these men, when they were done—a little disappointed, eager to depart. She retrieved her chewing gum. It was still moist and almost warm. She watched him search his trouser pockets and then the pockets of his leather jacket. He found his handkerchief and wiped his nose. He pressed a spray into his mouth and sucked on it, as if he wished to blast away the taste of her with Pine-'n-Chive. His face was red, but weren't they all, and with good cause? But this one did not rapidly turn pale. His breathing was not free. His chest was quivering as if his orgasm was trapped and heading for his lungs. She did not care. He'd only paid for fifteen minutes and time was up. Another girl would want the room. She picked his trousers up and put them in his hand.

"You'd better get some fresh air," she said.

She waited by the door until he put his spray away and pulled his trousers on. She went alone down to the street where she had friends and where her face and chewing gum could stretch and soften in the darkness.

Rook had cleared his mind at last. He left the street and market area. And as quickly as he could—in other words not speedily at all, but chin upon his chest and hands upon his lungs and phlegm upon his lips—he returned to his apartment.

He lay on his bed and shut his eyes and could not disentan-

gle Anna, Signor Busi or the prostitute. They coiled like an-
glers' worms so that it was a puzzle where they ended or
began. He slept and trod the waters of a shallow dream. Too
much nebulizer. Joseph wore the uniform of a commissionaire. He threw Rook out of doors, apartment doors, office
doors, and doors to gloomy bars. He slept with Anna, and
Anna slept with Victor, and Signor Busi slept with Rook until
the bed became a market stall turned to leaf and root. The
prostitute was in his bed and would not leave, and Anna's
feet were on the stairs. And she was not alone. Now someone
joined them in the bed and put a hand upon his chest. "You
don't look well," she said. Her breath was garlic and cigar.
Her perfume was Boulevard Liqueur.

She sat in front of the mirror and let him wake. She took
her bracelets and her earrings off and started on her eyes and
cheeks with cotton wool and rose oil.

"How did it go?" he said.

Anna was too satisfied to tell the truth. How easy it had
been, with Signor Busi keener to secure her admiration and
her rapt attention than to lure her to his bed. He had not
touched her once. He seemed afraid that he might go beyond
the point where he impressed her. He was adept with wine
lists and cigars. Waiters were polite with him. The chef—a
fellow Milanese—came up and shook his hand. He thrived on
conversation. He could talk and eat and drink as neatly and
amusingly as a juggler with five balls. He flattered Anna
charmingly. He could let her go without seducing her and do
his reputation not a jot of harm. But if he tried his luck with
her? What then? At best he'd take her to his room and she
would see how papery he was beneath the suit and how his
posture—tall, erect—was aided by a spinal truss. It took him
minutes to remove his jacket. He had to shake his shoes and
trousers off. To see him climb onto his bed, undressed, was
(he admitted it himself) to watch a scene from *Marat/Sade* or
witness antiballet of the kind danced by the chorus of the dead
in Przewalski's "Crematorium."

So there they stayed, at table, in public safety. He was, he
said, excited by the prospect of spending a few months in

town. His junior partners were good at seeing ideas through, but not so good at nurturing the building itself. He was the old-fashioned sort of architect, he said. He liked to have a love affair with everything he built. He let this slogan do its work, and then he threw it out before it did him harm in Anna's eyes: "Excuse an old man his absurdities. I promise I'll be less extravagant at the press conference. No gibberish, I think, for journalists."

"Ah, yes, the conference," said Anna. "Victor will need another set of plans . . . before the conference."

"Of course, my dear." (He had not used her name or even asked her what it was.) "I'll send them over to him by courier."

"I'll take them now, if it'll help. That'll please Victor. I'll feel I've earned this splendid meal."

"They weigh at least ten kilos."

"I'm stronger than you think."

Signor Busi was not keen to go with her to his room, or, indeed, to do the round trip all alone. It was too far. He was too tired and full. He called a bellboy to the table. He handed him his key. "Be so good as to go up to my room and fetch a yellow file. It's this thick and so high." He mimed the file. "You'll find three of them leaning up against the window bay. Just bring me one." He gave the boy a hundred note, and then embarked upon an anecdote about a client's file that he'd once lost in New York, in a cab. The telling of it tired him. He lost the thread, and was relieved when the boy came back with the yellow file. He could not fight a yawn.

"I'll let you get to bed," Anna said.

Signor Busi stood and slowly straightened. His stomach squalled. He took her hand. "Good night, my dear," he said. "It has been a great pleasure." He watched her leaving for the line of taxis in the street, the bellboy and the file of papers at her side. She walked triumphantly.

"She really is the most enticing woman," Signor Busi thought as he began the journey to his room.

Rook was now sitting up in bed. "How did it go?" he

asked again. Anna pointed to the bedroom door. A yellow file, fat with plans and papers, leaned against the frame.

"Have faith in me," she said. Why should she tell him any more. Let him imagine what he wished. Rook did not betray his lack of faith in her. His conscience was not clear but smudged with two gray marks where he had placed his knees.

They sat in silence for a while, Anna at the mirror, Rook in bed, each with secrets to preserve, but only one of them felt sure enough to smile.

6

ROOK SMILED AT CON. "Let's talk," he said.

"What for?"

"Because, unless we talk, your market stall will fall to bits."
His arms were up and stretched. "All this will disappear."

"Get lost." Con smiled at Rook, but his smile was lipless.
It did not crease his eyes or pack his cheeks. It was tight. It
elevated "Get Lost" from curt indifference to chilling maledic-
tion. The smile dismissed Rook as a man not worthy of contempt. But Rook was not dismissed. He put his hand out to
stop Con packing for the night. He had counted on Con's
hostility. He'd hoped for it. It would not do if Con was a
conciliator who preferred *What's done is done* to the bald *Get
Lost.* Rook rubbed a finger and a thumb to mime the crum-
bling of a solid into dust.

"Get lost," said Con. "I've work to do."

"But not for long," said Rook. "You'll soon be out of
work and rattling round the streets like me. Except you won't
have the savings I've got to make your unemployment
pleasant."

"You're farting through your mouth," said Con, but he
was enticed enough to stop his efforts with his stall and turn
to look Rook in the face.

Rook had prepared his speech: "Pay attention," he said, as
if the trader were a six-year-old. "Don't be a fool. We've

more in common than you think . . . and I'm not blaming you."

"Not blaming me? For what?"

"For that stupid scuffle with the country boy, and all your poke and squeak with Victor. For losing me my job. What do you think?"

"You can blame yourself for that," said Con. He'd not bother to deny that he'd launched Joseph on the fumbled attempt to repossess his pitch payment. Why should he? It was reclamation, just and fair. He did not understand what "all your poke and squeak with Victor" might be or why he should be blamed for Rook's dismissal. Nor did he care. Rook was despicable, he thought, but as harmless as a snake that having lost its venom makes do with hiss. It did not matter what Rook knew about that farce with Joseph in the walkers' tunnel. How could Rook damage Con now that he was, by all accounts, truncated from his boss for good?

"You had it coming, and you got off lightly," he said. "I should have sent four boys, not one. You'd be on crutches now. Why should I feel guilty? I'm only sorry I wasn't there myself."

"Don't play the hero," said Rook. "If I was holding grudges I wouldn't be here at all. I'd fix you privately. I'm here to help you out. Not that you deserve my help."

"Get lost."

Rook wrapped his fingers round his keys. How he despised this man, his smell, his clothes, his tight and unforgiving face. But Rook had to persevere. His only route was Con. He put the yellow file of duplicate designs from the Busi Partnership on the trader's stall, amongst the bruised fruit and the waste that Con would jettison. He took the top drawing out. There were the melting glass meringues, the starfish corridors, the indoor trees, the relocated cobblestones in wash and watercolor. There was the legend: "ARCADIA—a sketch."

"What's this?"

"It's what dear Victor has in mind for you."

Now Rook was free to make his speech. He told how Victor was not satisfied with profits from the marketplace, how he'd been prompted by his bankers and his strategists to build, how Signor Busi and Arcadia had won the old man's ear—and eye. An easy task because Victor was demented with old age, indigestion, and his obsession with a statue of some kind: "A mother and a child, would you believe. And not a statue of himself!"

Rook made the most of his regrets that he was no longer in Victor's pay. It was his view, he explained with patient irony, that since the one man who knew the Soap Market "from the inside out" had been removed from Victor's side, then Victor had been free to run amuck.

"I protected you," he said. "Maybe you didn't like to pay for that, but I protected you—and see what's happened now that the Soap Market has got no one to speak for it inside Big Vic." He punched the drawings. "There's a press conference in three days' time," he said. "They think they've got the only set of plans. But your man Rook has earned his pay and got a second set." Rook recalled for Con the chilling boasts of Busi, "There's nothing to preserve," "We level off and take away," "We start from scratch."

"I don't hold out much hope for you or this, unless you organize, unless you defend yourself. Yourselves," concluded Rook. He'd said enough. He pushed the file of papers toward Con.

"Why me?" asked Con. "Why not one of those old wind socks you hang out with in the bar?"

"Because they're wind socks, like you say. Limp when things are fine, and when it's stormy full of air. But you, you're not a wind sock; you're one of life's malcontents. You're not afraid of fights. You were the only one to give me any trouble over payments for your pitch. The only one from what? . . . from two hundred and eight stall holders. You're one in two-o-eight. You, Con, are a natural troublemaker. And may you be in Heaven for an hour before the Devil knows you're dead."

"All right, so I'm a malcontent. Then why not you? You're

the maestro amongst mischief makers. You've got the plans. You know the innards of the man. God knows, you've got enough spare time to organize a global war. Why me?"

Rook spoke with passion now. He was not obliged to equivocate with abstracts. He spoke of his damaged reputation in the marketplace, how he might still be seen as Victor's eyes and ears, as some double agent whose loyalties were as brief and unpredictable as shooting stars. Or else the word would be that the sacked factotum of the millionaire, disgruntled, venomous, was using marketeers to settle his own scores. The press and television would make a meal of that. They loved bad motives. They preferred an intrigue to the simple justice of a cause.

Or else no one would trust him. The older traders would not forget how Rook's brinking leadership a dozen years before had been so readily tranquilized by Victor's check. His appeasement had impoverished everyone but himself. Unless they were as forgetful and forgiving as chastised dogs they would suspect him.

"Besides," said Rook, "I've got to stay out of sight. That architect has seen me with . . . the person from Big Vic who stole the plans for you. I can't name names. The less you know of that the safer she, or he, will be. With luck they won't trace the leak. But if Busi sees me with the plans he'll make connections. He's slow and foreign but he's not stupid. Our routes to Victor and to Busi will be blocked and our informant will get sacked, at best. As things stand our sharpest weapon is surprise. What do you say?"

Con did not say a word. He gathered up the papers on his stall. He pushed them in his bag together with his newspaper, his change of shirt, his takings for the day. He'd sleep on it. Then, next morning, he would call a meeting of the marketeers and take directions, not from Rook but them.

He set to work dismantling his stall. He was dispirited by what he'd heard, though, normally, when work was at an end and home was near, he felt at his most contented. He wished that Victor's man—he could not think of Rook in other terms—would take the hint and leave. He'd said his piece. He'd mixed his poison. He ought to disappear. But Rook seemed keen to stay. He was smiling even; the same smile with which he'd burdened Con before they spoke.

Rook took the end of Con's stall and helped him lift it from the trestles. He packed the produce boxes to one side. He unhooked the green and yellow awning and began—inexpertly, incorrectly—to fold the canvas. His hands and fingers were as soft and clean as soap. Con took the bulky canvas and unfolded it. He stowed it once again, so that it made an almost perfect square. He stood on it to clear the air. "I don't need help," he said.

Rook shrugged. "We all need help."

"Get lost," said Con and, as he had his back to Rook, allowed himself the briefest smile, but one which packed his cheeks and creased his eyes and put his lips on show. It was true what Rook had said. He relished fights. He was the one in two-o-eight.

7

VICTOR AND SIGNOR BUSI were taking breakfast on the twenty-eighth when Con and his two hundred colleagues set out from the Soap Garden. Press cameramen and a television unit from the local studios were there to film the marketeers' procession to Big Vic.

Rook, in his role of unacknowledged puppet master, had made the phone calls to the press on his own initiative. Even though he was not fool enough to join the demonstrators, he watched them from his usual café table and was pleased. Two hundred out of two-o-eight was good, though not all the men and women there were stall holders. Some were porters, some were soapie wives and sons. Others represented the cafés and the bars that Victor wished to level to the ground. There were some customers, too—a dozen men and women from restaurants and small hotels in the Woodgate district who bought fresh produce from the Soap Market and liked the cheaper prices. They all feared change. Yet they believed that change could be confronted and repelled. Remember how the residents of Stephens Well, a small and wealthy suburb, had beaten back developers, or beaten them down at least. They'd forced the architects to lop three storeys from the top of their new office block because it cast a shadow on the suburb's private park for forty minutes every day. That contravened the ancient Law of Light. Consider how the city's conservation groups had stopped the widening of roads when widen-

ing would bring down trees. Trees of that age and size were
protected by the Sylvan Ordinances of 1910. The marketplace
had trees and light as well. So there was hope.

Rook drank his coffee, and peered at everyone who passed.
His newspaper was spread out across his lap, unread and wet.
It did not matter what the headlines were, or what the world
was coming to, or that, if NASA got it right, an asteroid,
one kilometer in width and traveling at seventy-four thousand
kilometers per hour, would "wing" the Earth at noon, missing the Soap Market (also one kilometer in width) by an astro-
nomically narrow half a million kilometers of space. His mind
was focused on the detail of his life and not Eternity. Here—
within a stone's throw—he and the soapies were confronted
by a danger they could witness, understand and quantify in
human measurements. Here was a space they could protect.

Of course the market did not close. The marchers all had
partners, deputies or family to defend them from a trading
loss. Each stall was open and the crowds were much the same
as on any other day, at least on any other day that rained as
hard as this. The demonstrators used their placards as screens
against the rain. They pulled on hats. The television unit
clothed its camera in a plastic hood. Someone had thought to
bring a drum and he was ordered to the front by Con. They
set off through the marketplace a trifle sheepishly, routed and
regrouped by Cellophane. He'd never known such ordered
crowds, such unity, before.

It's difficult to concentrate on grievances when all around
are friends. Con had a dozen leafleters. The Soap Fund—a
reserve to pay for traders' funerals or help out widows or
support those injured at their work—had provided money for
paper and printing. The leaflet showed the Busi sketch in ink
and wash of Arcadia. Its black and gothic headline was ARCA-
DIA? WHO PAYS?—and then it listed, with more regard for
impact than for grammar, "*You*, the shopper . . . *Me*, the
trader . . . *Us*, the citizens . . . *Them* that value history and
tradition."

When they had regrouped, at the Mathematical Park, to
enter Tower Square and curve round with the traffic into

Saints Row, the leafleters set to work, walking in the road to
press their message on to drivers, dodging through the pavement crowds. The crowds, in fact, had slowed to let the traders through. They had no choice. Their umbrellas made it
difficult to negotiate a passage through the squints and alleys
of a throng. It only takes a drum to cause the gaupers in the
street to stand and watch, or to make those drivers with a
little time to spare twist at their steering wheels to see what
the drum might signify. Once a few had stopped to look,
then everybody slowed. The usual speeding lava of the streets
had cooled. Then there were horns and tempers. Pedestrians,
blocked on the pavements by the ones who stopped to watch,
spilled out onto the street and tried to hurry on between the
cars and vans and gusts of rain. A courier motorcyclist
bumped up on the pavement, and tried to clear a passage for
himself.

The soapies could not find an easy way. Only the drummer, whose pulse and drumsticks seemed to threaten anyone
that blocked his path, proceeded with much speed. The camera crew and the photographers walked backward through the
traffic. Their lenses squared the scene and transformed this
hapless chaos, unintended and short-lived, into an act of
scheming anarchy. Marching in a traffic jam to the formal
beat of drum and to the blatant discord of car horns, the
protest had undermined itself. It could hardly move. The rule
of modern cities is that wheels and legs must keep on moving
or keep out of town. At least they should keep separate. They
should observe the segregations of the curb.

The police arrived—a single officer, already wet and robbed
of patience—and there were comic scenes adorning both the
evening and the morning television news and the front pages
of the daily papers, showing the drummer and policeman eye
to eye. Both had their sticks raised in the air, both were intent
on beating skin. The policeman, though, had been discreet
and brought his nightstick down upon the drum and not the
drummer. The drummer was less restrained. He beat a tattoo
on the policeman's hat. In the photograph, two traders were
stepping forward through the jam of cars to intervene. They

held placards as if they meant to chop the policeman down.
One placard said, They Shall Not Pass—ironically, in view
of all the chaos in the street. The other exhorted, Save Our
Market from the Millionaire. That was the picture that the
city saw. Those were the slogans that introduced them to
Arcadia.

The traders were elated. Now they understood that, for a
while at least, two hundred citizens could bring the city to a
halt. They formed a crowd, a laughing, animated crowd, at
the top of the steps to the tunnel beneath Link Highway Red.
Soon they were chanting slogans with one voice, walking
unencumbered except by wind and rain down the center·of
the mall. Their voices ricocheted wetly off the office glass and
stone and sounded like a bullet sounds when it is shot in a
ravine and lodges in the buttocks of an elk. They were loud
enough to summon Signor Busi and his host from their breakfast to the parapet of Victor's rooftop garden, and to crowd
the tinted, toughened windows of Big Vic with staff, including Anna on the twenty-seventh floor.

The mall had not witnessed noise or passion such as this,
not since the builders had removed their huts and debris and
left the buildings clean and free for business. The architecture
said *Don't raise your voice, Don't run, Don't hang around.* Office
workers, coming, going, did what they were told. The mall
prepared them for the obeisances of the office desk just as the
aisles of churches subdue their congregations between the
door and the altar. But the procession of greengrocers was
not intimidated by the prospect of a desk. Encouraged by the
cameras, the echo and the camaraderie of rain, they bellowed
slogans down the mall. The closer that the soapies got to Big
Vic, the unrulier they became. To see their faces you would
think that they were mutinous and angry. In fact, these men
and women were having fun. What is more fun than making
noisy mayhem in a place where you're not known but, yet,
are flanked by a company of friends? For once they felt like
crusaders instead of selfish middlemen in trade. This day en-
riched them. Indignation and a drum would save their market
from Arcadia.

They lined up with their placards outside Big Vic, unprotected from the rain, ennobled by discomfort, emboldened by their fears of being driven from their stalls. What then? No one had thought to make a speech or send a deputation in or lobby for support and signatures from Victor's office staff.

"They only need to see us," Con had said. "And hear us too."

So they stood firm and wet; and they began to chant and clap and jeer and offer leaflets whenever anybody passed them by to enter Victor's fort.

Just before eleven the architectural press began to arrive for Victor's conference, but there were other writers too, from papers and from magazines that would not normally concern themselves with building schemes. Rook's phone calls, Victor's press release and invitation, the early radio reports of trouble in the marketplace and streets, had stirred the news editors and the diarists to send their representatives. The Burgher himself had come (again my face is hoist above the parapet), and I was keen to follow up the anecdote of Victor's coddled fish with something else to make the rich seem ludicrous. I noted what the placards said—Save Our Market from the Millionaire—and when I took their leaflet, saw what comedy The Burgher could construct from Signor Busi's pregnant domes. Already—and without, as yet, much cause beyond an appetite for mischief—the traders had a champion. The Burgher loathed those men who gained their power and wealth from trade.

"Who are these people?"

Signor Busi was glad of an excuse to leave the breakfast table and look out on the mall. An hour of nonbusiness conversation with Victor had obliged him to sit silently, engaged in food, or else—his choice, in fact—to hold a monologue. As Victor showed no sign that he was either bored or entertained, the monologue was free to range untrammeled and, perhaps, unheard, amongst the pleasantries of Busi's intercontinental life. He talked at length about New York, its obesity. Did Victor know New York? No? So Busi spoke about Milan, the town he loved and loathed the most. It was more

Celtic than typically Italian, he believed. Did Victor realize that London was closer to Milan than Sicily? Victor had not realized, but seemed prepared to accept Busi's word.

Now the architect was stuck. The more he said, the less he had to say. So he was happy to stand and help the old man to the parapet and relay—his eyes were sharp—what he could see; the banners, the picket line, the drama in the mall. No, Victor did not know what all the distant noise was for. He sublet twenty-three floors of Big Vic to fourteen different companies, so there were fifteen possible reasons for demonstrations at the door.

When Anna came to lead her boss and Signor Busi down to the press conference, she said that there would be delays. They had expected just five writers at the most and perhaps an agency photographer, but there were thirty journalists in all, including a film crew and two people from the radio. The meeting room was far too small. They'd have to find a larger venue.

"Then use my office suite," Victor said. "You might have guessed there'd be wide interest."

Anna thought it prudent not to detail the width of interest that had gathered in the mall. She replied to Signor Busi's urbane bow with a ceremonial smile and left to fetch the press.

Both men were pleased to launch Arcadia to such an eager group. The cameras were put to work as soon as the two men came down by Victor's private lift. Anna distributed plans and paperwork. Each file contained an architectural brief, a plan, a sketch, an article from the *International Gazette* about the Busi Partnership. Big Vic's Publicity Manager introduced the two men to the press. Signor Claudio Busi, he explained, would say a word or two, and then there would be questions and photo-opportunities and wine.

Signor Busi embarked upon his second monologue that morning, but on this occasion he had come prepared. The speech that he had already made to Victor would do for these people, too, except that now there was no need "to glorify the vision of the man who pays."

"My work is familiar to you, I think," he said, implying that the new Arcadia was all his work. "I have been called . . ." (here he laughed, to demonstrate his lack of vanity) ". . . a guru of design, a philosopher amongst journeymen. I introduced the notion, as you know, of 'building as event.' That is to say, that when we use a building we should experience narrative and drama in the way that on a mountain walk we experience the textures and elements of landscape."

As yet the pens and pencils of the press had made no mark. What were they building in the marketplace? A planetarium? A Disneyland? An operatic set? A wildlife park? Mont Blanc?

"We have nostalgia and we have experiments," he continued. "We also have modernity. I think it will be clear to you—if I can now invite you to open up your files and look at the impression of Arcadia—that we have opted for modernity, that is to say, for this city of today we replace the chaos of a medieval market with the harmony and dignity of a modern one."

He held his larger illustration of Arcadia up against his chest. "What does this recall to you?" he asked, and gave no time for anyone to make a guess. "Here is a landscape at the city center," he said, and then—encouraged by the smiles that greeted every word—Signor Busi added "an amusing confidentiality": "Something to make us laugh. My colleagues in Milan have called Arcadia the Melting Glass Meringues. You see their joke, I think?" I held The Burgher's pen. It went to work. Busi had given me a comic heading for that evening's diary. He had surrendered his confectionary Arcadia to my cartoonist and to my irony.

"Meringues? Are these cakes known to you?" asked Busi, unnerved that no one seemed amused.

Victor hid behind his desk, his eyebrows making Ms and Ws. Perhaps he wondered whether this Italian was entirely sound, or else was blinking back his mirth.

When questions came, there were the usual queries about budgets and time scales which Signor Busi and the Publicity Manager handled with unnecessary detail. Then the tougher questions came, "What consultations have there been with the

street traders currently at work in the Soap Market?'' and
"What provisions have been made to protect the interests of
the marketeers.'' The PR man made reassuring noises. It was
his opinion that the building scheme was in the interests both
of the city and the traders. "Why, then, are there a crowd of
soapies demonstrating in the mall?''

The Burgher rose upon my legs. I held the market traders'
leaflet up and read the question that it posed and then the
answers that it gave: "Arcadia? Who pays? You, the shopper.
Me, the trader. Us, the citizens. Them that value history and
tradition.''

"There are placards at this very minute at the door which
call on us to help protect the market from the millionaire,'' I
said. "I see the millionaire himself is silent. I wonder whether
we can ask him to reply to what the traders say?''

Victor did not stand. He did not want to speak, but had
no choice. Old men can take their time, and not seem slow.
He looked down at his hands. It seemed he would not speak
at all, but then he raised his head and looked, not at the
people in the room, but at the rain which swept into the
windowpanes.

"The market's getting taller. That's all,'' he said. "When I
was small the traders put their produce out on mats. You had
to bend to make your choice. Then we brought in raised stalls
with awnings on which bags and tresses could be hung. You
had to stretch to take your pick. So now we have Arcadia
with steps and lifts and balconies. The market's like a plant.
It grows and flourishes, or else it withers. There will be no
problems with the marketeers. Arcadia will make them rich.''

"The traders at the door do not share your optimism,''
someone said.

"They will,'' said Victor. "I'll speak to them myself.''

Quite what he meant no one was sure. They stood and
watched him as he turned his back and went into his private
lift, with Anna at his side, his papers in her hands. Would he
go up or down? He could have said to Anna, "Phone the commissionaires and ask them to select a couple from the crowd
who are presentable. I'll talk to them. And phone the police

to clear the others from the mall." Instead he said, "Let's get it over with."

"What? Up or down?"

He pointed at his shoes.

It was simple, icy curiosity, not pluck or duty, which determined Victor to descend. His earlier rooftop view of what was happening below—even with Signor Busi as his sharper eyes—had not been satisfactory. It all had been a little out of tune, a half turn out of focus, just as the television was these days for him, for all old men. Words and images had frayed for him. Their selvages had gone. When Signor Busi had spoken for so long that morning, over breakfast, Victor had simply stared, uncertain when to nod or laugh or show concern. His hearing aid was temperamental. It worked more clearly in shuttered rooms than in the open air. Weak light was a thinner filter for the sound. It left the consonants intact. It did not squeeze the words. At breakfast there was too much light, and too much accent in Signor Busi's speech. At times, it seemed to Victor, the architect had retreated into Italian, or else was speaking seamless prose in which the pauses were as crammed with words as the sentences themselves. Was that a question that he asked? All Victor did was shake his head—a gesture which he hoped would be appropriate. The animation of the younger man was tiring. What kind of dilettante was he that he chattered while he ate? What sort of breakfast guest was too insensitive to match his host's own reticence?

Victor had been relieved—though startled for a moment—when Signor Busi had so suddenly left the table to peer down on the mall. "Who are these people?" Victor had not got a clue. It seemed to him the tide was going out and beaching him with failing faculties. It ebbed, it ebbed, it ebbed. Quite soon the only sounds and images which were defined would be those troubling ones—of Em and Aunt and eggs and fire—which were his memory.

Now that he was in the lift with Anna, though, his hearing aid was working perfectly. He heard the whisper of the steel hawsers, the detonation of the papers which Anna was tapping on her leg, the brittle timpani of his own bones. He even heard and felt the air grow thicker as the lift went down. How long since he had last been to the lobby? How much longer since he'd passed through Big Vic's revolving doors? Three months at least. How long since God had last descended from the heavens to stand with mortals on the ground?

The power of the speech that he had been obliged to make for the journalists, the felicity of the words that came with such simplicity, had fired the old man with sufficient self-esteem to think he could anesthetize the crowd with "Arcadia will make you rich." He was not nervous in the least—except, perhaps, that he was uneasy in the lift. It had dropped through twenty floors and more and seemed to travel at a speed and with a purpose that was reckless. He had to steady himself on the lift's steel walls, and then on Anna's arm. He was not sorry when his first journey for three months at last came to an end. The single door drew back and Victor looked out on the foliage of the atrium. All the ground-floor staff—receptionists, security, commissionaires—were looking out onto the mall where marketeers were drenched in rain and indignation. Victor pushed his hair back—needlessly—with his hand. He buttoned his coat, and walked across the atrium and stood, the shortest, oldest man, behind the crowd who blocked the exit doors. No one gave way. No one deferred. No one noticed him. He did not pass through these revolving doors each day on his way to work or on his way back home. The man was not familiar.

Anna tried to clear a path, but did not have the voice or strength to cut into the crowd. But when the press arrived a minute or so later, packed into Big Vic's main lifts, the crowd was soon pushed back and Victor was identified by cameramen and journalists who wished to winkle from him some idea of what he meant to say to the soapies on the far, wet side of the revolving doors.

Now Security did its work. It cleared a path. It made the staff give way. It made the pressmen step aside, and let Anna, Victor, and the breathless PR Manager whose face they knew, proceed toward their confrontation on the mall. Rank, age

and power, and the circling quarters of the automatic doors—
too fast and intimate for more than one high-ranker at a time,
or so the doorman judged—conspired to send the old man,
first and singly, into the rain. The Taxi Captain knew his
boss's face. He'd been at Big Vic since the start. He hurried
over with a black umbrella and followed Victor as he crossed
from private territory into the public domain of the mall.
There was no sudden wind. The sun did not break through
to mark this unaccustomed meeting between the subjects and
their distant king. The rain was democratic and it fell as dully
everywhere—except that Victor was not wet. He had his canopy, and now a retinue of three—Anna, PR and the umbrella
man.

The stout commissionaire—the one who had escorted Rook
out of Big Vic with such inflexible diplomacy—took it on
himself to block the building's exits. If the boss was on the
mall, then it became Victor's private place and no one could
presume the right to go outside and join him there unless they
had appointments to do so. The newspaper and the television
cameramen had to press their lenses to the rain-splashed,
tinted glass, while the sound men and the scribes stood by
helplessly or made the best of their imprisonment by inter-
viewing Signor Busi.

Victor's hearing suffered in the air and light. He was surrounded by the banners and the slogans of the marketeers,
but he could not make sense of what they said. The news
that he was Victor had somehow spread. It rippled every placard there. It made each demonstrator briefly vehement in
preparation for the quiet they knew must come. They crowded
him. They waved their placards and their leaflets—and, one or
two, their fists. If only Victor could have separated sound
from sound he would have understood the essence of their
anger, that a man who lived in grandeur in an office pent-
house on a business mall could, by decree, destroy their liveli-
hoods, could build on them, could sweep them up and bin
them out like worthless market waste.

"Who speaks for you?" he asked.

They pushed Con forward and made him stand square on

to Victor so that the rain which ran off the black umbrella splashed at his feet.

"You have been misinformed," Victor told the man. "You've been misled." He took the leaflet from the trader's hand. "I don't know how you got hold of this." He pointed at the illustration of Arcadia, taken from Busi's confidential plans. "But had you been more patient you would have heard the good news that we have prepared for you. 'Arcadia? Who pays?,' your leaflet asks." He put his finger on his chest. "I pay. Who else? Sixty million US dollars it will cost, but not one dollar of that comes from you. I take the risk. I tremble at the bills. And who will benefit from this? Who will have dry and permanent premises? Who will no longer need to put up and pack away the stalls each day? Who will no longer need to barrow in the produce from the market edge, but will have storage space and access for the lorries and dumper lifts to bring the produce to the stalls?" He spread his arms to encompass everybody there. He promised them that he would not betray his "market friends." He spoke of meetings where all the details would be hammered out and all their worries could be voiced. He suggested there should be liaison every week, and a trading parliament inside Arcadia on which the marketeers could have their representatives, their ministers.

Victor looked round to check there were no journalists, and then he spoke again the words that had worked so well earlier that day.

"The market's getting taller, that is all," he said. "I'm eighty years of age. I've seen it grow. When I was just a kid and your fathers and grandfathers were the traders there, they put their produce out on mats and sat like Buddhists on the cobblestones. When we brought in raised stalls, the sort you use and seem to love today, your fathers rioted. They said they were a modern curse. They said no one would buy from stalls. But market stalls have made you wealthier. And now we have Arcadia with all its beauty and its benefits. Everyone will want to buy their produce there. Not just the poor. The wealthy too. Why else would I agree to invest so much in you? To make us all as poor as our grandfathers were? My friends, have faith. Arcadia will make you rich."

Now Con was saying something in reply. Though Victor could not make out all his words, he knew the mood had changed. The placards were gripped less resolutely. After all, the boss himself had come out. He'd treated them as colleagues. He'd promised them meetings, safeguards, parliaments. And what he said made sense. Why would he wish to damage market trade? Their business made him rich.

Victor made a show of shaking hands, and then he turned about with Anna and the umbrella in his wake and reentered Big Vic. He would not talk to journalists. His publicity manager (now surrounded by the traders) was paid for that. He felt immensely tired and disconcerted. It was not age, but anger that such private plans as his should suffer from such scrutiny, from press, from public, from market traders, and that despite his eminence and wealth he had to barter in the open air as if he were a boy of seven dependent on a tray of eggs.

He shared the lift with Anna. He said, "Now I suppose you'd better see to it that meetings are arranged. We must be democrats." He held up Con's leaflet for closer scrutiny. "Those plans were confidential. Someone's leaked." He looked at Anna. Looked straight through her. "Find out who leaked," he said. "Give me the name, it doesn't matter who, or what it costs. He gets the sack."

For a moment Anna almost gave the boss a pair of names, her own and Busi's. Would the old man reward her for her honesty? Would he send Busi home, Arcadia and all? She doubted it. But then, why should she take the blame? There was another name, a guilty name. Rook was the man, and he was safe from anything that Victor might do. You cannot sack a man when he is sacked. If she was ever cornered, then Rook would be the name to help her out, to keep her safe, to earn rewards. "I'll ask around," she said.

Victor ordered sweetened tea and waited for it, standing at the window of his office suite. The mall was almost clear. A

broken placard lifted slightly in the wind. A few of Con's
blue leaflets were plastered to the marble flagstones by the
grease and rain. Unhurried soapies stood in a circle by the
fountains, as unimpassioned in their manner as a crowd of
football fans discussing their team's uninspiring draw.

The evening paper ran the photograph of comic revolution
on the streets, the policeman and the trader beating skins. The
Burgher, on an inside page, led with some gossip about a
writer and his wife. His seventh item had the heading, "Victor's Glass Meringue," and comprised one, long-winded feeble joke—I must admit—at the expense of cakes and architects
and millionaires. But the front-page headline read YOU HAVE
BEEN MISLED. The newspaper group for which The Burgher
worked had financial interests in Arcadia and the trading
wings of Victor's companies. It did not wish the old man any
harm.

8

THIS IS THE SORCERY of cities. We do not chase down country roads for fame or wealth or liberty. Or romance even. If we hanker for the fires and fevers of the world, we turn our backs on herds and hedgerows and seek out crowds. Who says— besides the planners and philosophers—that we don't love crowds or relish contact in the street with strangers? We all grow rich on that if nothing else. Each brush, each bump, confirms the obvious, that where you find the mass of bees is where to look for honey.

The conspiracy is this, that we—the seemly citizens—obey the traffic lights, observe timetables, endure the shadows and the din. We do not cross, or park, or push, or jump the queue, or trespass, except where we are ordered to. We wed ourselves to work and tickets. We ebb and flow with as much free will as salt in sea. Yet we count ourselves more blessed, more liberated than the country dwellers whose tumult is a tractor and a crow, whose ebb and flow is seasons, weather, meals. And why? Because we townies are the only creatures in the universe to benefit from chains, to make our fortunes from constraint, to wear the chafing, daily harnesses of city life as if they are the livery of plutocrats.

Who is more harnessed, then? The docile banker whose life is squared and mapped and calibrated, or the vagabond? Which of these two is more blessed with power and with wealth but is most likely to observe the bulls and firmans of the street?

Who is the lag and who the libertine? Yet who would be a vagabond by choice? What ploughman would not hope to be a trammeled plutocrat? We flock in to the city because we wish to dwell in hope. And hope—not gold—is what they pave the cities with.

So Joseph, then, was happier than Rook. His life was more uncomfortable, of course. But he was rich with hope. He had more empty years ahead, more possibility, while Rook now knew that he was in decline. Rook's harnesses had been unloosed. His city held for him few promises, few hopes. What was he but an unemployed, unmarried and unhealthy man, a firebrand turned to ash? Who'd take him on? What woman, what employer, what company of friends, what neighborhood? He looked for sentimental comfort now, the first quest of the middle-aged. His life orbited round Anna, her gossip, what news she had of Victor and Big Vic. He was resigned to witnessing Arcadia.

Of course, he spent each morning at his table in the Soap Garden, drinking fewer coffees than previously, but more spirits and—foolishly—even smoking a cheroot. You could count on him to join in cards or dice or dominoes, and to win or lose more recklessly than most. He rested on his bed most afternoons, but did not sleep. He took no pleasure in the radio or television. He did not read (except the evening news). He rarely cooked a meal more complicated than some soup or egg. At first he met with Anna every night. She slept with him. She had her own drawer and a suitcase in his apartment. Her blouses and her cardigans shared hangers with his trousers. She used his razor on her legs. He used her perspiration sprays. They talked of selling both their homes and pooling what they had to buy a quieter, larger place a little out of town. They'd buy a car with the profit. They'd take a holiday—in Nice or Istanbul or Amsterdam. He'd look for work, he said, but did not look. He promised he'd bring brochures from the travel firms, but he forgot. He would not visit valuers to discover what the flat was worth, or what sort of home the two of them could buy on the outskirts of the town. He only *talked* of how their life would be if they lived as a pair. His only act of union was in bed.

Within a month or two, Anna felt she needed more time on her own. She was too tired after work for Rook's invasive restlessness. She enjoyed, instead, the short bus journey to her own home, the respite of the empty rooms, the opportunity to sit alone in casual clothes with no demands beyond the television set. So she took to meeting Rook only on Wednesday nights and at the weekends. Rook was not pleased, of course, but Anna's half-time absence suited him to some extent. It left him free to drink and smoke and gamble at night as well as day.

In time Anna's Wednesday visits became less welcome. She wanted only to relax, to recuperate from work, to cook, make love impassively, sit up in bed with silence and a magazine. She did not wish to go out in the streets, take snacks in bars, make love more frequently, more rapidly, more testingly. The sexual hold she had on Rook was episodic and capricious. To indulge it was to end it. The moments of their greatest unity—their mouths and chests and genitals wrapped humidly together, their hands spread on each other's backs, their legs in plaits—were the moments, also, when Rook became absolved of her. That is the turpitude of men and love. Rook's orgasms unharnessed him. They transformed him, in an instant, from a man obsessed with Anna and the universe of bed to one impatient to pull his trousers on and walk, alone and passionless and free, out into town. He'd leave her less rewarded than a prostitute. At first, she would get out of bed with him, to wash and dress and rush outside when all she wanted was a massage and some tea, a shower and some sleep. But Rook always led her to the Soap Garden as if it had the only bars in town.

"Why don't you sleep out with the beggars and the alcoholics in the market?" she asked. It appeared to Anna that Rook was obsessed, but not with her. He only wished, it seemed, to woo the Soap Market and its garden before they disappeared for good.

If Anna had been more certain of herself she could have taken charge of Rook. She could have gripped him by the wrist, as if he were a child, and led him to the valuers or to the travel firms or to employment agencies. She could have banned him from the market bars. He was weak enough to do what he was told. Instead she made do on his half portions. What choice was there? She made excuses for him.

One Wednesday night, he would not settle down to sleep, despite embraces on the counterpane and the postcoital sedative of sheets. He dressed again. He said he had to buy some milk. He needed some fresh air. He couldn't breathe. She waited for him, but could not fight off sleep. When he returned, the broken noise of traffic from the street made clear that it was long past midnight. She did not need to ask him where he'd been.

She did not come on Wednesdays anymore, and he was glad of that. When all the bars were shut he liked to join the vagrants in the marketplace. He liked to stare into their box and carton fires and share with them a song, a cigarette, a cob of roast maize, a throat of wine, a curse. They did not guess from how he dressed—his leather coat was old and bothered—that he was rich. They merely counted him as one of those, down on their luck but not yet down-and-out, who drank with them when all the bars were shut. They did not know, they did not care, what happened to him when he left. For all they knew he had a niche not far from theirs. In a corner of the marketplace, perhaps. Or in the sink estates—a tram's ride out of town—where what had not been vandalized had never worked, where ground-floor flats were tinned up with corrugated sheeting, where staircases and lifts were urinous and dangerous and dark. No one among them knew about Arcadia. When Rook described the changes that would come it did not move them more than any other drunken, midnight speech. Why should they be alarmed? The distant future made no difference to them. They only waited for the bottle, still half-a-circle from their grasp. They only hoped the wood would last till dawn.

By day, Arcadia was much discussed among the marketeers. Of course. Surveyors were at work, and questionnaires were circulated. Inspection ditches had been dug across the grass in the Soap Garden. Women wearing ID badges sat on stools to monitor and graph pedestrian usage of the different market sectors. Outline proposals and planning certificates were displayed—as law decreed—at focal points. The marketeers were bemused, but flattered, too, by all the attention they received and by the consultation meetings and the Soapie Parliament that Victor promised them. They had agreed amongst themselves that there was little point in fighting progress with more demonstrations or with petitions. What power had a line of people or a list of names against the will of money to be spent? No, they would be modern citizens. That is to say, they would suppress their passions and hope to profit from their pragmatism. The boss had given them his word. The demonstration on the mall had wrinkled Victor from his lair. He'd stood amongst them in the rain and what he'd said had been a challenge: change your ways and prosper.

They imagined working under glass: warm in winter, cool in summer, dry and windless, weatherfree. There'd be the same old camaraderie but air-conditioned. The fruit and vegetables would survive, be crisp and firm, be sellable, a few days longer. There would be less waste, and what waste there was would make a profit, too. Pig farmers on the edge of town would pay a fee for each full bag. The soapies saw themselves driving freely in vans. They'd save on porters' fees. They'd save on time. There'd be disruptions, naturally. How would they manage during building work? But, all in all, the traders were buoyant. In fact, they were impatient. They were tired of being soapies: make us Arcadians, and quickly.

Rook's bitter auguries did not alarm them. It did not matter how disgruntled Rook might be. Con was the man to listen to, and he, though cautious, shared the view that they had less to fear from progress than from torpor. Rook had fooled him with his Jeremaic prophesies, "All this will disappear," "You'll soon be out of work and rattling round the streets like me." Con now was more inclined to trust the word of

Victor. It angered him that Rook was such a fixture in the
marketplace and in the bars. Had he no self-respect? Had he
no tact? If Arcadia would put an end to Rook, then that was
fine by Con. Rook preached his words of warning, but anyone could see, and smell, that his views were distilled in alcohol and flavored with the bitters of regret. The time would
come when all his kind, the nighttime nestlers, the parasites,
the idlers, would be swept away. Welcome the day!

It took a little less than twelve months for the Busi Partnership to complete their plans and raise a Bill of Quantities and
put out the building tender. Architecture is a bureaucratic
art—and *Markitecture*, as some comic christened the attempts
to marry art and trade, was doubly bureaucratic because each
detail had to satisfy the pocket and the eye, the aesthete and
the businessman.

Victor provided offices in Big Vic for Signor Busi's
younger colleagues. The Philosopher Among Journeymen
was not involved. He'd been persuaded to spend the winter
in New York; the weekends in Manhattan, the weekdays up-
state at Cornell where he had been appointed Comstock Visiting Professor in Art and Design. He gave sermons there
on the Italian Masterbuilders—Giovanni Michelucci, Franco
Fetronelli, and himself.

Busi's colleagues wished he had not promised to make space
for Victor's birthday statue. They were the modern school
and saw no point in statues that were, they said, "as sentimental as Capo di Monte figurines, but without the benefit of
dwarfishness." They wanted something glass or plastic, something steel, something big and time-honored in concrete, a
symbol of Arcadia. But they were stuck with *Beggar Woman
and her Child*, style 1910, in bronze.

Victor had insisted on where the statue would be placed: at
that entrance to Arcadia which was the closest to the Woodgate district, halfway between where Em had begged and
died.

"Perhaps we could persuade a builder's truck to back up
and wreck it," one architect suggested: "We'd have a modern
sculpture then, *Flattened Woman and her Child*."

My God, how they were bored by meetings, and evenings spent in their hotels, and all the budget-bullied cutbacks from their plans which were required, and which themselves required new plans, new calculations, work. They did not like our city. Newcomers seldom do. They are not literate in what leads where, or how and when. These architects hoped they'd never need to know our city well. Their main desire was *Do the Job, and Home*. They set a day, the first day of the year, when building work on Arcadia—two years of it—would start. So New Year's Eve would close the market and the decade down.

There was a problem. You did not need to be a space-time engineer to spot a two-year gap between the closure of the Soap Market and the opening of Arcadia. Those rash and early promises that builders and merchants could work in concord, the market stalls amongst the scaffolding, trade amongst construction, could not be kept. Were they naive, or mischievous, these undertakings? How had anybody ever thought that tomatoes by the kilo could be compatible with six-ton shovels and ballast trucks and men in safety hats? No one on site! That was the builder's sensible demand. It only needed some old lady laden down with cabbages and onions to take a fall or take a bruise from building work and she'd be shopping for a lawyer and for damages before her bruise was brown. So Victor's managers were told they had to relocate the market stalls for at least two years.

Victor himself was sent a memorandum—but what did he employ managers for? Besides he only had to look out of his window to see the perfect and the only answer to the two-year gap. There were open fields of tarmac, parking for the mall's nine thousand staff and more for visitors. Two areas, three hectares each, were underused. They were too far from offices, and windswept, dirty from Link Highway Red which passed close by. Blue whisker herb and smog-nettle had taken purchase in the tarmac, making do with lime from the painted parking grids and puddled rain for soil. At night this was where lovers came and prostitutes who traded from the curb, with rocking cars and peeping Toms parked asymmetrically for privacy. By day it was as empty as a prison yard. With access from the highway and, for pedestrians, by tunnel, this was the perfect place for market stalls. Good news for everyone involved. Or so Big Vic would have the world believe.

People are ready to be fooled. That's optimism. "This is the price you have to pay for Arcadia," the stall holders were told, when they were trying to make light of their predicament, their exile to the car park. "If you want your share of wealth then you must expect to take some risks, to suffer inconvenience. We're talking business here, not charity."

Who told them that? Why, Rook, of course. He was amused to tease them with their foolishness, their gullibility. Why had they ever thought that Victor's plan was some crusade to make them more secure and wealthier?

"Con led you down a cul-de-sac," he said. "You may be sure *he*'ll turn out fine. They'll keep him sweet and quiet at any cost. The last thing that they want is trouble on the mall again—so Victor's men will take good care of Con. He'll get prime site, you'll see. But what about the little traders, the ones who don't make noise but just scrape by, selling from the backs of vans? Or those who've got five kids to clothe? Or those . . ." Rook was drunk and smart enough to make an endless list in which the only one who showed a profit from the move into the car park site was Con.

No one doubted Rook was mischievous. He'd ducked and weaved too many times before. He'd broken free and realigned too frequently for any of his alliances to count for much. But it's a fact that even fools and drunks and liars can sound alarms. What does it matter who shouts fire, or how, so long as there are flames? Here, then, was the Soap Market in its final weeks. It seemed the same as it had always been. There were no closing sales. No bargains to be had. Fresh food has a shelf life of a day, a little more in wintertime. There were no stocks to clear because in produce markets stocks are cleared each day and replenished overnight. But there was something stale upon the air, more pungent than the market waste or the odor of too many people in one place. This was the putrefaction of resolve, the enfeebling of that prod-and-nudge which got the traders from their beds each day at five to bargain with the wholesalers, which gave them pride and pleasure in the stall-top patterns they could make with what they had to sell, which made them cheeky, cheerful, quick with repartee. Now they did not wake with an appetite for work. They did not relish the day. They were offhand with fruit and customers. It did not matter which of these were bruised or handled without care. They left the business in the hands of sons and nieces and stood in circles, hands dug deeply into pockets, shoulders down, to hear the latest rumor or hard news about their prospects between the market and Arcadia.

The bars and restaurants which fringed the Soap Garden had most to fear. There'd be no place for them in Victor's car park. They'd been promised leases in Arcadia, and there was compensation to be paid, negotiated by lawyers from Big Vic. They'd have to look for premises elsewhere. But for two years? What landlord would let his premises for just two years? Theirs was a quandary impossible to solve—to move, to stay, to wait and see? Yet, as the New Year drew closer, so the market mood transformed again. Business boomed at all the bars. The marketeers were thirsty all day long. They stayed at tables, stood at counters, found perches on the weathered stones around the medieval washing fountains. You'd think they had no work to do, and had no end of cash. You'd think they were in celebratory mood, the noise they made, the bottles that they drank. Theirs was a carnival of despair, the despair of those whose rafts draw closer to the weir and see both the tumbling dangers and the placid pools beyond. No one is fool enough to swim, yet none looks forward to the rocks.

Of course, they played the game of *If*. What if they moved as docilely as lambs and did their best at what they did the best, that is, sell fruit and vegetables to people in the town, no matter where? Would car park profits be the same as those made in the Soap Market? By spring, would they be smirking at the fears they'd had and wishing, secretly, for Arcadian delays so they could stay and flourish in the car park? What

if, what if they'd stood their ground and said, We Stay!?
These cobblestones are ours. We don't want risks and challenges. We want the market as it is. What if that Rook, that
braggart Rook, that told-you-so, had not been sacked and
still held Victor's ear on their behalf? Would he have stopped
Arcadia, as he now claimed? What if old Victor had not lived
to be so old?

Rook was Cassandra now, the unregarded prophet whose
truth was trash. He and Anna were no longer friends. A
woman of her age does not need ballast of his kind. She kept
away, and when she thought of Rook she flushed with anger
not with love. As he grew freer of Big Vic so she became
more part of it, more loyal to work which now she thought
of as "career." She wished the boss to favor her and so, of
course, ambition ruled her tongue.

"I have a name for you," she told Victor. "Remember what
you said? The name of who it was leaked Signor Busi's plans.
You said I should inquire. I'm certain it was Rook, the day
that he was sacked. He went into your room, I'm sure. He
used the photocopier . . . I have informants in the Soap Market. They say he boasts about the theft." She knew the timing
made no sense, that Rook had gone before the plans arrived.
But she guessed—and hoped—the old man's memory was
logically unsound. He'd not know one month from the next
when both these months were over one year old.

Victor rewarded her with nods. He was content to believe
the thief was Rook. He would not have to endure the awkwardness of sacking someone else.

"That's good," he said. "We harmed him more than he
harmed us, I think." He was ready now to turn to other
matters. But Anna knew that silence would not earn much
from Victor. She had betrayed a one-time friend, at no cost
to that friend, perhaps, but still, it was a real sin and sins
should stir up wind: "Rook's work load has transferred itself
to me in this past year. I've worked here now for seven years.
I wonder if . . ."

"We'll see," he said, but it was clear to him what he would
do. Anna, when all was said and done, was already Victor's

eyes and ears. She did what Rook had done, except she knew
the innards of Big Vic more closely than she knew the Soap
Market. What could that matter now? He'd send a memorandum to her, giving her Rook's job, Rook's salary, Rook's
desk, Rook's access to his suite, his apartment, his rooftop
hermitage. He almost gave her the news right then, by word
of mouth. But he resisted such intimacy, and asked that she
present the checks and documents to sign. He was not fond
of gratitude. Gratitude was not the same as debt. You could
not settle gratitude by check.

So Rook and Anna were lieutenants in opposing camps. So
what? They did not meet again, or even glimpse each other
on the street. Their streets were not the same. And Rook
would soon be off the streets for good. There was bitterness
between them, unexpressed. Rook saw that Anna's name was
where his name had been, on letters to the traders from Big
Vic, on market documents.

"Don't trust that woman," he warned them, shocked at the
ease with which he told such lies. "She's loyal to no one but
herself." She was the one, he said, who'd given Busi's plans
to Con. What should they make of that? The woman who had
chanced her job by stealing documents was now promoted to
Victor's personal aide, the old man's buffer and his fixer. In
Rook's version, everything was clear. It had all been a plot.
"Don't underestimate that man. He planned your demonstration on the mall. He had the press on hand. He had his speech
prepared. No doubt that PR monkey labored over it for
weeks and rehearsed each word with Victor. "The market's
getting taller"? Oh, yes? And who is standing there out in
the rain while Victor makes his pretty little speech and promises to make you rich? Sweet Anna, that is who. His parlor-
maid. Who was it chaperoned old Busi at the Excelsior? Who
was it, actually, who sacked me from my job? Who's now
ensconced in my old chair? Anna goes from strength to
strength while you, poor fellows, pack your bags on New
Year's Eve for two years' hard labor at the gulag car park in
the frozen wastes of New Town."

Rook sketched for them a future made from rotting unsold

fruit, and yellow leaves, and roots gone soft and pliable. No one would last the two years "in the wilderness," Rook said. That was Victor's master plan—to shed the soapies so that he could have Arcadia himself. But Rook was talking to nobody. His bitter punditry, his ironies, made people turn their backs, and seek out less bilious company. And company like that was not in short supply. By mid-December the marketplace was frolicsome. For once the center of our city was in vogue. Perhaps it was not paradise, but then neither was it hell. The soapies knew of better places and much worse. Who'd volunteer, they wondered, to live, along with twenty million others, in Mexico City in ghettos so dirty and so packed that roaches fled to countryside and pig ticks came to town? Or in Hong Kong where, it was said, apartments were so small and public space so scarce that should you wish to twist around in bed at night you'd have to take the ferry and twist around in mainland China? Who'd spend a single night by choice in London? Half the population there could only sleep with pills. Who'd want to breathe the air of Tokyo—where the holy mountain of Fuji was no longer visible through the smog? Or drink the waters of Detroit, where the Rouge River was so thick with effluent that, in infrared satellite pictures, it showed up as solid ground? Who'd swap our modest traffic jams for those great constipations in LA? Compared to these great towns, the unromantic modesty of our city center was cause for gratitude.

As December drew to its end so everybody in the city came to see the market for the final time. They brought their children. They blocked the streets with cars. They bought their token vegetables, their memento fruit, and wandered in between the stalls remarking how engaging marketplaces were. Cellophane directed them. They did what they were told. They treated him with more respect than he had ever known. They stood transfixed to watch him swing his arms or block the passage of a wayward van.

The soapies loved this valedictory clientele, this slow and gauping audience who bought bad fruit and never asked the price, who swallowed every tale a soapie told. One trader—

asked a hundred times how he'd lost the last joint of his little finger—winked at his wife and told how he had found, the month before, a fruit snake in a tub of peaches.

"It was no longer than my hand," he said. "But those fruit snakes are poisonous. One bite and you're dead in thirty seconds. That's if you're fit and strong like me, and have the heart to last that long. What could I do? I took this billhook and cut the finger off there and then before the poison reached my heart." At other times and other tellings, he carried out the surgery not with a billhook but with a banana knife, a piece of glass, a razor blade, an ax, a coffee spoon. And once, "What could I do but hold my finger up and let my wife here bite it off? She spat it out. It landed in that carrot box. We haven't found it yet."

One apple trader, a man who kept a bottle by his till, lectured as he sold: "To bite an apple is to taste the world's most scientific fruit. It was a falling apple that gave us gravity—though none of mine have fallen from the tree. They've all been picked and packed without a bruise. And here's the apple tempted Eve. You see the blushes on its cheeks? And here are cooking apples like the ones that Einstein used in his experiments. It's got the mass, it's got the energy. It's very good with cheese."

Another found a *bon viveur*, or nectar bug, amongst his fruit, as swollen by juice as a ripe green grape. He held it up for all the customers to see—and, spotting children watching him, he did a sleight of hand and swopped the bug for a real grape. He tossed it in his mouth. It popped between his teeth. He poked his tongue out at the children. Squashed green flesh lay in the ladle of his tongue.

This new, naive and richer clientele could not conceal its pleasure. Was this a circus or a marketplace? If only parking was a little simpler or the journey from the suburbs not so long, they'd do their shopping in the Soap Market every time. The fruit looked better free from cellophane. You had a chance to touch and choose exactly what you wanted. And so much choice. And much more fun—if less convenient—than the bright and covered stores they usually used, close to the office, a short walk from home, two minutes in the car. What a gift, as well, to find this patch of greenery at the market heart. There were such cheap cafés there—and bars like country bars with slatted tables, trees for shade in summer and protection in the winter, waiters and waitresses who were neither servile nor imperious. They could test the strangest drinks, and eavesdrop on a tumult of conversations, profanities and propositions like they'd never heard before.

The buskers came, like wasps to beer. They played old songs and standards from America. It was so crowded that the gypsy with the concertina could hardly stretch and squeeze his notes. The waiters had to carry trays of beers above their heads. The fact that Rook sat preaching doom was only further evidence that here, in this grassed and cobbled relic, life was ripe.

Some stayed all day, most of the night. In fact, in that last week between Christmas and New Year, the night took over from the day. The alcohol replaced the fruit. Trade gave way to pleasure. Some single traders ceased to trade. They did not rise at dawn to fidget over crops or fuss with decorations to their stalls. They got up late. They stayed up late. They drank like camels. Who gave a damn what fortune and the car parks held? There was a party to attend. A wake? A christening? Or both? No one had time to wonder or to care. Even those five men who'd been with Victor at his birthday lunch and were too old to take much pleasure out of noise and drink were not allowed to go home sober. How could they refuse a toast to "Ourselves"? And then another toast to "All these years we've shared"? And more: "To all our loyal customers." "To the new year and the old." "To Health, Wealth and Women." "To Arcadia." Quite soon they had the gypsy and his bewitching concertina at their table and were dredging for the words and tune of

> Are you for sale, sweet market maid?
> (And if so, can I squeeze you?)
> How much a kilo of your breasts?
> (I'll take a pair, so please you.)

How much for thighs?
And how much eyes?
Oh, tell me that you're merchandise.
Sweet maid, I long to lease you.
What is your fee?
That's fine by me!
Now settle down upon my knee,
before my missus sees you . . .

These were nights too good to end, so full of sin and yet so blameless and so virtuous. The celebration would not last. On the morning of January 1 the market would be cleared. The hoardings and barriers would go up. The diggers and the trenchers would move in. The soil beneath the stones would be on show, flints and shattered cobbles blinking in the light for the first time in six hundred years.

Rook wished to save the cobblestones. And himself. There was no place for him in Victor's car park, or in Arcadia. They'd not marked out a site for him, where he could trade on having been the Woodgate boy, the firebrand of the marketplace, the boss's right-hand man, the soapies' champion. On New Year's Day his world would be reduced to the four small rooms of his apartment. He'd be the undisputed king of walls and furniture. He'd have no reputation on the streets. Unless, that is, he took this final chance to make his mark, to take revenge, upon the town.

On New Year's Eve there was no room at his usual table in the Soap Market. Young men and women he had never seen before, and all the residents from thereabouts, had joined the traders, porters, drivers to celebrate year's end and mark the closing of the Soap Market.

At seven, the mayor had come, with cameramen, representatives from the Busi Partnership, and Victor's development and trading managers. The police had cleared a path and set up metal barriers so that the city mayor could be the first customer to shop unimpeded in the Soap Market, without the pressure of a crowd. The route which he would take was set, as was the stall where he would pause, the conversation he would have with the chosen soapie, the single orange—already washed and wrapped by a town hall official—that he would buy and peel and eat. There'd be a photo-call ("Please bite the orange, Mr. Mayor. A wider mouth. Smile!"), an interview, a walkabout, a hasty departure to give a speech to city businessmen at their annual dinner. A secretary made a note that in two years' time, this mayor, or the next, would need to buy a second orange and eat it for the cameras to mark the opening of Arcadia.

So much for the proprieties. Now the traders were free—and glad—to dismantle and to stow their market stalls for the last time. They did not pack them in the usual way, or lay them down for rest on their trading pitches, but followed the instructions which had been sent to them from Anna in Big Vic. They folded their awnings and their trestles, packed and boxed their unsold fruit and vegetables, fixed on a numbered label, inked in their names, and carried their trading rigs to two collection points behind the bars. Victor's trucks would arrive at dawn to take the stalls across Link Highway Red to their new car park homes.

For once the cleansing teams could be as careless as they wished with their sweepers and their hoses. They washed the cobbles wet and black, removed the daily waste, and left the market clean for its dawn clearance. The traders joined the party in the garden, their grimy aprons and hats persuading people in the crowd that they were soapies and should be let through and served at once, much in the way that funeral crowds defer to family mourners.

The cobbled oval which surrounded the garden and the bars was emptier than it had ever been. The new arrivals took advantage of the space to park their cars close to the bars. It only took one car to brave the medieval cordon of the cobblestones, for a hundred, then five hundred more to follow. You did not need a ticket there. You parked for free. There was a short-lived symmetry in this—a car park lost to marketeers below Big Vic, a car park gained in market space at the center of the old town.

The Soap Market gleamed. The windscreens and the roofs

of cars caught, tossed back, the street and building lights. The
cars were silky, sated beetles, nesting on the corpse while it
was wet and warm. The wise drivers put their windows up,
retracted their radio aerials, locked their cars, before they
headed for the bars. They did not like the look of those men
and women who hung around, the beggars and the drunks,
the homeless, jobless, feckless, hopeless, ancient men, the
ones who counted cobblestones as bed, the petrol sniffers
overawed by such a choice of petrol tanks.

Where would the nighttime soapies sleep that night? Where
were their nests? Where could they light their fires? They
called to Rook, the ones that knew his face. "What's going
on?" they asked. The quieter ones just walked around between the cars with nowhere else to go. Some tried the han-
dles of saloons. Some pulled off petrol caps and dined on
vapor. Some sat on hoods passing bottles, bothering the passersby for cash or cigarettes. It was too late to think of somewhere else. This was a home to them, and they were as
nervous and volatile as if they were bereaved.

Rook stood and watched, debating with himself whether
now was the time—before he grew too troublesome—to go
back home, to see the old year out, soberly, alone, in bed.
He was not well. The evening damp was sitting on his chest.
His head was crammed. He felt close to tears. Then he saw
Joseph for the fourth and final time. The boy was sitting with
his back against the smaller pile of stalls, asleep. The only
sleeper there. Rook could not resist the opportunity. He
leaned to wake the boy.

"It's me," Rook said, the Devil shaking Faust. Joseph's nose
was running. His eyes were wet. He smelled of alcohol and
fuel. He could not hold his head up straight. His breath could
bubble paint. "I've got a job for you." Rook searched his
pockets, found his wallet, and produced the ten half-notes.
"You have your halves, I hope? I'll give you my halves tonight. I'll make you rich if . . ." If you can shake a wand
and make the market whole again. If you can mug me back
my job. If you can kidnap Anna from Big Vic and place her
in my bed. If you can trick the lines to leave my face, the

gray to leave my hair, and make me young and dressed in black again. If you can stop the city in its tracks.

"If what?" asked Joseph, half awake. Rook tapped the stack of trading stalls with his toe.

"We'll have a bonfire, eh?" he said. "To end all this, to see the old year out." He produced a book of matches—free from the Excelsior—and dropped them into Joseph's hand. "Set fire to all this wood and canvas. And then the other pile as well. That's all you have to do. It's money for nothing."

"What for?"

"Just do it. Either you burn that or I'll burn these." He flexed the ten half-notes he held. He put them back inside his wallet. "Wait ten minutes. Do your job. Then find me here tomorrow. Start the new year ten thousand richer than today."

Rook would not go home to sleep soberly or alone that night. He wished to see what mayhem he could cause. But he would need an alibi. He must be seen, a noisy innocent, when the fires began. He made his way between the cars. He pushed a passage through the crowds until he reached the scuffed winter lawns of the Soap Garden. He got himself an empty glass in time for midnight, and as the toasts for Health and Wealth were offered to the crowds Rook was the noisiest respondent, like the worst of sinners at a mass. He called out madly. He made ironic toasts for Victor, for Arcadia. He stood on tables, made a nuisance of himself with women, traders, young men in garish clothes. He let them know his name. "I'm Rook, and this is my backyard." He was unforgettable. No one noticed that there was orange dawn rising from the west, with clouds of smoke. And no one turned to sniff the old and woody smell that comes from country hearths and bakeries and forest fires.

The first to warm their faces and their hands upon the flames were the market's night guests. Their nests were going up in smoke, but they were cheerful with the light and colors reflected in all the windscreens of the marketplace. They squatted on their haunches with their bottles and let their faces redden with the drink and heat. They cheered as flames collapsed the tepees made from wood and canvas. The heat compacted and sent its front-row audience back down the aisles of cars where it was darker, safer, less intense.

The crowd was growing. Late arrivals who had parked on pavements in the Woodgate district and who were too elated by the date and time to go back home were making for the market bars when they were blocked by smoke and fire and crowds. They were not alarmed. The midnight fire was not a threat to them. It only marked the closing of the market or the closing of the year. It gave a cheerful touch to New Year's Eve. The drunks and beggars pestered them for cigarettes and one or two lit up their cigarettes with embers from the fires.

The fire itself was changing mood. It spat. It was exasperated, and trapped. Fires by their nature sink and spread. They smolder at their edges and colonize the land around. But cobbles do not burn. They kept the fire at bay. The heat grew angrier, but it could not do much except startle everybody there with the pistol shot of cobbles splitting underneath the fire and timber detonating.

There's a winter city wind we call the Midnight Wheeze. The nighttime warmth of city life is dragged up by the moon, and colder country air is sucked in underneath, along the pavements and the alleyways and the tram routes, and blows till dawn. It and the fires made rendezvous. They waltzed. Their gowns flew up and sent out puffs of heat. The flames were animated now. They dipped and reached, they stretched, recoiled, as the wind shadowboxed the night. The smallest of the fires had stretched the furthest—and, at last, it held on to the leafless twigs of two snag trees which grew behind a bar. It turned them black. The flames had hardly touched. But those who watched saw fifty airborne smokers draw on fifty cigarettes as the twig tips drew in wind and glowed as redly as an owlet's eyes. The cigarettes caught fire. The flames now skipped like elves amongst the branches, feasting on the bark. The revelers in the Soap Garden looked up to see two trees on fire and giving voice to wind as trumpets do. Already twigs were falling onto roofs, and roofs were chattering with debris and shrugging noisily at the sudden warmth. Already insects filled the air. And there were rats and bats and cock-roaches that sought to flee the flames.

The wind now turned. It let the trees collapse. It blew back on the marketplace where the crowd had grown quieter, less amused. The fires hissed. Flames curled like Chinese waves and broke onto the hoods and the windscreens of the nearest cars. A tongue of heat blackened, shrank, a linen football flag that some young man had tied to the radio aerial of his creaky van. It scorched the chrome on ancient bumpers, drew acrid smells from new ones molded out of plastic.

Rook saw the trees go up, and he was gripped with guilt and fear and exhilaration. He ran, when everybody ran, to see what happened. He joined in the panic, whipped it up, agreed with, echoed every shout from every trader who read conspiracy in every flame, in every car, in every stranger's face. "They've burnt our stalls!" Too late to recover anything. Too hot and dangerous. "They've set fire to us now," though who "They" were, they did not say. "They" were the mayor, and architects, and businessmen, and Victor. "They" were the men who came at dawn to "start from scratch."

Who was the first to overturn a car? Not Rook. He was too small and breathless and had no comrades. Some young men who loved their cars had tried to back them out of dan-ger, reversing into spaces where people stood, pressing their bumpers against the bumpers of the car behind, attempting three-point turns where there was not sufficient room to turn a handcart. Some drivers at the front tried to clear a path at the fire's feet. They blared their horns, were more concerned for paintwork than for flesh. They found themselves enclosed by men. Their cars were rocked and turned. They had to scramble free. One young man—his back tires melting smoke, his windscreen smashed—sought reparation with a flaming stick. He'd kill to save his car.

The Soap Market did not have enough exits for all the vehi-cles that were parked. Besides, the narrow roads and pavements which led away were blocked by other cars and more crowds, drawn to the place by noise and light and smoke. What chance then for the fire brigade? Their engines could get no closer to the fires than the hydrants at Tower Square and on Saints Row would allow. The hoses that they ran could not reach the market rim. The firemen did not care. This fire was self-contained. It could not leap the cobbles to the town. Besides, at dawn, as everybody knew, the demolition would begin. So "Let the fire burn out," the police advised. "We'll clear the marketplace of people. We don't want injuries." But try to separate a drunken crowd from fire, or owners from their cars, or market men from what was left of all their working lives. No one would budge, though the captain of the district police made announcements with his megaphone.

It did not take long for those two trees to burn. The flames climbed down the trunk and sped along the ground. They jumped like cats across the roofs of outhouses and drink stores and kitchens at the back of bars. The drinkers and the beggars took their chance to loot before the fire drank all the beer and wine. They dragged out cases, smashing open bottles. They helped themselves to anything to eat or spend or sell. They fought the fire with German lager. They egged it on with Scotch and rum and wooden chairs. The bars and gardens had no time to bargain with the flames. There was too much wood. Only the burgher laurels were reluctant to join in. Their leaves seemed proofed, their branches far too flexible for flames. But when they burned at last, their molten marzipan hung in a cloud of country cooking which settled on the night like frost on fields.

The city police are not as patient as their country brothers. It seemed to them that this was a market protest which had gone mad. They well remembered what the market traders had done to the traffic when they marched on Big Vic, and—years before—the mayhem of the produce strike. The soapies had a reputation for independence, for cussedness. The police had little time for marketeers. And they were not fond, either, of the "dross," the down-and-outs, who slept out there. Now these two groups were teaming up with young drunk men. A fearsome trinity. And there was fighting, looting, fires. Already there were pockets of disturbance on the streets beyond the Soap Market. Young men attacked big cars, blocked trams, uprooted shrubs in the Mathematical Park. They took revenge on everything and everyone as if violence was the only way to make the city notice them. They knew instinctively that they were invisible unless they rioted and smashed and stole. And then their faces made the television screen.

The local police—exhausted, shocked—did not need a permit from a priest or mayor to draw their truncheons, raise their shields, and bruise the crowd. What was the point in holding back, in softening their blows. If they did not put an end to this disturbance now, then who could tell where it might lead and what it might achieve?

9

SO FAR, SO GOOD. A little local trouble, nurtured at the festive chest of New Year's Eve. But though the cobbles held the flames at bay, the heat and passion spread. Emptied bottles soon were filled with fuel from cars and stopped with rags and lit and thrown. What had held beer arced through the night like fairground comets, falling short on cars, exploding in the air, or showering the firemen and the police in flaming rain. In other times the older traders would have called for calm for fear their pitches might be destroyed, their customers abused. But what had they to lose now that the marketplace was stripped, their trestles and their canvas already up in flames, their stomachs full of drink? "It shouldn't end like this," they thought, but not with sufficient certainty to interfere. Instead they raised their arms and voices with the mob. Midnight made them brave, eloquent and loud.

What wisdom caused the captain of the police to radio for help? Why did he lose his nerve? Was he alarmed he could not stop his men from cracking heads? Was it the flaming bottles? Was it the cars? Or was he simply calm and procedural, judging that his men were now outnumbered by a mob and that diplomacy and night would not damp down its fire?

He radioed for help at five past one on that first, smoke-filled morning of the year, though what he said to his superiors is in dispute. The public inquiry that was held could not unravel truth and lies. But this is sure, his plea for—so he claimed—another fifty policemen at the most, disturbed the brandy and cigars of the city's powered notables. The chief of police, the mayor, the owner-publisher of all three city newspapers (my remote, rotund boss), three of the city's four leading financiers (no Victor, naturally), their partners and their consorts (my boss's blatant wife), had all been top-table guests at the businessmen's annual dinner. They'd made their annual speeches, dispensed their annual handshakes and their pledges. They'd joined in the choruses of New Year songs. (Once more the buxom sisters of the Band Accord were wheezing music for a fee.) And now they were alone, except for waitresses and cocktail staff, in a private suite.

The chief of police was trying hard to understand an anecdote the mayor was telling when a waitress brought him a folded note on an enameled Persian tray. He read: "HAPPY NEW YEAR, and to celebrate the occasion there is organized rioting in the market area. Briefly: arson, vehicles and property destroyed, incendiary devices, injuries (fatalities?). The district captain is flapping like a scorched moth. Requests urgent help. What action?" The ornamented B.L. below the note was the signature of the chief's uniformed aide.

"At last, the Revolution," the chief said, and read the note out loud.

His wife raised her eyebrows. "I suppose this means we have to leave," she said. "Who'd be married to a policeman? I never get to finish meals. Or drink. Though duty never calls so loudly during working hours. Oddly."

"We stay," her husband said. "That is my resolution for the New Year. Never leave a party before you've smoked the butt and drunk the dregs."

"And what about the Revolution, dear? That starchy little man who calls himself your aide won't give you any peace until you've done his bidding. I'm never sure who works for whom."

The chief preferred his wife when she was sober, and out of sight. He passed her comments off as family jokes. "I do not need to leave the room to settle this," he said. He took a ballpoint from his jacket and added just two words to his aide's short note. "Deploy URCU." His signature, attempted with a flourish, pierced and tore the paper. He held the paper up dramatically.

"That should do the trick," he said. "Revolution ends before cigar, I think."

On public holidays, such as New Year, he explained, it was not easy to solve problems of this kind. District policemen, it seemed, were in short supply at such a time. The ones that were not working on the New Year's shift were either out of town or drunk or celebrating on the street. But there were young men in the barracks who'd been on duty all night long, denied a drink, denied cigars, denied festivities. Let loose a bored detachment from the Urban Rapid Control Unit, the chief assured the other guests, and there would be—he sought a phrase which could be both manly and dispassionate—sudden order on the streets." How simple it felt, amid such comfort and such company, to settle revolutions with a phrase. He called the waitress. He placed his two-word note upon the tray and sent her off whence she had come to activate his aide and URCU.

The district police had been extemporary. Their blows had been offhand, and improvised. Their strategy was unrehearsed. They were the jazzmen of the law. But URCU were the classicists, contrapuntal, harmonized, notated, drilled. Their last note was implicit in their first. And their first note was this: a barrack klaxon call that in less than four minutes filled the barrack yard with 220 men, selected for URCU duties because their deference, their height, their eagerness to please suggested they were loyal to orders and to masters rather than to class. Kitted out in Impact Hats and blue-black riot overalls and keen to stretch their limbs after an evening spent crouched over dominoes, letters home and boot polish, they listened to instructions ("Suppress, contain, arrest") with the queasy eagerness of footballers at a prematch briefing. Defenders had been issued with long, transparent, Perspex shields. The strikers, divided into eight snatch-squads of six, had short shields, nightsticks made out of toughened PVC, and lighter boots for running swiftly and for kicking with

numbing accuracy. The specialists had short-barreled weap-
ons, or plastic-baton launchers, or canisters of gas, or dogs—
and—perks for the elite—hip flasks of rum to keep them
warm and reckless until their specialties were called upon.
Someone set up the URCU "anthem" beating on his shield,
the unforgiving sound of PVC on Perspex. In seconds every
shield was shivering in unison. Dum dum dum-dum-dump.
Dum. Dum. Dum-dum. Dump!

URCU rode across the city in their sweepers—blue-black
riot coaches (to coordinate with overalls), their fishnet windows grilled, their foremost fenders prowed and aproned like
snowplows. Soon there would be field toilets, civilian backup
units, refreshment vans for officers and ranks, the paramedics,
and parasites. Already trams and traffic had been stopped
from entering the older parts of town. Already marksmen
with infrared nightsights were seeking out the attic rooms in
those offices and homes which looked down on the fringes
of the Soap Market. Camera crews, from police and television, buzzed and hovered like carcass bees. Police radio wave-
lengths were as overloaded and as chattering as a telephone
line sagging with its swifts and swallows on summer's last
warm day. Here was a city at full stretch, able—as only cities
are—to Suppress, Contain, Arrest the chaos of the human
heart as if it were as fettered and as mindless as a tram.

So when URCU came, what could the soapies do, that
undrilled coalition of beggars, fruiterers, revelers, ne'er-do-
wells? Disperse? They were "bottled up," to use the phrase
preferred by URCU foot soldiers to the euphemistic "contained" of their officers. Where could they go but back toward
the flames? Those few who sought to leave by calmly walking
at the police were driven off with dum-dum-dump, or driven
back by water jets, or knocked onto the cobbles by boots and
sticks, or told—if they were too old and smartly dressed to
be struck or kicked or drenched—"Get back in there. You
don't come out until we say."

The market drains—muzzled already by the leaves and peel
of fruit—could not cope with the water from the hoses. The
drains were hydrants, tumbling with water and not removing

it. They soaked and drowned the cobblestones. What flames there were found ducking, orange twins to dance with in the flood, and there were silver floodlamps for the dancers, too, from police and TV helicopters whose rotaries sent frowns across the water.

The wisest men and women stood at the market's heart, ankle-deep in water, breathless and demoralized in the smoke and clamor. Rook was there. He held his chest. He held a handkerchief to his mouth. He felt exultant and dismayed. Who now could doubt the power and the patience of the rich? They held the ground. They held the sky. The city was all theirs. Had Rook not told the soapies so? He looked toward the conifer of lights which was Big Vic at night. Was Victor the Insomniac looking down upon the Soap Market? Was his permission sought before URCU squads were sent to put a cordon round his tenants on his territory? Whoever'd given Victor his first name had chosen well. Who was the victor now?

Rook found his nebulizer. He held it to his mouth. He sucked on its fine mist. It was no match for damp and fire and night. He wished he had a desk on which to rest his head, or Anna's chest. He wished he had the skill to rise above all this, say twenty-seven storeys up beyond the smoke and noise and danger of the street. If Rook was silent at the center of the storm, then Joseph was at the typhoon's active edge. His jacket top was thrown off. His sleeves were up despite the time of year, despite the hour. He pulled at cobblestones. He helped with flaming bottles, upturned cars, with threats and challenges in the puddled, twenty-meter showground between the people and the police. He took his work shirt off. The smoke from the wet fires was just as gelid as the steam and vapors of the train, the Salad Bowl Express, in which he'd bared himself at home, when he had raised the produce boxes to his head and steadied them, his face well hidden, his body on display. Now he did not hide his face, and what he hoisted overhead and shook were fists. The noses and the foreheads pressed to glass were not rich women's or their daughters' on weekend shopping sprees but those of URCU; unpowdered, unpampered noses and foreheads, unpainted mouths steaming

up the Perspex of their shields and waiting for the order to
Advance-dum-dum, Suppress-dum-dum, Arrest-dum-dump.

It was Joseph who found the stacks of unsold fruit and
vegetables, as yet untouched by fire. He held a mauving
loose-leafed cabbage in his hand, as light, for all its size, as a
can of beer. He was a child. He had no self-control. He ran
out in the showground, hoisted the cabbage in the air with
all the might that comes from years of lifting sacks. Many
were the times when cutting cabbages he'd found a damaged
one and, just for fun, had launched it in the air to reach the
hedge or scare the girls or break the boredom of the work.
His training helped him now. The mauving cabbage held its
own against the pull of earth and seemed to hang inside the
helicopter searchlight from above as if it were a pastel moon
that had till dawn to land.

The men of URCU watched the cabbage arc toward them
through the night. Not one amongst them knew what threat
it posed, but certainly it looked more menacing than cobblestones or petrol bombs. What escalation did it represent? How
would their shields withstand a missile that was so large and
pale and full of flight? The line of long shields tensed. The
squad knee-ducked to halve the impact of the foliage bomb.
The cabbage, dropping now, unnerved them more than stones
or flame. Four men from URCU, directly in the cabbage
path, fell onto the ground in preparation for its blow. The
cabbage struck a shield square on. It hardly made a sound. A
chicken's egg could make more noise and do more harm. The
cabbage fell apart. Its leaves were sheets, were flakes. The
target URCU fell onto his back and, if blushes weighed as
much as stones, he would have died beneath the load.

The laughter and jeers from the Soap Market were louder
even than the helicopter blades. Now everybody ran to arm
themselves with fruit and vegetables. Never had shopkeepers
and shoplifters been in such harmony. They knew—this is the
lesson of the insurrectionist—that ridicule and laughter are
more subversive, more disarming than bullets. What can a
line of soldiers do against a fusillade of cabbages? Put down

their shields and face the leaves? Hold up their shields and face the jeers?

Quite soon the air was thick with greengrocery. Potatoes were quite damaging and could be thrown further than even cobbles or bottles. Apples, pears, and avocados beat tattoos—dum-dump—on shields. Tomatoes blooded them, or burst on blue-black overalls or overpolished boots. The comedians sent bananas through the air. "Like boomerangs," they said. Indeed, some did return. You can't control the tempers of young URCU men who're made to feel like village clods. They sent bananas back. An URCU officer was uncapped by an aubergine. A courgette caught a policeman in the corner of his eye. A TV cameraman took on his cheek the full deceit of a peach: first the tight and rubbery impact of the skin, and then the sticky embrace of the flesh, and finally the wrinkled bullet at its heart. The peach stone split. It cut his cheek. His blood was peach juice, and his juice was blood.

Joseph indulged himself. He was a citizen at last. He held the front of stage, and worked his way through fruit. The snatch-squad leader noted him. "We'll have him first," he told his men. "The comic with the birthmark on his cheek. We'll give that bastard birthmarks, head to toe." The police and press took Joseph's photograph. They had a picture of him with his fists high in the air. They had him holding cobbles in his hand. And cabbages. And Ogun melons. And pomegranate hand grenades.

At 1:45 A.M. the senior officer sustained a chest wound from a sugar beet. It struck him between his heart and epaulet and knocked him to the ground. What could he say, to all who'd seen him tumbling on the cobblestones, except "Enough's enough. Go forward. Clear the market. Let them know who runs this town." So they were beating shields again. Each blow upon the Perspex shields took the URCU cordon one step closer to the produce bombardiers, the upturned cars, the scorched remains of trees and stalls and bars, to vaunting, topless Joseph, and to Rook.

"This is the classic public order maneuver," explained the

police PRs. Undermine resistance with a show of strength and noise. And then send in the Short Shields to arrest the troublemakers. And then send up the canisters of Green Grief, the gas that blinds the rioters and dyes them green and makes them weep and grimace like Picasso's Cubist lovers. And then mop up.

They griefed the center of the market first. The police—though they had masks—did not wish to gas their own advance. Rook kicked a canister away. His legs and shoes took on the airborne moss. His skin turned ghostly, apple-white, while Grief, as light and volatile as gnats, rose to his waist, his chest, his throat, his eyes. It was a pity all the lemons had been used as missiles. Lemon juice, rubbed on the face, is some protection against gas.

Rook felt for safety. He found a car. He crouched. His eyes and chest were tight. Rioters should not mix drink and gas. Asthmatics should shun crowds. He clutched the front tire of the car. He alternated handkerchief and nebulizer at his mouth. He coughed. But coughing did not clear his chest. The sticky sputum that landed on the cobblestones and on the rubber tire and in his hand was lining from his lungs. Its release left him raw. It hurt to swallow smoke and Grief. It hurt to barter oxygen with CO_2. His bellows wheezed and tightened if they were opened wider than a crack. He had to pant as quickly and as shallowly as marsh frogs do, his chest distended, his lungs migrating to his throat, his upper orifices strung like candle tops with waxy phlegm.

The country people say a dying man is concentrated in his thoughts. He sees the heights and depths of life ranged before him like colored beads on a Chinese abacus. He's deft and concentrated, accounting for his faults and triumphs. "The dying never lie," they say. But Rook was lying to himself. His abacus was ranged only with the whitest beads. His thoughts were hardly concentrated. His brain was in his throat, buffeted by outer, wicked air and inner, pinioned breath, now damp with bubble blood and overladen with the weight of mucus. His tongue and nails and lips were blue. He sweated and he trembled as he sank from sleep into coma.

But then, perhaps, he was not dying after all. The rain, the breeze, the slight protection of the car, the gas-repellent sheet of water which cushioned cobbles (and in which he now fell forward, his cheek and ear submerged) might dampen down the asthma and save Rook from the suffocating embraces of the air. Perhaps he stood a chance, for help was close at hand.

What did the market look like, now that the police had broken ranks and were intent, like running boys with flocks of sea gulls on the beach, to cause disordered flight amongst the trapped and agitated crowds? Helmets moved amongst bare heads. Soapies grouped, regrouped, broke up like antelope before the snapping jackal truncheons of the police. It seemed that URCU—far outnumbered by the crowd—were deadened men who had no pity and no fear. They went to work as if their orders were to complicate the mayhem of the night, not bring it to an end. Joseph was fleeing for his life. He'd already taken blows to his bare shoulder and his back. The Short Shields had him marked. They knew his face. His torso had been photographed. He was the prize stag in the herd. "Get the one without the shirt!" He ducked and dived between the people and cars as lightly as he'd done when he'd played tag with other boys between the orchard sheds and trees when he was young. His life had led to this. He had a plan: to find an open car and force his way, between the springs and cushions of the rear seats, into the boot. Where else was there to hide or go? The URCU had the soapies bottled up, their clothing steeped in green, reduced by Grief from revelers to snivelers.

Joseph had tried two dozen doors before—exactly this—he stumbled over Rook. He recognized the face, the cough, the leather jacket that he wore. He sat Rook up. "What's up?" he said, too dull to find dramatic words. Rook did not speak. His eyes were shut. One ear was full of water. The other one was stained with Grief. He was unconscious now. The best of luck to him. To be unconscious is God's way of settling the lungs. He did not fight the inner or the outer air. He breathed more shallowly, more evenly, less frequently. Joseph placed him with his back against the wheel arch. Rook's head and chest fell forward. His diaphragm forced heavy air into his upper lungs. By chance, his breathing pipes were tipped at just the angle for recovery. Joseph beat him on the back. The blows expelled damp sods of air.

"Come on. Wake up," said Joseph. "I want my money now." He slapped Rook's face. The color of his cheeks had turned from green to pink.

"Give. Give," he said. "You've had your bonfire. Now you've got to pay for it."

Rook was peaceful now. Too comfortable to wake and speak. He made a noise that found a passage through his nose. It was the noise that athletes make when marathons are run. It was a snore of restitution. It repaid the debt of oxygen. Joseph's slaps and blows—who knows?—had saved Rook's life.

Joseph had no time to spare. He heard the heavy boots close in, the cries of pain, the lifeless impacts made by sticks on men and cobblestones on shields. This place of safety by the car's front wheel could not last long. He tugged on Rook's coat. It would not shift, not speedily at least. He took his "nife" from his trouser pockets. He placed it at Rook's stooped back. He did not say a word, but opened up the leather purse of Rook, along the jacket's backbone seam, the woollen shirt beneath, as if this were no man but some slain goat. The knife cut from the inside out. It meant no harm to Rook. He was not hurt, just robbed. Joseph pulled off the left half of the jacket and the shirt, by the sleeves. And then the right half too. He checked the inner pockets, found the outline of Rook's wallet, and would have cut the pocket out, but Short Shields were too close. He stooped and ran again—and as he ran he pulled the two half-jackets with their half-shirt linings on his arms and round his shoulders. His leather jacket had a stripe of flesh down the center of his back. His muscled torso had only partly disappeared. He looked like some stage punk, prepared for surgery.

Rook was not aware that Joseph had come or gone, or what he'd done to save his life. He felt the cold of New Year's dawn and all the fires put out and no shirt or jacket on. He shivered when he became conscious. He was startled by the noise and by his seminakedness. He almost stood, and as he almost stood two URCU saw his lack of clothes. He was the one without the shirt. They pulled Rook up. They hit his legs and then his back with swinging blows. They put the handle on their batons in his ribs and pressed. They kicked him in the face and testicles, their boots scooping water from the ground and skidding on Rook's skin. They were well trained. It was a rule that policemen who were obliged to assault a suspect on the street would not arrest the man, but leave him to be found by other officers. The two that roughed up Rook were wise enough to roll him on the ground and disappear.

Joseph, split in two, Rook's wallet on his heart, found a car at last of which the window could be forced. It took him half a minute to get in. Another half to squeeze into the boot. He was appalled at being trapped like that, but hoped that he was safe. Indeed he was. No one was checking boots, while there were people still free in the marketplace. Joseph curled up in the darkness. Once he felt the car rock violently as someone outside was thrown against the frame. He heard one cry. But mostly he heard nothing, except the pulse inside his ears, his nervous breath. He did not hear, six cars away, the cough and splash as Rook rolled over for his last time, his dead face half submerged on market cobblestones.

10

WHEN JOSEPH HEARD the ambulance siren, he reemerged from the warren of the boot. He squeezed into the rear of the car, and peered out on semidarkness. Dawn was a narrow silver bar across the windscreen. Already it had reached the edge of town and was advancing with the first trams along the boulevards. The upper storeys of Big Vic could not be seen. Low cloud enclosed them. New Year's Day would be a rainy one.

The few officials and the policemen that remained in the Soap Market had their backs to Joseph. They did not see or hear him open the passenger door and step out onto cobblestones. A pulse of icy light was flung out by the ambulance like an irrigation sprinkler watering a field. Joseph ducked each time the beam swept by, as if he feared a drenching in the light. Joseph thanked St. Joseph, the Patron of the Holy Corpse, the Undertaker of Our Lord, that he was well enough to leave the marketplace by foot and not by ambulance. He'd made it through to the New Year without the beating he deserved. His only bruise was in the muscles of his shoulder, from throwing too much fruit.

There'd been a thousand injuries between the midnight and the dawn, though some of those had been administered at police HQ, in the privacy of cells. But there had only been one death. The corpse had not been found until the market site was cleared of drunks and revolutionaries. They might as well pump air into a brick as try the kiss of life. Rook would have blushed at being caught like this, flat on his back in water, naked from the waist up, his chest a splintered prow, his stomach just a touch too plump for one so slight and vain. The market boy had died the market death, his back on cobbles, green from Grief, discarded like a bruised courgette, and looking now as dull and common as the stones which were his mortuary. Here was a most unlikely Martyr for the Cause— though, as time would prove, his name was good for martyrdom. Not easy to forget. We all remember Rook.

Joseph recognized the face, but did not wait to see the body wrapped inside the body bag. He stole a broom which had been left leaning on the side panels of an URCU truck. He soon became just one of dawn's sweepers, brushing up the missile debris for little pay and less respect. He was invisible. He swept his way across the cobblestones, past URCU men, reporters from the papers, gaupers on their way to work, young men returned to claim (they hoped) their unburned cars. He swept toward the market edge, toward the exit where the banana vans had been but were no more. He joined the early morning New Year crowd, his severed clothes hardly noticed by the late-for-work, the late-to-bed. He made his way through the squints and alleys of the Woodgate district, uncertain whether he was rich or poor. Perhaps Rook's death had been a cunning way to keep the two halves of the bank notes forever separate, as disunited as the clothes upon his back.

Joseph found a place to stop at last, a graveyard in a cul-de-sac with high tombstones and cypresses, and two plane trees, the perfect citizens surrounded by the sloughed-off litter of their toxic bark. There were no spectators, except for pigeons, and a pack of feral dogs. He pulled Rook's wallet from Rook's jacket and went through the spoils. He laid them out before him on cold stone. A photograph of Anna, inscribed "Let's meet and talk." A set of keys. The ten odd halves of the ten one-thousand notes. An ID card with a photograph of Rook, a grainy square in gray and black, expressionless, with—below—Rook's home address, his status "Single

Male," and his signature in neat green ink. A folded advert from a catalog, the model on the stool, the barmaid in his grasp, the suit, the unattended glass. Five untorn fifty notes. A contraceptive. Credit cards. A throat spray of some kind.

Joseph only kept the money and the keys. He lifted up a slab of stone and put the empty wallet and the rest beneath. If ever he had need for contraceptives or had a customer for stolen credit cards then he could find this stone again. He memorized the mossy name upon the stone, but the feral dogs would snout the wallet out as soon as he was gone. Already he had memorized the address on Rook's ID card, and set off looking for a bed and an inheritance.

He'd seen that Rook was "Status: Single Male" and knew there was a chance that Rook's home would be undefended. What better way to spend the dawn on New Year's Day than use the dead man's keys, and find some shelter, warmth, some food, some sleep between four walls?

He found a parcel of deliveries in the entrance hall of Rook's apartment block. He tucked the parcel under his arm and took his time upon the stairs. What could be more normal at that time of day, than deliveries? If anybody met him on the stairs they'd take him for an errand boy, a scruffy, docile errand boy of the usual kind. He met no one. He found Rook's door and tried the keys. Two locks. Two sets of teeth unclenched. The locks obeyed the keys. He was inside. This was the dream he had when he was loading produce onto trains: the day would come when he came home to his apartment in a city. He closed the door on everything. He'd never known such perfect carpentry or such a calm as this. He went from room to room. He opened every cupboard, every drawer. He looked inside the fridge. He did not touch, or eat, or steal. That could wait. He knew what he was searching for. A roll of clear tape. He found it in a wicker basket with some scissors. He sat down at the table and, breathing through his nose for better concentration, made for himself, from twenty half-notes—his and Rook's—a fortune and a future.

The police would say they found him looting Rook's apartment. Already he had stolen, it would seem, a parcel of antique books intended for the collector in the attic rooms. They said that every drawer and cupboard had been opened and all Rook's valuables had gone. They said he planned to strip the place, that his accomplices would come with vans to take the furniture, to make off with the fridge and television set, the knickknacks that were Rook. Who knows? Joseph was not a saint, though in a way he'd been a hero of a kind, for half a night at least.

They had his picture in the first newspapers of the year, but not for burglary. Not yet. They had him seminaked on Page One, his arms raised up, an aubergine in hand. He was "The Face of Discontent," "The Market Rioter." He shared the page with Rook. The headline was MAN DEAD IN CITY VIOLENCE, and underneath reporters reproduced what they'd been told by police, how "groups of Trotskyists and Anarchists, trained by foreign radicals and at secret camps in Germany, have been identified as orchestrating the disturbances." The dead man's name had not been learned officially, but on the street the word had spread that URCU men had bludgeoned him to death. He was an "activist," an innocent, a man who simply wished to voice his fears. The police had hit a thousand heads the night before. They'd hit this one too hard.

No statements came from URCU. They were beyond the press. But police PR was doing what it could to give the corpse a name, to find the cause of death. They had their answers by midday. The marketplace had witnesses. A trader had seen a seminaked Rook go down and not get up. He'd seen the URCU pair run off. The police had rioted, he said, "not us." He made his statement to the radio and to a journalist from the sentimental left-wing press. So Rook became a martyr to the cause. The man who'd been top brass in Victor's palace; the man who'd left Big Vic on principle because he feared for the Soap Market, the man who had fought offstage against Arcadia, the man who was a trader's son himself, this market boy, had been brought down—"assassinated," was the word—by police clubs and boots. Coincidence? Wake

up! They'd sought him out, the rabble-rousers said. They'd
marked him down for death.

The chief of police had hardly slept. He and the mayor and
two financiers had celebrated the New Year long after their
wives had been driven home. They'd smoked the butt and
drunk the dregs. Their waking tempers were not sweet. Their
throats were raw with talk and smoke and spicy food. The
chief was nonplussed by the headlines in the morning paper.
Where was the "sudden order" he'd requested in the night?
He'd sobered up to find a scandal on his hands. A middle-
aged man was dead, and rumor on the run. How long before
some busybody asked, "Where was the chief of police when
his men were clubbing citizens to death?" He took some comfort from hurried medical reports that the "victim" (a mistake, he thought, to have used that word) had died from
respiratory failure—"asthma, possibly." But there were broken bones and bruises, too. His ribs had sixteen fractures. His
testicles were torn. His back and legs were ribbed and grilled
with bruises. His scalp was peeled by blows from boots.
There were sole marks on his cheeks. His nose was pointing
east-southeast. A vehicle had crushed the corpse's knee. If
this was asthma then this man's lungs deserved a trial and
punishment, and we all courted death each time we sneezed.

"Come up with something better," the chief of police instructed his aide. He was in luck. The officers who went to
Rook's address to tell his next of kin, if he had next of kin,
found Rook's apartment violated, the keys left hanging in the
lock. They found the ne'er-do-well asleep, his elbows on the
table, his birthmark cushioned by the newly reunited notes.
They recognized the face—the boy in all the photographs, the
crazy anarchist from German insurrection camps. Within a
day they had the evidence that they required. Two witnesses
had seen this Joseph kneeling at Rook's side. One swore he'd
noticed blows rained down on Rook, slaps to the face,
punches to the back "consistent with the bruises on the
corpse." The other said he'd seen a knife. He thought it was
a knife. It gleamed. But, no, he could not be certain there

was not something blunt as well. A cobblestone, perhaps. The ground was strewn with broken cobblestones. A broken cobblestone can tear a testicle and fracture sixteen ribs.

What chance had he? He was the one in the photographs, assaulting policemen with vegetables and fruit. Just the sort to pick on someone middle-class, respectable, like Rook. Perhaps at first he only sought to steal a jacket for disguise, but then—ever the feckless, opportunist thief, so everybody from his village claimed—he'd seen the wallet and he'd killed for it. The prosecution case was clear. Here were two men who'd seen it all. Here was the stolen jacket and the shirt, in halves, on Joseph's back. Here was a "nife." Here were the black field boots with which he'd bludgeoned Rook. The muddy imprint from them marked the victim's face. Here was the accused man, fresh from the murder, in Rook's home, a fortune in his hands. And his defense? Joseph only had deranged and far-fetched explanations—the mugging in the underpass, the severed notes, the lighting of the fire—to show why he and Rook weren't foes, but partners.

11

VICTOR, AS USUAL, had not gone early to his bed on New Year's Eve. His nighttime wanderings from room to room in Big Vic had distorted fitfully the perfect conifer of lights. Just short of midnight he had gone out on the roof to clear his lungs by jettisoning and melting phlegm in the potting compost of his plants. The country people always cleared their lungs on New Year's Eve: "Spit out bad debts," they used to say if they were merchants, or "Last year's spit for next year's spring," if they were working on the land. The merchants spat like pellet guns; the farmers dropped their phlegm onto the soil like bakers adding egg to cake.

Victor was not obliged to spit alone on New Year's Eve. He could have chosen company. There'd been the usual annual invitation to be the mayor's guest at the businessmen's banquet. But Anna had sent off Victor's annual regrets and his donation to the Widows' Fund. He said he was too old to celebrate the passage of another year.

"You're there in spirit," Anna said, flourishing the widows' check for him to sign.

Yet being on his own as all the city clocks stuck twelve was not entirely to Victor's taste. He had been tempted to suggest that Anna ought to stop behind and join him for a drink—but why embarrass her. She was not family. Her duties ended at the office door.

On the twelfth stroke he'd almost gone down in his lift to

shake the hands of those tall men in uniform who kept Big
Vic secure right round the clock. He need not hold a conversation with these men, a modest gratuity would satisfy. For
once, he felt regret that Rook had gone. The man was neither
honest nor efficient, it was true, but he was more like family.
A flippant nephew, say, determined to amuse. And he was
skilled—Victor acknowledged this—at catering for veterans.
That birthday meal that Rook had organized had been the
highlight of the year, just like the village parties he had known
and never known. He hummed the march from "La Regina"
which Band Accord had played that early summer's day upon
the roof. The coming year would make him eighty-two.
Would he be there to celebrate?

   The midnight roof was cold. But then old men are always
cold, like fish. It's heat they cannot bear, and noise, and sudden movements close at hand. He shivered but was glad to
be outside—almost the only "outside" in his life, these days—
liberated from the humming equanimity of air conditioners.
The wind snatched at his spit and tugged his dressing gown.
He hurried through the darkness to the greenhouse door and
found the switch to light two meanly powered orange bulbs,
the "forcing lamps" of market gardeners. The orange light
expelled the night. The glass leaked wind. It moaned and
chattered in its frame. Two liquid-gas heaters kept the winter
greenhouse warm. They kept his specimens alive and made
the winter temperate for succulents, for palms, for greenfly
and for bugs.

   He found low staging for a stool. He found the brandy
bottle, amongst the liquid feeds and aphid sprays. He spat
again. He spat for spring. And then he filled his mouth with
brandy from the bottle. Its fierceness numbed his mouth. He
drank more manically, determined to gulp down the medicine, the sleeping draft. He held the bottle up against the light.
It looked like melted beeswax. He took his medicine until the
brandy was lower than the bottle's label. Enough to make
him moan and chatter to himself in unison with window
frames. Victor was neither hot nor cold. He was the temperature of plants. He pressed his nose upon the glass, staring out

at first toward the outskirts and the hills. There were no stars, just damp and glass and greenhouse algae acting as a screen against the night. He heard the fire sirens at his back. He turned to see the flames, the incandescent trees, the unprecedented sight of car lights on the market cobblestones. At first he could not place the flames. He could not place them geographically or in time. The oblongs of greenhouse glass made the distance two-dimensional. It was a film, a flaring, fading early color film, the print besmirched by water, algae, fumes. Here was a scene brought on by sleeplessness and drink. Here was a scene that was familiar. He dared not blink. He had to concentrate to bring the memory back. The flames were old and watery. But, at his bidding, people had appeared, and sound. There was an old straw hat. The smell of bread and urine. The disconcerted snufflings of sleepers on bare boards. The sirens were his mother's screams, the screams of Princesses on fire, of people separated from their homes, the screams of rain-soaked timbers made dry and hot too swiftly by the fire.

He drank more brandy, finished what was left. He stood and looked more closely at the market flames. He wiped the glass clean with his dressing gown. The film was three-dimensional at last. The flames waved and beckoned to him—the ancient and dramatic call to warmth that is so eloquent at night. The fires seemed close when viewed through dewy glass, so close, he thought, that they could have been candles mounted on the rooftop parapet. Victor blinked the candles into distant fire. He sent them off. He brought them close again. Now he saw his mother in the glass, packing her possessions in a canvas bag and strapping her only child across her chest with a shawl. She threw some grains of maize across the doorstep of their country home. She lit a single candle and left it—for too short a time—standing at the center of their wooden table. She closed the door.

When Victor focused once again, his mother's table was alight. The door was orange flame. She could not keep the fire away. She could not stop the timbers cracking. She called for Victor. He was gone. She went down on her hands and

knees. She could not breathe. She curled up in the smoke and
flame. She did not know if he was safe or dead. They'd find
her well-cooked body in the morning, the rain its undertaker.
They'd find a blanket for her, a morgue, a box. They'd give
her earthen eyelids in the common grave. Victor blinked the
fire back into candle. He blinked up tears, but then old men
are used to having water in their eyes without good cause. It's
part of growing old. Besides, the heating of the greenhouse let
out fumes, and fumes are just as sure as sentiment to make
men weep.

By now the helicopters were aloft. Their searchlights left
Victor in no doubt—once he had wiped the past away and
focused on the night—that there was trouble in the Soap Market. The helicopters sobered him. They were a match for
brandy and self-pity and for the apprehension that he felt. He
left the orange bulbs to burn. He chanced the rooftop wind
and made his way to bed. For once he slept quite readily. He
did not dream or need to wake to urinate. When dawn came,
his body on the mattress formed an arthritic question mark,
his right ear on the pillow, his torso curved, his knees and
legs brought up for comfort. His question was—Why do I
feel so scorched and dry?

It was New Year's Day and—not for the first time in his
life—Victor was plagued by an anxiety which he could not
name. Who's dead? What's dead? he asked himself. What
could the fires and helicopters mean? He had a hollow in his
chest that only getting out of bed could displace, that only
going out into the town and seeing for himself could fill. He
tried to conjure up his mother's face, but failed. He saw his
aunt. But more than Aunt he saw the market as it was when
he was young and poor. He sat cross-legged upon the ground.
A tray of eggs at his feet. There were no customers. It seemed
that this imagined market was piled with produce—but, when
he looked more closely, the sacks and bags, the spuds and
watermelons, turned to corpses. There were a thousand bodies on the ground. The cobblestones were corpses too, as still
and stiff as graveyard flesh, as implacable as eggs.

So it was, when Anna came on New Year's Day to rehearse his duties for the week. Victor was prepared.

"You've heard the news," she said. He shook his head. She showed the morning papers and the police reports. Joseph straddled the front page, "The Market Rioter." And naturally there was an unnamed corpse. A man of middle age, stripped naked to the waist, softened, bruised and split like an old banana by the beating he'd received.

"I had a dream like this," he said. "I dreamed this death."

"It's not a dream," she said, unnerved that he should mention dreams. "It's pandemonium downstairs. The phones are smoking—traders, press, the police, the architects, the building contractors. Arcadia will have to wait a day. I don't think we can go in with clearance gangs until they've buried that poor man at least." She pointed at the subheading, MAN DEAD IN CITY VIOLENCE.

"Condolences are due, perhaps," he said, "if he has family. Please organize a check for me to sign."

She made a note. "It's all in hand," she said, "though there are problems to be solved."

"Please specify."

"Such as, the market stalls. They are all destroyed. What will the traders use tomorrow when the car park site opens? The city must be fed."

Victor did not seem alarmed. It was his view that merchants have to cope. They did not need their trestles to do trade. They were the sort who'd sell fruit off the floor or from their vans and be content so long as money bruised their thighs. He might have been alarmed, perhaps, if fire and riot had reduced Arcadia to rubble on the ground. Yet no damage to Arcadia was done, or could be done. Not for a while at least. The riot was benign as riots go. A riot on an empty building site could do no harm.

He shrugged at Anna, as if to say, Don't worry me with trifles. But what he said was this: "It would be diplomatic, don't you think, if I went down to show my face?" The shrug was meant to hide his awkwardness.

"Down where?"

"To the Soap Market. Where else?" And then, "I feel I ought to demonstrate concern. But privately, you see. No need for fuss. Or press. I simply want to satisfy myself, with my own eyes, that all is well."

It was the early afternoon when Victor's black Panache was backed up to the entrance to Big Vic. "The old man's going out," the chauffeur had been told. He hardly had the time to air the car, to polish off the dust. Security held the rubberneckers back as Victor came out of the lift, with Anna at his heels. Her new winter coat was black and long and astrakhan. His coat was alpine wool, and gray and fifteen years of age. They knew how cold it was on New Year's Day, and how the wind could grip the knees and thighs, how rain could bounce off paving stones, how colds and rheumatism were unforbearing muggers on the street.

Anna had already lost the final kilo of the three she'd targeted, and so she felt the cold more keenly than before. She wore a business suit beneath the astrakhan, the same creamy color but a more expensive cut than Joseph's *On the Town*. It did not tug across the chest or pinch the waist. Her hair was short and razored still, though her hairdresser had added "just a little fire" by lightening her quiff. She was not the jolly Anna anymore, and glad of that. Jolliness is a despairing refuge for women of her age. It tries to take the place of youth and looks, and is not dignified. Anna was now as solemn and as trim as the clothes she wore. She'd had enough of men, and she had vowed, for this New Year, to do without their oily approbation. She would not seek their sexual patronage. She would not be their carrion. Let them fear her for a change. She held the keys to Victor now—and anyone who sought the chance of sitting at his desk, enveloped by his cheesy old-man's breath, must knock upon her door.

The doormen did not wince a smile at her as they'd once done, as she followed Victor onto the rainy mall. They almost called her Sir, she was so manly in her self-regard. And she herself no longer had the need to smile from 9:00 to 5:00, or be polite, or defer to the men in suits and uniforms. Promotion had redeemed her from the curse of growing old. She had an office of her own, an office staff, the power of command. She'd use that power to the full. She'd not be loose at work like Rook had been, his feet and cake crumbs on his desk. She'd not emulate his lack of *gravitas*, his office improprieties, his open door. She'd not be Rook, or Mrs. Rook. She would, though, welcome just one chance to see the man again, to let him know how disengaged she had become from him. To let him see—and rue—her power and her sleekness and her pride. She'd have him on his knees. He'd be like Victor, like a child.

The old man now was in the car. His door was closed. His face was purposeless and spoiled. He needed her like no man ever had, that is to say he had no need for love or touch. Where should she sit? Beside the chauffeur? With the boss? The doormen knew the protocol. They opened up the front and near-side door so that she could sit in the servant's seat, where Rook had sat on those rare occasions when he'd shared a car with Victor. But Anna walked round to the driving side, emboldened by her freshly minted resolution for New Year. The chauffeur was too slow to open up the far rear door. She opened it herself and sat down on the same bench seat as Victor, one upholstered meter between their hips. He would not try to hold her hand. He would not try to touch her knees, or even look at them, despite their newly nobled shape, now that they sat as colleagues side by side. She tapped the glass behind the chauffeur's cap and they set off into the city. When they cleared the mall she spoke for Victor into the intercom. "We're going to the Soap Market," she said. "We'll need an umbrella when we're there." Then no one spoke. The chauffeur hid behind his cap, disturbed by the breach of protocol which placed a woman at the boss's side. The old man closed his eyes and mouth, in disapproval, surely. The chauffeur could not see him breathe or move.

Anna, sitting with her fingers laced across her lap, sucked on a granny mint to make her breath and stomach sweet and anodyne. What would she do if she saw Rook where Rook was bound to be, amongst the soapies in the market-place? She let herself imagine he was standing there, among the idlers on the cobblestones, with nothing else to do but watch the limousine, with Victor getting out, and Anna hovering behind. She'd look him in the eye if he was there, if she had pluck enough to lift her head and face the crowd. She'd have no need or time to smile. It was too windy and too wet to smile. She closed her eyes and mouth to match the old man at her side. The windscreen wipers sounded like an oxygen machine, pumping air into their lungs. If it stops raining we will die, she thought. Her heartbeat matched the wipers. It pulsed beneath the astrakhan. The black and courtly limousine advanced through the rain. There was no haste. They were like mourners in a hearse, composed, embarrassed, fearful for themselves, gray-eyed, but from weariness not grief.

When Victor's chauffeur took the car through the Wood-gate district to the edge of what had been the Soap Market, all appeared quite well. Much of the debris had been re-moved, and nearly all the cars that had been parked were claimed and driven off. Already work had begun on the wooden palisade that would enclose the empty oval while Arcadia was being built, and city laborers were taking down the hazardous charred remains of bars and trees. For the first time for six hundred years the fountains and the gar-goyles of the ancient washing place were unattended. They were as disused by the city now as pyramids. Soon the trenchers and the laborers would come to harvest cobble-stones and box them up like sugar beets for their deploy-ment in Arcadia.

The police had cleared the site of everyone but the work-men and themselves. Detectives had set up a caravan at the market edge to interview those witnesses who volunteered to speak. They looked through the rubbish for evidence of organized disruption and put the charred and broken bottle-bombs in plastic bags together with examples of the fruit and

cobblestones that had been thrown. They interviewed the last
few young men who came to claim their cars. A fixed-frame
canvas shed had been erected above the spot where Rook
had died, but no one stood on guard. Inside, placed on the
cobblestones, were six or seven lighted candles and a spray
of greenhouse blooms, making the inside of the shed a warm
and makeshift corpseless shrine. Who'd put the candles there
no one was sure. But they'd been left to burn themselves into
the ground.

Two uniformed policemen controlled all access to the market site. They hesitated when they saw the black Panache,
but were persuaded by the chauffeur's cap and the imperious
flashing of the limousine's front lamps to lift the makeshift
barrier. Victor and Anna were driven a further twenty meters.
Then they stopped. The chauffeur's umbrella matched the car
and Anna's coat. Now Victor and his female aide were thigh
to thigh beneath the chauffeur's outstretched arm. She took
her boss's elbow to help him walk. He was no longer used to
cobblestones or hazards such as broken glass, wet leaf mush,
splintered wood. She let him lead the way, but he was lost.
There were no markers in this empty space for him to recognize. Where had the women sat with their shallots? Where
had he stood with eggs? Where was the thoroughfare of stalls
which seemed, by day, as ancient and as permanent as a
Roman road? Who'd start a fire, who'd die, to save a place
so empty and so dull?

Victor was not the sort to share his memories. He seemed
just like the old, rich man he was—too grand to feel the rain.
So this was his diplomacy, to shuffle on the cobbles for a
while, and not share what he felt with those two aides who
kept him dry and upright. They walked, this threesome, to
the public washing square. The trees and shrubbery which
had been there were reduced to blackened stumps. The lawns
were stubble, stiff and dead and black. But fire could not
harm stone or water, and the medieval fountains, with their
gargoyles and their pitted scrubbing stones, were just as they
had been the week before, the century before. The fountain

water, augmented by rain, was like all mountain streams, like every brackish spring, indifferent to every living thing on earth.

They watched the water for a while and then turned back toward the car, but took a slightly different route, enticed by what might be beneath the canvas of the blinking, well-lit shed.

"That man died here last night, I guess," said Anna. "They've made a shrine for him." She knelt and rearranged the flowers so that they made a neater shape between the candles. "It's sad."

The two men did not speak, so Anna rose and spoke for them. "He's someone's husband or son or dad. Or else he's one of those no-hopers who sleep out here. Perhaps they'll never find out who he was. They'll put *The Unknown Soapie* on his grave."

"My father's buried over there," the chauffeur said. "In the Woodgate cemetery. My mother, too. We used to live round here. I've soapie blood . . ."

They stood like tourists in a foreign church, familiar with the funereal intimacy of candlelight, but ill at ease with dispositions they'd not met before: the flapping walls; the cobblestones; the rhythmic catechism of the rain on canvas. The weather worsened. They could hear it growing sullen. The candle flames curtsied in the damp, cold air which pierced the fabric chapel. Water made its way between the cobblestones and crept inside to puddle beneath their feet. They might have been upon some Afghan plain, three hundred years ago, pinned in by space and sky and frost. The office blocks and tenements which circled them, though distantly, invisibly, were ancient cliffs, shrinking in the cold and wind and rain.

"I'll bring the car," the chauffeur said, glad to leave the candlelight. "It's raining pips and pods."

"Exactly," Victor said to Anna after they had stood still and silent for longer than made sense. "It's pips and pods. Just listen to the rain. I never hear the rain inside Big Vic. It's pips and pods. She used to use that phrase. You can hear exactly what she meant."

"Who meant?"

Victor did not dare reply. He did not wish to make himself seem foolish as the chauffeur had, weak with sentiment. He crouched as best he could to look into the candle flames.

"I think," he said, "we'll take a lighted candle with us when we leave. The fellow who died here won't mind." He broke the waxy seal which fixed a candle to its cobblestone. "A country ritual, that's all. You take a lighted candle from the old place to the new. That way you keep the goodwill of the past."

"I'll carry it." Anna held her fingers out. Just as she'd thought, the boss was like a child.

"No, no."

"What 'new place' will you take it to? Arcadia? That candle isn't long enough to burn for two years."

"We'll take it to the car park site. It's just a symbol."

Anna's nod displayed her patience and obedience, but not a sign of understanding.

"It's true you don't grow rich on sentiment—not in the market trade," said Victor. "Hard work is what it takes, and common sense. But ritual has its part to play. We should not underestimate . . ." He did not finish what he had to say. He was an undramatic man.

"All right," he said. "You carry it." He held the candle up for Anna to hold. "Take care the wind and rain don't put it out. A rain-soaked wick is bad luck for a hundred years."

Who phoned The Burgher? I can't be sure. I did not take the call. The chauffeur, maybe. Anna? No. The policeman who controlled the barrier and let the Panache pass into the squints and alleys of the old town? A worker at the car park site? Some restless, spying spirit of the town? There's always someone in a city with a tale to tell, and there are always Burghers to dress it up and publish it. Prompted by the memo on my desk from this unnamed source, I wrote a paragraph for The Burgher column. They ran it on the morning after Victor's market pilgrimage on the usual inside page of the edition which had pictures of both Rook and Joseph on the front. The headline was SOAPIE RIOTER CHARGED WITH MURDER. Rook was described as being "an executive assistant in the produce market industry, until his recent redundancy."

By nine o'clock on the morning of January 2, when Anna walked down the mall and entered Big Vic, Rook's name was known throughout the town. Office workers in the atrium pored over copies of our newspaper, regretting, relishing the fate of one so popular as Rook.

Anna sat before her untouched desk. She breathed as evenly as her tightened ribcage would allow. Could she now make more sense or less of what had happened in the canvas shed, of the strange journey in the car protecting that small flame as they sped through the town? The day before, the words she'd used had seemed too strong. "It's sad," she'd said. But now "It's sad" took on a fugal note. She could not find the words to go beyond "It's sad." She could not comprehend the burden of the news expressed so solidly in print.

The Burgher—steered by me—took the lighter view, of course. "It's rare these days," I wrote, "to see Victor, the city's octogenarian Vegetable King, out on the streets. But if you could see through the tinted glass of limousines you might have spotted the old man in the recently truncheoned Soap Market yesterday afternoon. No doubt he came to creak his respects to Rook, his one-time accessory, who was struck to the ground in the small hours of New Year's Day.

"Sharp-eyed citizens report that Victor did not come away empty-handed. The greenhouse recluse who is not, you will recall, averse to transporting fish fillets to his table in a taxi, departed from Rook's market shrine with a lighted candle in his hand. The candle made the journey across town by chauffeur-driven limousine. Of course. Who says the rich aren't ludicrous?

"My colleague, our religious affairs correspondent, tells me as he passes between the city's clubs and bars on some lifelong mission of his own, that 'candles light the darkened alleyways through which we all must pass when time is up, and all our bottles emptied to the dregs.' Is it the fashion in these straitened times to pay respects to recent employees by *removing* candles from their place of rest? Victor's 'spokeswoman' could not say when I phoned on your behalf to put that simple question. She only knew the price of beans.

"I'm sure a man as practical as Victor will find a use for Rook's half-candle, if only to grease the elevators of Arcadia. The old greengrocer might, too, like to pillage the cemeteries and morgues of our city for further spoils. Gravestones make good foundations. So do bones."

PART FOUR

Arcadia

1

TODAY THE PRESS CLUB BUFFERS have their monthly lunch at Victor's-In-Arcadia. We have the private room, beyond the mezzanine restaurant. There the finest produce of the market floors is served al dente for the city's swiftest, trimmest, smartest clientele: I am not one.

The female maître d' of Victor's-In-Arcadia—"Madame" to us, but Sophia to the younger men—conducts me past the rising stars, the upstart businessmen, the skipjack currency kings, whose mobile phones and calculators share tablecloths with button mushrooms à la grècque and vegetable brochettes. I pass the inner bars, and then the Conversation Pits where men and women half my age strike deals and attitudes in easy chairs. This is not the populace at lunch, and these are hardly citizens at all. They are—forgive my want of charity—Invulnerables, protected from the town by bottled water, parking permits, air-conditioned cars, and by the jaundiced deference of waiters, commissionaires, receptionists, the police. Their tables are reserved. Their clubs, their tailors, their dentists and their apartment homes are "Private and Exclusive," meaning they are closed to those who are not dignified by wealth or birth or fashion. They seldom need to queue or step onto the street, but organize their lives through fax machines, credit cards, and home deliveries. Or else they delegate these tasks to secretaries, adjutants and housekeepers who are employed to keep the world at bay. No wonder that, despite

the stresses of the street, their faces are so cool, their suits and
skirts so crisp and clean, their tempers so dispassionate. No
wonder I am tempted to topple bottles into laps as I pass
slowly by.

Our room is on the highest level of Arcadia. Sophia leaves
me to go alone upstairs. She is too busy to escort those Buffers whose hearts and lungs and legs are so abused and slack
that they climb slowly. Not one of us is less than sixty-two.
What journalist, at sixty-two and more, could climb a stair at
speed? What journalist would climb the stair at all unless there
were good food and drink and gossip at the top? Not one of
us is so required at work that he—yes, every Buffer is a
man—cannot take time away from his desk to lunch with
fading comrades. We're of an age, when we toast "Absent
Friends," to mean those colleagues who are dead, or those
few and tough successful ones too busy to be there—the managers, the editors who've grown gray and powerful like griz-
zly bears, while we are as gray and powerful as pigeons.

But us, the Friends too idle to be Absent? We undertake
the stairs at Victor's-In-Arcadia unburdened by wealth or status or by energy. We're winding down our working lives.
We're dining out on what we were, before they took our
offices away, before we were reduced from editors to columnists, from publicity executives to small-ad men, from roving
correspondents to custodians of the Letters Page, before our
bylines were removed.

The Burgher now is someone else. A younger woman has
my job. She is not interested in the fate of millionaires or city
councillors. The power that she follows is power of a different
kind. She spends her afternoons in bars and restaurants and
hotel lobbies. She writes a column cast with television hosts,
and dance club managers, and rich men's sons. The term "Invulnerables" is hers. She never misses trysts or tête-à-têtes.
She lunches out on indiscretion, celebrity tantrums, scandal,
flagrancy. Her sources are the city's maître d's, the waiters
and receptionists, the hotel boys who take the breakfast trays
to guests.

I'm bitter, naturally. What trickery of physics allows the

world to spin, yet leaves me motionless? They've moved me
sideways to the Waiting Room, their mordant description of
the office where the older, *valued* men like me are asked to
wait until, at best, our underfunded pensions turn us out. I'm
known as Back-End Editor. I have the weather and the law
reports in my control. Obituaries, as well. You see how
comic these professionals can be with words? And grimly
accurate? Of my four predecessors three have died of heart
attacks. The fourth has cancer of the throat. The Back-End
Editor? The Waiting Room? The Press Club Buffers? My
laughter thins and hastens as I grow fat and slow.

Today I am the first Buffer to arrive, and glad of it. I have
the chance to catch my breath and fuel myself with drinks.
We like to formalize the lunch, to listen to each Buffer give
his news before the meal. Today I'll tell them what I know
of Victor, the man who built Arcadia and gives his name to
this restaurant and bar, the man who is too old these days
to interest my substitute. His ninetieth birthday passed by,
unremarked by her.

Why Victor? Here's the news which almost gives a skip to
my edgy pacing of the room. Six months ago I prepared the
old man's obituary for the Pending File. I turned—the well-
trained journalist—to the trusted testimony of the cuttings
files. What could I learn of him from what's in print. I
searched the archives and the only items on the man, apart
from industry and trade reports, were those I'd written up
myself. He'd brought fish by taxi for his birthday once, from
the station to Big Vic. He stole a candle from a colleague's
grave. Enough to deepen interest in the man, of course. But
not much of an epitaph. I phoned Big Vic. Anna, his deputy,
a woman in her fifties now, sharp faced, a little overdressed,
but winsome still, did what she could to help. And then—
when she had checked the accuracy of the obituary—she said,
"He's looking for an author to prepare a memoir. Might you
be interested? . . ." And so I am the one retained to write his
Life. Luck has landed me a paying task for my maturity. A
contract's signed, and already I have spent some—mostly silent—time with him, though he has told me anecdotes of a

fat man in the Soap Market and he has talked a little of his
childhood. Is that the word? Is "childhood" not too innocent
for how he passed his urchin years, for how he says his
mother died in flames? The old man had a mother, yes. Her
name was Em. He's not the product of a melon and a cucum-
ber after all. I have, through Anna, some access to the files,
her private memories, and—more crucially—some pointers to
the old man's early life which seem to bear his story out. But
Anna much prefers to talk of Rook, and of the boy who
murdered him. She has procured court depositions for me to
study, and can arrange, she says, for me to visit Joseph on
the prison farm (he's working in the fields again!) where he
is serving Life. She mistakes me for a detective-journalist, a
Woodward or a Bernstein, and wants me to investigate what
truly happened all those years ago to Rook. I have asked her
more than once to dine with me, to socialize about the book.
But she declines. She gives more thought to Rook, it would
appear, than she gives to her boss's Life. She shows no interest
in his childhood or his youth. For evidence of Victor in his
later years I have no need to search. I only have to look
around—at our hired room, at our refurbished town.

I'm in a tree house made of glass. On two sides there is
stretched netting screening off the market concourses below.
The netting supports creepers, cycads, vines. They are the
building's drapery. They grow from elevated beds, together
with other hothouse plants such as philodendrons and spider
palms which can breathe and neutralize the atmosphere. It is
their task—for nothing here is idle or unplanned—to filter
from the air the carbon monoxide, the benzene and the form-
aldehyde, the fumes and vapors, the leakages and pungencies
of Arcadia.

The plants define the frontiers of Signor Busi's "largest aviary yet." One hundred cockatiels, one thousand finches, sixty
pheasant doves, a throng of budgerigars, and cockatoos and
parakeets and myna birds, a petal storm of buntings, are bil-
leted up here. They seem to like the glass and framework of
Arcadia better than the trees. They make their nests and
perches on the tops of the suspended humidifiers which—

under the direction of a computer christened Zephyr—blast compressed air into the tropics of the aviary. The birds shuffle on the metal girders and the arching glassmounts, pecking at the paintwork made loose already by the eczema of the rust. Rain forests cannot keep rust at bay. But glass has kept the day-hawks out. They hover at the transparent domes of Arcadia, like children at sweetshop windows, hopelessly drawn to candied parakeets.

Imagine what so many birds can do to glass. They settle on the window frames and jettison their chalky waste in reckless, heavy streaks which provide food and habitation for lime flies, silver thrips and fleas. What architect could plan for that? What glazier could outwit birds and coprophagous parasites? What scaffolder could foresee the territorial conflicts that take place above Arcadia's trading concourses, its restaurants and bars? I look out through the room's streaked glass to see what causes such raucous purpose amongst the rainbow flocks. A small brown interloper from the city streets, a sparrow in its business suit, has found its way inside Arcadia. Busi's "hermetically sealed megalith" is no match for a hungry sparrow. It has squeezed through the cavity of an expansion joist, and then found passage through the ill-docked heating duct. The bird now seeks to feast on sunflower seeds, mixed nuts and grain put out in feeding trays by the custodians. The doves are beating at it with their wings. A cockatiel has caught the sparrow's underbreast. Down in the folds of netting which separate the people and the birds, a dozen corpses can be seen. Dead sparrows that have reached this dripping, heated heaven and have died.

The third side of the room has unstreaked glass. No birds. My view is unrestricted, except by bamboo leaves and vines and slight myopia. I look down on the building's centerpiece, its hub: the garden court to which the trading corridors and halls, the stairs, the patios, the terraces and balconies defer. I spend a little time watching the light show on the fountains, its blushes and its loops, exactly like the blushes and the loops which decorate the chamber music being played by three young women and a man on the concert podium by the open brasserie. The entertainment's free all day. Six Africans will play their drums this afternoon. A girl will juggle with some market fruit. The Band Accord, those aging sisters and their friend, will squeeze out melodies for tea.

The tourists take their coffee and their photographs, with views across the rebuilt medieval washing place toward the thickest foliage of Arcadia. The camera with a narrow lens can take a photograph which shows just water, washing place and leaves, a flash of cockatoo, a beam of sun. Arcadia, so framed, could be a part of Yucatan or Abyssinia. It's true the tourists cannot sit and pose amongst the resurrected gargoyles or the repaired stone, or trail their fingers in the water as they smile on film. A man in uniform is there to see they don't. "What next," he'll say, if they protest. "Let people touch the water, then they'll want to wash their feet in it? Swim in it? Piss in it?" He's down there now. I see him prowling at the water's edge, a two-way radio reverberating in his hand. He helps and points, reproves and redirects. He shows where handicapped visitors can find the Courtesy Wheelchairs, where children can be left in the Jungle Crèche while parents or au pairs shop and take a snack in the Picnic Basket, the Texas Pantry or the Hunger Monger. No eating on-the-hoof, of course. It is not done to take an apple or an orange from your bag and munch it as you browse. There's pith and skin and core to clear. No dining on a sandwich that you've bought outside. There's paper then, and crust. No cigarettes, except inside the bars. This is the price you pay.

Yet, Arcadia is a triumph. Let's admit it. It weathers as I watch; it settles in. There is no complacency, just the swagger and ambition that cities flourish on. I'd stand here happily— glass in hand, alone—all day, and not be bored, and not grow tired, and not be stifled by its flamboyant uniformity, by its recreant geometry, by its managed cheerfulness. Give me the chance. Give me the time. Give me the bottle and the glass. I'd sooner look upon Arcadia than anything in town. Yet I'm obliged to socialize. The room is filling now, and we are making phatic conversation, amongst the vines and birds. We put the world to rights. We are as vehement about the rain

as we are sanguine and ironic with politics and trade. We do
not merchandise our gossip, yet—not till our sixth or seventh
glass.

When we have eaten, swopped our formal news, we leave
the table and our muddied plates to stand in groups about the
room, to stand in pairs in conversation as we look out
through the bird-stained glass at birds or through the cleaner
glass at Victor's earthly paradise. What must we look like,
standing here engrossed in our last drinks? I press my nose
against the glass, twenty meters up above the market concourse, and watch those citizens, those purchasers below. I
look, no doubt, like Victor looks, up on the rooftop garden
of the twenty-eighth. I look like every suited, grandee looks:
untouchable, untouched. Yet, this I know, as I grow older, I
must descend the stairs and join the populace before my day
is done. The city claims its citizens before they die. The taxicabs are full of younger men. The trams—soon to be replaced
by subway trains—are slow with pensioners who cannot find
their money or their step. The streets these days are for the old
and weak and poor. I'll leave no monument to me. No bar or
restaurant, no market hall, will bear my name. My book, if
I survive to see it done, will have my name in print—but
think how big my name in print will be compared to Victor's
name, a banner on the cover. My labors print his mark more
deeply on the town. His labors press me deeper in.

So the lunch is done, and we go back to work or home, a
little drunk and overfed. I've time to wander in Arcadia. I
fool myself this is research, that everything I see is Victor-
manifest. Certainly it is not dull, though Victor-manifest
should be more dull than this. It is a work of art and industry
and arrogance, but, then, where would our city be without
these three? We'd be a village still. Arcadia hunches its four
backs against the town, the sky, the world. Who, passing
through its halls, its barrow-vaulted sublit aisles of glass, can
tell or care if it is night or day, or north or south, or spring,
or windy, wet or bright? Arcadia is—that word again—
Invulnerable.

I take the route, along one trading corridor, which would

have led from the old bars to the edge of the Woodgate district. I am besieged by color and by smell. There is no wind
or cold, and any sun that filters through is bounced by angles,
shed by glass, and spread by glossy walls as if it were the
bogus light of theaters. The music and the smells are piped:
fresh bread with Paganini; oranges augmented by the quintets
of Osvaldo Bosse. I cannot hear the birds. Even the humidifiers—roaring in the heavens of the building's carapace—are
silent at ground level. The fountains cast their strands of water
as quietly as a jug pours milk. The traders do not shout. They
do not cry their wares. They have found out what only now
I discover for myself, that—removed from wind and open
air—man-made sounds are quails. They cannot fly. They cannot travel far. They tremble on the ground. No screeching
indoor parakeet can pierce a flight path with its cry. Any
raucous marketeer evangelizing fruit would find no echo to
endorse his claims. At best, the sound he'd hear—if he were
close enough—would be the sullen impact of his voice on
toughened glass.

Though the noises of Arcadia are flat, the fruit and vegetables have never seemed so polished and so uniform. The traders, beneath their matching awnings, seduce the passersby
with produce of the gene bank and the science farm, enhanced
by Spray-Dew, Frost-Ban and by packaging. Recessed orange
lights warm and flatter every radish, every grape, every hy-
brid superfruit. Together with the onions and the swedes, are
Kingquats, a kumquat bigger than a plum and every part of
it—the peel, the pith—is edible. And there are orange grapes,
and bananas from Barbados shaped like avocado pears. And
avocado pears without a stone. And lab-grown lettuces (red
or green or white). And greenhouse broccoli with flowerheads
as big and tight as cobblestones, achromatic rhubarb force-
grown under fluorescent lights, and biotechnic aubergines
which some chemist-gardener has artificially bloated in diox-
ide pods. Young men in search of romance can still buy their
loves a Courting Quince, just as before, but more romanti-
cally presented in a silver nest with a heart-shaped, perfumed
top. Each purchase has its plastic bag, each plastic bag its

colored logo for Arcadia; each colored logo is a dancing apple with a hygienic, grub-free smile.

If I were rich I could buy jewelry and suits from boutiques which trade side by side with salad stands. If I were ill I could select a dozen cures for my maladies from the fresh herb shop; some adder buckthorn for my bowels (recalcitrant), some juniper for failing sight, some chamomile to help me sleep, some cuckoopint to keep alert my hope of finding love, some mistletoe as sedative, some poisoned laurel sap for the new Burgher's gin. If I liked fungi (I do not) I'd have the choice of fifty sorts from Mycologia, The Mushroom Shop. Should I prepare a fritto misto for my supper from an edible bolete. Or should I select a honey mushroom or a chanterelle?

If I were looking for a gift, a set of gaudy stamps from the philatelists might take my fancy. A first edition (slightly stained) of dell'Ova's *Truismes*, complete with margin notes by Pierre Loti's bastard son. A pair of handmade gloves. A pastry house with stucco-marzipan and flaked walnut tiles. A T-shirt printed with my name, or any name I choose. A postcard hologram of Arcadia. Or I could light a candle for the birthday of a friend. The Market Chapel is a shop and pays the usual rent, so needs to sell as many candles as it can. Nothing is cheap, of course. Don't rummage for your bargains here. Arcadia is built to shake out pockets, unzip wallets, cash checks, debit bank accounts. It is a monumental Dip. Victor has created the perfect cash machine. The traders pay, on top of rents, percentages to Victor, too, like feudal peasants paying "overage" on everything they sell. You see, Arcadia observes tradition after all. Something medieval is preserved intact! (If I were still The Burgher, there'd be a paragraph in this.)

Is there not cause to celebrate this new diversity, this innocent variety of goods, despite the claims of oracles and pamphleteers who say our city's in decline—and money is the force? Yet how could those greengrocers who once traded out of sacks and boxes in the Soap Market meet the rents and standards of Arcadia? They had to modernize or close up shop. Every shop that closed was taken up within a day, by businessmen whose visions were much looser and much wider than the soapies they replaced. Who needs so many outlets for a grape? One grape these days is much like all the rest. It makes good sense to let a market such as this diversify.

You only have to see the crowds to know these changes work. See how the middle classes flock from shop to shop, a bunch of parsley in their bags along with a batik headscarf that they've bought, and a piece of blue goat's cheese. See those valet-attended dowagers braving arthritis and discretion in the couturieres. See how the bars and restaurants are packed with men and women who never used the windswept bars in the old Soap Market for fear of chaos and antipathy. See the foreign faces here; the tourists who have come to witness what Fodor calls "the city's triumphant fusion of modernity and tradition, order and spontaneity, Life and Art, business and entertainment."

Of course, you will not see the nighttime soapies here. The bylaws say there can be no loitering, no Unlicensed Trading, no begging, no entertainment without a permit, no vehicles (including skates and skateboards), no animals (except for guide dogs), no unrestricted access to the sort who clutch a bottle or whose dress and cleanliness would strike a sour note. "Shop in Safety at Arcadia," the adverts say. "Attended parking for two thousand cars." There is no need to taste the city air at all, for those who drive, then shop, then drive. But who's so fearful of the city air that they dare not venture into the open forecourts which surround Arcadia? Here an open market still survives—three stalls of fruit (no vegetables), with staff in rural uniforms of dirndl skirts, straw hats and clogs. There's a take-a-number, wait-your-turn lunch stand. There are greenstone benches, and official buskers more impromptu and eclectic than the bands and string quartets inside.

I browse amongst the pushcarts there. Their tenants are the city's fireside artisans. I have the choice of jam or wooden beads or necklaces or cameos. One man sells woven bags. A woman and her dog have candles of a thousand kinds. Another deals in landscape prints and postcards of the town. I have the choice of riding on the garish carousel (restored from an original) or touring the old town by pony and trap, or visiting, with a bag of feed, the pigs, rabbits, goats and llamas of City Farm. I also have the choice of sitting here, bathing in the bounce-light of Arcadia, or going back to work. I would return to work, except that life is comforting here, and entertaining too. It's fun to watch the browsers shop, to watch the drama of the door staff turning back a drunk or turning out a bearded man with leaflets and a coat weighed down by badges. It's better fun than work to watch the "flamingos" operate their upturned litter scoops so that the market site is clean enough—if it were not against the market law—to sit upon the ground and doze.

It is, of course, the spirit of research and not distaste for work that takes me strolling round the wind-stroked, whistling outer rim of Arcadia. The Glass Meringue indeed. The Lobster Trap. The See-through Octopus. The Pumpkin. It has a hundred names. But one has stuck amongst those people rarely let inside or rarely rich enough to browse and buy. They call the place Fat Vic. It's Big Vic's plumper sibling. One stands, one squats. They are the city's strangest twins.

I come at last to Victor's birthday gift, the statue cast in bronze, commissioned by the merchants of the Soap Market. The move amongst the bleeding hearts, some time ago, to pull it down and put a statue up for Rook, has come to nothing. Victor's birthday gift survives. A woman sits cross-legged before a bowl. The artist has welded real coins inside. The woman has an infant at her breast. Its eyes are open wide, and fixed upon Arcadia. There was a time when children clambered over her, when office workers used the plinth for lunch, when young men wrote the names of their sweethearts in felt tip along the woman's arms, or colored in her nipple, darkly. But, pretty soon, they railed her and her infant in. The statue's called *The Beggar Woman and Her Child*, but we all know it as *The Cage*.

So this is Em. And this is Victor, an infant at the breast. They are so still, you'd think their abject happiness could never end. Yet end it did. In flames. And here she—resurrected—is. Too rigid now to take the painted cart, piled high

with melons—honeydews, casabas, canteloupes, and musks—
and far too late to set off, as she had promised, toward the
city hems where blue fields match the sea-blue sky, with her
small son her only passenger. I have the first line of his Life:
"No wonder Victor never fell in love."

2

I'M IN THE MOOD to take my time. I walk across the last few patterned slabs and cobblestones of Arcadia and head off into town. The Woodgate pavements are old and cracked and buckled. They are ideal for puddles, weeds and saunterers. I peer down squints and alleyways. They seem more festive than they used to. Perhaps the presence of Arcadia has enlivened them. They are not back streets now, but brisk with bars and antique shops, and second-storey studios.

You cannot park. The wardens and the police make sure of that. How can they stop the soapies though? At first it was just one or two—disgruntled fruiterers who'd been displaced from Fat Vic's corridors. They had to work and feed their families, and so they set up shop in backs of vans and parked across the curbstones in dead ends, blind alleys, cul-de-sacs, providing low-grade, cheaper fruit for those in too much hurry for Arcadia. Quite soon there were a bunch of makeshift stalls, some colored awnings set up at the backs of vans, some trays of produce set out on the pavement. You've never seen such rugged mushrooms, such unselected fruit, such tattered sugar-snaps, such unwaxed oranges, such blemished pears, such unwrapped chard—poor man's asparagus—and mulberries and radicchio still moist with country rain, already past their best, so cheap.

Quite soon, of course, the displaced market had a name—Soap Two, just like a film. You think its characters are dead,

and then the sequel comes along, as lively as the first. So now
we see that it's not true that "cities swallow up the small,"
that "soufflés only rise the once." The pygmies flourish on
the street. I used to think that buildings were all that could
endure in cities. But people, it would seem, endure as well.
They hang on by their nails. They improvise. They kick.
They leave a legacy which is not brick or stone.

The first to come and trade are well established now. They
have their clientele, their daily pitches, their regimens. Some
clever spark has improvised some light for dawn, and after
dusk. Soap Two trades in the night when Arcadia is shut and
under guard. The soapie trading light is pilfered from the
streetlamps, by an illegal wire connected and undone a dozen
times a day as uniforms approach. Who'll get the bill? Who
cares! Not Cellophane. He does not give a damn. He is untouched by bills. He's shielded by the corset of his cellophane.
He waltzes, as sheenily as a stage sardine, through the market
all day and all night long. Sometimes he takes it on himself
to direct the traffic as it squeezes past the stalls. Sometimes
he lies down in the street to block the passing cars. He begs.
He steals. He shouts obscenities. I've never heard such words
before. He kicks the windfalls from the trading stalls. He's
always at the market's edge, a cellophane commissionaire. As
Soap Two expands then, so he moves out from the core, to
summon people in. It does not matter what their business is,
or if they have no cause at all to pack into the streets. He
simply hopes to share—and complicate—the ecstasy of
crowds.

Now the Woodgate district, once so lifeless and depressed,
is as noisy and congested, lively and unsafe, as the Soap Market used to be. Merchandise is stacked in piles which challenge
sense and physics—towers of potatoes, conifers of oranges,
trembling with every passerby. The makeshift market flourishes on noise and filth and rain. It would even flourish—and
it does—on poverty. "All Life is Here," according to the market chauvinists, a claim no one would make for Arcadia, with
its policed doors, its creed of Safety from the Streets, its ban
on pimps and tramps and tarts and bagladies, street vendors,

rascals, teenagers, drunkards, dogs. All life is here, despite the wind, the rain, the airborne dust, the litter at my feet.

The New Age meal I ate at the Buffers' lunch has left me hungry still. I buy one sleepy pear. Its skin is bruised and weather-beaten like a ploughman's face. The trader comes down from his perch on the bonnet of his car. He leaves a conversation with a friend, and his meal half eaten on the metal, his teethmarks in the boiled egg; the ripped white loaf, the plastic flask of over-sweetened coffee. He wipes my one pear on his trouser leg to take away the marks of harvesting. He pirouettes it in a paper bag. He twists the paper bag a pair of ears. He takes my cash. I take the fruit. I'm free to eat it when I want. I eat it now. My chin is wet. I cannot walk and eat efficiently. I stand back from the crowd, against a wall between a bistro and an odd-job shop to watch the Man in Cellophane cause mayhem with the cars. I cannot say where I prefer to eat, Soap Two, Fat Vic. The prospect of them both seduces me. I'm free while there is sap inside my legs to make my choice. I am not Invulnerable. Thank God for that. I am not Victor and too old and dry to be at ease down here. He'll have a book (perhaps) to celebrate his life. Arcadia. A statue, too. But all his pears, I guess, are brought by train and taxi to Big Vic. He takes Life on a plate. He has a serviette. He cannot simply—as I do now—toss the sodden paper bag which held the pear to the ground and find a warming corner for himself.

There is a little sun which falls directly on my face, my shirt, the damaged pear. I eat it now. I eat it now. The eye, the core, the stalk are given to the pavement, and flattened by ten thousand feet, as everyone is flattened by the town when they are done, when they are waste.

The sun is fully out for just an instant. It is radiant, then it is gone. The blocking bollard which has kept the weather dry has moved before the wind. The time has come for it to rain. It's hard and sudden as it always is in our city. It drizzles in the countryside but here the rain is bouncing berries on the roofs of cars. The squints and alleys cannot cope with this. They flood. They overflow. Their drains are blocked with

cabbage leaves, handbills, discarded pith and peel. The pavement turns to green and slimy rinks of foliage. To walk on
them is to gamble with your bones. What should we do but
huddle underneath the awnings that are there, but gather in
the doorways to the shops, or sit in cars, or seek refuge—and
a drink—inside a bar?

I cannot quite escape the rain, despite the umbrella which
my neighbor holds. My suit is sodden at the shoulder. My
socks and shoes are wet. My forehead sweats with rain. The
entertainment never ends. The weather is a ballet for the
streets. But then there is a more substantial dancer too. Cellophane is kicking water in the air. He thinks we're going to
throw him coins for the show. He bows. And as he bows the
rainbow arches up, connecting the old town and the new. It
is a bridge beyond the wit of architects reflected in the glass
of Big Vic and Arcadia. The rainbow relishes windows. There
is no need to draw conclusions though. We all know rainbows
start and finish everywhere, that they are simply sun, shining
from behind to trick the light from falling rain, if we look
east in the middle afternoon toward the clearing shower of
the day. They are not omens—but they are signs that it is
safe to walk onto the streets again. The rain has almost done.

My face and eyes are wet. I have to frown and squint for
focus as I pass between the glare and darkness, as I cross
streets and circumscribe the puddles, as I avoid collisions with
people and with cars. So many people with so many purposes.
Too many people to know well.

I would not wish to be too grand for streets. To be removed from them is to lose the blessing of the multitude.
The tallest buildings throw the longest shadows, it is said, by
those who spend their lives in contemplation of their monu-
ments, and those for whom the shadow life is better than the
real. But most of us who live in cities die and take our shadows to the grave. We don't outlive the masonry or glass. It's
said that great men have the grandest tombstones, too, and
throw the longest shadows even after death. The cemeteries
prove the truth in that. But I prefer to think that worms and
damp and degradation are open-minded democrats which

treat us all the same. We are all citizens at last. At least until
we are all soil.

I make my mark upon the city, too. My living mark. I
stretch my legs as best I can and set off slowly down the
street. My rainy footprints on the pavement will soon dry,
but footprints and the thousand sodden paper bags which held
a thousand pears, the eyes, the cores, the stalks, the rinds of
daily life, are more substantial—are they not?—than shadows.
They swell the middens of the town.

There are people, wet and poor, who walk the pavements
with a skip as if the puddles and the cracks are civic birthday
gifts. And there are many whistlers around. My legs are old.
That's all that holds me back from skipping on the spot or
kicking up a puddled loop of rain. My tongue's kept busy by
the scrap of pear skin lodged between my teeth. That's all
that stops me sucking in our city air, and whistling.